Peculiar Pilgrims:

Stories from the

Left Hand of God

Peculiar Pilgrims:

Stories from the

Left Hand of God

Linda K. Wendling

Guest Editor

With a Foreword by

Gregory Wolfe

Debra Dean, Ron Ebest, Sally Barr Ebest,
Jenni Ferrari-Adler, Jackie Gross, Cathy Lichti,
Marlene Muller, Sarah Steinke,
Lonnie Whitaker

Associate Editors

CHICAGO

www.hourglassbooks.org

Cover Artwork by Randi Layne Scheurer
www.randiworks.com

ISBN 978-0-9725254-4-2
LCCN 2006933202

Printed in the United States of America
on acid-free paper

Published by Hourglass Books
www.hourglassbooks.org

Contents

Contents

Contents

Contents

Foreword
Gregory Wolfe

Reading Linda Wendling's exquisite anthology of short stories has stirred something within me that few thematic collections ever touch—the place where conscious reflection meets deep-seated memory. Brooding over this book in the light of its subtitle, *Stories from the Left Hand of God*, reminded me just how disturbing was the discovery of my left-handedness. I must have been five or six when it happened. Of course, I'd probably been using my left hand to draw for some time. But it took going to school—encountering others—to make me aware of my difference.

My mother was so besotted with me, her first-born, that she kept me home until I was six. Having missed the glorified playtime of nursery, I plunged into the rigors of kindergarten. Children are acute observers of difference and uninhibited about pointing it out. When we began to practice penmanship, I became painfully self-conscious, aware that my letters were clumsy and deformed. I compensated by gripping pen and pencil tightly, bearing down on the paper—more of an incision than a flowing movement. As I pushed across the lined paper, the accumulating ink and lead on my fingers made smudges on what I had already written. Whereas I had to push, the others merely had to pull, their right hands moving, with seemingly no effort, into virgin territory.

I have a memory from this period of my mother sweetly suggesting that I try to use my right hand. As I recall it, I felt her anxiety and love in the proposal, but I also sensed that she, too, felt some discomfort about my difference from the others. Perhaps I also felt a little betrayed by her well-intentioned suggestion, as if, like my classmates, she agreed that I was a benighted soul. But then I may be making this memory up, projecting my childish insecurity onto her.

Throughout history, religion has often taken the form of the "right-handed" banishing the lefties into outer darkness. It's an ancient dialectic: us and them, sheep and goats. And the dichotomy is always charged with moralistic fervor, the assertion of the moral superiority of those on the inside. Indeed, I would venture to say that the single most powerful reason motivating people to abjure organized religion is precisely this tendency to define reality in binary, self-righteous terms.

But here's the irony: the us/them mentality is a corruption of a genuinely religious insight. Nearly all religions begin with the primal human experience of feeling different—being out of place, exiled, a stranger in a strange land. It is true that this sense of displacement has been too easily associated with sin—the moralistic instinct rearing its head again. But neither should the idea of sin be utterly dismissed. After all, another universal human experience, to paraphrase St. Paul, is that of not being able to do what we ought to do and of doing what we ought not to do.

But sometimes our sense of displacement and difference goes beyond our personal responsibility to the world around us. Countless millions of human beings have felt the haunting suspicion that there is something not quite right about this world, that there is or should be a way to redeem it. That this world is our home—and not our home.

The biblical phrase for this experience is that we are "strangers and pilgrims on the earth." The paradox is that most of us seem to share this feeling; in an odd way, it unites us. Geoffrey Chaucer understood the paradox perfectly: his rag-tag group of pilgrims on the Canterbury Road are as earthy a rabble as it is possible to imagine. But they are never more earthy than when driven by the desire for forgiveness and understanding—for a fleeting encounter with the sacred that might give meaning to their rambunctiously profane lives.

Chaucer's pilgrims are forever on the road—Canterbury, like Heaven or Nirvana or the New Jerusalem—lies off in the distance. The worldly equivalent of sacramental confession is storytelling, the urge to use narrative to explain (perhaps discover) who we really are. Thus their tales become milestones along that road, helping to guide them that much closer to their destination.

This is how the short story works: by presenting us with a character who feels different—perhaps even blighted or cursed—but whose travails reveal to her just how like her fellow travelers she really is. In this sense, the best short stories are profoundly moral, but never moralistic, because the event that befalls the protagonist calls forth a transformation, even if that change comes in the form of the recognition of a truth rather than a radical overhaul in behavior.

A wise man once said that the religious sense begins at the moment we love the truth more than we love ourselves. The same could be said for the *peripeteia*, or reversal, that sets a short story on its way to a climax. So it is, again and again, in *Peculiar Pilgrims*, from the truck driver whose devotion to ancient Chinese wisdom enables him to love a woman the world would call unattractive, and to endure injustice, to the "bad Jew" whose life slowly becomes defined by the religion she doesn't practice, to the abused young woman who lies and steals and yet who writes love letters, suffused with ecstatic gratitude, to those she has wronged.

In a number of religious traditions, God actually demonstrates a marked preference for those on his left side. Because it is precisely there that we can come to the realization that there are no sides, only one screwed-up, yearning human family. In the stories that follow, that place of reversal and recognition is the first step on the pilgrim's path.

❈

---

*"...All of that cavern was piled high with bales of wicks . . .
[and the old man answered,] '. . . tell him that the wicks are
ready...'"*
                                    —Howard Schwartz, *Gabriel's Palace*

In one of his many books of folk legends and magical realist
tales, Howard Schwartz, winner of the National Jewish Book
Award (*Tree of Souls*, Oxford University Press), offers a translation of an oral-tradition Hasidic tale from Eastern Europe,
called "The Cave of Mattathias". In the story, every Hanukah,
a Hasid carried newly made oil to Reb Menachem Mendel of
Riminov. Then, in his presence, the rabbi would light the first
candle of Hanukah. One year, a terrible blizzard came, but the
Hasid was determined to set out on his customary pilgrimage,
despite his family's dire warnings. Quickly lost in a blizzard,
the Hasid is forced to use the rabbi's oil and the lining of his

own coat to create a flame in the forest. What follows is a vision and an otherworldly miraculous recovery—and most important of all, a message of hope to be delivered to the rabbi.

"The Cave of Mattathias," like so many of Schwartz's masterful tales, achieves something unexplainable, and something that we all need. First and foremost, this is the tale of a pilgrimage, a journey of homage paid yearly by a devout man. But it quickly becomes so much more than that—all of those favorite elements of a tale are here: a catastrophe occurs—a blizzard! Then—and this is key—the Hasid sets out on the journey despite dire warnings from his family. And then—we see the gift that results. The miracle and the message…despite dire warnings.

Stories of pilgrimage, of searching, are stories of renewal in one way or another—and not necessarily of a religious nature. And does it matter? Madeleine L'Engle once said that God will use art to reveal Truth and Beauty. The artist's religion, or lack of religion, is of little importance in this delivery system. Religion and spiritual pilgrimage are, after all, far from the same thing.

Why do stories of pilgrimage, stories of seekers, whether religious or not, compel us? Isn't it because that's what we're here for, in the end? To journey? To seek? And for many of us, the revelation is in the journey itself and not always in its elusive end. As that humble bard James Taylor writes, "The secret of life is enjoying the passing of time." A pilgrimage implies an enjoying of the journey, finding meaning there as much as in its destination.

This is what stories teach us most of all—all stories, if they are good ones: to enjoy, to appreciate, the mere passing of time. What good is a love story if we skip to the happy ending and miss all the wooing? Isn't the wooing a great deal of what all love and all searching is about?

We woo our lovers.
We woo children.
We woo our aging parents—
We woo the Stranger Among Us.
We woo The Mysterious.

All is in the wooing—the journey—more than in the conquest of the heart or the clutching of the secret. What strength lies in the meaning at the end of any journey is what the experience of pilgrimage has made of us ourselves, long before we get there.

Discovering the stories meant for us has been, for this editorial team, a winding, twisting, mysterious, hilarious, and sacred journey. It was a wooing. We cast a wide net when we searched for and invited the stories for this anthology. The theme was deliberately broad—what would pilgrimage mean to our contributors? And what unity would we find among those that compelled us to embrace them in the end? Our editorial team found that what attracted us to these final stories—out of so many, many outstanding choices—too many more jewels than we could finally choose from—were those that conveyed three peculiar aspects of the pilgrimage—

- The first? The search for a meaningful sign or more precisely, that one singular moment of unbounded grace.

- The second—the aching sojourn toward reconciliation or healing.

- The third? The innate desire for some kind of transcendence, in any of its myriad forms.

I am grateful for my amazing Editorial Team—it was heartening at every turn to see how sensitive, gifted, and insightful these editors have been—not to mention compassionate. They cared tenderly for each story that came to them; read each one with an open heart and mind; wrote me long, aching, impassioned letters over those they accepted and those they could not. With such readers as these, there is hope for the writers of the world. I thank Gregory Wolfe at *Image* for keen advice on the journal's title and vision, and Lonnie Whitaker, the editor who came up with the subtitle, "Stories From The Left Hand of God." And I am grateful, of course, to Bill Scheurer, our publisher, who does it for all the right reasons.

But most of all—not surprisingly—I am grateful for my family and my friends; my parents (all five of them, the newest no less dear than the first), my astounding children—Greg, Laura, Hannah, and Lorita—but especially my husband, the one and only love of my life. There has never been in this world a friend quite like him. There has never been a sweetheart, there has never been a father or a kindly stranger who is a safe haven for other pilgrims—quite like this one. I can't believe he has been lent to me for all these years.

Part One
The Search for One Moment of Unbounded Grace

John Dalton
STORY

BOOK OF SONGS

MY wife, Juanita, and I lived for ten years in the town of Times Beach, Missouri. We had a used trailer home and a two-acre lot which sloped down to the banks of the Meramac River. We painted the trailer a light, cloudy, hopeful blue. I would like to say here that it was this light blue tone that separated us, at least in spirit, from the other dented and diminished trailers of our neighborhood. But in truth, we shared the same bad habit of letting things slip. I substituted sheets of cheap plastic for storm windows, and Juanita hid boxes of rubbish under the trailer foundation. Things accumulated in our yard, and not just the usual tires and broken toys either. We had the pipe section of a church organ and the weather-eroded skeleton of an old wooden canoe and a solid white stone monkey, minus the tail of course. A hard rain would wash gravel and road dust into our yard causing the grass to die and the earth to wear away into long, thin, meandering gullies.

Now we live in Eureka, some five miles up Highway 44 from Times Beach. We live, along with several other Times Beach families, in the Monument Trailer Park where I work as the caretaker. Here, Juanita and I enjoy a much nicer trailer, two trailers actually, placed side by side and connected seamlessly down the center. We have wall-to-wall carpeting, and a dishwasher, and cable television and much more room to carry on with our lives. Just beyond the Monument Trailer Park, they are finishing up the Deer Run Estates. These estates—notice I do not use the word homes—are spaced evenly along the rising hill behind us. They are very large, impressively complex in their design, especially the wooden decks jutting off their sides and backs. Decks upon decks leading into other decks. An amazing thing to see. The billboard on Highway 44 reads simply, "Deer Run Estates: Believe The Difference". We of the Monument Trailer Park have walked up the hill and seen the display homes. We are believers.

Still, the home owners and visitors and prospective buyers arriving at Deer Run Estates must pause briefly at the stop sign next to our trailer park. They stop as the law requires them to do, and through their car windows we witness, but do not hear their conversations. Clearly, our community of trailers is not what they expected. It is an odd thing.

Juanita and I and other Times Beach families have discussed it. We now have our dishwashers, our cable TV, our seamless trailers, and yet we find ourselves suddenly poorer.

I have read that in ancient China, about two thousand years before the birth of Christ, someone decided to begin writing down important happenings and the lives of the ancient big shots. One thing led to another as they often do. Archives were set up. More and more information was added. These archivists began to gather more sophisticated and poetic material which later became a series of folk and court songs and temple hymns called "The Book of Songs." In this book, rulers like Tan-fu and King Wen became models of virtue. Whether they were virtuous or not is beside the point. What eventually mattered was that they came to represent values and ideas of correct behavior which could be passed on to future generations. It was an old idea, perhaps not very original, but a good one nonetheless, I think.

In Times Beach we had our own personal histories, our own as yet unwritten and unsung temple hymns. Here's one about Mick Tarbell:

Mick came back to Times Beach from Vietnam in 1973. He was discharged a year earlier, and nobody is quite sure where he spent that year. Mick rented an old A-frame hunting cabin near the river not far from his family's home and our own blue trailer. He was thin and pale and shook slightly when he stood in the bright light of day, which was not often. Juanita and I saw him only now and then, walking to the town grocery store with his government check, coming back with a bit of food and a lot of cheap beer. He was visited by a number of undesirables that year, and the townspeople suspected they were bringing in drugs. When Mick stepped out of his A-frame to greet them or bid them good-bye, he stammered and trembled and slurred his words.

I decided to help.

I snuck down early one morning and left copies of the *Tao Te Ching* and the *Confucian Analects* on his doorstep. From the *Analects*, I underlined the following lines:

Hold loyalty and faithfulness to be fundamental. Have no friends who are not as good as yourself. When you have made mistakes, don't be afraid to correct them.

In the months that followed nothing appeared to change. But then there was a loud argument one night. The police were called. The undesirables left and when they returned several days later, Mick greeted them with shouts and curses.

He kept to himself that summer, spent his time fishing on the Meramac. He was not drinking. He lost his paleness and gained his weight back. Sometime that fall he met Beth Anne Gordon.

During our negotiations with the state and federal government at a nearby high school gymnasium, it was Mick Tarbell who stood before us and defended our claims. We had our lawyers of course, but there was something in the solidness of his character that demanded attention. Mick gradually became a physically strong man, and when he stood and made his point, when he lashed out at the air around him with quick, forceful jabs, the boys in the suits leaned back in their chairs and waited for him to finish. "Don't you dare apologize to us," Mick demanded. "These are *our* families and lives at risk. 'I'm sorry' doesn't cover it."

We were all there, every resident of our sad, troubled town. Beth Anne was there with her two little girls. She concentrated on her husband's words and on his anger.

"That's right Mickey," we said. "You tell him Mickey." We were all sitting behind him and shifting our weight on those uncomfortable foldout gymnasium bleachers. We voiced our support by shouting out "Yes!...Uh huh!...You got that right!" At times we clapped or booed and made a hell of a racket.

5

People have sometimes mistaken me for an educated man, which I am not. It would be better to think of me as a Civil War buff, or a baseball fan, or a gardening fanatic, although I know practically nothing about these three subjects. I know only ancient China. On the television show "Jeopardy" I would die a quick, humiliating death.

I moved into Juanita's trailer home at Times Beach in 1972. We lived together without the benefit of a marriage certificate for one year, and in Times Beach this meant that we were poor and lazy rather then trendy or liberal.

One warm evening I took Juanita by the hand and led her to our favorite shaded point along the Meramac. With my right knee in the leaves and dirt, I proposed marriage and then held out a thin gold ring.

She cried.

"No," she said. "Why do you keep doing all of this?"

She had been struggling with this question for some time, and though I tried to assure her, I could never fully convince Juanita exactly why I stayed on with her, why I loved her so damned much.

I slid an arm around her plump, soft waist and we walked further into the woods, near the bank.

It was the summer of '73. Mick Tarbell was fishing somewhere along the river. I had completed the *Tao Te Ching* and the *Analects*, and I was halfway through my first history of ancient China.

I said, "Imagine that for one day, or even one hour, that everyone in the world loses their face and hair and bodies and everything, and for that one hour they become pure light. The light of their own souls. Imagine that Juanita."

Juanita paused. After a year of living with me, she was used to this kind of talk.

"If that were true," I continued, "then you would shine brighter than anyone I know, anyone I ever met. You would be a kaleidoscope of yellows and oranges, a little green and a lot of jasmine. If jasmine could be a color then you would be just like that."

She asked me what color I would be.

This was easy.

"A light, cloudy, hopeful blue," I said.

During the dry weather we always had trouble with road dust. A pickup would speed by and if you happened to be walking along the road you would cover your face and side-step quickly into the trees or else choke on the dust.

When this happened, the Times Beach Mayor would call in Russell Bliss, and he would ease along the town's gravel roads in his truck laying down a light film of waste oil as he went.

Between 1972 and 1976 the oil he sprinkled on our streets was mixed with dioxin. It seems he received this dioxin from the Northeastern Pharmaceutical and Chemical Company that filtered out dioxin, a hazardous by-product, from a surgical cleanser they produced called hexachlorophene. The people at Northeastern claimed their hexachlorophene was so clean that the dioxin levels were undetectable in the finished product. Sadly, they were not so rigorous when it came to disposing of the dioxin-tainted water, filters and clay-like sludge used in the manufacturing process. Much of the dioxin-contaminated water was stored in tanks, which eventually rusted and leaked into the Spring River near the factory. The worst part of the waste—a concentrated, thick, smelly residue—was given to Russell Bliss for disposal. To this day he maintains that he had no idea the materials he received from Northeastern were dangerous. Mr. Bliss mixed six truckloads of this residue with his own waste oil and then went on to contaminate Times Beach and more than thirty other locations in the state of Missouri.

In English there is one verb which we have adopted from the Chinese language, and when it is my turn to speak at the negotiation meeting, I stand, clear my throat and say, "The citizens of Times Beach will not kowtow to the Northeastern Pharmaceutical and Chemical Company."

One day I was walking back from the Kwik Trip with a gallon of 2% milk. I had just crossed under the Monument Trailer Park entrance, when I passed three teenage boys also on foot, but on their way out.

"Can you imagine poochin' that fat old hag?" the tallest, leanest one of the three said to the others.

"I wouldn't touch her with a ten-foot slime pole" his friend answered.

"But can you *imagine*?" the tall one said again.

By now they had already passed through the gate and had turned right at the stop sign.

"I can imagine very well," I called back to them. "I can imagine very easily."

I paced by two trailers and I was home. Just as I suspected, Juanita was outside. She was on her hands and knees pulling weeds from a bed of marigolds that bordered the trailer porch. I waited as she rose slowly from the lawn. She was wearing my old warm up suit and the material stretched unevenly over her big tummy. Outdoor light is never kind to Juanita's complexion, the old acne scars appeared more defined, and the only smooth patches of skin, at the top of each cheek, seemed blanched and puffy.

"Can you believe it?" she said, and with a grand sweep of her arm, she presented two rows of flowers staggered alternately orange and yellow. "If I'd known I could actually keep 'em alive, I would have bought twice as many." She favored me with a closed-lip smile, and though her glasses were slightly filmy, I could see her green eyes widen and focus on me in a loving, familiar way. I wished the boys had seen these eyes, which are absolute wonders in their ability to concentrate and reflect. And as unlikely as it may seem, I wished that they had stopped and talked to her, wished that they had given her a chance to lavish some of her attention on them. My Juanita is 55 years old and I have never seen her condescend, in even the most subtle ways, to the young or the aged. In her mind, everyone is guilty of some secret enchantment, and she is so earnest in her approach to people that I believe she can eventually win anyone over.

When there was no longer any doubt that we had all been exposed to dioxin, a meeting was called and we filed into the gymnasium and arranged ourselves on the bleachers. A medical researcher was present and he carefully explained the word "carcinogen." Then he broke the bad news and told us that the dioxin-fed rats had developed cancer and died.

What little hope the newspaper reports had not yet smothered, now deserted us all at once. We surprised ourselves with our silence, our awkwardness in having no composed response to the research man.

But there was more bad news. The effects of exposure to this type of carcinogen were uncertain. There was a waiting period, a time of twenty to thirty years before we were out of danger.

Here, the researcher wisely chose to pause. There was a tremor of emotion spreading through the crowd and we were still not yet sure if this emotion would turn to outrage or despair. Small gestures of nervous energy caused the bleachers to wobble beneath us. A woman turned and hid her face in her husband's down jacket. Mick Tarbell began clenching and unclenching his fists.

He stood and asked, "Does this mean twenty years down the road *we're* gonna' get sick? ... And our kids?"

"Possible," the research man answered, "but not likely."

Our neighbor, John Crawley stood and waited to speak, but even before he opened his mouth, we knew what the words would be: three dead in his family alone, all of cancer. After John, others stood and reported their losses. Colon, prostate, liver, brain, lung, skin, tongue and testicles: we heard them all described from the initial symptoms to the hospitalization to the struggle itself and then on to recovery or death. We also heard complaints of blurred vision, coughs and colds that never quite went away, hearing loss, taste loss, smelling loss, bad dreams. Juanita and I listened but did not speak.

The researcher, who had been standing patiently through all of this, finally interrupted and told us we had reason for hope. Preliminary findings from the "Ranch Hand" study on Vietnam veterans exposed to dioxin in the form of Agent Orange showed no higher than average rate in cancer deaths. He told us that 25% of any population in America would eventually have some form of cancer.

"Do not jump to conclusions," he said. "Don't forget that many things in life occur randomly. Don't forget coincidence."

To illustrate this point, the research man told us that a man in Ontario was at home listening to Frankie Laine's "Cry of the Wild Goose" when a giant Canada goose crashed through his living room picture window and died at his feet.

"Pure coincidence," the research man explained and then frowned when he noticed we were not amused.

During the previous winter, I discovered that I could no longer fulfill my duties as a husband in bed. Juanita was calm and assuring. "It will come back in the spring," she promised. The springtime did not revive me. I felt quiet stirrings of desire, but for the first time they formed as abstract ideas, difficult to hold and manipulate, impossible to channel into any real physical sensation.

While the research man was speaking, I turned and whispered in my wife's ear, "Have I got a coincidence for him."

Times Beach was not the first place to receive Mr. Bliss's dioxin tainted oil. The first location was Shenandoah Stables, an indoor horse arena near the town of Moscow Mills. Immediately after the arena floor had been sprayed to hold down dust during the shows, the stable workers were overwhelmed by a fierce, burning chemical odor. The following week, birds began falling from the rafters in such numbers that each morning a stable hand was assigned the job of raking their bodies into a pile and shoveling them into plastic bags. The stable owner's daughters, ages six and eight, both became sick; one was hospitalized with severe bladder inflammation and bleeding. As for the horses, they ate and digested dioxin contaminated hay and absorbed this same chemical through their hooves. During the next two months, they grew increasingly nervous, refused to eat, bled internally and finally became feeble and emaciated. Sixty-two of them died in their stables or were led outside to a hitching post where the stable hands soothed them with soft words and familiar strokes, distracting them from the veterinarian's final injection.

From The Book of Songs:

Teddy Barnes moved his family to Times Beach sometime in the mid-seventies. Still, it took a while, a year or more, before I really got to know him. Juanita got along well with Teddy's wife, Clara, and we would now and then share Sunday dinner together inside their two-story farmhouse just down the road from our trailer. At that time, there were a number of my Times Beach neighbors that I could call friends, but Teddy was my favorite, someone different, someone I could connect with. One reason for this was that, like me and ancient China, Teddy had interests that stretched beyond Times Beach and his job as a carpenter with the Postal System. He did not try to school himself in any particular field, but instead, using the public library, Teddy apprenticed himself in such diverse areas of study as the Alaskan gold rush, the history of Venice, Proxima Centauri (our nearest star), American sports cars 1962-1972, and the Easter Island Statues. He stayed with a topic until he could declare himself knowledgeable which by Teddy's standards meant an impressive mental reserve of information, close to expertise and usually exhausting all the library resources. When I knew him well, he was researching Britain's deportation of prisoners to Botany Bay Australia, but already he was making lists of future study topics.

As things turned out Teddy finished his Botany Bay research and was halfway through American Indian sundials when his mind began to unravel. Juanita and I were visiting the Barnes's for dinner one evening, and just after we sat down at the table Teddy leaned over and started eating right out of the large bowl of mashed potatoes. He slid the wide serving spoon back and forth between that bowl and his mouth while we looked on, unsure as to exactly what kind of joke this might turn out to be. Then Teddy's youngest son, Raymond, a quiet, high school-age kid and the only of

Teddy's five children still left at home, this Raymond reached over and pulled the spoon out of his father's hand and used it to set a mound of mashed potatoes on Teddy's plate. After that, Raymond walked softly to the screen door, stepped outside and began sprinting across the yard.

It seemed that Raymond had noticed a great many small details before any of us, including Clara. He had witnessed his father pause far too long over the easy TV quiz show questions, had seen Teddy's tools hung incorrectly on the garage pegboard, had even noticed the family pick-up truck parked off center in the driveway.

During the years before the dioxin discovery, Teddy grew steadily worse. The Post Office retired him with full benefits. The doctors' diagnoses bounced back and forth between organic brain dysfunction and Alzheimer's disease. Clara did her best to keep her husband comfortable and safe, but Teddy liked the outdoors and spent most of the daylight hours in the yard, pacing about, rearranging objects, edging closer and closer to the road as if he might make a sudden dash and escape.

The Barneses were one of six Times Beach families who moved with us to the Monument Trailer Park. I'm sorry to say that Juanita and I are not frequent visitors to their trailer at the end of the court. It is a difficult thing to spend even a few hours with Teddy Barnes who has grown wiry, anxious, and irritable with age. He does not recognize either of us, and his talk is wild and emphatic, sometimes paranoid. In addition, Teddy has come to believe Raymond has been kidnapped and is being held for ransom. While Raymond, who now lives in California, has not come to visit for some time, he has telephoned to reassure his father that he is safe and sound. "That's exactly right," Teddy responds, "and don't you worry either because I'm comin' to get you out of this mess."

Recently, Teddy has begun sneaking out early in the morning and literally running amok through our trailer court. Clara has changed door locks several times, but Teddy's carpentry skills have not entirely deserted him, and while she sleeps, he tinkers with the locks or removes the door hinges and makes good his escape. When she wakes and finds him missing, she places an urgent call to the Eureka Police Department where the officers are familiar with Teddy's indiscretions. Clara worries that he may eventually be hit by a car, and so at night, before she sleeps, she dresses Teddy in a navy blue running suit with thick white stripes on the sleeves and legs. Once he is outside, Teddy is unbelievably fast. He charges through our neighborhood and occasionally runs up the hill and into the Deer Run Estates. More often than not, he crouches next to the stop sign near the trailer park entrance and waits for an early morning commuter to roll to a stop. Then Teddy springs out and raps his knuckles on the driver's side window. His approach is not subtle. "Open the damn door and let me in for Christ's sake!"

On a mild December morning in 1982, we looked out through the clouded, plastic-covered windows of our trailer home and saw white, buoyant figures moving along the gravel roads of Times Beach. Juanita and I opened the front door for a better view. Standing on the opposite side of the road, dressed in stiff, bloated coveralls was a man wearing an air mask with a long, ribbed, black hose that led from the muzzle of his mask to a filter system inside his clothing. A hood, with interior flaps that folded down beneath the mask, covered his head. There were two sets of circular clamps: one set fastened his white sleeves to his thick rubber gloves and another set kept the ends of his trousers tightened around his boot tops. He began leaning and applying his weight on what appeared to be a slim version of a posthole digger. Soon, he was joined by another white-suited man who leaned down and scraped mud from the digger's open claw into a plastic container. This container was quickly labeled and the two moved on.

Our phone rang. Juanita answered and talked to a neighbor. She hung up and initiated her own call. Our phone was alive with news that day. The people of Times Beach were uncertain as to what the men in white coveralls may have represented; however, these men were certainly easy to nickname. Juanita covered the receiver with her hand and informed me, "There are more moon men working there way along the river."

This sampling continued the entire day. At times they gathered together and then dispersed like straying sheep, pausing to remove golf-hole size specimens from our lawns. They had a master plan, a map, which they pulled from their pockets and unfolded clumsily with gloved hands. They took samples from our roads and then moved across yards and patios where we spent our lives working or idling away our leisure hours. On the banks of the Meramac, even on the wooded point where I proposed to Juanita, they were especially meticulous, forcing their diggers deep in the soft river shore and pulling up murky silt.

Towards evening the air took on an oppressive density. Heavy grey clouds rolled in. It was not storm weather, but there was an expectant humidity to the air that would normally have drawn us outside to examine the sky, but the moon men caused us to reconsider stepping so bravely into our own back yards.

When the clouds did break loose, the rain swept into town from the Southwest in one of those rare lines of advance that is visible to the eye. The moon men grabbed their containers and lumbered awkwardly across the roads and clearings. Their white coveralls became splattered with mud, and they were extra cautious in wiping down their trouser legs before getting into their vans and driving away.

The rain did not let up. It pounded down on the roof of our trailer throughout the night. Inside, Juanita and I cushioned ourselves from the sound of resonant drumming by turning up the TV volume. We slept with our pillows over our heads. In the morning, we woke to the same relentless rhythm.

The moon men returned that day, but they stayed for only a few minutes and did not wander far from their vans. They decided to rush their samples to the Center for Disease Control in Atlanta rather than wait for the rain to cease. This turned out to be a wise decision. The following day Times Beach was underwater.

From The Book of Songs:

A newspaper reporter came to Times Beach and did a story on Lorraine and Carl Hopper. The story, titled "The Plight of Job," detailed Lorraine and Carl Hopper's intense spell of bad luck. It began in April of 1982. Lorraine and her husband and two small children were away for the weekend with relatives in the countryside. When the family returned to Times Beach, they discovered that their new home, completed the previous summer, had been hit by lightning and burned to the ground. Carl had fire insurance and because of his work as a building contractor, cleanup and reconstruction began almost immediately. By late October a second version of the house, lower and less ornate, but certainly impressive by Times Beach standards, stood in its place.

Six weeks after they moved in, the Meramac River swelled and reached flood levels unheard of in 25 years. But this time the disaster did not plague the Hoppers alone. The entire town suffered, and therefore the Hoppers were one family among many in complaining of chest-high watermarks on the living room wallpaper, broken appliances and water-logged furniture. Carl Hopper did not have flood insurance. The floodwater eventually receded and like everyone else in town they threw out most of their possessions and scraped buckets of river sludge from their floors. The family returned to their home and spent a total of three nights distracted from sleep by the dank river odors seeping out of the floors and walls before the EPA announced positive test results for dioxin. The agency recommended that those still forced out by the flood not reinhabit and strongly urged those who had already moved back to Times Beach to find accommodations elsewhere.

By the time the government buy-out finally came, Carl Hopper had lost a good deal of his resolve. His contracting business had failed largely due to the fact that most of his customers were now displaced residents of Times Beach. I suspect that when he moved his family to the Forest Summit Trailer Park, just two miles south of Times Beach on Highway 44, that he was thinking of pulling back for a time and gathering his resources and strength. Two months later the family was forced to abandon their mobile home when the EPA discovered that nine years earlier Russell Bliss had also visited this trailer court with his oil truck.

The newspaper article described Mrs. Hopper as "unsmiling but not unfriendly." When I run into her at the Eureka grocery store or post office, I see her differently. Lorraine Hopper behaves like a woman placed under a secret and incomprehensible curse. Yes, it's true that she does not smile, and although she observes the rules of neighborly etiquette, I can't help but feel that she will never be able to extend genuine human warmth until she discovers who exactly has brought this plague upon her family. I read Carl Hopper much more easily. Certainly, he is aware that he is a ruined man; however, there is an air of hope and expectant good fortune about him, and when I see him I smile to myself because I understand so thoroughly what he is thinking. Carl believes that he has used up all, or nearly all, of his bad luck in this life. It is not simply that he has reached bottom and things can only improve, but also that once he has returned to success, he will not be bothered by formless and irrational fears of failure. As in nearly all matters concerning chance, I remain confused, but I do wish the Hoppers well, I truly do.

The ancient Chinese did not believe in coincidence. They placed their trust in a sense of fate which was wide and flawless, beyond questioning. Even Confucius believed in a theory he called "Waiting for Destiny" which meant that a man should do his best to be virtuous and moral, but occasionally events took place in life that were beyond a man's control and therefore man must wait for fate to run its course. In the Chinese language there is a popular idiom which the Chinese recite both in times of tragedy and during moments of far less momentous sorrow and anxiety. "Submit to the will of heaven and one's fate," they say.

After the flood, Juanita and I lived in a small apartment set behind the nursing home where she worked. I set about finding us another trailer and lot. We had managed to save most of our valuables by filling my Buick with hastily packed boxes of books, clothing and small appliances and driving away before the water was high enough to spill in through our back door. We told ourselves that what happened to the trailer could have been worse; that is, it could have been pulled into the swollen Meramac River and lost for good. Instead, it was pushed by the rising water farther in toward the center of town. Juanita and I found it battered, stretched on its side like an exhausted swimmer, the interior fouled with river sludge.

The Center for Disease Control report found dioxin levels exceeding three hundred parts per billion. Additional testing completed after the floodwaters receded showed the dioxin level had not decreased. The state and federal government were gradually pressured into a complete buy-out of Times Beach.

Late the following summer we began receiving our settlement checks, except for the Stewarts who refused their government offer. We smiled to ourselves thinking that Charles and Marge, now in their late 60's, were holding out for a bigger piece of the pie, a lump sum that would settle them in a Florida retirement community. We were wrong. The Stewarts were not just refusing the money; they were refusing to leave.

"I'm too damned old to move now," Charles said.

His refusal was puzzling. It was not as if he had grown up and lived out his life in Times Beach. Charles had retired from the Marines ten years earlier and he and Marge had come to Times Beach and picked out a shaded, grassy and somewhat isolated lot near the river. He had refurbished the lot's modest timber house and had it set up on stilts—Charles grew up in a Louisiana floodplain and took no chances—and Marge gradually built up a complex maze of flower beds utilizing everything from diesel truck tires to colored rows of power line resistors.

We were patient with them. We explained all the advantages of accepting the money, pointed out all the potential problems of staying on, told them how alone they would feel in their quaint log house on the outskirts of town.

"We understand all that," Marge insisted, "but we're still too damned old."

Not long after the buy-out was over, the state and federal government and the EPA made a concerted effort to erase our town. The highway sign announcing the Times Beach exit was the first to go. Then construction teams jackhammered the paved exits into pieces and hauled the ruble away. Grass was planted to fill in the scarred earth. The Stewarts are able to exit and enter Times Beach on a gated access road leading to nearby Eureka. To this day, the two main roads leading in and out of town remain barricaded with weighty concrete lane dividers. Signs on the barricades read "NOT ACCESSI-BLE. NO TRESSPASSING BY ORDER OF THE STATE GOV-ERNMENT OF MISSOURI.

But people have trespassed. The have browsed through our deserted houses and trailers. Windows, frames, TV antennas, wall and ceiling fixtures, and copper pipes have all been looted and carried away under the cover of darkness. Even the town's electric power lines have been cut down and stripped of their valuable copper. Stories of gangs of bandits and homeless travelers inhabiting our abandoned Times Beach persist. We suspect the Stewarts may have some interesting stories to tell.

The buy-out did not allow most of us to migrate far from Times Beach. I recall a few of the town's residents leaving for Florida and Arizona. Most of us remain in the immediate area. If we have jobs, we drive by Times Beach each day, and I am certain that we all must ease off the accelerator, turn and study what remains of our community.

The largest and nicest homes are visible from Highway 44; perhaps this is what tempts people to trespass. Paint peels and falls from the exterior walls. Gutters and siding hang loose, but if we remember the old Times Beach, if we are honest with ourselves, these are not legitimate signs of decay. What disturbs us most are the holes left by missing windows, doors hanging open in the cold weather, the unwanted pieces of cheap furniture and fragments of our homes which the looters have left scattered in the yards.

Like hundreds of other cultures, the Chinese believed there were important truths to be found encoded within a dream or nightmare. Yet dreams were of special significance in ancient China because it was believed that the dreamer's soul was able to transcend the body and move on to a kind of meeting ground where the lives of mortal men and women could connect with the otherworldly. In dreams, sons and daughters could commune with relatives long dead, or, during the course of a dream, a dreamer could pass hours inside a heavenly palace as a specially summoned guest of a god or goddess. In the background, just within range of hearing, celestial maidens would recite long poems and songs chronicling the dreamer's life history and offering subtle clues concerning the dreamer's earthly fate.

From the age of 29 until Juanita and I moved from Times Beach, I earned my living driving a tractor trailer for the J & B Interstate Transfer Company. My routes were almost entirely in the South and Midwest. It's no secret that a diesel rig sits much higher than an automobile, and there is always that feeling of gliding above the road rather than driving on top of the pavement. With this in mind, I recall drifting through Florida, Georgia, North and South Carolina, Tennessee, Kentucky, Indiana, Illinois, and into Missouri. I drove without music. The tires whined, the rig hummed and shook, and I listened to that. I enjoyed the sensation of being insulated from everything outside the cab of my truck, and yet stepping down from the running board, feeling the solidness of a restaurant or motel sidewalk beneath my feet always made me tense and apprehensive.

The only remarkable thing about truck driving which stays with me to this day is how I managed to memorize long stretches of interstate just like the streets and lanes of a small town. Billboards, ruined barns, oddly angled fence lines, cracked or uneven highway exits; they all became part of my own intuitive map of America. Over the next rise, I would tell myself, there will be a dark and rusted oil drilling platform. And I was always right. Always.

Inside the cab, I would daydream which I have been told is a dangerous activity for a truck driver. And while most of my daydreams were silly and inconsequential, I remember one in which I slip back in time to the year 1952. I go to the Immaculate Mary High School in Louisville, Kentucky and find Juanita quietly pacing the school parking lot. She is there, just as I always imagined her, sad and serene, her face sore and irritated with acne so that its prettiness is unrecognizable to everyone except me. "Juanita," I call to her and she turns in surprise, lifts her glasses, and takes a few hesitant steps toward me. I lean against the wire-linked fence, my fingers poking through the wide silver diamonds. I stand there knowing we have floods and toxic waste still yet to live through, and I say, "Don't be afraid, Juanita. Submit to the will of heaven and one's fate."

One morning last week I woke early as usual, showered, dressed and made coffee while Juanita continued to sleep. As I sat down to the kitchen table, I remembered I had left several library books under the Buick's front seat.

I threw on a light jacket and stepped outside. In early October I am often surprised by the mornings, which are far cooler than the long Missouri summer has prepared me for.

There was a sharp briskness to the air, and the grass between the trailer and driveway was damp and stiff, a near frost.

Inside the Buick, I rested my head on the passenger-side seat and ran my left hand along the shadowy floor of the automobile. Suddenly, I was jarred up into a sitting position by a loud and rapid tapping on the windowpane. I looked over and saw Teddy Barnes dressed in his blue and white-stripped jogging suit. His face fluctuated between expressions of expectancy and confusion, that is, he expected me to open the car door and then appeared confused when I would not.

"Well for Christ sake, open the door Mister!"

I did not open the door; instead, I drew myself out of the car and talked to Teddy across the roof of the Buick.

"You really should go back to Clara and the trailer, Teddy. After all, it's cold out this morning."

"Mister, you wouldn't say that if your son was being held up the way mine is."

"Teddy, your son is in California."

"Not any more he ain't. He's being held up back at the old place."

"Times Beach?"

"That's the one. Which way is it?"

I pointed towards the east and a growing arc of light flooding up over the horizon. "That's the way, but it's at least five miles."

"How 'bout giving me a ride?"

"No, I can't do that."

"Well," he said, "that's a shame because I'd do it for you, Mister." He then took off jogging toward the trailer park exit. At the stop sign, he turned right and headed for the highway.

I dashed back into the trailer, found my car keys, and placed a quick call to Clara. I told her that I would pick Teddy up on the highway and try to talk him into returning home, but if I couldn't then I would drive him on to Times Beach and

23

she should call the police and have them meet me there. I didn't want to argue or wrestle with him, I told her, I just wanted to make sure he was safe.

I found Teddy pacing quickly along the freeway entrance ramp getting close to Highway 44. I pulled over and pushed open the passenger door for him.

"I changed my mind," I explained.

"That's better," he said leaning into the car. "Much better." He patted his hands up and down his running suit before easing into the seat.

We gathered speed and moved east toward Times Beach. I drove slowly though, and kept to the far right lane, near the shoulder. Although Teddy was winded from his jog, he could not quite relax. His fingers jittered their way along the dash and brushed dangerously close to the release handle on the door.

"Won't this car go faster?" Teddy asked.

"Sure, but what's the hurry?"

Teddy lowered his brows and eyed me skeptically. "I believe I explained this once already. It's Raymond. They've got him. I'm gonna' get him back."

"Who's they?"

"The boys from the government, state and federal, and the boys from the EPA."

"I called Clara before I picked you up and she told me Raymond's back home at the trailer."

"Ha!" Teddy laughed, "I bet she did."

Once we were close enough to look down off the highway and see the outskirts of Times Beach, Teddy leaned against the dash and said, "It was just like Venice, Italy, I mean the sinking part of it, one fifth of an inch per year. The big mistake was we should've been hooked up to the county water line all along instead of using water from the town wells and sucking ourselves down. We were sinking further and further each year and we didn't even know it."

I guided the Buick off Highway 44 and onto a grassy slope—previously the highway off ramp—and rolled forward until we came to the concrete barricades. As soon as the car rolled to a stop, Teddy was outside making his way around the barrier.

"You might want to wait here for a while," I suggested.

"No thanks. The sooner I get going the better." He slipped behind the barrier and was gone, but then I could see him again hiking swiftly along the obstructed road leading into Times Beach.

A car braked behind me. I turned and saw a police cruiser, the lights flashing but the siren mute. The officer emerged from his car, a paunch-bellied man who appeared hemmed in by his own brown uniform. He spotted Teddy making his way toward town.

"Oh Christ, I don't believe this. Why didn't you hold him for me?"

"I'm not going to wrestle with Teddy," I said, "I thought you'd be here when I arrived."

The officer cupped his hands around his mouth and shouted, "*Teddy*, this is *Officer Duffy*! I want you to *return* to the barricade *right now*!"

No luck. Not only did Teddy refuse to turn back, but he broke into a nimble jog.

Officer Duffy returned to his cruiser and began making a call to the dispatcher. I stood outside my idling automobile and watched Teddy reach the outskirts of town. He slipped through a line of mulberry trees and into someone's unkempt back yard, all the while maintaining the precise and crafty step of a commando. I watched him move like that until he was out of sight, obscured by houses and trees. And I continued to watch for a long while afterward, taking a sad and strange kind of inventory of our ruined town. During those moments, I carefully considered both coincidence and fate.

Here's a question. Given the accidental poisoning of the streets of Times Beach and the far more lethal events at Shenandoah Stables, and my own mysterious inability to show my wife physical love, given all this, don't Juanita and I worry about other, perhaps more dangerous, threats to our health, the unraveling of our own fate? The answer to this is, of course, yes, but this worry does not dominate our lives, and when we do discuss the matter, we do so quietly and mostly to ourselves.

From the follow-up studies done on Times Beach and its scattered former residents, the outlook appears encouraging. Some studies show no higher than average cancer rates. Another believes that Times Beach might be ready for the return of its citizens, though it also suggests that sealing the town under a half-foot of concrete and turning it into an airport might be a better alternative.

In all truth though, Juanita and I are not particularly health conscious. We are both pack-a-day smokers and love our barbecued red meat. We do not exercise, nor do we enjoy weekend getaways to the countryside. If Juanita and I are anything, we are stay-at-home types. Like the trailer, our lives are small and insulated. Our living room is a couch, coffee table, twenty-seven inch TV, carpet, drapes, and a bookshelf containing books, stand-up photographs, and one decorative plate emblazoned with a mallard duck. This is what we are familiar with, and we seldom, if ever, rearrange the furniture, and we hardly ever mention cancer. And to be honest it is not truly cancer or illness or death that we fear so much as being left alone. We each have life insurance policies, and during one of our rare discussions on being alone, Juanita said that if

I die first, she will move back to the apartment near the nursing home and use the money in some manner helpful to others. I could not think of a reasonable plan for myself were the situation reversed. A return to truck driving seemed out of the question. It was then that Juanita suggested that I use the money to travel to China. I thought about that, about boarding a plane in California and gliding for hours over the Pacific, maybe looking down on Japan or Korea. I have never in my life flown in a plane, yet I can imagine the bump and squeal of jet tires setting down on a foreign runway. I can also picture the rolling staircase, which I have seen in photographs of Chinese airports, pressed up snugly beneath the side of the jet. I see myself, outside the protective shell of the plane, taking that last step onto the hard surface of the runway, feeling its solidness beneath my shoes, a country so wide and real that I would certainly tremble upon my arrival.

Alice Fulton
The Gettysburg Review
Pushcart Prize XXIX

THE REAL ELEANOR RIGBY

EDNA Livingston was the loneliest girl in North America. She was the only Catholic High student who subscribed to *Zen Teen: The Journal of Juvenile Macrobiotics* published by the Youth in Asia Foundation (Euthanasia! Someone should point out the unhappy homonym), the only member of the Sodality of the Blessed Virgin who'd read *Tropic of Cancer*. Once when she mentioned Henry Miller, the entire group thought she was referring to the amiable, goateed host of the popular TV show, *Sing Along with Mitch.*

Arthur Miller maybe, but Mitch!

In a weak moment Edna had joined her school's chapter of Up with People, the moral rearmament choral group. She'd performed with them once or twice, but she was asked to leave after taking liberties with the windshield-wiper waves. Now she spent her weekends immured in her room, cataloging items in *BeatleLuv Unlimited* magazine and *IshMail*, the Melville Society newsletter.

"John, Paul, George, and Herman!" her mother said. "If you ask me, *Moby Dick* is one dull book. Where's the romance, the love interest? If you ask me, Herman was a fink."

Edna felt deeply misunderstood. Like Melville, she wanted to ship out to Liverpool.

No one shared her obsessions except Sunny Metzger, a Lutheran who attended Troy High. The two girls were desperate virgins, isolated by their attraction to the non-Troy and exotic. Edna had heard all about Sunny's brief fling with an Estonian boy who wanted her to eat borscht while he snapped Polaroids. She heard how one famished night, Sunny agreed, and afterwards during the sad, postculinary intimacy, the boy drove her to Albany Airport to watch the planes take off. They had sat in the car outside the runway's chain-link till Sunny's hair smelled like jet fuel, a musky residue of adventure that Edna envied, though the Estonian boy never called again.

Every night Edna fell asleep with her transistor radio under her head like a renunciate's stone pillow. The local station was always holding contests. Their call letters, WTRY, stood for Troy, but in their elastic ID jingles, she heard the command *to strive*. Third caller, try again, fifth caller, try again, the deejay would say. One lucky midnight she became the ninth caller and won a pen touched by the Beatles. It arrived by mail a week later.

"It's a second-class relic," Edna said, placing the sealed envelope in the middle of the kitchen table. Her mother was ironing nearby. Sunny was sipping a Diet Rite.

"Well, I call it pretty chintzy. At least they could give you a first-class prize," Mrs. Livingston said.

"C'mon, Ma. First-class relics are rare." First-class relics were taken from the body or any of its integrant parts, such as limbs, ashes, and bones. How many times had she explained? But her mother was an Easter-duty Catholic. What could you expect.

"Well, I still say it's pretty darn cheap."

"A third-class relic, now that would be cheap," Sunny offered. "A third-class relic is anything that's touched a first- or second-class relic. You can't take a relic like that theriously." Sunny lisped when she got excited. Sometimes she stuttered. "Hey, Ed. Now we can make our own third-clath welicths," she said. "We could thell them."

They had learned about relics during a special weekend retreat taught by a foreign priest full of discouraged Catholic lore. Sunny had sat in the back, and the visiting cleric did not recognize her as an interloper. His presentation was part show-and-tell, part autopsy. He explained how a particle extracted from a saint had been placed in a locket, covered by crystal, bound by red thread, and sealed with the insignia of office. Then he opened the back cover of the locket and showed them a swatch of red wax that looked like a hundred-year-old heart, wizened and dripping with antiquity.

Sunny raised her hand. "Father, I know a second-class welic is an object that has come in contact with a living saint, like the instruments wherewith a martyr has been tortured, the chains by which he was bound, the clothes he wore, or objects he used. But what about Saint Peter's shadow or a saint's bray-bray-braces? I mean, it's just a high-high—"A couple of boys snickered, and Brew Thudlinsky, the school bully, belched derisively—"hypothesis, Father, but what class would a saint's con-con- contact lenses be?"

And though the priest spoke perfect English, he had sighed in Spanish. "For the sake of simplicity, let's stick with the bones," he said.

The pen the Beatles touched was enrobed in a red plastic pencil case. Edna eased the zipper back. As the tiny metal fangs gave way, a faint gas, a perfume of petroleum products, essence of black vinyl and steel strings, escaped, and there it was: an instrument of monastic plainness nestled in the scarlet darkness. A cheap black ballpoint. A new warmth possessed her. Hope, the thing with feathers, was perching in her soul.

"Are you sure it's not the albatross like in that other poem?" Sunny asked.

A relic might be *coronse spinse D.N.J.C.,* taken from the crown of thorns, or *de velo,* from the veil. It might be *ex parecordi,* from the stomach or intestines; *ex pelle* from the skin; *ex capillus,* from the hair; *ex carne,* from the flesh. It could be *ex stipite affixionis,* from the whipping post, or *ex tela serica quae tetigit cor,* from the silk cloth that touched the heart.

"Or maybe it's the liver. That extinct bird Liverpool was named for."

"This is Hope," Edna said. "You'll know it when you feel it." Hope felt like a summer clearance when the worn merchandise was offered up and whisked away.

Her mother hung up a blouse with a vehemence that made the hangers shriek. "It doesn't take much to make you girls happy, does it?" she said.

"Knock, knock!" Mrs. Livingston had yelled on the day Herman Melville entered Edna's life. She was sequestered in her bedroom, which resembled a clipping service run by a poltergeist. The floor was a brittle strudel of back issues and loose paper. Narrow paths had been cleared between the door, bed, and stereo.

"What a booby trap," her mother said, walking the plank of carpet. "It kind of makes you glad paper has only two sides." She placed two books on the bed next to Edna. "Old junk from the Phoenix." The Phoenix, an old residential hotel, had belonged to Edna's father. He had died a year ago.

Typee: A Peep at Polynesian Life by Herman Melville, Edna read. New York, Wiley and Putnam, 1846. Volume I popped like an arthritic knuckle when she opened it, and a dank, riverish smell rose from the pages.

"*Typee* is a cookbook and a sex manual," she told Sunny during their nightly phone call. "It's a hunger novel."

Melville's book told the story of two starving pals, Tommo and Toby, on their perilous journey into the heart of the Marquesas. The infinite care with which these deserters parceled out their sea biscuits, the division of a little sustenance into less, worked upon Edna's imagination. Every night she gave Sunny a synopsis. *Tommo and Toby have been captured by natives! Toby has escaped, but Tommo is being treated well! Today the island girls gathered a thimbleful of salt. They spread a big leaf on the ground, dropped a few grains on it, and invited Tommo to taste them as a sign of their esteem.* "From the extravagant value placed upon the article," Edna read, "I verily believed that with a bushel of common Liverpool salt, all the real estate in Typee might have been purchased."

"I verily believe it, too," Sunny said.

The girls passed *Typee* back and forth, reading and rereading. They went to the Troy Public Library and checked out everything on Herman Melville. One night Edna called with a major discovery. "Herman wrote *Typee* in Lansingburgh. He was living on 114th Street, near the Phoenix Hotel." The next day, she called the Lansingburgh Historical Society, and they gave her the phone number of a ninety-year-old man named Tim Brunswick, whose father was rumored to have actually known Herman Melville.

"I'd like to meet him," she told her mother.

"I wish you could find someone your own age."

"Don't you mean *from* my own age?" Edna said.

When Mrs. Livingston realized the girls were determined to visit the ancient Melville expert, she offered them a ride. Tim Brunswick lived in a trailer on the banks of the Hudson River. He met them at the door with a quivery little dog in his arms. A toy poodle? Sunny asked.

"A Maltese," said Tim Brunswick. "Name of Blimey." He led them into a tiny parlor lined with gray file cabinets. A picture window showed a dismal river view, and a saxophone gleamed dully in one corner like the esophagus of a golden beast. The room shivered when the wind blew, as if it might lunge into the Hudson at any minute. Edna felt a little seasick.

"Did your father really know Herman Melville, Mr. Brunswick?" Sunny asked.

"Everybody in the 'burgh knew him. Dad went to school with his kid brother, Tom. Those boys worshipped Melville." Blimey buried his tiny nose in his master's shirt, and Tim Brunswick peered at Mrs. Livingston over his bifocals. His eyes were a vibrant baby blue. "I also knew your husband, Sammy Livingston. He was a serious person. Quiet, but accommodating."

"That's why he needed me." Mrs. Livingston crossed her legs and started swinging the top one with aggressive abandon. "I was fun-loving as all get-out."

"Lansingburgh was quite a place in his day. It has quite a history." And Tim Brunswick told them how the first Dutch settlers had named the village Steen Arabia and how in Melville's time, the 1840s, peach trees and willows had grown along the Hudson, which was then a busy shipyard. "Melville and a local girl, Mary Parmalee, used to stroll on the riverbank, reading Tennyson to each other. 'Far on the ringing plains of windy Troy. I am a part of all that I have met—' "

"Mary Parmalee!" Edna's mother interrupted. "What a pretty name! How did I wind up being plain old Annie Livingston?"

"What was Herman like?" Sunny asked eagerly.

"Like a real sailor, Dad said. Suntanned. And he walked with this racy kind of swagger, what they called the sailor's roll. It was considered very suggestive in his day."

"Yeah?" Sunny smiled encouragingly.

"Yeah. Melville walked like he was on a rocking boat, kind of bowlegged like—" And Tim Brunswick set the dog down on his chair and lurched around the table, demonstrating. Then he came to a halt and swayed tipsily above the little Maltese.

"Blimey!" exclaimed Sunny.

"You betcha!" said Tim Brunswick. "The ladies love a sailor. All the belles of Lansingburgh were after Herman Melville. Ladies led sheltered lives in those days, and he was a man of the world, swashbuckling, like Errol Flynn. He was what we'd call a sex symbol today."

"I don't understand symbolism, do you?" Mrs. Livingston appealed. "That's why I don't understand *Moby Dick*." She shifted restlessly on the narrow love seat. "It's full of symbolism."

"Some books you have to read twice to understand," Edna said.

"And some you'd never understand if you read till time immortal. *Gone with the Wind!* Now there was a book."

Edna handed Tim Brunswick her copy of *Typee*. "This was in my father's safe at the Phoenix Hotel."

He opened volume one and examined it. "You'd better take good care of this, young lady. This is a first edition. It might even be an association copy."

"Wow!" Sunny said. "What's that?"

"A book Melville owned himself. He might have given it to the innkeeper in payment for his drinking tab."

"You mean Herman touched *Typee?* That makes it a thecond-clath welic."

"Say again?"

"An object rich with spiritual electricity," Edna translated. "An object made luminous by contact with a radiant being."

As they walked to the car, she looked for evidence of peach trees by the Hudson. She felt the past must exist behind, beside, inside, or under the present. The problem was time. Time came between things, shutting them off in loneliness and ignorance. And time had dimension. It wasn't flat like paper. Time had substance, yet it was invisible, like all important things.

"All the lonely people!" Sunny exclaimed.

Edna had long believed she had the power to pull things toward her with her mind. Now she sensed something desirable approaching, and she urged it on, envisioning a limo with dark windows, a single-masted schooner. A yellow submarine.

A week later Mrs. Livingston came running upstairs in a state of high emergency. "The Beatle Buggy's outside!" she said. "It looks like a Ford Fairlane. Hurry!"

WTRY was giving away tickets to see the group at Shea Stadium. The winners also would attend the junior press conference in New York. Edna and Sunny had sent in a hundred entries with "Jay Blue is sexy!" scrawled all over them. They'd found the deejay's name in the phone book under *Blue, Jay* and called to say they admired his jingles. Now he sat in her mother's living room, a palpable absence of sound taking shape around him. His quietude felt lifeless, as if uttering inanities at the speed of light for a living drained him of élan vital. Maybe he's a mild-mannered mortician by day and a swinging deejay by night, Edna thought. "It'll be a gas," Jay Blue said in the forced baritone that was his air voice. He scratched his head and his mod-style toupee, said to be made of genuine mink, slipped down and touched the top of his sunglasses. Then he stood up and handed Edna the tickets, and Mrs. Livingston burst into applause. "Since her father died, she's hardly left her room. Maybe this will get her out of the house."

"Say, that's a good idea," said Jay Blue.

Edna held the receiver at arm's length after telling Sunny. "We have to stop screaming and think," she yelled into the mouthpiece.

"Thop threaming and think!"

"We need a way to get close to them. We need the perfect gift."

The usual offerings—gum wrappers woven into an eighteen-foot strip, a life-size portrait of Ringo made entirely of uncooked elbow macaroni—would not do. All that chewing and plaiting and dying and gluing did not reflect well upon the giver. They'd have to come up with something unique. Something the Beatles might actually want. The perfect gift could open doors. It must be something that would not melt or die on the bus to New York, something that could be carried while sprinting in a miniskirt.

"For the man who has everything," Edna continued, "a relic would make a very special present."

"Why would the Beatles want a pen they touched?"

"Not that, Hairspray Brains! *Typee.*"

Sunny squealed in shock. "If we give them *Typee,* what are we going to re-reread?"

"There are other books in the world, you know." Edna affected a supercilious tone. "We could read *Billy Budd*. Or *Moby Dick*." In fact, she was tired of second-class relics. If she could get close to the Beatles, she might achieve the hands-on, naked knowledge that came from touching a primary source.

"Why not give them uth," Sunny suggested.

"Give them us?"

"Remember Regina." This cousin of Sunny's had lost her virginity at Jose's Deli, and her description—the really amazing pain, the counter boy's commands to open wider—made sex sound like a terrible trip to the dentist. Now Sunny said she thought they could do better. Since Herman was unavailable, she thought the Beatles might be equal to the task. Try the best, then try the rest, she said, and the concept appealed to Edna's perfectionism.

And so over the next few weeks, they set about starving their bodies into bodies the Beatles could want: model bodies, twiggish and ravishingly thin. Sometimes at the end of a meal, Sunny would pick up her plate and lick it clean. She was so hungry!

"Zen cookery uses four yangizing factors to achieve change," Edna said. She and Sunny were eating their usual dinner of brown rice with brown rice. "Heat, time, pressure, and/or salt."

"You girls need more variety in your diet," her mother remarked. "You need more color. 'A bright color on a brown gruel is like a song in the heart.' I made that up myself."

"Was Jay Blue anything like his image, Mrs. Livingston?" Sunny asked.

"No. In real life he's dead timber. Not my type." She took another bite of Irish stew.

"Who's your type, Ma?"

"Tyrone Power. He had bedroom eyes. And Sam, your father, liked Kay Francis." Her mother set dishes of pink pudding before them.

"I don't want any," Edna said.

"Sam was the only one who thought I was swell." Her mother sighed. "He was the only one who liked my cooking. Though when I was a visiting nurse, I had admirers. I once had a patient change her name to mine, you know."

Edna rolled her eyes. "This patient changed her first name *and* her last name," she told Sunny.

"I know it!" crowed her mother. "She became Annie Monahan. That was before I became Annie Livingston, of course."

"Did she change her name to Livingston when you did?" Edna asked.

"Huh?" her mother's mind was back in the 1930s. "We'd lost touch by then. Who knows, she might have. She thought very highly of me, that's for dang sure."

"Well, I like your cooking, Mrs. L.," Sunny said.

Mrs. Livingston gave another martyred sigh. "I eat to live, I don't live to eat."

"The body is water, but the mind is sea," said Edna. "The body—"

"The body is water, but the mind is at sea! What's that supposed to mean?" Mrs. Livingston interrupted.

Since earliest childhood, whenever Edna tried to speak, her mother's voice had drowned her out. Rather than compete for conversational space, she had become a seriously silent person. Her father had mistaken her reticence for arrogance. He'd accused her of caring more for John Lennon than her parents. And what could she say? The Beatles are my Polynesia?

"The ripe raw breadfruit can be stored away in large underground receptacles for years on end," Edna quoted from *Typee*. "It only improves with age." They were sitting at a card table in the cellar of her house. The cellar, fusty with oilcloth and light-absorbing knotty pine, reminded them of the Cavern, where the Fab Four had begun. Now that school had ended for the summer, they spent much of their time there, playing the one folk song they knew over and over on their warped guitars. "Danger water's coming, baby, hold me tight," they sang in loud, flat voices.

"Were it not that the breadfruit is thus capable of being preserved for a length of time, the natives might be reduced to a state of starvation."

"If I could get my hands on a breadfruit, I'd know what to do with it," Sunny said. But breadfruit was not available at the local supermarkets, and when they asked after it, the produce managers became churlish and depressed.

"What was Jay Blue like?" Sunny asked.

"He was like—nothing. He seemed kind of lonely."

"Troy must be the loneliest place on Earth. I bet we're one of the only places on Earth without a sister city."

"One of the only! That's a redundancy," Edna said.

"Wow!" Sunny dropped her guitar with a metallic boom. "Herman's first voyage was to Liverpool, right? And he was living in Lansingburgh then, right? Well, it's obvious. We'll start a petition to make Lansingburgh and Liverpool sister cities, and we'll ask the Beatles to sigh-sigh-"—her voice sounded as if she'd been breathing helium—"sign it!"

"We can't do that! It'll ruin our image. They'll think we're fans." Edna fluffed her hair near the crown to give it more height. "Anyway, it's so—municipal."

"Your mother can do the embarrassing part, asking for their autographs." Since the girls were only fourteen, Mrs. Livingston insisted on accompanying them to New York. "We need more than one idea," Sunny said. "We shouldn't put all our begs in one ask-it."

"Wouldn't we have to get somebody's approval, like the lord mayor of Liverpool or at least the mayor of Lansingburgh?"

"If the Beatles sign, do you think those guys will say no? They're politicians! They know which side their butt is breaded on!"

And Edna didn't argue. *Do I dare to eat a peach?* she often asked herself. Lately, more often than not, the answer was yes.

On August 22, Edna, Sunny, and Mrs. Livingston took the bus to New York City. The girls were using years of baby-sitting savings to pay for a room at the Warwick, where the Beatles were staying. They spent the hours before the junior press conference donning their Beatle girlfriend costumes: hip-hugger skirts, net stockings, paisley shirts with white cuffs and collars, ghillie shoes of golden suede. Do I look like a fan? No, do I? they asked each other.

The press conference was held on the second floor. Girls waited outside, trying to insinuate themselves to the front of the pack, and at last the doors swung open. As the crowd trampled past, Edna was stabbed in the clavicle by someone's JOHN IS GOD button. She hugged her copy of *Typee,* which she planned to present at a suitable moment. An aide appeared and said, "The Beatles are about to enter. Would those in front please kneel?" All the girls sank like barn animals on Christmas Eve. "I mean," he amended, "so those in back can get their picture. Make room." Edna and Sunny were pressed against an emergency exit when suddenly it opened, hurtling them back into the hall. A long, navy blue arm reached over their heads and slammed the door, stranding them outside.

"We won passes!" Edna wailed.

"Win some, lose some," the policeman said.

"You're supposed to be a community helper," Sunny scolded.

"I'm helping those rich fairies stay alive." He patted his gun holster. "If you ask me, those guys are a little light in their loafers."

"Nobody asked you," Sunny snapped. Muffled munchkin squeals erupted from within the room, followed by deeper, foreign inflections that flipped up at the ends. Edna and Sunny pulled their hair and groaned in frustration. When the doors opened they rushed in, but the Beatles had been whisked away. We've been cheated! they told each other through disbelieving tears.

"Yes, they do that to your mother, too," Mrs. Livingston remarked, when they returned to the room. "But I don't let them get away with it."

The girls were prostrated in shock on the bed. "They're above us right now," Edna said. "Just one floor up." And they listened to the footsteps on high, trying to guess their identities.

"C'mon," her mother said, putting on her pumps. "Let's meet the Beatles and get it over with. Then we can go out and have some fun."

As soon as the girls had repaired their eyeliner, Mrs. Livingston hustled them onto the elevator. When the doors opened at the eighth floor, a guard blocked their exit. Edna peered into the corridor and spied the Beatles' road manager. "Neil As-As—" Sunny called, as the elevator door slammed into her side. "—Aspinall!" The road manager paused, and Edna told him how they'd missed the press conference. He asked her age. Eighteen, she lied, and for once her mother didn't contradict her. Follow me, Neil said. When he saw Mrs.

Livingston was with the girls, he hesitated. Then he unlocked a door, and with a sweeping gesture, bade them enter.

Four dove-gray suits with plum-red stripes lay draped across the bed, gleaming in the lunar light of the TV. Edna reacted like a Geiger counter sensing uranium nearby. Her teeth began to chatter, and she had to suppress high-pitched trills of impending revelation. "If you wouldn't mind doing us a favor," Neil said. "These have to be ironed before the show tomorrow." He pointed to an ironing board in the corner. "I'll be back," he promised.

"Always leave the door ajar when you're in a strange man's hotel room," Mrs. Livingston instructed, propping it with the telephone book. She examined the suits. "What elegant tailoring! You have to take everything out of the pockets, or they won't lie flat. Oh, name tags."

The girls exchanged thrilled looks. "Which one do you want?" Edna asked.

"Paul, of course," Sunny said. "Paul is All!"

"Is he the single one?" Mrs. Livingston inquired.

"He's the Cute One," Edna said dismissively. "I want John, the Sexy One."

"Paul's had a very hard life, you know," Sunny told them. "His mother died when he was fourteen."

"John's mother died, too," said Edna. "And his father deserted him. He's an orphan."

Mrs. Livingston sighed. She'd been born near an orphanage, and as a student nurse she'd worked in the New York Foundling Hospital. "Poor motherless boys! At least they're young and healthy."

"Oh no," Edna informed her. "Ringo had peritonitis as a child, and George had nephritis. They're actually kind of sickly." She knew her mother had sympathy for physical ills, though disturbances of the mind only made her irritable. Mrs. Livingston respected reality and those who kept in touch with its firm facts. Now she sat on the bed, watching TV, while Edna and Sunny took turns ironing. John Lennon came on the screen, apologizing for saying the Beatles were more popular than Jesus. The report that followed said the group had been nearly crushed to death in Cleveland, picketed by the Ku Klux Klan in Washington, D.C., and almost electrocuted in St. Louis. They'd received death threats in Memphis, where someone tossed a bomb on stage, and today two fans had promised to leap from the ledge of a New York hotel unless they met the Beatles.

"Silly girls!" Mrs. Livingston frowned. Edna and Sunny were caressing the suits as if they were alive. They ran the zippers up and down, unbuttoned the waistbands, rubbed their faces against the lapels. "Don't be getting lipstick on their outfits. And there's another thing I won't stand for."

Edna held her breath.

"I won't have you throwing things at those boys while they're trying to play their music. They have enough trouble."

"The only thing I want to throw at them is myself," Edna said. She ironed lasciviously, stopping to inhale the faint scents—shaving crème and sweat, patchouli and dry cleaning fluid—liberated by steam and heat. She felt delirious. "How many pleats go in each leg?" she asked.

"Give me that iron," her mother said, pushing her aside. "I can't believe we came to New York for this. This is just like home."

At last the suits were finished, but there still was no sign of Neil Aspinall. "That dress manager of theirs. He has what are called 'craggy good looks.' Do you girls know what that means?"

"Like Frankenstein might have looked if Frankenstein had been good-looking?" Sunny suggested.

Suddenly fragments of song—"Summer in the City"—burst from a room at the end of the hall, a door slammed, and voices came lilting along the corridor. Edna, Sunny, and Mrs. Livingston rushed to the threshold in time to see a fantasia of flowers and paisley, polka dots and stripes, mossy velvets and sun-bright satins levitate down the hall. Then the mirage vanished in a Beatle-scented breeze. Edna and Sunny grabbed each other. Did you see them? Did you see them?

"Had a glimpse of the gardens of Paradise been revealed to me, I could scarcely have been more ravished with the sight," Sunny quoted from *Typee*. "Didn't they look— mythical?"

"Mystical, yes," Edna said. She had expected the Beatles to sense their intimate bond with her and stop. How could they have mistaken her for a stranger?

"If you knew that was them, why didn't you speak up? You missed your chance," her mother said. "Here comes their handsome valet." Mrs. Livingston showed Neil the ironed suits. She pointed to a little heap of Beatle detritus on the dresser. "That was in their pockets."

"Oh, you can keep those things." The road manager's eyes looked dreamy and glazed. "As souvenirs."

"When do we meet the Beatles?" Mrs. Livingston asked.

"The boys are tired. They've had a hard week."

"Listen, we kept our part of the bargain." Mrs. Livingston folded her arms across her chest, preparing for battle. "These girls have come a long way. They've waited a long time."

"Okay," Neil said reluctantly. "All right." He extracted three red press passes from his wallet and handed them out. "Come by the suite tomorrow around four, and you'll meet the Beatles."

At the appointed hour the next day, they showed their passes and joined the line extending from the Beatles' suite. Edna spotted Jay Blue just ahead of them, talking into a cassette recorder and punching the air for emphasis. She clutched *Typee* with clammy fingers. On this day of days, her bangs were wrinkled, her hair full of flyaway, her Beatle girl-friend ensemble disheveled from dress rehearsals. And how could she meet the Beatles with her mother tagging along? She wanted to be back in her room, copying their song lyrics with the patience of a scrivener. Last year she'd ordered some bromeliads from Florida, and when she opened the carton, the pots were swarming with centipedes. She had shrieked and thrown the shipment away before her mother, always disgusted by forays into the strange, could find out. Now she felt the same hysterical alarm. "You go, I'll wait here," she said.

"The heck you will," her mother said, pulling her through the door.

The Beatles' suite was crawling with gifts. *It's like Christmas morning in here*, Edna thought. *Your riches taught me poverty.* What she had to offer seemed shabby in comparison. By the time they'd edged near enough to see the group, everyone else had been ushered out except Jay Blue. The Beatles were holding court from the sofa. There was a gritty orb before them on the cocktail table, and they were staring at it as if it might hatch.

"Is that egg really one hundred years old?" Jay Blue asked.

"No," John Lennon said. "The Chinese only call it that so ignorant Westerners will think they'll eat anything."

"Say, that's a good idea!" said Jay Blue.

The Beatles seemed disgruntled, almost crotchety behind their granny glasses. Apathy poured off them, and joyless waterfalls of worry. Edna yearned to make them happy, if only for an instant. Five minutes, their press agent called. "There's no time like the present," her mother hissed, nudging the girls forward. Edna knew Sunny would not speak for fear of stuttering. She wanted to be introduced as a mute painter who spoke only in watercolors of a halcyon refinement.

"Hi," Edna whispered.

The Beatles went on talking all at once and only with each other above the insect whir of the recorder. They seemed to be discussing the hundred-year-old egg. "Looks like snot I suppose you could wear a blindfold whilst eating it my son please don't use the word *snot* in my hearing snot nice I deplore having used it smells disgusting take it to the loo if you must burn incense," they said.

"Hey, fellas!" Mrs. Livingston interrupted. "These girls have brought you a special present."

The Beatles nodded and mumbled sleepily. George Harrison yawned. Edna and Sunny had decided they must return everything they'd taken from the suits except one relic too precious to relinquish. Now they stepped forward and emptied their purses onto the table before the group. Out tumbled guitar picks, chewing gum, half a cigarette, a little box of perfumed incense papers, a ballpoint pen, and a sticker that said "I Still Love the Beatles."

"It's from your pockets," Edna said.

"Are you thieves or magicians?" George Harrison asked. He lit one of the incense papers, and they began talking about the explosion during their Memphis show.

"You know how George is the Quiet One, I'm the Big-mouthed One, etc.," John Lennon told Jay Blue. "We were looking around to see who was going to be the Dead One." And Jay Blue told them about a friend of his in the music business who'd been shot in the heart. Doctors had removed half the bullet and left the other half in his chest, and now he was fine. He just had some tear duct problems.

"Perhaps we shouldn't have called our album *Revolver,*" George said, twiddling his thumbs.

"You know the old saying. Those who live by the song, die by the song," Mrs. Livingston put in.

John Lennon looked up, aware of her for the first time.

"My husband was musically inclined," Mrs. Livingston continued. "He was shot in the arm during Prohibition."

"Has Prohibition ended?" John asked.

Mrs. Livingston chose that moment to produce the Sister City petition. The quartet picked up pens, and John was about to sign when the TV began to report on anti-Beatle demonstrations in the South. "They're burning my book," he said.

"Shame on them!" Mrs. Livingston seized the "I Still Love The Beatles" sticker, licked it, and pressed it onto the petition folder. "There! That'll show them!"

John blinked slowly. Edna thought it might have been the first time he'd blinked in several years. He said something to the others in a dialect that even she, with her scholarly knowledge of the Scouse language, could not translate. Then Paul McCartney hit the stop button on Jay Blue's recorder, and they all started to speak in a rich mishmash of code that seemed to be their native tongue. Their press agent, sensing a change in atmosphere, came charging over. "Get Brian," John told him. And the Beatles fell silent.

"Well, a lot of people still love you," Mrs. Livingston assured them. "It's not just us."

George, Paul, and Ringo lowered their eyes demurely. John gnawed delicately at his index finger. At last Ringo spoke. "We're very fond of you, too," he said, and with his words some hidden signal seemed to pass between the four, a vibration more enigmatic than a glance. Yes, we loove you too, they insisted. We loove you too!

"That's good," Mrs. Livingston said, grabbing the petition. "It was nice meeting you fellas, but we don't want to wear out our welcome—"

"No!" the Beatles shouted, and the force of their voices almost knocked Edna's contacts off her eyes.

"What's your name?" Paul McCartney inquired gently of her mother. Yes, which one are you? John Lennon added.

"Annie. I'm the sensible one, and these two—" she nodded toward Edna and Sunny—"are the dreamy ones."

"And what can the Beatles do for Annie and the Dreamers?" John asked, with a pleasant smile. Yes, what can we do, would you like a cup of tea? the others echoed. And it was as if they'd morphed from petulant pop stars into solicitous male nurses, custodians of perfect love.

"Well, if we're staying, could somebody make these girls a peanut butter and jelly sandwich?" Mrs. Livingston said. "They haven't had a thing to eat all day." Edna tried to kick her mother discreetly.

"Would you care for some macadamia nuts?" Paul McCartney said, tearing the cellophane from a gift basket piled high with exotic produce. Their manager, Brian Epstein, arrived then, looking impeccable yet flustered. He asked them to wait in the vestibule while he conferred with the boys.

"Gosh, Mrs. L., you've got the Beatles wrapped around your little finger," Sunny gasped as soon as they were alone.

"Listen to this," Edna said, opening *Typee*. " 'The natives, actuated by some mysterious impulse ... redoubled their attentions to us. Their manner towards us was unaccountable ... Why this excess of deferential kindness, or what equivalent can they imagine us capable of rendering them for it?' " She gave them an astonished glance.

"I was kind of surprised myself," her mother admitted, "by how grateful they were that we still love them. I guess everyone needs a kind word. Then they all started speaking in Gaelic or Liverpuddle or something—"

Brian Epstein returned. His eyebrows met in a furrowed point. He cleared his throat and said there had been a slight mishap. Apparently some medicine of John's had been affixed to the back of the "I Still Love The Beatles" sticker that Mrs. Livingston had licked. This medicine, lysergic acid diethylamide, was used to enhance creativity. Thus it could have disquieting effects. One could expect to feel rather odd. One could expect visions, hallucinations—

"You mean it's like someone put a Mickey in my drink?" Mrs. Livingston interrupted.

"Rather."

Nothing scared Edna's mother more than an unquiet mind. "Listen, I'm not the creative type," she said. "I've never had a vision in my life! I don't believe in visions." Then all her bluster faded. She clutched her throat with a trembling hand. "I'm a registered nurse, and I never heard of any medicine being administered on a stamp."

"But you haven't practiced in thirty years," said Edna. "Times change."

"Quite," said Brian Epstein. "This drug makes one highly suggestible. Whatever your companions suggest becomes your reality. But you musn't fret. You are amongst friends. The boys and I would like you to join our entourage tonight so that you might be in the safest, indeed the happiest, indeed the most—" he searched for the ideal hyperbole—"fabulous place on earth."

"Where is that, Mist-Mist-Mr. Epstein?" Sunny wondered.

"The Beatles' dressing room." And his eyes fluttered briefly, involuntarily, heavenwards. "Please." He adjusted his cravat. "I implore you. Do not share this with reporters."

"Don't be a snitch, that's my motto," Edna's mother said. "Nobody likes a tattletale."

"Quite."

"Is this drug habit forming?" she asked.

"On the contrary." And Brian Epstein smiled benignly, glad to be the bearer of good news at last. "You might wish never to take it again."

And so they had been driven by limo to Shea Stadium, escorted to the locker room, and abandoned in that windowless bunker. The lockers were painted gunmetal gray; a few benches and folding metal chairs were the only furnishings. "Are we buried alive?" Mrs. Livingston asked.

Edna was distraught. The Beatles had terrified her. Their godlike confidence brought out her awkwardness. She'd been crushed by their surliness, confused by their kindness. Worst of all, they'd been too busy doting on her mother to notice her existence. She missed the cell-like safety of her room. Yet she could not quit until she had given them her gift. This might be her only chance to achieve the metaphysical-physical contact of her dreams.

"Are you all right?" she asked her mother. Mrs. Livingston looked a little wild eyed.

"This must be the dreariest place on earth," her mother said.

Edna browsed through *Typee* in search of a soothing passage. "'When I looked around the verdant recess in which I was buried, and gazed up to the summits of the lofty eminence that hemmed me in, I was well disposed to think that I was in the 'Happy Valley,' and that beyond those heights there was nought but a world of care and anxiety.'" Footsteps. Her pulse quickened. Her contacts were dirty. She was seeing everything through the oily shimmer her optometrist called spectacle blur. When the Beatles came sprinting in—day of daze!—each was haloed by his own greasy rainbow.

"How are you feeling, all right?" Paul asked her mother.

"I'm feeling kind of—" The Beatles leaned forward, attentive. "Creative. I want to hold your—" She paused, distracted by their raised eyebrows.

"Hand?" Paul said hopefully.

"Guitar," her mother said, and he obligingly extended his Hofner bass. "No, not that little one. I want to hold that big one," she said, pointing to a sunburst Epiphone Casino in the corner. George brought it over and began trying to teach her a chord. "Are you the Orphaned One?" she asked. No, I'm the Lonely One, he told her. His guitar made an empty thunking sound when she strummed it. "Gee, this is harder than I thought. Don't you fellas have to practice?"

"All we have to practice is smiling," John said. He took a long drag on a hand-rolled cigarette.

"Are those roofers you're smoking?" The air was thick with rank, weedy fumes. Before he could answer she said, "Do you know these girls are your biggest fans?" Edna froze, her shame revealed.

"No, but hum a few bars and I'll fake it," said John.

"That's an old one."

"We're old at heart." He rubbed his sideburn reflectively.

"You do seem kind of tired for young fellas."

"We had to perform twice on Sunday," Paul explained. "In Cincinnati and St. Louis. We had a contract." And he squinched his face into a frown.

"Well, don't be making any more contractions," Mrs. Livingston commanded. "Take a rest."

"Say, that's a good idea!" Paul said in a fine imitation of Jay Blue. Once again some unspoken agreement buzzed between the four, and they fell into a pensive silence.

"Cheer up, boys!" Mrs. Livingston said, springing to her feet. Then, to Edna's horror, her mother began to do the dance they called her routine: a high-spirited cancan with kicking Rockette variations performed to her own sung accompaniment. Edna knew it well.

"Mom, stop," she pleaded. But the Beatles were yielding little ironic smiles. Ringo started clapping, and George began to play along. "Julia," Paul said. Julia was John's mother who'd died when he was a teenager. Every fan knew that. Edna felt sullen with envy. She wanted to rise into the Beatles' consciousness, if only for a minute, but even in close proximity it seemed impossible. Her mother kept getting in her way.

At last Mrs. Livingston stopped prancing, out of breath. "Now why don't you sing to us?" she asked.

"They can't," Edna said quickly. "They can't sing now."

"Course we can sing," said Paul. "Don't believe everything you read."

John wearily picked up an acoustic guitar. He strummed the first chords of "Anna," an oldie about a girl who'd come and asked him to set her free. He changed the name to Annie, in honor of Mrs. Livingston, and sang that all his life he'd been searching for a girl to love him, but every girl he ever had broke his heart and left him sad, what was he supposed to do? And the other Beatles chorused "like his mum," "I deplore," and "drink my sweat." After a verse or two, John forgot the words, and the song broke down.

"It's now or never," Sunny whispered. "*Typee*." George was closest, so Edna thrust the book at him. "It's about sailors held captive by a group of man-eating cannibals," she said.

"The fans would devour us if they could." He nibbled on his guitar pick. "It's because they love us. And it's the thought that counts."

"This is a first edition. It belonged to Herman Melville." She paused for effect. "You can have it."

"I don't want it," he said, handing it back. "It'll only get lost or left behind. It'll only get ruined." The room whirled. Her fears were realized, her gift rejected. "Try John," George added quickly. "His father was a sailor."

The walk across the room to John Lennon seemed long and fraught with obstacles. "This book is set on a remote island where there's no religion or possessions, no greed or hunger," she began. He listened to her ragged exegesis with half-closed eyes, impassive as a Buddha. Then he opened Typee and read aloud. " 'Her manner convinced me that she deeply compassionated my situation, as being removed from my country and friends, and placed beyond the reach of all relief.' " He stopped and stared off into space.

"Can I ask you something?" Edna said. Everyone else was across the room, admiring her mother's earrings.

"Sure," he said. "Shoot."

"What would you do if you were in love with someone who didn't know you were alive?"

"Love really tears us up, doesn't it?" He paused. The pause was delicious, eloquent. "But we always get another chance."

The other Beatles were taking their stage suits out of the lockers. They called John over, then George spoke up. "We have to turn off the lights so we can change," he said. For a second Edna imagined them assuming another identity, like Gregor Samsa becoming a bug. "You won't be upset now, will you? We won't be long. Just stay put." He asked her to work the lights, and she nodded, feeling a new sense of power.

The Beatles hummed and whistled like a human meadow as they dressed, and the darkness amplified their chirping and rustling. They shouted reassurances—we still loove you, Annie!—and in no time at all, they called for the lights. But Edna must have lost her bearings because she could not find the switch. She stroked the cinder blocks and shuffled to the left, groping blindly. Then she tripped over a guitar cord and crashed against a texture she knew well. A suit of summer wool, now sculpted into three dimensions. Her previous experience of the Beatles had been so flat, so limited to pictures and screens, that the depth and breadth of this actual body felt almost wrong. She clung like a barnacle nonetheless. Now that she had him, she would not let him go. And instead of pulling away, he stood patiently, perhaps resignedly, in an attitude of forbearance, emitting an aura of—was it possible?—understanding. His face felt gritty as a beach, and through his shirt she heard the rock-solid four/four of his heart and an ambient hum like damaged nerves. "Let there be light!" her mother called. "Quick, before I have a vision!" His hair sifted through her fingers then like salt dissolving, silky with escape. And she let him go.

She found the switch, and by the time her eyes adjusted, the Beatles looked perfectly composed. John, Paul, and George had assumed their guitars like shields. Only Ringo had nothing to hide behind. "How do we look?" he asked.

"Like stars," Mrs. Livingston said with satisfaction. "Like brothers. Like you should."

John, meanwhile, was searching his pockets. Now he held up an "I Still Love The Beatles" sticker for all to see.

"Mine is missing," Paul said. "And there was nothing funny about mine."

"You mean—she didn't take that drug?" said Edna.

"Looks like your trip is over before it's begun," George told her mother.

Then Neil flung the door open, and a noise like a force of nature rushed in. John gave *Typee* to the road manager for safekeeping. The PA system boomed "Now ... The Beatles!" And they were gone. Edna, Sunny, and Mrs. Livingston hurried out onto the field to watch them play. Flashbulbs splashed the night as John launched into "Twist and Shout," his legs braced like a sailor's on a tossing ship. Brian Epstein stood near second base, nervously chewing gum on the downbeat. Edna was struck by how solitary the Beatles looked on stage, on their private island of fame. If a string broke or an amp exploded, if they needed a drink or felt unwell, there was no one to help them. They were at the mercy of the fans and police. For thirty minutes the Beatles were the loneliest people on earth.

One of Mrs. Livingston's earrings fell off, and she pitched it at the stage. Sunny, meanwhile, was screaming Be-Be-Be-Beatles! Rah-Rah-Rah-Ringo! Edna had kept one item from their pockets, a scrap from a cigarette pack. Now she dug this second-class relic from the depths of her purse. "Rich Choice" was printed on one side, a set list of songs handwritten on the other. She crushed it and tossed it toward the stage like an offering, a flower over a burial at sea.

"Those Beatles work a short shift, don't they?" Mrs. Livingston said. The parking lot was covered with tickets like fallen leaves. Sunny spotted a taxi with a model of a yellow submarine secured to its roof, and the driver said he'd take them to the city as soon as he had a full cab. He had one other passenger already, an older girl with a Beatle haircut, wearing a dress made from the Union Jack. A pin identified her as PaulMichelle, a stringer for *Teenbeat*. Enjoy yourselves, ladies? the cabbie asked.

"We had the time of our lives," Mrs. Livingston said. "The Beatles autographed our petition."

"No," Edna corrected. "John never signed."

"Well, you gave him your book," her mother said proudly.

The driver checked the moorings of the yellow sub on his roof. "I want to shake the hand that shook the hand of John Lennon," he said to Edna.

"Gosh, Ed, your hand's become a second-class relic," said Sunny.

"We didn't shake hands."

"But he sang to us. And George let me play his guitar," her mother boasted.

The *Teenbeat* stringer looked skeptical.

"It's true, PaulMichelle," Sunny said. "The Beatles really liked her. They thought she was—"

"Swell," Mrs. Livingston interrupted. "The Beatles thought I was swell. And they were nice, too. I felt like I'd known them forever."

"So what are those guys really like?" the driver asked.

"Not what you'd expect," Edna's mother said. "They seemed old as the hills. Believe me, those boys are century plants. Those boys were born old."

"But what were they *like?*" PaulMichelle persisted.

"Real regular and down-to-earth. They were so ordinary! That's what I loved about them."

"Ordinary!" Edna scoffed. "Little do you know." Was it possible to love someone, with the love the Beatles sang in their close harmonies, without ever knowing that person?

"Well, I know one thing," her mother asserted. "Paul explained the hidden symbolism of that Eleanor song to me."

"'Eleanor Rigby!' What is it?" Sunny asked.

"I—uh—I can't remember. It was very hidden. But he told me, he explained it all."

"C'mon, Ma. Try to remember. It's important."

"It was something about lonely people. Where they come from, where they belong. There's a priest in it, a loner who never connects with Eleanor. They never get to know each other, then she dies, and it's too late. They're like two ships that pass in the night."

"That's not hidden," said Edna. "That's really obvious."

Then PaulMichelle started talking about a relative of hers who had emigrated to Liverpool many moons ago and met the real Eleanor Rigby. This relative had revealed the secret meaning of the song to her. In fact, PaulMichelle considered herself an expert on the boys, for she had traveled with the tour since Boston, almost a week, and Neil had given her two of John's guitar picks, which she'd had made into earrings, see? And she shook her head to make them swing.

"Who was your favorite, Mrs. L.?" Sunny asked.

Edna felt her mother weighing her answer. "George," she said finally. "I liked George Harrison best."

"But George is the Spiritual One," Edna argued. "He's not your type at all. What about the two motherless boys? What about John and Paul?"

"George has a mind of his own. He calls a spade a spade, and I admire that. George was my favorite Beatle. But my favorite guy is Neil. Neil has dreamboat eyes."

"John, Paul, George, and Neil!" Edna exclaimed in disgust.

"Who did you like the best, Hon?" Mrs. Livingston asked Sunny.

"Paul's her favorite," Edna said quickly.

"Paul is All," agreed PaulMichelle.

But Sunny twirled a strand of her long dark hair. "There was something about Ringo."

"Paul," Edna said firmly.

"Remember when the others put on their guitars, and Ringo had nothing but his drumsticks? He looked so unprotected. I guess that's when I fell for him. And now that I've met him," Sunny continued, "I think Jay Blue is kind of cute."

"I don't get you," Edna said. Stars were easier to understand, celebrities on elevated stages illuminated by giant lights, who could be resurrected anytime at will within your head.

"Who was your favorite, Ed?" Sunny asked.

Headlights from buses pierced the warm August darkness. Edna saw Jay Blue standing alone by the WTRY Beatle Buggy, dabbing at his eyes under his sunglasses.

"I'm not sure," she said. Her favorite was the one who'd understood her wish for contact in the dark. But if she lived to be a hundred, she'd never know for certain who that was.

She felt her mother scrutinizing her. "Those fuzzy blonde hairs under your chin," Mrs. Livingston said. "I never noticed them before. I have those, too. My own!"

And she seized Edna in a bone-crushing hug. It was the first maternal embrace Edna could remember, and she endured it stoically, amazed to be touched by this stranger, her mother.

❄

Anthony Farrington
Glimmer Train

BARTLEBY

> Deliver my soul from the sword;
> my darling from the power of the dog.
> —*Psalms 22:20*

IT was the summer of plagues. I was invaded by spiders and scorpions; I was plagued by dogs, children, and things that wouldn't go away. Things that weren't my business. I lived in a rundown neighborhood on the edge of town. On the very edge of civilization. And despite the drought, or because of it, there were crickets everywhere. Sometimes, they were an inch thick in the corners of my carport—a writhing mass of kicking brown and gray. Mysteries are sometimes messy things. But crickets are generally harmless. Still, poisonous creatures liked to hunt these crickets and use my house as base-of-operations. I had scorpions in my cabinets, fire ants scouring my lawn, and spiders tiptoeing along my carpets. I had a dog that refused to go away and a neighborhood child who broke into my home with astonishing frequency.

The rental house wasn't my first choice; it was my only choice. I was divorced and newly unemployed. I quit my job in southeast Iowa to start a brand new life in southeast Arkansas. Call me crazy. Ostensibly, I moved here so my children could be closer to their mother. She worked for the United States Post Office and had relocated to a more profitable position a year earlier. But seven hundred miles or a measly seven, I knew my ex wouldn't go out of her way to see our children. Her own guilt kept her away. If you ask me, every village has its idiot, and every village has its dog. I would soon learn that Monticello, Arkansas, was blessed with an overabundance of both.

I was a history teacher, and my new job at the local high school wouldn't start for three months. I was at the end of my financial rope. My ex found the house for me—or cursed me with it—and I moved, sight unseen. When I first arrived, the front door of the house was unlocked and ajar. When I stepped inside, a small child dashed through the kitchen and was out the back door before I could say hey. I could have thrown a fit or chased him down. Instead, I dumped Comet in the sinks, Drain-O in the drains, and bleach in the toilet. I flipped on the master switchbox, lit the water heater, and the house groaned reluctantly to life. There was no central air, no air conditioning at all. So I installed window fans to blow out the stink. I vacuumed furiously. I cut back vines that had crawled up the outside of the house and over the filthy windows. There were gaps beneath and above my doors. A few tendrils of vine grew inside. The insects loved my house. My undiscerning children did too. I did not. But there was little to do except sweep aside the cricket carcasses, sew up the holes in the window screens, shrug off the scorpions, and make do.

Before even ten boxes were unloaded from the moving truck, and I was—I admit—in the blackest of moods, a woman pulled into my driveway, got out of her car, and marched toward me. Her hair was dark and wild. So were her eyes. She wore an enormous blue tee shirt that ballooned over her breasts. "I am the previous renter," she said.

I looked at the unmowed lawn—the undergrowth, more like it. The grass was knee-high and menacing.

The woman unhinged a large, leather purse like a trap. She peered into its recesses. And out of the yawning darkness—under a fierce sun—she pulled a black checkbook. She dropped the purse at her feet without ceremony. I was sweating. Some flying bloodsucker kept dive-bombing my ear. I waved at it helplessly. I had to get the rental truck back by tomorrow morning, and not even ten boxes were unloaded. My children were too young to help unload and too old to remain motionless. They were seven and eight, and they were already racing each other up and down the street on their bicycles.

Regardless, I am not an unkind man. I stooped to pick up the woman's fallen purse, but before I could touch it, the woman waved a check in my face.

"Here," she said. "Fifty dollars. I know it's not much."

I was struck dumb and stood up.

She waved the check and glanced at the neighboring homes. "What I have to ask," she said, "is not much. Just a tiny thing. Take it. No strings."

"I don't understand," I said.

"I ask that you take care of Bartleby."

For a brief moment, I feared she meant the child who broke into my home. "You must have me confused," I began.

"No," she said and put her fingers to her temple. Her skin was flushed, and she was trying to be patient. "You must take care of Bartleby. I can't take him with me. I've tried. He won't go."

"Ma'am," I said.

The woman heard something behind her and put her hand to her throat. My eight-year-old son pulled his bike behind me. "Dad?" he said.

"Just a minute," I hushed him. He knew the drill, and he stood a little out of breath, balancing his bike, waiting. "I'm not interested," I told the woman.

"No," the woman said. "You must." She touched my arm lightly, surprising both of us, and then withdrew. She had a pair of reading glasses nearly lost in her frizzy hair. She explained rapid-fire: This was *her* house. Bartleby was her *dog*. A white dog. Like a ghost. "Named after Bartleby," she said. *"Melville?"*

I had work to do. There were more bugs buzzing. And I wiped the sweat from my forehead.

"The dog doesn't do anything," she said, pleading. "Just lies around. Never leaves. Never causes trouble." She looked at me expectantly. "He's around here somewhere," she said. "Always is. All white. Some kind of pure breed or high mix."

"Ma'am," I said. "I'm not interested."

"Look," she said. And her voice lowered. "I'll *pay*. All you have to do is *feed* him. Just set out *food*. That's it. I'll *pay* you to do it. It's no work at all. Really. Please. You *must*."

It was getting late. And the moving truck was begging to be emptied.

"I have to go," she said, throwing her purse strap over her shoulder. She looked at her watch and then quickly at the neighboring house. "Just say yes. There's a bag of food there." And she pointed with the check to a feedbag leaning against the brick home. I had noticed it earlier, but what it meant hadn't registered until now. I was exhausted. "Here's fifty dollars," she said. "There's a dish behind the bag. Just set out food, please, once a day." She was anxious and out of breath. "I'll send more money," she said. She was nearly in tears. "Another fifty dollars. Just keep feeding him. Here's fifty for your efforts. *Please.*"

I didn't take the money, and she began to panic. She bent to my son and talked to him as though he were a small child. "You'd like to feed a cute doggy, wouldn't you?" And the woman turned to speak to me again. "You can give the money to the children as allowance. Just please. *Feed Bartleby.*" The woman gave my son the check, and—being eight years old—he took it. He was saying, "Can we, Dad?" And I was hesitating. *Fifty dollars.* And despite my better judgment, I let the woman leave without stopping her. She nearly ran to her car. Sweat was running down my forehead and into my eyes, stinging me blind.

The next day, the kids and I went to Wal-Mart. The house needed everything—not that I could afford much: some weather stripping for the gaps beneath the doors, a six-pack of bug-spray, and a few sacks of groceries to feed my children. When we returned from the store, my daughter went to her room to play, but she came back immediately. She said there was a boy in her room. And indeed, there was: the same boy who ran from my house the day before. He was maybe a year younger than my daughter. He had a teardrop head and a light brown face. His hair was buzzed short.

I said, "Who are you?"

"Solomon Boyd," he said. He wouldn't look at me.

I said, "Who's your daddy?"

And Solomon Boyd pointed directly through the walls of the bedroom. "Right there," he said.

"What are you doing in my house?"

The little boy shrugged.

So I walked with him to the neighbor's, and I knocked. A tall and slender black man opened the door. He wore brilliant, bleach-white socks and paisley boxer shorts.

I introduced myself. His name was Jack Boyd. I was hoping for a pleasant introduction and a parental apology promising me that his son would stay out of my goddamned house. A wink of understanding between two affable parents. But I never got to that point.

"I met your son, Solomon," I said. The boy had wandered off to play with my daughter.

"I don't call him that no more," Jack said.

"What?" I said, disarmed. I received no response. In the first place, I was a careful man, long-studied in the art of social conduct and domestic order. Everyone who knew me said so. But here—far away from my home in the Midwest—where the accents, the homes, the children, and even the insects were unfamiliar, I lost footing. Jack thanked me for no reason whatsoever and shut the door.

That night—the second night—I fell asleep on the couch without a fan. I woke up sweating. I wasn't used to the humidity or the sounds of this place. I was sore from lifting boxes and moving appliances. I ached. So I went into the kitchen, wishing desperately I had a beer. Better yet, an entire bottle of whiskey. I couldn't find my aspirin in the moving-box labeled *meds*, so I took a dozen chewable children's tablets instead. I turned on the carport light just to look outside, my mouth flooding with sweetness. And I saw Bartleby for the first time.

He was, at best, bedraggled. A dusty white. He wasn't a *he*, though. He was obviously a *she*. Misnamed. Bartleby seemed to be about a year old and looked something like a bull terrier. I was surprised to see that she had a collar on. She stood up and looked at the door, curious and unafraid. Her teats were swollen and black; she was obviously pregnant. My children had left food for her earlier. But it was untouched. All day, the children had wanted to find her, to pet her, but I told them to leave her be. Who knew? Dogs, like crickets, swarmed the place. A proliferation of unclean pups. "Any one of them could be sick," I said. "Any one of them could have rabies." I knew I was being unreasonable.

Bartleby stood in the carport light, looking up at the kitchen door. She looked like she wanted something. She cocked her head. She looked singularly gentle. Kind. I don't know if she saw me in the darkness of the kitchen or not. But when I opened the door, she ran like shot. As long as I stayed on my side of the window—I would learn—or more than twenty feet away, she tolerated me. In the morning, like the mornings that followed, the food was gone. And so was Bartleby. Into thin air.

I was still living amid boxes and insect carcasses a week later when a personal letter arrived in the mail. Her address, but not her name, was typed on the outside of the envelope. It didn't take me long to figure out who had sent it.

"Dear Sir," the letter began. "Like Bartleby, the dog won't go away. The allusion is to a story by Herman Melville. I am an English professor," the woman wrote, "and I can't help it—

> I think I owe you an explanation.
> Bartleby wasn't *my* dog initially.
> But he stayed with me. To drive him
> away by calling him hard names would
> not do. My husband threw rocks. He
> told me not to feed him. Still,
> Bartleby *preferred* to stay.

```
    Poor fellow, thought I. Poor
Bartleby. If I turn him away,
chances are he will fall in with
someone less indulgent. He will be
rudely treated and perhaps driven
forth miserably to starve. Besides,
Bartleby has seen hard times. He
ought to be indulged. My husband
thought otherwise.
    So again, thank you. I can tell
you are a kind man. Do write me and
tell me how Bartleby is. Let me know
that he is well fed. Write me about
the neighborhood, especially the
children. Tell me what I am missing.
Please. Charity.
```

Two days later, another letter came.

```
    Addendum: I never felt so private
as when I knew Bartleby was there.
My mission in this world was to fur-
nish him with room for such a period
as he saw fit to remain.
```

```
    Your turn. Charity.
```

I declared war. My yard was filled with fire ants. There were wasp nests the size of sunflowers in my eaves. My children brought home a black widow spider in a jar. Normally calm, I freaked. That none of us had been killed was clearly a miracle. I'd only found two scorpions inside the house so far, but that was two too many. (My landlord's secretary insisted that scorpions, like cockroaches, were pests. There was nothing she could do. Moreover, she insisted, there were *no* scorpions in southeast Arkansas. I told her I'd mail one to her alive.) The house began to wear on me. I would turn on the light before I walked across a dark room. I shook my shoes before I put my feet inside. There were cottonmouths in the nearby swamp and hundreds of tree frogs ricketing all night. There were swallows and dragonflies and bats everywhere—squadrons of them—battling the countless mosquitoes. They were woefully outnumbered. Score: good creatures, a-dozen-or-so. Evil creatures, infinity. I had to admit, the place was abuzz with life. With children running. Life screaming. I wanted to kill most of it. My own children excepted. So I went to Wal-Mart again to buy some steel wool to fill the cracks, ant poison, and just enough beans and rice and fat-back to get us through.

When we returned—even though I'd made sure to lock the door, I was *sure* of it—my son came into the kitchen with obvious impatience. "Solomon Boyd is here again."

"Don't call him that," I said.

"That's his name," my son said.

"Not—" I almost raised my voice, then caught myself. "Not according to his father."

My daughter was standing in the bedroom doorway watching Solomon. What else could she do? He was sitting in the middle of my son's floor playing with my son's trucks.

I was exasperated. "What's your name, Solomon?"

"Solomon," he said.

"No. What's your daddy call you?"

He shrugged.

"How'd you get in my house?"

He shrugged.

"Well stop it," I said, which didn't make sense. I was losing control. My house was more like a sieve than a house. Children apparently walked through the walls on whim. Hornets raided my kitchen. I found a live scorpion trapped in my wok. Spiders the size of saucer plates stalked crickets and small, invisible mammals on my carpet. That's when the third letter came. Folded inside it was another fifty-dollar check with *for dog & humanity* written on the memo line. I didn't read the letter this time. But I cashed the check with guilt and decided to take my chances. I walked the three letters over to Jack's place. He stood in the doorway, unfolded the letters, and read them with interest.

"*Bartleby,*" he finally said. "That's funny."

I was desperate and eager. Jack, standing on his stoop, towered above me. I needed to establish some sense of order in my life. "Tell me about Charity," I said.

"What?"

"Charity. Your old neighbor. The nutcase."

"Her name ain't Charity," Jack said. "There are no whores and no dogs in *my* house." Jack watched me. "Deuteronomy," he said. And he closed his door. He still had my letters. I went home and paced for maybe twenty minutes before going back to his house. I would *insist* this time. So when he opened the door again, I was ready and stepped inside.

It was cool and lush in his living room. Not a cricket in sight. A real house. And I stood there in awe, just letting the central air wash over me. There were oriental rugs on the walls and plants in the windows. A baseball game was on the large-screen television. And there were a million books. Shelves and shelves of books. Books on top the television. Books opened on the couch. Books everywhere.

"Shit," I said. "You must like to read."

"Not much," Jack said. His hand was on the doorknob.

I was afraid the earth would give beneath me. "Look," I said. "I'm not getting off on the right foot. This old neighbor of yours—whatever her name—is a nutcase. She sends me money to feed her dog." I let that sink in for a second. "I have enough money for dinner at a restaurant. How about I take you and your boy out for dinner? A neighborly gesture."

Jack Boyd seemed suddenly puzzled. His face fell flat.

"I could use the company," I said. "Please."

Jack hesitated. He put his fingers to his chin. "Why the hell not?" he said, and then he smiled wide. "Mysterious ways," he said and slapped his thigh.

I had a large steak generous with black pepper. And the children each had restaurant chicken. I felt hedonistic. I hadn't had beef in nearly six months. During the whole meal, Jack was in a glorious mood. We were talking about whole-roasted hogs and buckets of boiled crawfish. He insisted on buying me a drink with his own money. It was the first cold beer I'd had in a year. I nearly wept.

"Here's to betrayal," Jack said and raised a big hunk of prime rib with his fork. Then he raised his beer to my beer, "Here's to whores that leave and dogs that stay," he said. "And fine beef." He drank long and deep.

The kids were being kids. Solomon was literally yodeling. "You eat up, boy," his father said loudly. He wiped his mouth with his wrist. Everyone in the restaurant stared. "This food is ill-begotten for everyone but you," he said to Solomon. And he placed a good portion of prime rib on the boy's plate.

"What's that?" Solomon asked.

And Jack just grinned. "That's charity, Boy. Sweet charity."

Jack waved to me all the time now. He thanked me more than once. He said he had been in a funk. He was sorry. I learned that he was a single father himself. In the midst of a custody battle. And he was struggling mightily with it. Forgive him. Jack came over in boxer shorts and a loose tee shirt one late afternoon. He was nearly always barefooted. Apparently, his feet were impervious to fire ant stings and prickles in the grass. Jack asked for some eggs. He told me he was going to make peach cobbler for his son. His son's mother had made blue-ribbon cobbler, he said. But she was gone. Almost five months now. And Jack insisted that his son still needed baked goods. So I gave him two eggs. Ten minutes later, Jack returned and asked for some sugar. He was running much lower than he thought. Two hours later, he came back again. His mood had obviously turned. "You don't happen to have any peaches do you?"

Around midnight, Jack saw that my light was on, and he brought me a plate of cobbler covered with pink cellophane on a blue paper plate. There was a plastic fork wrapped separately on the side. He was obviously proud of himself. The next day, I told him his peach cobbler was the best I'd had. He laughed, and he promised to make me more. To tell the truth, though, I had the children cast the goo to the dog. Not that she ever ate, as far as I could tell.

In their enthusiasm, my children fed Bartleby three or four times a day. Whenever they walked by the bag of dog food, they added more to the dish. It was usually overflowing. I never saw Bartleby eat from the dish, but I saw other dogs occasionally. A possum or two. A few cats. Ants by the hundreds, of course. Flies. And once—I'm not kidding—a Vietnamese potbellied pig. That single bag of dog food fed the entire animal population of the neighborhood for nearly three weeks before finally running out.

I didn't buy another bag. I doubt that I ever intended to do so. I simply pocketed the hundred dollars, and Bartleby continued to live at my house, at the edge of the carport. As far as I could tell, she lived on air. Sure, I felt guilty. But windfalls weren't common. And I was desperate. I ignored Bartleby, but she wouldn't go away. Twice, for no reason whatsoever, I shooed her away in the middle of the night. She had been sleeping on a ratty rug that stunk. I threw it in the garbage. But what the woman had written was true. No matter what, Bartleby preferred to stay.

In the morning, I saw Jack outside, watering his tomato plants with a five-gallon bucket of water. Everything grew here: gardens, children, as well as bugs. I went over to talk. Jack seemed to like my company.

I asked Jack why he supposed a stray dog had a collar. I meant Bartleby.

He said it was the remains of a failed noose.

"No Jack," I said. "Someone's address must be on the collar."

"I'll tell you what the collar says," Jack said. *"I'm my own dog. Whose dog are you?"* He grinned and set the splashing bucket down.

My daughter and Solomon interrupted us. My daughter said, "Daddy," to get my attention. Jack threw up his hands in mock surprise. "I'll get you, my pretty," he said to her. "And your little dog, too." My daughter had a good-sized puppy in her arms. We all laughed.

But Jack and I noticed that the puppy wouldn't move. Its reddish fur was caked brown. Blood was in its nose. It was mostly bones. Probably starving. The puppy didn't whimper when Jack took it from my daughter. Its eyes stared. I suspected the puppy had been hit by a car. Jack did too. He handed me the puppy, took the shirt off his back, and placed it on the ground. He inspected the puppy in my arms carefully. He felt its legs and pushed along its body. There was no collar around its neck. The children had never seen this puppy before. Then Jack took the puppy gently and set it on the shirt. He stroked it once while the children watched and said everything would be okay. He told the children to go play. And they did. Jack tied the shirt over the dog gently, pushed the puppy into the bucket of water, and placed a large stone on top to hold the puppy to the bottom.

He turned and saw my face. "You offered the same drink," he said. "Get the fuck off my back."

Then a rare thing happened. In the middle of everything, Jenny, my ex-wife—the Queen of Disruption—stopped by to visit our children. *Back again.* But instead of sitting at the kitchen table waiting for them to appear from wherever they were playing, Jenny sat outside in her car with the door wide open. She honked her horn twice on three separate occasions. But my children failed to show up. She stayed for maybe fifteen minutes. More like ten. She could surprise me, even then.

Jenny—the most enigmatic woman on earth—lived nearby, though it didn't seem like it. She said her work at the post office kept her busy. I wasn't surprised. She said that the post office—desperate to rid itself of the plague of crickets—sprayed poison everywhere. The patrons had been disturbed by the unsettling crunch of live crickets beneath their feet as they checked their mail. Once everything started to die from the poison, though—moths, crickets, June bugs, roaches—it was infinitely worse. Dead bugs still crunch.

Jenny was tired of waiting for the children in the hot car, so she handed me a shoebox with a moth inside. A Polyphemus moth—one of those startling, bark-colored moths the size of your opened hand—with a blind, purple eye on each wing. Jenny said that the moth had been poisoned at the post office. "Isn't it beautiful?" she asked. She wanted the children to see it. And she left the box with me to show them when they came home.

I asked her to stay, but let's not go there. I remembered my married life as a series of one-act plays that always started with *back again* and ended with *gone again.*

Inside the box, the moth was losing control. Its legs were collapsing. It may have lived another twelve hours; I don't know. I couldn't look. When I finally checked the next day, the moth was dead. *Gone again.* Its purple eyes, though, were still open and watching.

Jack was erratic. Ever since the drowned puppy, he was pushing me for some reason. I was hoeing out some poison ivy around the trees that divided our plots. Bartleby was lying on my driveway, surprisingly close, and minding her own business.

"Watch this," Jack said. I was shocked to see him in my yard. He had a gun. At first, I thought it was a .22. I stood there stunned, unable to speak. Unable to do anything but watch Bartleby die. Another kind of drowning. I would have yelled stop. I would have screamed. But some things happen. They just *happen.* Jack closed one eye, laughed, said, "One-eyed Black-Jack," and the shot was on its way, ringing true.

Bartleby yelped. Hollered. Ran for the woods. It was only a BB gun.

"That's it," Jack said, and he chopped his hand in the air. "I just fired Bartleby. Relationship terminated." He laughed again. Then he stood there long and certain. His torso glistened. And he was breathing deep and confident. "Since she will not quit me," he said. "I must quit her."

He looked at me. "Beer?"

```
    Dear Sir: Once you have taken in a
stray—once you have provided for it &
its life is dependent upon you—aren't
you obligated to it? The concept of
justice & charitable grace. The narra-
tor in the story deals with matters of
fairness & natural justice rather than
specific laws. The story—& ultimately
everything—is really a matter of eth-
ics, isn't it?
    The narrator recalls a "divine in-
junction": the eleventh commandment:
```

```
"that ye love one another." After re-
jecting retribution and condemnation,
the narrator gives in to charitable
grace. He cares for Bartleby. Charity
becomes our salvation. Indulgence our
only hope.
     Regardless, the narrator ultimately
betrays Bartleby by denying him. &
Bartleby dies.
     I beg you, Sir. Save me from what I
have started.
```

The impact of a BB is like a wasp sting. Something to forget. Of course Bartleby came home. Like a patch of snow that refused to melt come spring. Lonely. But solid. She lay in the cool grass beside my house. When I walked toward her, she got up and disappeared. When I went away, she came back. Sometimes, I would talk to her late at night. I would sit in my lawn chair on the porch, drinking ice water, knowing she was around the corner. And I'd say, "What was it like living with a crazy woman?" Laugh at myself.

Other times, I would get in my jeep and just drive, trying to get to know this country. And we would come home late—my children sleepy—and there was Bartleby. Sure as life. And my yawning children would say, "Hi Bartleby." And she would get up and walk away, stand at the edge of the woods, and wait for us to go inside. When I looked from the kitchen window, I could see she was back. Sleeping by the house. Watching the sky. I felt safe with her outside, with my children sleeping peacefully in their bedrooms. When Bartleby barked, it was always something of interest. A strange dog. An unusual car stopped on the street. Teenagers walking through my yard. I could momentarily convince myself that nothing would ever sneak up on me again.

"What agreement is there between cat and dog, man and wife?" Jack asked. "What peace between rich and poor?" He was talking about something I didn't understand. I began to see less of him. There was a new car parked in his driveway at night. There was a pretty lady in a turquoise dress standing in his doorframe, back-lit with yellow light. I was sitting on my porch. Jack waved to me once and gave me a thumbs-up sign. The lady smiled. She waved too, even though we were strangers. I didn't see Solomon anywhere, but Jack pulled the lady inside and closed the door. I watched and watched, through late night, through a lonely, sprinkling rain, but I didn't see her leave. I fell asleep on my couch sometime in the early morning. I had been unpacking pictures. Some had fallen to the floor. My snarling daughter as a Halloween witch with fluorescent spiders painted on her fingernails. A single photo of Jenny—her hair flowing from beneath a blue bowler—happy. A long time ago.

I woke to a noise, and I went to the kitchen to see if Bartleby had risen. But I didn't see her in the darkness. So I went outside. Jack's lady-friend was gone. And under the clouded moon, Bartleby was there, lying down in the wet black grass. Very still. I walked right up to her. "Did you hear anything, Girl?" She raised her head. Sniffed warily. She seemed hurt. Worried. I wanted to touch her. But her fur was bone in this light. And I felt a low growl inside my own chest. I was suddenly afraid. So very close and completely unable to surrender myself to a new story.

Continued resistance. I decided that if I killed the lawn, I could eradicate the indigenous chigger population. So I was mowing the grass and choking in the dust. The blade of the mower was set very low. Dangerous. Later, I would seed the fire ant hills with delicious poison. When I went inside to ice my throat with water, Solomon was standing in my kitchen. He was hurt and bleeding bad. My children ran inside. They had been looking for Jack. Solomon had wrecked his bike on the concrete road. Blood was leaking from his nose and mouth. His elbow was hamburger. His knee was worse. The side of his face was bloody as well. On his forehead was a purplish-black bump. I told my children to find Jack. But they said he wasn't home. They didn't know where he was.

I stopped most of the blood, got a pack of ice, and tried to clean him up. Other than a lot of serious bruises and nasty scrapes, I couldn't see much wrong—except that Solomon kept bleeding from his nose. I thought maybe he had broken it. He kept asking what happened. I told him, "You wrecked your bicycle. You hit your head." Then he looked and looked and asked what happened again. I asked Solomon where he was, but he was stumped; he was whimpering but not crying. I asked him what he had for breakfast. He didn't know. He asked for his mother. "She's in Memphis," he said. "Stop her."

I couldn't get him into my jeep easily. He was wobbly, and I became scared. I shouted for my children. I held my hand on Solomon's shoulder. I sped to the hospital the whole way—telling him his father was coming; he'd be here soon. Tears washed continuously down Solomon's face.

At the hospital, people parted for me. *I* was covered in blood. Solomon was frightening. My children bopped right along next to me, proud to tell anyone what happened. Their friend was bleeding. He wrecked his bike. They were proud.

It was a long time before Jack ran into the emergency room. He was panicked until he saw me. I nodded that everything would be okay. And in the morning, there was a case of beer in front of my door with a green ribbon stuck on top and a card signed, "thank you thank you thank you. JB & Son"

Like a trap sprung, the blow came from nowhere. Sniper fire. A sudden sting on my foot. It felt like a wasp was between my toes. A hammer blow. It was a scorpion. In the half-dark, I had stepped on it in my bare feet.

After flipping on the light, I unceremoniously picked up a nearby shoe and killed the scorpion. My toe ached. I worried that my legs and lips were going numb. But in the end—an enormous surprise to me—it was just another blow. One of thousands received and thousands to come. Nothing to write about.

> Dear Sir: It was good to see the old place again. You've trimmed the hedges. You've planted flowers. I notice these things. You make the place sing. & I am sure that Bartleby is happy.
>
> *I would rather be innocent than know something evil. Knowing something had befallen Bartleby would be unbearable. His harm—my own fault—would be a millstone around my neck. Useless as a necklace. And afflictive to bear.*

> Thank you for helping the boy.

Goose pimples rose along the backs of my arms. I felt, suddenly, as if I were being watched. This woman, this lunatic, was somewhere spying on me, gauging how I was *not* taking care of her dog. I felt the infinite eyes of the world upon me. I suddenly felt my own enormous inadequacy, my own selfishness, my own guilt. I heard laughing. A mental self-portrait dropped from the sky, painfully ugly and true. When someone is watching you, you're supposed to straighten your life. But me? I swallowed like the condemned man I was.

She surprised me a few days later by coming around the corner of my house. I had been in the back yard. I nearly screamed. She had a bag of dog food in her arms.

"His dish looks empty," she said.

There was so much junk in this world, so much to do, I never thought to get rid of the dish. Boxes were still half-unpacked in my bedroom. I couldn't find my blank envelopes in all the clutter. I planned to mail the scorpion to my land-lord. I needed help from the outside world. UN troops. Otherwise, I would come unhinged.

"Possums," I said. "They eat her food most nights."

The woman said, "Is he around?"

But truth was, I hadn't seen Bartleby in quite a while.

The woman's hair was wavy, now. She was quite pretty, about my age. She had a familiar face. She set the bag of food under my carport; she looked around and cast a glance at her watch. She peeked behind my house. She watched my children carefully as though she were memorizing their faces. My heart began to race. She had to know I wasn't feeding Bartleby. I felt the suspicion.

"You never write," she said and turned to me. She gave me her business card.

"I'll try," I said. And at the time, I really meant it.

She was relaxed. And she wasn't all that interested any-way. Soon, the woman was in her car, backing out slowly, waving to me as she pulled away.

Almost immediately, Jack was pounding at my door. "What the fuck did she want? Why was she here?" He was talking to me through my own screen. "Where's Solomon?" he said. It was the first time I heard Jack speak the name of his son. A panic had descended upon him. But then he saw Solomon coming from the woods by the train tracks. I stepped outside. Solomon had a stick, and he was beating the leaves off a small tree.

"I got papers," Jack said. He was so angry his voice was shaking. "I got papers says she's not supposed to be here." He rattled my screen door by smacking the frame with the back of his hand, and he went away. I was shaken and uneasy and alone. I was trying desperately to forget the complications of my life. Rather, I was trying not to think at all. The sun was going down, and the rest of the evening Jack sat on his porch in the heat even though it was cool inside and his television was running. I could see the blue light flickering in his window. I could see a man's broken heart.

That night, I saw Bartleby for the last time. Under a bright moon, a small, white, speckled thing bounded out of the black woods and pounced. Bartleby followed, then walked by with a purpose. The puppy ran to catch up. The puppy nipped and jumped at its mother's mouth. Months later, I would wonder what had happened to Bartleby. What was *her* story? Was she hit by a car; did her puppy starve? Was she shot by a farmer? Maybe she simply moved on, like the other women in my life. Maybe I drove her away.

When I saw Jack the next morning, I had news. I was excited with it. But he wouldn't listen. He talked about the woman instead. And I could sense a growing dread. His custody battle was going poorly. He said Solomon's mother had put out food for Bartleby every night. She'd put out water. She tried to pet it. She tried to love it. And after she offered Bartleby her own home, she kept saying, *She had done all she could possibly do.* "But it wasn't true," Jack said. "It simply wasn't true."

"But Bartleby," I said. "Bartleby has puppies. I saw one."

He said, "Who?"

I said, "What game are you playing this time, Jack?"

"I'm in denial," he said. "I don't know what you're talking about."

"*Bartleby*," I said. "Melville's dog."

"Ah," he said. "That's just a story." And there were real tears in his eyes.

I still think of her name as "Charity." But her business card said: "Gail Boyd." Gail Boyd. I realized I had stepped into the middle of something, something that grew bigger and uglier the more you looked. It was like a traffic accident you couldn't see coming. No exit. No escape. No preparation. This was simply something you had to ride out.

But I was angry too. Thinking that Jack Boyd and Gail Boyd were laughing at my expense. But no, I thought. I was not a piece of foam in the rapids. I followed my own current. Which was not their current. A flood of water with Solomon drowning in the middle.

Jack was eating ribs. He had been smoking them all day. The whole neighborhood smelled of hickory chips and smoked pork. The whole neighborhood tasted the air. Jack and his self-made smoker were local celebrities. And now, Jack was testing cuts from a few slabs of ribs. He was down on his haunches. His fingers were greasy. His black face was shining.

"You were married to her," I said.

"Rib?" He held one in the air, like a finger, like a vague question mark.

"You were married to her," I repeated.

"Actually," he said, "it was a common-law marriage." He dropped a stripped rib to the ground, between his feet, and picked up another one loaded with meat. He bit into it.

"She lived in my house?" I asked.

"She wouldn't live in that scorpion nest," Jack said. "Just look at her." He meant that she was beautiful, that she wouldn't lower herself. He wiped his chin with his fingers.

"But she said she was the previous renter," I said.

"She lied. The previous renter was a grade-A asshole; a real slob," Jack said. "Then there was you. Rib?"

I'd done all the swimming I could. *The fifty dollars?* I asked. He shrugged his shoulders. *Bartleby?* A stray dog she occasionally fed for a few weeks before she left. No one could touch it. "Someone must have beat it bad," Jack said. Then he smiled, "She was surprised to find out Bartleby was a mother."

"She's a professor?"

"She's a college graduate," Jack said.

"She teaches at the university," I said.

"No. She's a legal secretary in Memphis. She's well paid. I don't take a dime on principle."

Solomon?

Yes, he was their child. Named after the book of love in the bible. A name that hurt Jack so deeply, he wouldn't speak the name. I could see Solomon's face in her face. They had another child, too, Jack said. Just a tiny, tiny baby. They were sorting through things.

Separated?

"Common-law divorce," he said. And he laughed at the irony. But he didn't look at me.

"Did she leave you, Jack?"

"Nah," he said. And that's all he said.

So I went into his house without asking. I got two beers from his refrigerator, and I handed him one. It was hot outside and humid, and the beer cans were already sweating. I sat down on the concrete beside Jack.

"Fuck," I said.

"You and me," Jack said and shrugged his shoulders. "A living dog is better than a lion."

I looked around. The pines were set against the blue sky. The butterflies were flying. My kids whizzed by on their bicycles. Solomon was yelling something, waving for my son to come look. The smoke from the smoker hovered just below the green of the pines. And I took a good drink from my beer. "Fuck," I said.

"Rib?" Jack said.

I said, "Uncle."

The last letter from Gail Boyd:

```
    Like lightning struck. Good-bye,
Bartleby; I am going—goodbye, & God
some way bless you. I should have
lain still & been quiet. Written
words are nothing but dead letters.
I should have let lying dogs lie. I
should have rested with kings &
counselors. With infants who never
saw light.
    Beware the dog & especially love.
```

After the children went to sleep that night, I went outside as I usually did. And I saw Jack sitting on his own porch. Rather, I saw his legs. His upper body was in shadow. I saw him lift a can of beer. And seconds later, he set it on the ground beside his chair. The world was a different place.

Where Bartleby slept was here. There was something about this spot. It was where I saw her nearly every night for an eternity. The grass was bent over, perpetually. Little else. Just a pinkish oil rag on the harsh grass. And the lingering smell of dog. If you looked closely in the light that fell from my kitchen window, you could see white hairs flicking back and forth in the southern breeze. I felt so miserably alone.

Suddenly Jack was yelling. He was laughing too. He was shouting something. And he threw a can of beer like a football. It crashed in my yard. It burst open and sprayed.

"A little hair of the dog that bit you!" he yelled. And he was laughing like an idiot. And I had to admit, I found it funny. But I also knew what state he was in. I had been there myself once.

I shouldn't have gone over, but prudence only involves my children. I grabbed the beer that landed in my yard. I drank from it despite the dirt and grass. It was horrible. Flat.

"A dog returns to his vomit," Jack said. "A fool to his folly."

"You're full of shit," I said.

"Proverbs," he said. "Proverbs is full of shit."

I said, "Are you okay, Jack?"

"I am poured out like water," he said. "All my bones are out of joint: my heart is like wax." He took a long drink, exhaled loudly. "Psalm twenty-two." And he patted something beside him that I couldn't see.

I said, "Save me at least *one* for later."

"Your ass," he said.

Jack's house seemed empty in the morning. It was peaceful. I was sitting on my porch. A cold front had gone through recently, and I was enjoying the breeze and the depth of the amazing, clear sky. My son came to me with his hands cupped together. He was shielding a glowing treasure. When his cupped hands bloomed open—like an offering—there was a small lizard inside. A skink with an electric blue tail.

I liked lizards for two reasons. One: they ate crickets. Two: unlike every six, eight, and two-legged varmint, they stayed out of my house. There were dozens of them here. Lightning fast. Energetic. And very well fed. I tried to take the lizard from my son's hands. But when I did, the small skink shook itself violently in my hand, snapped its own tail off, and escaped. I was thunderstruck. Between my fingers was a wriggling blue tail.

"They do that, Dad," my son said. "They always do that." He was growing so fast.

Some things you have to hold gently. Others you have to strangle. But the truth is, to hold anything—to truly possess it—takes more tenderness and strength than we will ever have. We eventually lose everything. But hold on. Regardless. Sometimes a touch will suffice. Or a cold beer. To sit finally still with the whole world buzzing around you.

Surrender yourself. Over again.

Angela Hamilton
Natural Bridge

RUSTED NAILS

IT was a fine Wednesday, my only day off that week. I decided to splurge on a cab up to Seventh Avenue. I thought that since it was probably going to be the last warm day of the year, I'd take my Great Aunt Joanie with me. (Maybe she'd treat me to a cheap lunch at Carol's on Pine Street and after, we'd get a quick look at those statues of important men in front of the fountain.)

Aunt Joanie turned eighty-two last spring. She was a beautiful salt-and-pepper-haired woman. I had to search my soul for this beauty, though. I basically grew up with the lady. Well, from seven on anyway. At eighty-two, she looked it, acted it, and complained like it all the time. But I loved her. And the shopping excursions, where we never actually bought anything, neither of us having the money, became fairly regular in the last couple of years.

On my twentieth birthday, Aunt Joanie said that she finally considered me an adult. It could be a coincidence that this was right after I dropped out of the "college rigmarole," as she called it. Aunt Joanie thought that sitting in lectures and studying was a waste of energy. But then, she also told me to find a man I could bear to have sex with for the rest of my life and marry him, fast.

"No spark," she motioned to her eyes, "no sizzle," and acted like she was going to pinch my nipple. I hated that.

But she knew what she was talking about. Aunt Joanie was married for fifty-two years before Uncle Joe died. He was the love of her life. They gardened together, smoked together, they even sunbathed together in the Botanical Garden – two turtled heads on a park bench with the chrome-looking face tanners.

A couple of months ago I'd taken Isaac, my last boyfriend, over to her house. She'd called and had some old books she wanted to unload on me.

"I want this shit cleared out before I die," she said.

I could hear the phlegm rattle in her lungs from smoking a pipe for sixty years or more. I was surprised she'd hung on so long.

So, I took Isaac for some help. We rode the bus over and planned on taking a cab back to my place with the boxes. I had built-in bookshelves and not a lot on them besides burnt down candles and old newspapers. Books would be nice, and titles didn't matter so much. I'd probably never read them anyway.

The three of us sat talking for a while at her dining room table with a cocktail or two. When Isaac went to the bathroom, Aunt Joanie got up to go to the kitchen. She motioned for me to follow.

When the kitchen door swung shut, Aunt Joanie turned to me. "Elly, you can't date a man like that." She pinched up her mouth. Her eyes looked like raisins, salt-dried.

I rolled my eyes at her. Of course she had to get me in the kitchen to tell me this.

"Christ, Aunt Joanie. Give him a chance."

"Oh, Eleanor, please." She waved her hand in the air, waved me off. She opened the freezer door, and I waited for her reasons. I listened to the ice cubes clink in the empty glass that smelled of gin. I could only see her sagging stomach down to her Kathie Lee Gifford shoes, labeled neatly on the side. The enormous mouth of the freezer door swallowed her head.

"Aunt Joanie, hello?"

She shut the freezer door. "Don't waste my time, or yours, with that boy."

I forgot about the books, making an excuse to Isaac that I felt lightheaded, that maybe we should get some food. He didn't ask. We got our coats. On her stoop, Isaac told me he didn't like Aunt Joanie's mouth, and he didn't like that I drank with an eighty-two year old woman.

Aunt Joanie opened her window and started banging her Gifford shoes together.

"Aunt Joanie, go back in. Shut that window."

"Go home," she said, looking straight down at Isaac.

"Yeah, go home," echoed Mrs. Giunta from her steadfast position at the first floor window.

Isaac walked away, ending our conversation and three-week relationship with a quick catch of the number fifty-two headed west.

I waited for the number eight for forty-seven minutes. Forty-seven minutes. All I'd wanted to do was stop by to get some old books. I looked up from the bus stop to the warm glow of Aunt Joanie's living room. I thought better of going back up. I thought I might yell at her, or say something mean like, "Why did you wash my Mickey Mouse ears when I was seven?" or maybe, "You should shove that pipe up your ass." I suppose I was protecting her from me. She knew that Isaac was wasting my time anyway, just looking for a window to climb out of quickly, a clean break, a swift end to something he really didn't want. I suppose I did want more than that from a man.

At Pop's Blue Room later that week, I saw Isaac's friend, Harry. Harry's a good guy, very nice. I trust him. Harry'd had a few, becoming a little loose lipped. Isaac had a girlfriend the whole time. And I felt like I was getting too old for this. Maybe Aunt Joanie knew what she was talking about, even if she didn't know what the hell she was talking about.

So Aunt Joanie and I were on our way to Barney's at one in the afternoon. We always tried to look our best on such occasions. We cheaply copied outfits we saw other, financially capable women wearing. We'd keep quiet until we reached the door of Saks, Macy's, or any smaller independently owned boutique. Then, we talked about the couture.

"Did you see that lady's scarf? She didn't even have to dress up. The scarf did it all. I could pull that off," I said, as we walked by other shops on our way home.

"Yes, Elly. I think you could. Jeans, nice fitting t-shirt, scarf, maybe some Kathie Lee Gifford shoes. Her shoes are the best copies I've seen. You could fake it with those for sure. In fact, you should get some, they have good arch supports."

Aunt Joanie bought her Gifford shoes from Ona, a woman who sold shoes on a blanket by the bus station. Aunt Joanie was the biggest Kathie Lee Gifford fan. If Kathie Lee told her to buy the side of Mount Rainier she would, as long as she could afford it on a fixed income.

So we were a couple of blocks from Barney's that afternoon and a button, the button on my orange organza blouse, popped off. Aunt Joanie saw it happen. She stooped over and shuffled down the sidewalk like she'd lost a contact or something. She swore she'd watched its trail.

"It's okay," I said, rummaging through my purse for a safety pin.

"No, look at you, Eleanor. We can't go anywhere like this."

I kept rummaging while she held my blouse closed right where my breasts ended and my stomach began – like her stomach, pooched and sagging from too many frozen dinners.

"Look, I found a safety pin."

"We still can't go in anywhere fancy, Eleanor. We can't go in Barney's now."

I started walking again in the direction of Barney's, holding the pin in my mouth, arranging my blouse just so.

"Eleanor."

"What?" I turned and faced Aunt Joanie on the sidewalk again.

"Your button." She held it up to me, her hand shaking slightly from pipe withdrawals.

She died one week later, old age. Attached to her will was what the attorney called an admissible addendum. To me, a scrap of paper clipped on. It claimed that I was the new owner of her 1976 General Electric piece of junk sewing machine and seventeen hundred dollars of her fifty-four hundred net worth. She'd given the rest of it to PAWS in Brooklyn, an AIDS pet charity. At the bottom of the admissible scrap was written, "For all the days of shopping with the old lady."

I wore the organza blouse, fixed, to her wake. She looked peaceful finally. I had her in a Gifford dress, a nice warm one. Mrs. Giunta and the other neighbors were there. They even let me bring Mitzi, Aunt Joanie's Bichon Frise, who was being adopted by old man Garrison on the fourth floor.

The paper docked me a day's pay when I went to the attorney's for the reading of the will. I sat alone in the office with the untouched books, wondering who Carl was working with since I didn't show.

I work in between 43rd and 102nd most of the time, filling the newspaper boxes in Manhattan. Carl drives; I load. Carl says that if I'd done nine months in 'Nam, I could drive the truck. For now, he was head of that domain. He drove well, I had to admit. I suppose when you've been doing it as long as he had (since 'Nam), with the same truck (since '83), you have your say. Carl, I swear, could steer that truck like a thread through the eye of a needle. When he parallel parked, he'd back up quickly and snake it right in, one hand on the wheel and the other flipping off the cars that would honk behind him.

"Elly, jump at the next light and look in Garner's store window!" Carl called this from the cab while he was driving.

"What for? I'm busy!" I said, re-lacing my new boots.

"Look at the ring, seventh from the left, I'm gonna buy that sucker for Etta. It's called an anniversary band. Take a look. Tell me what you think."

I sighed heavily, hoping he could hear my tired bitterness.

"Oh, is the non-driver gettin' tired?"

I grabbed a bundle and jumped off before succumbing to the desire of giving Carl the ol' one-two on the back of his head. The sidewalk by Garner's Jewelers smelled like piss and curry. As usual.

I looked in the window and kept my eyes pinned on the ring selection the whole way by, feigning interest for Carl's amusement. Then, I focused on the newspaper box at the corner. Some days I didn't see one person, even though I saw thousands. Other days I saw thousands, but I never really saw anyone.

A fleece-lined shoulder bumped me hard.

"Watch it," I said, even though I never got a response from anyone.

I loaded up the box and jumped back on the truck.

"Beautiful, huh?"

"Yeah, almost made me cry." I faked a wipe at the corner of my eye.

"You're just jealous."

When I got home that night, I told myself I was going to the store. I was going to buy some veggie burgers, maybe some of those blue corn low-fat tortilla chips to go with them. I'd seen the vegetarian highlights on the cooking show on channel eight. I felt I was ready to make the move, the move away from frozen beef burritos and chicken a la king every night.

But instead, at six p.m. I fell asleep to the news on my couch. I woke up two hours later and got in bed. I heard Marion's heels on the hardwood floor above me. I stirred, then looked at the ceiling wondering why. Why heels on in the house all the time when a newspaper girl lives below? I heard her bed squeak. Then it was quiet for five minutes or so. I was almost back asleep. Then her bed squeaked again and Marion moaned, or was that her boyfriend from 3B?

I tossed around, then thought about going back to the couch until I had to get up at three a.m. The moans got louder, sounding fake, rehearsed. I'd seen the boyfriend from 3B. He was a film geek. I'd assumed he was gay until he started fucking Marion. But who knew? He probably still was.

I moved into Chelsea two years ago when I got this job. That first day, I met Marion on the stairs and asked if I could use her phone. We went up together talking about the cool breeze in the hallway and the nice looking tomatoes she'd just bought down the street at Joe's. Her apartment was exactly like mine—same layout, same amount of space. She gave me a tour and showed me where to put things in a habitat big enough for a small family of rats.

"Watch these guys." Marion slammed her checkbook down on a roach crawling across the counter. I watched her cigarette dangle from her lip, stuck with spit.

I took her ideas and set up my bedroom and living room just like hers, for optimal space. I thought it worked well. I thought it was the only way it could work. Then I realized that Marion was a thirty-year-old single woman who had sex, a lot. During the first year, I thought maybe it was her job. Now I know she just likes it that way.

So her bed is exactly above mine, shoved into the northeast corner like a kid gone wrong. 8:07 p.m.—Marion's getting her brains fucked out. 8:10—I become disgusted when I realize that if I just lie still on my back and remove Marion, her bed, the floorboards and cockroaches, take away the air in between us (keeping Mr. 3B), and there he'd be, fucking me (assuming we were all in missionary position).

I got up and stumbled to the bathroom. I blocked my eyes with my hand, flipped the light on and stood staring at the floor to adjust. Two cockroaches scattered for cover like vampires. I sighed. In New York, it wasn't even worth the effort. Most cockroaches puckered up and kissed the plastic nozzle of the Borax bottle, their constitution too strong for anything but an iron shoe.

I thought I'd brush my teeth then bed down on the couch. I opened the mirrored cabinet and the facial scrub dropped into the sink. So I gave myself a scrub instead. After rinsing, coming back up for air, I looked into the mirror as the drops of water dove down my young face. I saw an eyelash on my cheek. I picked it off and thought of blowing it from my fingertip with a wish in mind. Instead, I settled on the fact that my finger was wet, and I was alone. And wishes like that, the ones with the eyelashes, are only in movies and the main character is never, ever alone.

It works like this: the *New York Times* wants every driver and pusher to know each route like the back of God's hand. Our normal route in the east part of Manhattan, nine square blocks, is what driver Carl DiMiglio and pusher Eleanor Dugan, get three to four days a week. It varies. The other days, Carl and I get an alternate route. Carl's favorite route is by the East River – Old Slip down past Vietnam Veterans Plaza. He takes his hat off every time we round that first curve, no matter what. If we get stopped in traffic, his hat lays limp in his grasp until we drive off and the memorial is out of sight.

I appreciate the Battery Park rounds in the lowest of the low of Manhattan. Then we get to see the Franciscan Sisters of Mary. In nice weather you can see them out doing crafts at a picnic table or yoga on the lawn in full habit. Just seeing a nun-in-habit trying to do macramé for homeless people brings Carl and me into fits of laughter.

"Hey, Elly," Carl calls over the seat in the cab, "check out the old nun sitting Indian-style. Maybe we should stick around and watch her try to get up."

All of this in front of the huge crucifix that was displayed at the top of a stack of boulders behind the chain link fence, and always on spotlight. The old J.C. himself, staring down, looking disappointed and ashamed, probably wondering if Carl and I were really the pathetic reason why those nails were in his feet.

Neither of us talks about religion outside of the usual comments of, "Jesus H. Christ" and, "Holy shit!" Most of the jokes Carl tells have more to do with the various origins of people who live in his apartment building in the Bronx. Carl has a thing for Armenian jokes about his loud, dark neighbors who, he says, cook rotten cabbage every night for dinner. And where, he asks, did I get off finding cheap rent in Chelsea—a rich, predominantly gay neighborhood?

"I'd still take the Armenians, though," he always says. "At least I don't have to live with a bunch of faggots and artists."

"Don't forget the nymph upstairs." I easily provoke him.

"Yeah, and that hooker. Faggots, artists, and a hooker, all the same."

I never let him see that any of his ponderings jarred me. I'd only been on the job two years, nine months of it assigned as Carl's pusher – as long as he'd been in Vietnam. I hadn't yet developed a thick skin with him. Some guys never did and just refused to ride with Carl anymore. Most of the time, I ignored him or turned my back to him and sat on the stacks watching the street spill away from the back window.

When I got the check from Aunt Joanie's estate in the mail, I truly realized that I had seventeen hundred dollars that I'd never had before. My rent was manageable, but I afforded myself no luxuries outside of a well-made coat every two years and good boots for winter. Seventeen hundred dollars could have bought the "real deal" dress at Barney's or some silk pajamas at Henri Bendel's on Fifth Avenue.

I decided there was probably a better way to make both Aunt Joanie and me proud. On my next day off, I took a train to Welland, Connecticut to see an old friend, Jacob, the only college friend I'd hung on to. I hadn't seen him in three years. Of course, he finished the obligations of NYU, and I took off after only two years, surprised that I'd had the patience to get that far. I just knew that it wasn't in me. I was salutatorian of my class in high school, which is basically the consolation prize for second place. I got myself a little burnt out on the books, but a full scholarship and the principal from my high school in the Bronx told me I should suck it up and do it.

I'd probably hung on to Jacob because he was easy. We'd slept together a few times while we casually dated, or hung out, as we called it. He'd always been sort of a loner at school. We lived down the hall from each other and had the same hours every semester. When the dorms were cleared out at noon and everyone was in class, Jacob and I would cook lunch in the community kitchen. Engineer hours, we called it, both of us studying the same major. Now he was living in Welland, designing Contour chairs, which were making a comeback in senior citizen homes, while I was engineering a hotheaded, Italian driver through rush hour with the daily.

I never pulled punches with Jacob. That would never change. The attraction dissipated after I left school and our paths split, but the commonality of two years of lunch in the kitchen together would always leave a comfortable feeling between us.

Jacob was an individual trader, heavy in the online stock market. He worked out of his house most of the time, and he made more money trading stocks and secrets than designing the lumbar cushion that vibrated just right.

I laid the check on the table and told him to invest it. With no hesitation, Jacob picked up the check, then laid it back down and picked up the newspaper. He spread it out before me.

"What do you want to invest in? Risky, aggressive, passive, no losses?"

I scanned the columns of letters and numbers – hieroglyphics to me. Then it caught my eye, right there in the bottom corner about to fall off the page—Kathie Lee Gifford, Inc. I put my finger on it. Jacob grabbed a pen and handed it to me as he stamped out his cigarette.

"Circle it plainly. Get this check in your account. You can pay me. I'll buy it in the morning. The whole thing?"

"The whole thing."

I didn't stay for the late dinner of fish and macaroni and cheese he offered. He kissed me on my forehead and said, "Maybe I'll come up for a visit sometime."

On the train ride home, I thought of Aunt Joanie. She would have been so proud of me. I would earn money with the gift she gave me, and I would support Kathie Lee's business, the leading maker of quality clothing at affordable prices.

For two weeks I didn't think too much about the money. I felt the release of socking it away, saving up on a memory of Aunt Joanie. I didn't know how to check the stocks. I knew it opened at twenty-four the day I bought. I didn't even really know what that meant.

At Benton's Grocery, I stocked up on the healthy items in the first two aisles. I bought St. John's Wort shake mix, organically grown mushrooms, spinach lasagna, black bean burritos, and raspberry nectar. I was on my way up.

Carl seemed like he was in a good mood, too. He bought the anniversary ring for Etta and all seemed right with him and the world. He confessed that it was the ring that had given him sex on a daily basis for the entire week and three home-cooked meals.

"Last night meatloaf and mashed potatoes and a little snooky after the national news." Carl rubbed his belly. I thought he might be slightly blushing from the images he was giving me.

"When you gonna settle down, Elly?"

"When I settle."

"Yeah, yeah. You women, you think we're all bad."

I was stooping over in the back of the truck sorting for 38th. I glanced at Carl who still had his hand on his belly, savoring the feast from the night before. He noticed, and casually moved his hand back to the steering wheel.

"I don't need a man to support me."

"No, you're right," Carl said, in a serious tone. "You need money."

We both smiled at each other. Then Carl pulled out of the lot so fast that I rocked against the side of the truck. I grabbed the leather grip hanging from the ceiling to stop my fall.

"Jeez, Carl. Watch it."

"Someday, Elly, you'll really know what it's like to be knocked on your ass."

"Yeah, if I win the lottery or something."

"Nah, the man who'll give you good lovin' after the seven o'clock news."

He just never gave up.

When I got home my answering machine was blinking in that good news sort of way. It was my boss calling to tell me our route was switched for the next day. The second message was Jacob. He wanted to talk to me, something about going all the way. I wasn't sure what he meant. When I called him back I got his answering machine.

"Jacob, it's Elly. I'm returning your phone call, something about going all the way-"

"Elly?"

He sounded out of breath. Did he just discover the perfect coil for the heating system of the lounger?

"What's up?"

"I gotta tell you, kiddo... uh, well things aren't too good."

How do you really tell someone like me (whom he calls "kiddo") that the money is, well, gone?

Something about sweatshops, something about a news announcement a couple of days ago. Kathie Lee Gifford, down eighteen points, crash and burn. Aunt Joanie, in the loving memory of... yada yada, crash and burn. No more Barney's. No more seventeen hundred dollars.

He made apologies, profuse ones, as they say. I heard them—didn't keep his eye on it closely, just heard about the news coverage that day, a day too late, but I wasn't really listening. I thought I might strike gold with this one. But Elly Dugan never really struck gold. Self-pity kicked in hard. I grabbed my coat and got the blue line down to Battery Park. It was six thirty p.m., December 20, 1996.

On the way down I tried my best to sit alone. At commuter's hours, it was hard. A bum came and sat down next to me. He fell asleep almost immediately. His knee knocked against mine. I moved closer to the blackened window but somehow his knee kept finding me, like he was running in his dream.

I thought about Aunt Joanie's asparagus mushroom casserole, her hateful looks, her gut, her money, her memory. What was she thinking with giving me that money? Did she know I was going to fuck up? Was she giving me the chance to show myself how badly I could fuck up? It was all pinpointed now. What had I done right? I thought that I was abiding by Aunt Joanie's floating carefree mentality, that of – Do what makes you happy. Don't like school? Quit. Don't like that guy? Don't date him.

For two weeks I had known what I wanted – a monetary return on a gift, a chance to buy something at Barney's besides a votive candle or a coffee mug. And Jacob, he was sorry, but what happened? This guy knew what he was doing. He'd funded all of his college expenses on buying and selling. I didn't get it. Sweatshops in Honduras? What did that have to do with anything?

He told me he'd take the train up the next morning to try and fix things. He asked me if I'd be around. I told him not to bother. What could he fix? It was gone. It was a fluke. It was just me, not striking gold again. For the millionth time.

A shot of electric blue came through the window and woke me up. An ad for a new men's fragrance, available only in fine stores. Fine stores.

"Battery Park, exit to your left."

As I stepped over the bum's legs, my coat knocked his hat off. I looked back at him when I was getting off. The man who was sitting behind us picked up the hat and laid it precariously on top of the old man's head.

I walked past Maury's Pub where Carl and I always got lunch when we were on the sisters' route. There was a biting cold wind that night, the kind that would chap my nose and cheeks. It wouldn't let up, it would keep on me, push me until I worked my way back to the subway. I walked past the faded picnic tables on the sisters' lawn and up to J.C., who was still looking down.

I stared at him through the diamond-shaped pattern of the fence. The lines of worry were in his forehead, just like Aunt Joanie's when I stopped confession at twelve and mass at thirteen. She would put her hat on, grab her coat, and never say goodbye. Just out the door. We never talked about it. There was no hidden agenda. I just didn't want to go. I didn't have this strong faith in what I considered to be the unseen. I wanted to sleep late and watch the weekend matinees in my nightshirt.

The subway car was empty on my ride home. I read the latest edition of the *Times*, which I swiped from the seat in front of me. The travel section told me I'd find hidden treasures in Costa Rica. I could barely afford a cab once a week and these people thought I'd go to Costa Rica? Who wrote this crap anyway? This is what I was delivering to people like me? Or were these readers not really like me, Elly Dugan, at all?

I walked the couple of blocks to my building and went around back to the fire escape to avoid the always-bustling lobby, full of people with cell phones and dogs. I got into bed with all of my clothes on, even my coat. It was ten p.m. I fell asleep before I could think about the money anymore.

We had the sisters' route the next morning. Carl and I were on the road by four. He'd brought a steaming cup of hot coffee just for me.

"You didn't have to do that, Carl." I sipped the coffee — on the burner too long, my sentiments exactly.

"Well, just this once," he said. "You'll probably score big with this inheritance thing you got going on, then you'll leave me or something. Become a supermodel or something. Move up in the world, live with the supermodels instead of the faggot artists."

"I doubt it." I looked at Carl whose face seemed worried. Not about me, or the workday. Just an overall life's worry, right there in his face. Like my father who died twenty years ago, a bad liver.

"Carl, I lost it."

He didn't look at me. There was no surprised gasp, or a gaping mouth, or a "Why, Elly, why?" He just kept looking at our old truck, like I'd simply said, "I need to buy some new boots this winter" or "This job is gonna be the death of me yet."

We loaded up and pulled out. I warmed up in the cab with Carl until the first string of stops. Then he made me stay in back so that he wouldn't have to feel the cold gust of December air which made his arthritis worse. I didn't mind. I was glad I was young and didn't have these worries.

The five hours of fitful sleep the night before didn't do it for me. The coffee sat in my stomach, acidic and bitter. Cold beads of nervous sweat prickled my forehead. That money, that stupid money, was gone. Kathie Lee Gifford and her sweatshops.

I thought about the tired limp arms of the shirts hanging in my closet. Cheap fakes, all of them. Right down to the orange organza blouse with the re-sewn button.

We hit some slow traffic at the west end of Battery Park by the sisters' place. We slowed to a stop across the street from J.C.

"Elly, it's gonna be awhile. I can feel it. No progress in this city. One accident and the whole place shuts down. Who ever heard of traffic at this time of the morning anyway?"

I nodded, then looked over at the crucifix and moved closer to the back window to get a better view. It was still dark and the spotlights were shining on his forehead, his chest, his feet.

"Oh, wait a minute. I see it, Elly. It's a main break *and* a fender bender."

I opened the back door and jumped down. I surveyed the situation: endless lines of cars, the unified blare of variously pitched horns, and the ugly loud mouth of an old cop on beat who was trying to clear one lane. I walked in between the stopped cars to the chain link fence. Tiny flakes of snow dusted J.C.'s head. The sky was a muted gray, carrying the burden of a heavy, wet snow.

There were no nuns around. I opened the gate and walked up to the rock formation. I chose a jutting stronghold and made my way up quickly, as if it were built for climbing.

I was right in front of him before I knew it. His eyes, which were always on his feet, were now looking down at me. I was right. He was ashamed, but hopeful.

I climbed up closer. All of the honking and yelling swelled into white noise, white angry noise.

I reached up and touched his foot. I always wondered what it felt like. The perfect gray stone he was carved from, the rusted nails hammered into his feet. Who took that hammer and nailed those into the stone feet? Was it hard to do? Was it out of love and artistry, or the simple task of a mainte-nance man hammering away?

"HEY!"

A sister came out of the Frandscan door approaching me, approaching J.C. I looked down at Carl in the truck. He sat there in the warm cab staring at me in disbelief.

"Get down now. I'm calling the police."

She ran back to the door and called to someone inside, then came running out to us.

"Don't touch Him!" She was now directly below me.

"I'm getting down!" I looked for a foothold. Why was getting down always so much harder? The color rose in my face. I avoided her eyes. Her arms were crossed over her chest.

"Can you help me down?"

"I have half a mind to make you stay there for the police." She looked out to the street and suddenly noticed the traffic, which was slowly snaking out with one lane now cleared.

So I jumped. It was about an eight-foot fall to the ground. I landed on my feet, stumbled, then ran through the gate.

"Young girl!"

She didn't attempt to follow me. I didn't want her to see me getting in the truck. She'd report me for sure, and I would lose my job, the only thing I had.

I ran around the truck to the driver's side and Carl opened the door.

"What the hell were you doing, Elly? Trying to get yourself arrested?"

I put my hand on his arm and gently pushed it. I looked up at him, into his eyes. "Carl, move over."

And then I was driving the 1983 Ford down through the one-lane traffic of Battery Park. Carl didn't say a word until we were out of sight. Then he started to laugh.

"For a minute, I thought you were up there trying to find God or something."

I didn't say anything. At the next box, I pulled over and went to the back for my bundles.

We ate at Maury's that afternoon. Baked cod sandwiches. They were the best in town, by far. Carl sat across from me in the old wooden booth, breathing through the bread in his mouth. He kept smiling and looking out the window. Once, I heard him mutter, "Finding God."

When I got home that afternoon, Jacob sat on my front steps with the late light of the December sun.

"I took the train up. The 1:57. I gotta get back home soon. Here's your money." He handed me a personal check, seventeen hundred dollars.

I stared at it.

Jacob threw his cigarette against the wall of the building and got up to leave. He hugged me tightly. "Buy a Certificate of Deposit or something." He stepped down two stairs and stopped. "Or," he said, raising his finger, "spend it on yourself."

I stood there watching him. He turned around to go.

"But how did you get this back? Where did you get this from?"

Jacob kept walking and waved goodbye to me over his shoulder.

"Jacob!"

"It's all the same!" He called up to me as he approached the street, heading for the cover of the subway stairwell.

I ran to the railing and caught my last glimpse of him in the dying light.

"It's not the same!" I yelled.

I sat down on the fire escape stairs and thought about how I'd never been given back anything I'd lost. Was this my moment of striking gold? Then I thought about the speed of that sister – running out to her savior, the feet of ol' J.C. and the perfect wrinkles in his loincloth. He was looking at me from way up there. All those times passing right by J.C., he was looking at me with those rusted-through nails, still in his hands, still in his feet.

✳

Quinn Dalton
Kenyon Review

LENNIE REMEMBERS THE ANGELS

LATELY she's going back to the two tall sisters in their white choir robes standing next to the box she put her mother in, looking at her, not like somebody you pass on the street, but staring *into* her, eyes marching right inside her like she's just a house with the doors flung wide open. The two of them like any other woman in her church, wide-shouldered and big-busted, black hair and honey brown skin shining, the way she'd look someday, she thought then. The women stood there while Reverend Earl was preaching by the grave, robe hems lifting in the hot air, moving like someone sighing, only no one heard them and no saw them. And it wasn't no dream. It was what happened, Lennie holding the paper bag one of the women had handed her, the bag gone soft and furry with the sweat of her hand, a bag full of cash, which she used to

pay for the box and then the hole in the clay and some flowers, too, even though her uncle, her mother's own brother,
said her mother didn't deserve flowers. *A whore like her.*

Storm coming up now, air heavy on her forehead. She
rolls over, pulls a pillow to her chest out of habit so she won't
feel the flatness, the breasts gone and now just bone and
ribbed, scarred skin. She rocks and cradles the pillow and
tries to remember what the women were telling her without
moving their red lips, that everything was going to be fine,
she had her whole life ahead of her, the past didn't matter.
This was what she knew she'd heard that day, and she'd believed it. She was sixteen, small for her age, small like a child,
and men loved that about her, the way they could put their
hands around her waist and touch their thumbs and middle
fingers without squeezing. Only they did squeeze.

The first crack lights up the room, everything bone-white
and then black, even though it's only late afternoon. Another
thump like it's in her own walls and she's on her feet, down
the short hall, past the row of Cedric's school pictures, past
the State Farm calendar, finding the ash tray and cigarettes on
the coffee table in the front room. The rain starts, fat, slapping
drops. Another thump and she screams. "Gimme that goddamned lighter," she commands the room, and then she sees
its metal tip glinting next to the stove, she had used it earlier
to light the gas, she remembers now. She lights her cigarette
on the third try and stands by the kitchen window, shaking
and watching the storm mix up the trees.

Another thump and she pounds the counter to keep her
fear and her rage at the fear, after all this time, in the bottom
of her throat where it belongs. Then she sees what's making
the sound, not really the storm but a little man coming out of
the apartment next door, screen slapping the outside wall as

he hurries down the back steps and tugs at a mattress in the back seat of a long green Chevrolet. His skinny body jerks back and forth as he pulls, shaking his head to get the rain out of his eyes. She wonders how he can reach the pedals in a car like that. Finally the mattress gives and one corner splashes into a puddle before he can stop it. Lennie puts a hand over her mouth because she feels like laughing but she knows it isn't right.

She watches him stagger as he pulls the mattress to his shoulder and makes his way back to the door, rain rolling down the bedding like the side of a roof. She steps back from the window, even though she knows he won't see her. He's Asian; she can't tell what kind. The last family that lived next door was Vietnamese—four kids and so noisy she prayed they'd be deported. She heard they got evicted for cutting a hole in the floor and using the basement for a toilet. She doesn't know if this is true, but it did take four months to get anyone new in there and a lot of people looking at it. Meantime, she had gotten used to the quiet.

The man makes one more trip to the Chevrolet and comes back with two bulging garbage bags. He grimaces against the rain. "You go on and make a face," Lennie whispers to him. "Ain' no one want you here anyway."

***

Sometime during the night the storm clears and the claws unhook themselves from Lennie's stomach. She wakes up on the couch, the sun already high and sucking the blue out of the sky. Another hot day. Sunday. Her birthday. She sits up, presses her fingers to her forehead and thinks of fifty years. Born May fifth, 1950. Five-five-fifty-fifty. Some numerology type would get all over that. "Maybe this my year," Lennie says, pushing herself to her feet. She makes coffee, scrambles an egg, toasts and butters some white bread. She eats at the kitchen sink, gazing at the trees lining the gravel parking lot, their leaves glossy and deep green, still wet and heavy from the storm. She thinks about propping her door open to catch a breeze, then thinks better of it. Then she's glad she waited, because the little man comes out the back door, walking fast, screen clapping against the outside wall again. Her wall. She'll have to talk to him about that. He rolls down his car window and backs out, and she gets a good look at his face as he turns his head to see behind him. He's older than she thought, maybe fifty, maybe older than that. Hard to tell with men, with Asian men especially.

Lennie finishes her breakfast, showers and dresses for church. As she pulls her hair scarf from her purse and checks the lock on her back door she sees the green Chevrolet; the man is already back from wherever he went. She goes out the front door, squinting in the sun, locks up and starts down her steps.

"Hello."

Lennie hears the voice and the accent and knows it's her neighbor before she turns to see him standing at his open front door. He is smiling, nodding at her as if they're already friends having a pleasant little conversation. Small talk is for small people, Lennie thinks. Who had said that to her once? She presses out a closed-mouth smile. "Hello," she says.

The man steps onto his stoop, and Lennie steps off her last step into the warm wet grass. He sees this and stops, puts a hand to his chest. "Duc Li." The sound in "Duc" is something between "oo" and "uh."

"Duke?" Lennie says.

"Duc Li," the man says again, nodding.

"Duck," Lennie says.

"Yes," the man says, although Lennie knows she wasn't even close. Why do those people have to talk up in their nose like that? She wonders.

"And, you, name?" Duc Li says, the last word swinging up in his throat like he's just remembered he's asking a question.

"Lennie," she says. She takes another step away from him, wet grass brushing her ankles and marking her hose. They need to take a mower to this place, she thinks. She sees her bus turning the corner. "Nice to meet you," she says, although this isn't true, it isn't nice, but she doesn't want to miss her bus.

Lennie walks quickly to the curb, watching the bus, which is waiting to make a left turn onto her street. She hears Duc Li sing out, "And you!" in a thin reedy voice that sounds like a sick child's. She throws her arm up in a quick wave but doesn't turn around.

* * *

This isn't the church she went to as a child, where her mother was buried. That church burned down while she was in Atlanta trying to get clean, her small son left with her Aunt Olivia, who was actually her mother's aunt. She heard they moved the bodies before they built the shopping center, but her mother's grave never had a marker except a few stones, so Lennie figures she's still in the old church yard, under all that concrete, where it's cool and quiet and no one can bother her.

The church Lennie goes to now is beige brick with thick beige carpet and long, blond wood pews, a far cry from the splintered folding chairs that cut into the back of your thighs and nothing but packed dirt for a floor. And no organ, not even a piano. And no air conditioning. When she went to that church all she could think about was getting out, first so she could play with her girlfriends, and later so she could get with the boys who were turning into men, who couldn't be made to go to church anymore, and if they did, they sat in the back so she felt their eyes moving over her neck and arms like a slow fire.

Today the sermon is about Jesus turning the water into wine, and Lennie thinks of when she joined twenty years ago, having just come back from AA in Atlanta, still shaky, her son ten years old and not sure who she was. The preacher is saying the wine is a symbol for something else. Lennie sits up straighter in her pew to see where he goes with this. He says the wine is a sign for the joy of life.

"Not that you got to drink it to be happy," he says, and people laugh. He's young, round-faced. Most of the brothers and sisters are grey-headed.

A woman moans an Amen to Lennie's left. She doesn't think this preacher is going to last—he'll go on to bigger churches that put their services on TV—but his hoarse, microphoned words makes her think of other signs: Her mother's death a sign of sin's punishment, her own burning house a sign for starting over, her breasts cut away a sign that she would no longer be the woman she was.

The preacher's asking people for prayer dedications. Over the years Lennie always called out her mother's name, Celia, because it's true, she was a whore, at least for one man, who kept her in drugs until he got tired of her, then beat her unconscious one night and dragged her into the road and drove back and forth over her until she was in pieces. Broke Lennie's father's heart in pieces, too, because he died soon after that. If she'd had a daughter, Lennie would have named her Celia, and raised her to become the kind of woman her mother might have been, if things had been different. Instead she had Cedric, and then she left him when he was only four and didn't come back until he was ten and then he looked her in the face and said his mother was dead.

Pray for me, Lennie wants to say. But nobody ever asks for that. So she doesn't either.

* * *

On the bus home she thinks about taking a trip, maybe to the ocean, which she has been to once, when she was a child. It was before her father's heart attack, the one that put a scar up his middle and the end to his working. It was before her mother left them for Dag, who always had money and rings, thick gold on every finger. Lennie remembers not believing her father when he said they were going to the beach, because the ocean in her mind was so clean and blue, she didn't think whites would let coloreds near it.

But they did drive to the beach, right onto it even, sand stinging her arm where it hung over the side of the car through the open back window, sand spraying the wheel wells like rain on their tin roof at home, sand flying in the windows, sticking in her teeth. She collected the grains with her tongue and swallowed them, and thought about where'd they'd been, where they'd had to travel, to land in her belly. In the water, she opened her mouth to the warm salty wet, closed her eyes, let wave after wave roll her body into the surf, water rushing in her ears, drowning out her father's warning calls and sounding like somewhere she'd been before. And the most amazing sight: chocolate and coffee and caramel skins of other children, of men and women, shining wet in the light that came from every direction, everyone laughing and walking as if this was all there was — sun, water, sand and brown people in their own paradise.

The bus chokes to a stop at the curb in front of Lennie's apartment building. She takes her time getting off, crossing the street and the lawn, glancing at the apartment next to hers, trying to judge if her new neighbor is watching. She doesn't want to try to make conversation. Inside she splashes water on her face, changes clothes, waits to check the red light on the answering machine in the small bedroom until she has nothing left to do.

The light is blinking. She holds her finger just above the button, listening, as if she might be able to tell the voice before it starts. There are words and then there are the words behind the words, her father used to say, especially when she started staying out late with men, and he sat up waiting and watching for her, knowing that getting angry would've done nothing but drive her away, like it did her mother. What did he think of women, how they left him when he was too weak to even argue?

Cedric. Like she hoped. "Mama, Nina and me wanna come over and take you to lunch, OK? Maybe over to Herbie's. Guess you at church. Call me."

So nice to be called. So right. She walks through her house and inspects it, straightens a rug, smoothes the bedspread. Opens all the curtains. She spritzes the couch pillows with her favorite perfume, sits down and lights a cigarette, watches the bluish ribbon rise and spread and curl like a storm cloud, like a woman's hair, loose and flowing, underwater. She thinks of her little girl's braids standing around her head for the seconds she could stay under the waves, all that water and deep around her and she wasn't even scared. She walks back down the hall to call Cedric, who's a good son even though he's had his share of turnaround changes, and as she dials, she thinks she might look into a bus ticket to the coast. Maybe Myrtle Beach.

Answering machine. Probably they're outside with Nina's kids. She tells them she'd love to go to Herbie's. "Hi Sally," she says to Nina's older daughter. "Hi Lola."

She hangs up, stubs out the cigarette, changes back into the dress she wore to church and smiles at herself in the bathroom mirror, even though she's feeling the first ache of worry in the soft space between her ribs, the way she feels when the clouds gather over the development down the hill and lightning winks behind the trees. She can hear the man moving around in the apartment next door, rustling like a small animal behind the walls. Then she hears his back door open and she steps to the side of her window, where she can see. He leans out with two plants, pink impatiens and some kind of a cactus, both in green plastic pots with the price stickers still on. He leaves them on the stoop, proof he's there to stay.

She stretches out on the couch, balancing her feet on the arm. Passing cars sigh on the road, and she thinks of the two women in their choir robes, the air around them alive somehow, looking at her in a way that moved through her, telling her: *you gonna be OK.* But asking, too. She thinks of her job at the nursing home, turning all those poor bony bodies, wondering who will turn her someday.

"Stop it," Lennie says to the air, and right after that, she falls asleep.

When she wakes up, it's nearly five o'clock, sun in her eyes. She knows it's late without checking, she could always tell time within ten minutes by the light, the way her father taught her. But she looks anyway at the black lines on the clock, and she walks slowly to the smaller bedroom, her hips stiff, to check the answering machine, knowing she wouldn't have slept through any rings.

Red light steady as a stare. "Fine," Lennie says to the room, to the dust floating in the sunlight. "Fine."

She smoothes her hair, finds her purse and keys, heads for the bus stop on the curb before remembering Sunday bus service cuts off at five. She decides to walk to the Kentucky Fried Chicken a half mile down Church Street next to the gas station. She'll take herself out to dinner and pick up some cigarettes, too.

She's stepping off the curb, checking to make sure she's remembered her wallet, starting to cross the street, feeling around in her purse, looking down, and then there is a metal flash and sound so great she can't tell the two apart, and she feels not pain, really, but weight, like the waves rolling her down into heavy sand, and she can't tell where her body is, and then there is nothing.

* * *

Someone is crying. Lennie tries to comfort her, but the more she tries, the louder the moans.

"You steal," a voice says, right above her head somewhere.

"No," Lennie says. She's done a lot of things in her life, but she never took anything that wasn't hers.

"Steal!"

She tries to respond, but she is too tired, and it's too bright to open her eyes.

"No! No move!"

"Oh my god," a woman's voice says. A voice she recognizes.

She hears scraping footsteps near her head, fading, then returning. And her back and arms are hot, so she tries to roll on her side, but someone gently pushes her back, "Goddamn you," she mutters, and she opens her eyes and there is a face above hers, a boy's face she thinks, but the sun is behind it. Cedric? She thinks or maybe says. Then she's being lifted and the pain moves through her like a wedge of hot metal from her leg to her shoulder, and then she passes out.

* * *

There's no reason to be confused, she keeps telling herself every time she opens her eyes, sometimes when a nurse comes in to check on her, to change one of the bags dripping clear liquid into her arm. But she is. Once she sees herself tearing out the needle and getting up to leave, but when she looks again, it's still there, and she doesn't know whether it was a dream or not.

Then she thinks it's her breasts again, the doctors telling her they were poisoning her body and they would have to take them. She laughs at the word *take*, like they're children she can't control, like they can be brought back once they learn to behave. But then she looks down at her chest and it's flat as a girl's, the white gown like a field of snow, like the choir robes the angels wore. Well, they were angels, weren't they? Meeting her in front of the church like that, and she only had five dollars in her pocket, wasn't even enough to have the hole dug. They handed her a paper bag, twisted tight at the mouth like around a wino's sack, only it was so light it felt like there wasn't nothing in it. They handed her that sack and walked away, leaving her in the dirt churchyard like this was the kind of thing people did every day.

How did she know to walk to the back of the church and find Sarylee, the secretary, and dump that sack all over a chair? Money falling out and tumbling to the floor, damp and folded. Almost five hundred dollars. She had always said she'd remember the exact number forever, because that would be her lucky number for the rest of her life, but then she'd forgotten it right away, almost as soon as the money was spent. Enough for the hole and the preacher and a pine coffin. And flowers too. And even some left over, which she had promised herself she would put down on a grave stone, a big white marble one, but then she'd spent it on a dress for getting married to Tony, and it was that dress she wanted to save when she woke up one night in that drafty country house he stuck her in, the fire heat holding her down on the bed, its sound like people whispering, laughing. She thought of the dress even before her own son.

It was lightning that started it, turned that house to black bones, as if to say *this is your heart, this is what it looks like*. She wants to get on her knees and pray about it, even now, but she can't move, can't even think of how she would bend to kneel.

Then there is the policeman, his chest a gray wall, the loose pink skin of his neck wagging as he asks her what she remembers. She remembers a lot of things, things she'd rather forget, and here they are lined up in front of her like Judgment Day. The policeman asks if she can tell him anything about the car.

"The car?" she asks, her throat surprised at its sound.

"That hit you?" Metal pen tapping a clipboard. Clock hands clicking in their circle. Ticking her to sleep.

* * *

"You got a nice young man here to see you," the nurse says. "You gonna be fine."

"Who?" Lennie says. Then she sees her son in the doorway, looking at her with a smile that says he'd rather be somewhere else. His church smile. His good son smile. The one that seems to hurt him from the way he squints. Shifting from one foot to the other.

"Hi mama," he says. "How you feeling?" He jingles some change in his pocket.

"She a lot better, ain't she," the nurse says to Lennie. She wheels a chair to the side of the bed and presses a button to push Lennie upright. Lennie can feel her insides folding hotly as she rises.

"No," she moans.

The nurse peels back the covers. "Gotta start somewhere," she says. "You gonna be OK."

* * *

Home. Right leg broken, five broken ribs—two on the left and three on the right. Contusions on the left shoulder. *Upper extremities* they called it. Where she threw herself against the door of her burning house. Where she burped her son. Now she can't even think about lifting that arm. The car hit her leg first, then flipped her over the hood onto her shoulder. Then left her to die. The worst part: scrubbing the asphalt from her skin, the palms of her hands where she had evidently tried to break her fall. She had cried like a child during that.

Nurse coming twice a day. Aqua blue uniform, skin so white it's almost blue, too. Nancy. Wears her hair in a pony tail with a rubber band and no makeup. No wedding ring either. Lennie wants to tell her she could fix herself up a little, probably find herself someone, but then what does she have to say about men? Chasing after Tony with his almond eyes and the muscles in his shoulders like something molded, not flesh, two tear drops that slid from his neck and fanned over her in bed, how she loved his size, she loved men who towered over her, and most did, but she loved the biggest, the ones who made her feel like a little doll. Thinking of him, if she lets herself go into that first year, the year Cedric was born, can still make her thighs twitch and tighten with the heat.

That year, before his drinking set his anger on fire, before he started accusing her, asking her to prove that was really his son and how could she do that? It was him that was cheating, and she started drinking too because it was something they had in common, and because sometimes when he was drunk he got slow and soft, usually after he'd gotten paid and the money stretched out in front of them like a long velvet cushion until Tuesday of the following week, when there was only beans or those yellow noodles in the crinkly sacks to eat.

That first year they lived in that country shack of a house with nothing, and he was happy she was pregnant, telling her she was so beautiful, that first summer the fireflies were thick in the trees and some nights when it was too hot in the house they laid down in the grass and made love with crickets trilling all around. One time she looked up, past the blue-black sheen of Tony's hair, past the swell of his back and the twin slopes of her drawn-up knees and saw a plane sliding silently across the sky. She had never been in a plane, and had always wanted to, but that night she felt sorry for the people inside, that they could not know the pleasure that ran down to her very fingertips, so much of it she thought she could die right then, never even get to see her baby, and be happy enough to let go of it all.

Nancy sponges her down in the morning and helps her dress and eat. This morning Lennie's in her recliner in a slip and underpants. A nylon bandage buckled around her ribs like the tightest girdle she's ever had. The hospital doctor told her Medicaid would cover fake breasts to put in her bra; but she said no. Who is she going to impress?

"Which one?" Nancy asks, holding up two dresses, one red with white flowers and one a yellow check. Lennie looks at them but doesn't see them yet; she's not quite ready to get up off that dewy grass, to give up all that roundness—her breasts and belly, Tony's buttocks and the tip of his purple brown penis.

"Ms. Williams?"

Lennie sighs, lets go. "I don't care."

Nancy hugs the dresses to her like limp children. She cocks her head to one side like a schoolteacher. "Ms. Williams, would you like me to help you do your make up today?"

"What for? Huh? Where am I going?" Lennie asks. The itch under her leg cast is hot sandpaper on her skin. She claws it anyway, knowing it won't help. She doesn't know why she likes being rude to Nancy. Maybe because she will take it; she'll just be more and more polite until she freezes in place, all that blue skin and pale brown hair still as death.

Nancy gives up. "OK, the yellow one." Lennie lets her arms go slack and Nancy gently lifts the hurt one first, her fingertips like cold little stones, then the other. Then she helps Lennie stand so that the dress falls down her back, and Lennie buttons it herself.

Nancy sits down on the couch across from her. "Are you sure there isn't anything more I can do for you?"

"Don't you have your next appointment?"

"You know, it's OK to take help right now. You need to let people take care of you until you're better."

Lennie tries to lean forward in her chair, but the pain stops her. She grunts out her words, using her best white talk to try to get through to the woman. "For your information, my son is coming over in a while. I am not some charity case. You look at me and you think you know what you see. But you don't know anything."

Nancy's lips get straight and thin; Lennie can see she's made her point. Nancy stands, gathers her brown purse and her white notebook. "See you tomorrow, Ms. Williams."

Front door pulls closed, and Lennie sighs. She nods to her father's picture on the wall, next to it her parent's wedding picture in front of the courthouse, her mother wearing a stiff white dress with lace at the wrists and throat, looking serious, her father in a dark suit, sweat shining on his high forehead, smiling. Their features narrow and spare. She wishes she could step into that picture and touch their soft faces and warn them about everything, tell them they can save themselves. But what about her? She doesn't even have a picture of Tony—all that floated into the air the night of the fire—and after that they moved in with his parents since hers were already dead, and he was never there, and when he was there he hit her or sometimes they drank together until she couldn't even wake up when her son was crying. And then she left Cedric, left him with those brown stick arms wrapped around her aunt's leg, his shoulders capped with those tear drops of muscle just like his father's, except small and nowhere near as strong.

Maybe an hour passes, her just thinking, waiting for Cedric to come, until she's sure he won't come, and she starts crying, thinking of that day two weeks ago in the church when she wanted to ask everyone to pray for her. "Please," she says into the quiet. "Please."

* * *

The knock wakes her, and the pain comes first to certain places, and then everywhere at once. "Mama, it's me, open up."

She has to unlock it herself. "OK," she tries to say, but she can barely whisper with the effort of pulling herself onto the crutches. She crab-steps past the coffee table, then leans against the back door as she turns the lock. She sees her son's sagging white truck next to her neighbor's Chevrolet and wonders why she hasn't heard the little man lately. She steps away from the door. "You can open it now."

Cedric steps in and she's hit with the smell of him—sweat and cologne and smoke. He follows her slowly back into the living room. She tries to sense his mood while he's still behind her—she's always been able to tell more about a person if she closes her eyes and listens to them. She can tell he's tired, maybe worried about something, from the way his feet shuffle and his breath comes out too fast from his nose. "Help me back down in this chair," she says, and winces as he grabs her too strongly and lowers her. "Now, there's a tall bottle of white pills, and a smaller bottle of blue pills on the sink in there," she says, pointing at the bathroom. He comes back with the pills and she doesn't bother to ask for water; she just swallows them as quickly as she can, waiting for the slicing pain in her arm and leg and ribs to subside. He puts them back in the bathroom.

"Mama, you don't look too good."

"Thanks, Cedric."

"No, I mean it. They feeding you?"

"Yes, they feed me nasty crap and I eat it. Got me a white nurse named Nancy who don't know how to fix her own hair, not to mention mine."

This makes Cedric laugh. He slaps his knee and falls back against her couch cushion. "Mama, you a mess." And Lennie feels a warmth that starts in her chest and spreads into her neck and then her face. Her son, a grown man right in front of her, laughing with his wide mouth that turns up at the corners just like his father's. I made you, she thinks. She smiles. She goes through the things she won't ask, like where he's working now, or if he's working, or whether he's talked to his father lately. "How's Nina and Sally?"

"They fine, they fine. Listen, I got news for you." Cedric's face looks serious and Lennie pulls in her breath to steady herself. The pain medication is flowing over her, and she knows she can live with it if he's going to ask her for money again, because he's alive, and as long as he's alive, she is too. Cedric sits forward, folds his long fingers. "Nina gonna have a baby."

"You?" is all Lennie manages to say, and then she flings her arms out to him, never mind the stab in her shoulder, and Cedric comes around the coffee table to her and kneels between her cast and her good leg and she pulls him to her and rocks him like she used to do when they laid awake in that leaky house, listening to the rain splashing in all their pots and pans. She can already see the baby, slick from just being born, being handed to her, and it will be light-skinned like Nina but wiry like Cedric. She can hear its thin mewling, oh and see the head turning, rooting for milk. She knows she will be there.

Cedric pulls away and sits back on his heels, looking down to check the beeping pager clipped to the waistband of his baggy shorts. The bands of muscles in his arms roll over each other and Lennie allows herself to think of Tony, how he kneeled, asking her to marry him, except he almost fell over because he was so drunk, and they both laughed because they were so young, and it was so, so funny. They were young and black and poor and the world had nothing to give them, but it didn't matter because they didn't need anything then, they would have laughed like hyenas at anyone who thought they were good enough to pity them.

Cedric's on his feet. "Let me use your phone, Mama." While he's down the hall, Lennie is listing all the questions she has to ask, but when he comes back he's jingling his keys. "I gotta go."

"Wait, now," Lennie says. "You gotta tell me more! When's it due?"

Cedric's shifting his feet now, finding the right key. "I don't know. Nina just took a home test."

"She going to the doctor, ain' she?"

"I guess so. Look, Mama, I gotta go."

Lennie wants to get to her feet but can't. "Was that her calling?"

"No." Cedric bends to kiss her cheek. His lips are dry, quick. "You want me to bring you some dinner?"

"OK, if you can," Lennie tries to act like it doesn't matter either way, but she's hopeful.

"You want some fried chicken?"

Lennie gets her purse from under the recliner, hands him a twenty. "Why don't you get some for yourselves too and bring Nina and Sally over?"

Cedric smiling, pushes the bill into his running shorts. "OK then." Then he's out the door and all that's left is his smell and the heat from where he was standing.

Lennie closes her eyes, thinks about the baby, which is carrying a little bit of her inside it, unfurling inside Nina. She liked Nina before; now maybe she can love her. She lets herself slide into a light sleep. Then she's seeing the women by her mother's grave, telling her she would be OK, meaning there would be a day when all the pain she had felt and made for herself would somehow come to something good, and on that day she'd find her way to something like grace. She drifts on this, waves swelling underneath and lifting her salty body to the sun, and she is sleeping lightly when there's another knock on her door. She opens her eyes and listens. "Cedric, that you?"

"Hello," a man's voice says, but not Cedric's, thinner.

"Who is it?" Reaching for the crowbar she put under her chair, next to her purse.

"Duc Li. Next door?" That swinging upward at the end of his voice, like he's always surprised.

Lennie lets the air out of her chest. If not Cedric, then at least it's someone to help her pass the time. "Come in."

She hears her screen slap, and she wants to ask this man if anyone ever explained to him about not letting doors slam. He comes into the living room where she can see him, and he's holding something white in both hands. She squints to see it better. It seems too dark all of a sudden—did she sleep later than she thought? He bends and places the bundle on the table, and then she can see it's a package of candles, bound in twine. He points toward the ceiling. "Stome tonight," he says.

"What?" Then she understands. Storm. And as soon as she understands the word, she's looking out the front window down the hill toward the development, where the weather always comes in, and even though the sun is still shining on the street, the sky down there is a bruised gray. Her chest gets tight again. She can hear the air moving in and out of her lungs, feel the gathering pressure at her temples. Duc Li is watching her. He is so short that he only has to bend a little to get to her eye level. "You OK?" Words halting, like a water-bug zigzagging.

Lennie nods. "Thanks for the candles."

"In case the lights go—" he makes a slicing gesture with his hands. "Bad," he says, shaking his head. Lennie looks at the clock. Two hours since Cedric left. She thinks about call-ing about dinner but doesn't want to beg. She's too old for that. He said he was coming back. He's a man now, and his word has to count for something.

Duc Li is cutting open the package with a pocketknife. "You want?" he says, miming putting a candle in a holder.

Lennie shakes her head. "I don't have any."

"OK," Duc Li says, smiling. "OK." He holds up one finger signaling her to wait and goes out the back door, screen slamming, making her jump.

"Goddamnit!" Lennie yells at him. She's hungry, her son isn't going to show up—she knows this even if she wants to pretend otherwise—and the sky is going to crack open any minute. Truth is, after the fire she never liked candles. She keeps a flashlight by her bed, but didn't think to put it in reach since the accident.

Duc Li comes back with a roll of foil. He tears a piece and makes a mound of it and presses the base of one candle into it. Then he makes another. Lennie doesn't try to stop him. "You see?" he says, and Lennie nods. She sees. She's going to sit in this apartment alone, waiting out the storm, hoping the lightning doesn't burn her alive like it almost did the last time. She's going to sit here until her body knits itself together again, and then she'll go back to work, and when she can't work anymore she'll go back to sitting again, and then she'll die alone. Yes, she sees.

"I made," Duc Li says, pointing to the candles. "Carter Candle Factory." Except he says it "Carteh Cander Fahctree." Lennie wants to laugh at him for his cartoon talk and jerky gestures, the comical grin on his face. She wants to laugh at him for thinking this country would be so much better for him, that he'd ever belong here. But then the first thunder hits, and she hears it pushing through the air almost before it explodes into sound, but she can't stop the yelp that tears itself out of her throat.

Duc Li jumps back, and for some reason she sees no point in not telling him the situation. "I'm scared. Storm," she says, pointing at the ceiling like Duc Li did, and feeling ridiculous. "Can you get my pills?" She points to the bathroom.

He brings them, sets them on the table beside her. "You stay steel," he says, and goes out the back door again, and she keeps hearing the word "steel." She knows he means "still." But where did she hear it before? She closes her eyes and what she sees is a boy's face—maybe a man's—looking down at her, sun behind him so she can't make out the features. She's on her back and the pavement's burning her, and she's thinking someone's accusing her of stealing. Then she realizes he's the one who found her. He saw her get hit.

Duc Li comes back with two bowls of steaming rice and vegetables, one fork, one set of chopsticks. "Here," he says, holding one out to her.

"No, that's OK," she says. "I'm not hungry." She isn't. She's angry—at her fear of mere weather, the picture of Duc Li standing over her in the street, the stupidity of not seeing the car coming, the pain that's coming back. Duc Li places the bowl on her coffee table. She reaches for the two bottles of pills, the pills rattling like ice in a glass, all those glasses of gin she drank, toward the end with no ice at all. No glass even. She opens the tall bottle and finds that most of the pills are gone. A lot more than earlier today. Cedric. Always nipping a little here, a little there. She squeezes the bottle and shakes her head. Tears dripping off her nose. What did she expect?

Duc Li takes the bottle from her. He reads the label, counts out one white pill, two blue pills. He takes a glass from the drainer in the kitchen, fills it with water from the tap, hands her the glass and the pills. He sits on his heels near where her son was sitting just hours before, telling her about a baby, filling her with hope even as he was stealing from her. Duc Li takes the glass from her and offers her the bowl. "You eat." She shakes her head, but he leans forward and pushes the bowl into her hands. "Eat," he says. He sits back on his heels again, prepared to wait.

Lightning now, turning his face gray, then darkening it. No more sun on the street, just the heavy air, the waiting still-ness. She holds the warm bowl, holds her breath, listening for thunder. Duc Li picks up his bowl and begins to eat. His fingers are narrow and long, like a woman's, his chopsticks click lightly against the bowl. The thunder rolls into the room and he looks up at her, smiles while she grips the chair arm with her free hand, bearing down on the urge to scream. Alone, she could let it out into a pillow, but not with him here. Do you think this is funny? Lennie wants to ask him. Me, trapped here with you? But Duc Li is back to shoveling in mouthfuls of food. He is almost finished by the time Lennie manages the first bite. The rice is sticky and warm, and the vegetables, bell pepper and snow peas, crunch loud like the thud of blood in her ears. She keeps going until her bowl is empty. Duc Li takes it, stacks it into his own. "Thank you," she says. He nods, rises fluidly to his feet, heads for the back door.

"Wait a minute," she says. "Do you remember my name?"

Duc Li seems to think this is funny. "Len-nie," he says with a pause in the middle. "Like my wife. Li Ni." No smile now.

"Where is she?"

"Gone. Long time."

Lennie doesn't say anything to this. The medicine is loosening her muscles, relaxing her jaw. She barely twitches at the next roll of thunder. The room is almost dark; normally she would turn off all the lights and unplug her radio and television and smoke cigarettes until the worst had passed. Tonight she doesn't even have the energy to ask him to hand her the pack. He stands in the shadow of her doorway, waiting, she thinks, for her to say something, but she can't. She's thinking of her mother now, her broken body nailed into the pine box, how only a week before Dag killed her she was standing on his rickety front porch yelling, 'You ain't my daughter! You get outta here you little bitch!" The drugs had carved deep holes under her eyes and cheekbones. Lennie's thinking that's what death is, not being known. She's thinking of the quality of the brown sisters' voices, like breath over a bottle, telling her not to worry—weren't they saying she could one day live in grace? She lifts her hand, reaches, waits for it, the dry pressure of Duc Li's hand closing over hers.

David Evans Katz

THE WANDERING BARD OF NETHER SAWREY

ROBERT Jenks Fredet got his middle name from his mother, but nothing else, because she died within a few days of his birth. His father called him Jinx, either for his middle name or because the old man thought he was a bad omen. The name stuck, and that's how I always knew him.

Jinx and his older sister, Annelise, lived with their father beyond the old coal yard in a rented four-room frame house that hadn't been repainted since it was first built in 1923. No one knew what Jinx's dad did for a living, but we all knew he never thought much about feeding Jinx. And so Jinx became a regular dinnertime visitor at my house, where the food was always plentiful, if not fancy.

Jinx and I grew up in a small town in northwestern Connecticut, hard by the Little Sawrey River. The village of Upper Sawrey was where rich New Yorkers kept their weekend and summer homes; we lived in Nether Sawrey with the hoi pol-loi. My father was a product line salesman for a paper company down in Torrington, and he earned a good living, but not a great one. He never went to college, and he was determined that I do so, so he worked hard and saved, hoping to buy my way into to a private college. My end of the bargain was to study hard and earn good grades.

Jinx made no such bargain. He was a sorry looking kid, too tall for his clothes and too skinny to fill them out. When he wasn't in school, he spent most of his time outdoors, usually fishing the Little Sawrey, rendering his complexion permanently sunburned. Our school was small, so we shared classes together all the way through high school. While I was at the top of my class, Jinx always hovered near the bottom, not because he wasn't smart, but because the faculty tagged him early on as someone not worth teaching, and he lived down to their expectations.

Once, during an English test in seventh grade, I heard a commotion behind me. Mrs. Alois jumped up from her desk and walked past me with an angry, thrusting stride that threatened impending disaster for one of my classmates. I turned around in time to see her snatch Jinx's test paper from his hands.

"Robert Fredet, I will not tolerate cheating in my classroom. March yourself to the principal's office immediately."

"But, Mrs. Alois," Jinx protested, "it wasn't me."

Mrs. Alois glared at him, cold fury emanating from her eyes. The only thing she hated more than cheating was backtalk. "Don't lie to me, young man. I saw you copy from Leonard's paper."

Mrs. Alois pinched Jinx by the top of his ear and pulled him out of his seat. She led him down the aisle between the desks, still holding his ear between her index finger and thumb, and hustled him out the door. As he passed my desk, I saw tears forming in the corners of his eyes. I looked back at Leonard Bligh; his face was red.

Jinx never returned that day, nor for three days afterward. During his absence from school, he didn't show up at my house for dinner, either, and I began to worry that something awful had happened to him. I couldn't call him, because the Fredets didn't have a telephone, and I didn't dare go to his house for fear that his father would chase me away. I cornered Leonard Bligh in the schoolyard and tried to make him tell me about the test, but he had a good twenty pounds on me, and he knew I couldn't take him in a fight.

When Jinx returned to school, he looked like a frightened animal. He avoided eye contact, and it took me two days of badgering to get him to talk.

"Leonard tapped me on the shoulder," he said. "He wanted me to give him one of the answers, but I turned around and told him I wouldn't. That's when Mrs. Alois caught me. Mr. Higgins suspended me."

"Why didn't you tell them Leonard was cheating?" I asked.

Jinx looked at me as though I were stupid. "I tried to tell them, but they wouldn't listen."

I was furious with Mrs. Alois and our principal, Mr. Higgins, and with the sniveling Leonard for letting Jinx take the blame.

"Let's go make Leonard tell the truth."

Jinx laughed. "You and me? C'mon, Willie. Leonard won't fess up, and you and I can't make him."

Jinx was right, of course. Without admitting our collective weakness, I changed the subject. "What did your father say?" I asked.

Jinx averted his eyes. "Whaddayou think? He whacked me in the head and locked me in my room for three days. I woulda gone hungry if Annelise hadn't snuck me some food.

The old man wouldn't even let me out to take a crap. I had to climb out the window and go in the woods."

After the cheating incident, Jinx bore the mark of Cain. Teachers didn't trust him, and our classmates didn't believe him. For the rest of our time in the Sawrey school system, he became introverted and sullen, and I was his only friend.

Right after we finished high school, Jinx's father took off for good, leaving him a one-sentence note that read, simply, "You can take care of yourself from now on." It wasn't even signed. Annelise had been married for a few years by then, and she lived in a big farmhouse with her husband, Max Durran, a dairyman whose family had been in the Sawreys for generations. He and Annelise took Jinx in.

That fall, I matriculated at Avon College in Vermont. Christmas break of my freshman year was the last I saw of Nether Sawrey for a long time, because my father was promoted to regional sales manager and he and my mother moved to Rochester. It was also the last time I ever saw Jinx Fredet.

When I paid a holiday call at Annelise's house, Jinx told me what he planned to do with his life.

"I'm gonna get out of Nether Sawrey and travel the world, Willie. I went to the library and read about how cheap you can travel overseas if you book passage on a cargo ship."

"Are you going to work your way across?" I asked, astonished at the thought of Jinx as a merchant seaman.

Jinx shook his head. "Nah. I'm going as a passenger. These ships – they take passengers for next to nothing. You just can't be too particular about where you wanna go and when you wanna get there."

"But how will you live? How will you support yourself?"

He shrugged his shoulders. "I'll find work. I don't need much to live on. I'll figure it out once I get there."

"Get where?" I asked.

"I don't know. Outta Nether Sawrey. I'll write you and let you know where I end up."

The following spring, as I was studying for finals and struggling with writing a short story for my Freshman English class, I received a large manila envelope in the mail marked with Annelise's return address. Inside was another envelope addressed to me, and inside that was a letter and twenty pages of Jinx's scrawl. I read the letter first.

Dear Willie,

I finally did it. I booked passage to Dakar on a cargo ship called the Standart. It's increddable here. I'll write you more about it after I get me a job. I figure I'll stay in Senegal for a bit, at least till I save up enough money to move on. Meanwhile, I've inclosed some notes about my boat trip I thought you might like to read.

I'll be moving around a lot, so if you want, you can write me in care of Annelise, and she'll forward it to me. It's cheaper for me to write you both at the same time and inclose both letters in the same envelope and send it off to her. She'll post it in Sawrey and mail it to you as long as you let me know where to find you. I hope colledge is fun for you. Take care of yourself.

Youre pal,

Jinx Fredet
P.S: My [something] is [something].

Jinx's spelling hadn't improved, and neither had his handwriting. He'd used a fountain pen, and the ink bled through the paper, rendering his post-script unintelligible. I was proud of him for pursuing his dream, and more than a little jealous. College life in Vermont had been an interesting change from Nether Sawrey, but the campus was just as isolated. I yearned for the kind of adventure my friend had found.

I put Jinx's letter aside and read the notes of his voyage to West Africa. He described the officers and crew, and each of the fourteen passengers in rich detail. He related anecdotes about shipboard activities during the slow trans-Atlantic crossing, as well as observations of each passenger. By the time I finished reading, I realized that, despite his poor spelling, Jinx had painted a montage of characters who came to life on each page.

I'd been struggling with my own creative writing assignment for days, unable to complete a coherent beginning for a story that would count for forty percent of my final grade. As I placed Jinx's papers on my desk, I thought about what he had written, and I decided to compose a story based upon his adventures. I placed some paper in my portable Smith Corona and typed a title page: "Write of Passage" By William J. Goodrich.

I wrote for hours, absorbed in creative fervor inspired by Jinx. The experience was his; the story was mine. When I finished, I gave no thought to having stolen someone else's ideas. I submitted the paper to Professor Appleton the following day and returned to the business of cramming for finals, happy that I had completed the last of my writing assignments.

Two weeks later, after I finished my last exam, I received a note from Professor Appleton requesting that I stop by his office.

"William, I don't know any other way to put this, except to say that your story is remarkable."

I was overwhelmed. Receiving praise from Professor Appleton was rare – he was a perfectionist who delighted in skewering aspiring writers with acerbic editorial comments. Once, during my first semester, he had circled one of my split infinitives in red and wrote in the margin, "Intolerable." He then handed the paper back to me and said, "Mr. Goodrich, this is unworthy of an Avon College student. Giving you an F for this work would inflate its value."

Now, however, he smiled and informed me that "Write of Passage" had earned the Freshman Writing Award for fiction, which consisted of a hundred-dollar honorarium and publication in *The Bard*, Avon's prestigious literary annual.

My gratification over Professor Appleton's praise dissolved into consternation. At Avon, plagiarism was tantamount to a capital offense. It was bad enough that I'd submitted a story that wasn't entirely original; having it published would only compound the crime. I sat before Professor Appleton contemplating the implications of what I'd done and what I needed to do next. If I spoke up immediately, I might avoid expulsion and suffer only failure of the course and academic probation. If, however, I permitted the story to be published and the truth later emerged, I'd be branded a liar and a cheat.

Professor Appleton mistook my silence for incredulity. He said, "It's permissible to smile. The Freshman Writing Award is a prize, not a punishment."

Haltingly, I explained to Professor Appleton what I had done. As I spoke, his expression transformed from pride to disdain, reflecting a blend of anger and disappointment. I found it difficult to continue, but he gave me no quarter. He curtly asked for my source material, which, for better or worse, I had with me in the briefcase my father had given me as a high school graduation present. I handed over the sheaf of Jinx's notes along with his cover letter, knowing that with them went my academic career.

Professor Appleton read the letter first and then scanned the pages of composition paper. Gradually, his expression softened. At last, he put the papers down and leaned back in his chair. He glanced up at the ceiling and interlaced his fingers, resting them atop his stomach. I edged forward, awaiting his verdict.

"William," he said, more to the ceiling than to me, "it's obvious that your story was inspired by your friend's journey and the notes he shared with you." He lowered his chin and looked at me earnestly. "Thank you for disclosing this, but I assure you it isn't plagiarism. The words are yours; you merely co-opted someone else's experience and turned it into fiction. In that, you share a literary tradition with many other writers."

My sigh of relief was audible and profound, but I still felt guilty. Professor Appleton suggested that I append an acknowledgment to my story, giving Jinx credit for its inspiration.

When I received my hundred-dollar check later that month, I sat down and wrote Jinx a letter, explaining what I'd done and enclosing a copy of the story along with fifty dollars in cash. He had earned a share of the award money, and I knew the cash would come in handy in his travels. About five weeks later, I received his reply – just as before, a smaller envelope enclosed in a larger one postmarked from his sister's address in Nether Sawrey. He wrote to say that he enjoyed my story and appreciated the money. Fifty American dollars in Senegal, he said, was worth twenty times what it was back home. He promised to write again with more observations about his adventures.

Shortly after *The Bard* published "Write of Passage," I received a letter from *Occidental Magazine* asking to reprint it for two hundred and fifty dollars, a veritable fortune. I accepted immediately, and forwarded a money order for half of it to Jinx in care of Annelise. Jinx wrote back to thank me for the money, and he suggested that half was too much, since I was the one who had actually turned his ramblings into a story. He enclosed another twenty-something handwritten pages about the village where he had been staying near Dakar, and he asked if I could provide any necessary editing and try to get it published for him. He imposed a condition: if I sold it for him, he wanted it published under the pen name "Fred Roberts."

I read Jinx's new offering, hoping for the same magic he'd produced before. I was disappointed. He had attempted to emulate what I had done, and the attempt failed. Whereas his previous writing had been natural and unaffected, his most recent effort didn't resonate with the same warmth or honesty; his words were stilted and artificial. It was as though he had swallowed a dictionary and spit it up on paper.

Reluctantly, I composed another letter to Jinx, suggesting he try to replicate his earlier writing style. As soon as I mailed it, I regretted having done so. I feared my criticism would cause my friend to think I'd developed a swelled head.

It was a long time before Jinx wrote back to me – at least seven months – by which time I was already late into the spring semester of my sophomore year. I had published another short story, not as good as my first, but good enough to earn fifteen dollars from a small circulation literary magazine. Jinx's new letter came enclosed with a revision of his previous story about the Senegalese village. I resolved to read it with more sensitivity than I had given his earlier effort and, to my surprise, I found he'd taken my advice to heart and produced two well-written vignettes about the people with whom he lived and worked.

They were related stories, each with a different point of view. The first, "The Water Bearer," concerned a teenage girl's infatuation with a visiting older boy from a neighboring tribe; the second, "Intruder at the Well," gave the boy's perspective of the same situation. His words were vivid without being sentimental, and they stirred a feeling in me similar to what I experienced the previous year when I read his description of crossing the Atlantic.

I cleaned up Jinx's spelling and made a few minor edits. For the next week, I thought about how I could sell his prose. I even consulted Professor Appleton for advice, and he encouraged me to submit them to *The Greater Bostonian*, a national literary journal. To my astonishment, *The Greater Bostonian* picked up both and published them together six months later.

Within a week of the magazine's release, in the fall of my junior year, I received another letter from Jinx telling me that he had left Senegal and was traveling across Africa by rail to Cairo, from where he hoped to catch a ship to Southeast Asia. I replied in care of Annelise and enclosed a copy of *The Greater Bostonian*, along with an American Express money order for his stories.

I wrote to Jinx regularly, but I didn't hear back from him again for almost two years, by which time I had graduated from Avon and had moved to Boston, having secured a job as an assistant copy editor with a small advertising agency. The job didn't pay much, but the hours were tolerable, and it provided me with the resources I needed to write in my spare time.

Jinx's next letter arrived in the usual way, enclosed in a manila envelope with a Nether Sawrey postmark. His cover letter said simply, "Dear Willie, see if you can sell this. Your pal, Jinx Fredet." His familiar sheets of composition paper were there, this time numbering more than thirty pages of text. I was pleased to note that he hadn't committed a single spelling error. He'd been in Burma for more than six months, and he wrote about his experiences from his outsider's point of view.

I hadn't written anything worthwhile since leaving Avon, and I was beginning to realize that I was more suited to a career in advertising than creative writing. I read Jinx's new story with more than a little jealousy, resenting his natural ability as an affront to my expensive college education. I tried editing his work, hoping I could improve it, but it was no use.

At last I typed Jinx's story, just as he wrote it, and sent it to the fiction editor at *The Greater Bostonian*. She telephoned me within the week and offered to publish it. "Rangoon Sunset" earned "Fred Roberts" two hundred dollars. When it appeared a few months later, I sent a copy to Jinx with another money order.

Over the next several years, Jinx wrote me at intervals of six or seven months, always enclosing a new story about his many travels. Each time, I was able to place the stories with consumer magazines or literary journals. And with each success, Jinx grew more prolific, to the point where he became a regular contributor to *The Greater Bostonian*. I lived vicariously through his nomadic adventures in Southeast Asia, the East Indies and the South Pacific. I fantasized that I was traveling the world and writing fiction instead of editing copy for car-dealer and department store ads.

I heard nothing further from Jinx for about a year. I was considering telephoning Annelise to ask his whereabouts, when another manila envelope arrived from Nether Sawrey.

This one was larger than the previous ones Annelise had sent, and inside was the usual letter from Jinx and a ream of paper. He was in Vladivostok, Russia, having spent the past eight months traveling from Moscow aboard the Trans-Siberian Railway, stopping intermittently along the route to soak up the local atmosphere. The result was *Cold Horizon*, the story of an expatriate American's journey of self-discovery from European Russia to the Far East.

Jinx's writing this time was more than good. From first page to last, it was captivating – I stayed up all night reading and stayed home from work the next day. When I finished, I poured myself a cup of coffee and sat down again for a second read-through.

I had long contemplated writing a novel, but I was daunted by the challenge. Now Jinx had done it. He'd written a book-length manuscript worthy of publication. I drafted a synopsis of Jinx's book, fleshing out a chapter-by-chapter outline, and then brought it to *The Greater Bostonian* and asked the fiction editor for a critique.

She was enthusiastic about it, and eager to help. She introduced me to a literary agent who, over the next few months, submitted *Cold Horizon* to publishers. Three months later, Jinx had a contract with Hornblower & Meade, with serial rights going to *The Greater Bostonian*. The publisher wanted to know all about "Fred Roberts," but I was sworn to secrecy. On Jinx's instructions, I handled all the financial matters, arranging for the advance and royalties to be sent to a post office box in Nether Sawrey.

When the author's copies arrived, I forwarded them to Nether Sawrey. Three months later, Jinx sent me an autographed copy, signed, "To my best friend, Willie Goodrich, from the Wandering Bard of Nether Sawrey." I smiled, all trace of jealousy gone.

Cold Horizon was a modest success. It didn't win any awards, but it sold over fifty thousand copies. A few months after *Cold Horizon* was released, I received a telephone call from Annelise telling me that Jinx was dead.

I was grief-stricken. A part of me had always hoped that I would someday join him in his travels, but I never had the courage to do what he had done. I was too conventional ever to consider taking off for parts unknown without any idea of how I would support myself. Jinx was the adventurer. He had lived more in his thirty-three years than most people do in a lifetime, and he had done it on his own terms, despite the skepticism of his teachers and schoolmates.

"How did it happen?" I asked Annelise.

She stifled a sob and said, "He was fishing the Little Sawrey, and he must have forgotten to cinch up his chest-waders. We figure he tripped on a rock and water filled his waders, dragging him under. Another fishermen found him downstream."

"Annelise, I didn't even know he was home. When did he come back to Nether Sawrey?"

"What do you mean, Willie? Come back from where?"

"From Russia, I guess. That was the last place I heard from him."

She was puzzled. "I don't know what you're talking about. You've been writing him here for years."

"Well, of course I have," I said, frustrated that she didn't understand my question. "I always wrote him in care of your address because I never knew where he'd be from one day to the next. You've been forwarding his letters to me. The last one came from Russia."

"Russia? You're crazy," she said. "Jinx has been living in my guest house for the past fifteen years. I don't think he's ever been more than twenty miles from Nether Sawrey his whole life."

I was stunned. "I don't understand. Jinx has been writing me from all over the world, and sending me stories. *Cold Horizon* – what about that?"

Annelise didn't respond immediately; she was as surprised as I was. "Jinx never traveled anywhere. He was a fishing guide right here in town. When he wasn't on the water, he was down at Finch's Tavern or at the public library. Hell, Willie, you were his hero. When you started writing your stories, Jinx started reading everything he could get his hands on, and he took up writing too. You and your stories and your book were all he ever talked about."

"My stories? My book? What do you mean?"

"You know – the 'Fred Roberts' book – *Cold Horizon*. I never read it – too far beyond me – but it was all Jinx ever talked about. He was flattered that you used a variation of his name to write by."

I didn't know what to say at first. When I told her everything, Annelise didn't want to believe me. But she did, at last, reluctantly.

She asked if I would be one of Jinx's pallbearers and deliver a eulogy. I agreed without hesitation. The following morning, I drove the three hours from Boston west on the Mass. Pike and then south on Route 7 to Nether Sawrey. It was the first time I'd been back since I left for Avon College so many years before.

Nether Sawrey was still as hardscrabble as I remembered it. I drove straight to the white clapboard Congregational Church in the center of town, where Annelise and her husband Max and their two teenage boys waited for me. Much to my surprise, the church was filled to overflowing. I recognized some of the faces. There were more than two hundred people turned out to pay tribute to Jinx Fredet, humble fishing guide and would-be world explorer who never left the confines of the town in which he was raised. I had tried to compose a eulogy, but words failed me; I decided that when my turn came, I would speak extemporaneously.

The service was brief. After the prayers were said and the hymns sung, Reverend Hill remembered Jinx in the way that ministers do at funerals – with a mixture of banalities and exhortations to the Almighty to intercede in the salvation of the deceased's immortal soul.

At last, it was my turn. I rose from my position next to Annelise in the front pew, cognizant of the honor she had accorded me by inviting me to sit with the family, and I walked slowly up to the flower-bedecked altar. I gazed out at a sea of wizened Yankee faces and began.

"Jinx Fredet was the most well-traveled man I ever knew…"

❄

Erin McGraw
Image

A HISTORY OF THE MIRACLE

WHEN the pebble flew out from the gravel truck in front of them and cracked the windshield, Iris wasn't even looking; she had leaned over to tighten her daughter's seat belt. She jerked her head up at the sharp pop and looked into a lattice of hard lines. Lisa, of course, started to cry. "Hush," Iris said, fighting unsuccessfully to keep the snap out of her voice. "It's just an accident."

Lisa wailed.

They were on their way to Lisa's third day at school, and the girl had been crying for a week, threading herself around Iris's legs, refusing in the mornings to pull on her own socks. "This happens all the time," the kindergarten teacher had assured Iris, but Iris, drained of patience, knew better—she remembered how Lisa's brothers had whooped and torn into the classroom. Now the girl was thrashing under the seat belt as if it were a harness, screaming "I hate it! I hate it!" Iris pulled over by yanking on the steering wheel, and the car bumped hard against the curb, sending the girl's screams up half an octave.

"You're too old for this," Iris said, trying to still the quiver in her voice. "You're a big girl."

"No!" Lisa squalled, pointing to the explosion of lines. Iris couldn't begin to guess the replacement cost. She sighed, shifted the car into park and smoothed her daughter's hair. "All right," she said. "Let's calm down now."

"No." Lisa subsided, but Iris could see her calculating a victory; the car had stopped. "It's broken," she said, nodding at the windshield.

"It sure is," Iris said. "But isn't it pretty? Look," she said, running her finger along a line that caught the morning sun in a bright channel.

"Pink," Lisa said, pointing her own small finger at another line.

"You wouldn't have seen this if it didn't get broken."

"I hate it," Lisa said.

"Me too. But at least it's pretty." Iris shifted the car back into drive before Lisa could cloud up again, and they made it to school only five minutes late. Lisa dragged morosely into the classroom. "See?" the teacher said, smiling. "They always come around." Iris smiled back, too depleted to think of a snappy answer.

She felt tired all the time lately. She had hoped for wide drifts of time now that all three of the children were in school, but her energy dribbled away into PTA and Cub Scouts. If she hadn't known better, she might have thought she was pregnant again; her own body seemed mysterious and alien and exhausting. She stooped for a drink at the water fountain outside Lisa's classroom door, then went down to the teachers' lounge for a cup of coffee. She might as well stay; she was scheduled for 10 a.m. playground duty.

By the time she made it out to lean against the fence and watch the fourth graders play kickball, Iris's mood was perfectly sour. The preliminary telephone bids for the windshield were each enough to break the bank; Jack would be furious. By the third call she simply hung up and went out to the playground. The children played ferociously; games ended when some bruised child sat sniffling and shrugging her away, and Iris wondered what her presence there was supposed to do. She had never once prevented an accident.

She listened, keeping a distracted eye on the game, while Frances Holmes fretted about next week's parish-wide crab supper. Frances was hoping the event would bring in at least five hundred dollars. Plans for the outdoor chapel were way behind schedule, but Frances didn't know what people expected her to do without any budget.

Iris sighed and stared unhappily at her feet. Sheer guilt would force Jack and her to go, although seafood made her queasy. Why couldn't the committee have set up a steak dinner? She was about to ask, and nastily, when she glanced to her right, toward the boys, to see the red kickball shooting at Tommy Pointer and catching him on the throat; the boy dropped as if he'd been shot.

Iris took off. Tommy had fallen hard, straight back, and on the asphalt beneath his head there was a tiny seepage that Iris looked away from the moment she saw it; she could only stand so much.

Tommy was silent, and his face had already turned a rubbery gray. Iris, wincing as sharp pebbles cut into her knees, took his hand. "Tommy? You're all right, aren't you?" A moment passed, and Iris was aware of the boys jostling behind her to catch a glimpse, though none of them made a sound. Then Tommy opened his eyes and pulled his hand away from hers.

"Sure," he said, scooting onto his feet. He wiped his nose with a gritty hand and ran toward the water fountain while his friends jeered. Iris felt a rush of relief, and for a moment she stayed on the ground, too soft with gratitude to stand. When she glanced at the spot where Tommy's head had lain, there was no moisture at all, and she thought it was amazing what a panicky mind could invent.

"They're indestructible," said Frances when Iris rejoined her at the fence. "Did you hear about Pat Kenny's boy?" Iris nodded. Pat's four-year-old, left for a moment in the car, had slipped off the emergency brake. The car had rolled across an embankment and four lanes of traffic before settling underneath a speed limit sign.

"God keeps an eye out," Iris said, surprising herself, and then let Frances go back to costs and logistics. Iris's head pounded with children's laughter and shrieks; she felt like an overfull cup. Five minutes later, when the recess bell sounded and the children formed wavering lines, she had to look away, weak at the thought of looking after so much sweet, unscarred skin.

The night of the crab dinner, Jack and Iris entered the church auditorium warily. Iris's sourness had lingered and spread to Jack, so that they had spent all weekend sniping at each other. On the drive over, ducking and craning to see through the windshield, Jack said, "We'll get stuck with the Logans. Bill will talk all night about his important work for TRW and his important work on the steering committee and his important work with the Boy Scouts. And then we'll come home and you'll throw up all night."

"We don't have to sit with them. We can't not show up. People expect us." Iris was trying to get the clasp on her necklace to catch, taking deep breaths—her stomach already felt wobbly.

"We certainly wouldn't want to let people down," Jack said, pulling into a space by the rectory and jerking up the parking brake. "My head feels like it's breaking in half."

"What do you expect? You diddle around in the basement until it gets so late you don't even have time to take an aspirin. Ben wanted to talk to you, you know. He wanted to show you his project."

"I thought you wanted the water heater fixed. I thought you'd asked me to look at it."

"For God's sake," Iris snapped. "Here. Let me rub your head for a minute. We can't go in there looking like murder."

"Ah hell, nobody notices anyway," he said, settling his head into her lap. She could feel the tightness quivering around his eyes, how hot he was, and she brushed his temples with the tips of her fingers, unable to keep herself from slumping. Her weariness seemed able to deepen infinitely.

"That's better," he said.

"Relax."

"I mean it. It's better." He held her fingers still against his head for a moment, then straightened up.

"It can't be. I hardly touched you."

"Well, it's gone, Magic Fingers. Let's go in. Maybe we can still get home before the news."

But Iris was exhausted; Jack had to help her to the door, where Frances met them and said, "We almost started without you. Thought maybe you'd decided not to come."

"Who, us?" Iris said faintly. "Bells on."

The auditorium seemed to rattle with laughter and the banging of steam tables. Above the racket, Iris heard the buzz of Kay Wendell's wheelchair and winced—Kay had been diagnosed with MS ten years before, only a month after her husband was killed by a hit-and-run driver. She persisted in attending church functions, Iris was convinced, because she could trap people into listening to her pathetic litany. Iris turned, but Kay was already on her.

"Well, you finally made it. I guess I shouldn't expect people with children to be on time."

Iris felt Jack stiffen beside her, and she put her hand on his arm to keep him from bolting. "Nice to see you, Kay."

"How many wee ones are there?" Kay cackled. "Six?"

"Please. Only three. That's plenty."

Kay looked down and fiddled with the controls on her wheelchair. "When you live alone, everyone else's house seems so full of life."

"I see plenty of life in you yet, girl," Jack said, and took Iris by the wrist. "Look, dear. There's Bill Logan. We'll be seeing you, Kay." He steered Iris to a table already heaped with red and white crabs while Iris ducked her eyes and glanced back at the other woman, who at least wasn't following them; she had caught Betty and Frank Marsh at the coat rack.

Iris survived the meal by industriously separating meat from shell and then eating the hard French rolls—first her own, then Jack's. Jack and Bill Logan carried the conversation, Jack laughing forcefully at all of Bill's jokes. Jack wiped his eyes. Iris wished he wouldn't try so hard. By the end of the meal, her plate and lap were covered with crumbs, and she thought of her house and robe with a yearning that bordered on the erotic.

As Jack was encouraging Bill to tell him more about the Scout trip, a cry rang out directly behind Iris. She turned to see Meg Price choking and flailing at her husband, who shrank away from her. Meg's shoulders jerked and her face turned the color of iron. Iris scrambled up before she had a chance to think and started pounding Meg on the back, while the woman grabbed her and whined desperately. Iris turned Meg around, clutched her under the ribs, and pulled up so hard she felt something in her own back give. She had no idea what she was doing. Meg was still choking, so Iris tried it again, half hanging onto the other woman for support. After the third try Meg barked and spat out a piece of shell an inch across that gleamed as it hit the plate. She fell forward, hanging onto the table, and Iris reached for a chair. Her lower back seemed to have separated into distinct, fiery pieces.

The auditorium clamored. People rushed in on Iris and Meg, exclaiming over what they'd seen, congratulating, marveling. Iris's knees quivered, and the damp shadows of nausea swept across her stomach. "Lucky for Meg you knew how to do the Heimlich," Jo Salton was saying. "I keep meaning to learn."

"Instinct, I guess," Iris said. "I just found myself doing it." She saw Jack studying her from across their table, looking startled and uneasy. "If it wasn't me, somebody else would have helped," she said loudly, looking straight at him.

"That's right," Kay called out, whirring over from two tables away, her mouth bunched up like a paper bag. "Anybody would have done as much."

"Not that I wasn't glad to help," Iris said.

"Purely human nature," Kay said. "Reflex."

"You know, it's harder than you think. Next time . . .," Iris began.

"Somebody else will get to do the saving," Kay said, grinning at the speechless Iris until Jack picked up his coat and said that they'd better get back, before someone needed saving at home. He had to let Iris lean on him all the way out to the car; her ankles kept buckling as if she'd been drinking.

Jack stalled a week before he asked, diffidently, how Iris had known what to do for Meg, and Iris looked out the window and told him the truth: "I don't know. I found myself grabbing her." He didn't ask any more, but she felt him tracking her as she made her way around the house.

She wished he would stop it. He snuck looks from around the newspaper, watched her dry dishes as if she might reach into her pocket at any moment and produce a hissing fuse. "Here," she said, setting a cup of coffee in front of him. "Please just drink this."

"I don't know if I want it that bad."

"What does that mean?"

"You're acting like Joan of Arc at the stake because you fixed a cup of coffee. I didn't even ask for it. What is going on with you?"

"I'm trying to be a good wife. I'm trying to do my job around here."

"Well, quit trying. It didn't used to take you all this effort."

That night, while she was brushing her hair, Jack came and laid his hands on her shoulders with a gesture so proprietary she jerked away despite her best intentions. "I'm tired," she said, which was the level truth.

In the morning she apologized, but Jack grunted; mornings were not his best time. And still she felt nervy, full of prickles; she swore at the agave by the door when she stepped too close and snagged her stockings. Later, she drove to the guild meeting snags and all, barely avoiding a dog who got lost in the fractured windshield, and when she was nominated to head the outreach committee, she said with embarrassing passion, "Please! Anybody else." At the break Mary Lou Betts asked compassionately whether everything was all right at home, and Iris smiled, shrugged, and nodded, afraid of what might fly out of her mouth.

At home the kids' noise filled the house, and Iris found she could get by on nods and shrugs, which at least kept her from picking more fights with Jack. He didn't understand; she was scrabbling to keep solid ground under her feet. When Ben came down with the flu, she made Jack take the boy's temperature and dole out antibiotics. "I can't afford to be exposed," she murmured as an excuse. "We go to the clinic next week."

In fact, she was in charge of the guild's annual visit to the free clinic downtown, the one committee duty she didn't mind. Iris enjoyed watching the young doctors and nurses who volunteered there. The clinic patients were mostly immigrants—entire enormous families—and Iris listened happily while the doctors prescribed blood-pressure medication and iron supplements for the grandmothers, dark green vegetables for the children. Here was real help; she was glad to be a part of it.

For weeks the women in the guild had been collecting medical supplies from their own family doctors—drug samples, tongue depressors, disposable gloves and basins. The bags of supplies always seemed impressive to Iris until she got to the clinic, where the stack of tongue depressors rattled into an empty drawer. A nurse smiled at Iris. "There's never enough," she said.

As always, the women stayed to serve lunch to the doctors and nurses. Iris took on sandwich duty in the clinic's tiny kitchen, where she methodically sliced the ham they had brought and slapped it onto slices of bread. She was good at this; the line of sandwiches was scarcely different from mornings at home.

A woman, one of the patients, slipped into the kitchen with Iris. She was thin, and had a lump the size of a tangerine under her jaw. She wasn't supposed to be in the kitchen. The guild couldn't bring enough food for patients, so they tried to be discreet about lunch. Iris wondered whether she should say something, or simply escort the woman back out to the waiting area. She stared at the woman's lump; the skin over it was stretched so taut it was lustrous. "Would you like a sandwich?" Iris asked.

"Yes."

Iris handed it to her, watching while she took her first bite. The lump didn't prevent her from swallowing, and so Iris smiled and went back to the ham. "Thank you," the woman said, and then the door clicked softly after her. Thank you, Iris thought, pleased with herself. She made three more sandwiches before she heard the door open again and looked around to see the woman standing with a crowd of children—seven? ten? The woman looked at her calmly.

Iris felt the small of her back sag. She gestured at her meager provisions—two loaves of white bread, a small ham and the mustard Renee Cox had remembered to bring. "There isn't enough." She looked at the woman with the lump. "I'm sorry."

The woman said nothing, and played with the hair of the boy standing before her, who was looking at Iris with eyes so soulful they seemed impertinent. "Oh, for heaven's sake," Iris said, and began to hand sandwiches around. She would go out to a grocery store. Lunch would just have to be late. The children chewed their dry sandwiches, and she returned to the counter, hacking at the ham. She felt a tug on her skirt. A little boy pointed to the oranges, and she handed him one. "Thank you," he said.

Then Iris heard the door open again, and Renee saying, "What are you doing?"

"Things got out of control."

"There are medical professionals out there, volunteering their time for these people."

"Give them these." Iris filled her hands with sandwiches and a few oranges.

"Now everybody wants to eat. Iris, we never feed the patients."

"They never asked before," she said, reaching into the bag for more bread.

Before long, the guild members began coming into the kitchen in shifts to collect sandwiches and oranges. In a minute, Iris told herself, I'll have to go out and get some more. But her hands, greasy with fat, kept slicing and stacking, and she stood at the narrow counter and made sandwiches even after Renee told her that she had made enough, that everyone had eaten. There was still the butt end of the ham, half a bag of oranges. Renee had to take her by the elbow and force her to sit down, when finally Iris felt blind with fatigue. Renee pressed a sandwich into her hand, but Iris couldn't lift it to her mouth.

"We didn't have that much food," Renee was saying. "You know we didn't."

"Hush," Iris said.

Monsignor Laoghrie was calling when Iris walked in her front door, and after him neighbors, half-strangers. People had heard reports that Iris had been bathed in light, had talked in languages no one had ever heard. Suzanne Muller asked if it was true that the oranges tasted like sacramental wine. "Mine didn't," Iris said, talking with her head propped against the wall.

It was after four, and none of the children was home. Iris shivered. She felt naked in the house without their comforting uproar. She tried to remember—was this the afternoon of

Jim's rehearsal, Lisa's soccer practice? She was hanging up the phone for the seventh time when she finally heard a shuffling at the door. "Hey," Iris called. "There are cookies in here."

She heard them file back to their rooms. Fear rose in Iris like a quick flood; she set the phone off the hook and went to the boys' room. Jim, face down on the bed, didn't move, and Ben sat with his back to her, his jaw hard and quivering. Sometimes he looked so much like Jack that Iris caught her breath. "Don't you want anything to eat?"

"No," Ben said.

"What's up? How come you were late home?"

He shrugged. "Leave me alone."

She went to Lisa's room, her mouth dry. Like Jim, Lisa was stretched out on the bed, but Iris heard her sniff and she crouched by the bed, laying her head beside her daughter's on the pillow. "What is it, honey? What happened?"

Lisa edged away from her, and at first Iris thought she wouldn't talk at all. "Sister made us stay. The whole school. She made us all stay after school and said you'd performed a miracle." Her shoulders were rigid. "She said you were holy."

"Oh, honey," Iris said. "Honey. I'm just your mom." She put her hand on Lisa's steely shoulder. "Everything is just the same."

"It is not. Everything's wrecked."

Iris looked at her daughter, who lay with her head twisted away from her. Wildly, she wanted to laugh. "If I'm holy, maybe I'll be a better cook. What do you want for dinner? Do you want spaghetti? I'll make you anything you want."

"Leave me alone."

"You'll see," Iris said. "It will go away in a few days, and you'll see that nothing has changed." She reached out to stroke her hair, but then let her hand drop in the air between them.

Jack came in an hour later, and they looked at each other warily across the width of the living room. "Well," he said. "I hear I'm married to Our Lady of Sandwiches."

"Is that supposed to be a joke?"

"You are some kind of famous," he said, his tone so non-committal that Iris felt like slapping him. "I've been getting phone calls telling me the history of the miracle all afternoon."

"What do they say?"

"It's the loaves and the fishes, right here in River City."

"The food went further than we thought. Nobody thought we had enough, but we did. That's all." She stood blinking at him, her hands clenching and unclenching.

"A committee will be over later to take the measurements for your shrine."

"Listen to me, dammit. I sliced the ham thin, and it went around. Who are you going to believe here?"

"A hundred people say it was a miracle. You say it wasn't. How do I know who to believe? Hell, Iris. How do you know?" He shrugged.

"You never believed in miracles before."

"You never performed any before."

Iris shook her head; frustrated tears were crowding her throat and eyes. "Wait till you hear what Sister did," she whispered, fighting for control.

"I heard."

"The kids won't speak to me."

"They'll get over it. They're scared."

"So am I. Aren't you?"

"Terrified," Jack said flatly.

That night, after Iris had burned the potatoes and broken two dinner plates while loading the dishwasher, the doorbell rang. It was Sandra, the little girl who lived next door. Her parents didn't belong to the parish, so Iris only saw the girl when she happened to be outside playing, a tiny, weedy thing, smaller than Lisa. "It's late, honey," Iris said. "Do your parents know that you're out so late?"

Sandra nodded. "I hurt my elbow."

"Where?"

"Right here," the girl said, jutting her knobby elbow at Iris, who couldn't see any scratch or bruise. "It hurts," Sandra said. "I hurt it."

"Do you want me to kiss it for you?"

Sandra nodded again, and Iris bent swiftly. When she straightened again, the girl's expression was rapturous. "I knew it would feel better if you kissed it. I'll bet it will never hurt again."

"Kisses don't last that long," Iris said, but Sandra was already backing away, her hand cradling her healed elbow, her face radiant. "Shit," Iris muttered.

"Suffer the little children," said Jack, coming in from the living room.

"Very funny."

"Come on, honey. Kids love saints." He skimmed his fingers lightly up her sides, and she jerked away. "Stop twiddling at me. I am not a saint. I don't do miracle cures."

"Not on the home front, that's for sure."

"Then quit looking at me like you're expecting something."

"Lately I don't expect one thing from you. Some miracles are just too much to hope for."

Iris nearly collided with Ben as she stormed to the bedroom. He was still sniffling, and she rested her hands on his head as they passed. She listened after he went into the bathroom, but he wasn't crying any more. God damn it, she thought.

The next morning the phone was still off the hook and notes were stuck under the welcome mat; Iris had refused to answer the door again after Sandra's visit. Jack left early for work and the kids shuffled and muttered, refusing to look at their mother. When Ruth Dowers, who was driving carpool that week, swung into the driveway, Jim and Ben and Lisa raced out the door like escapees.

Iris trudged into the kitchen. Sugar was scattered across the table and floor, milk was already hardening at the bottom of glasses. The frying pan Jack had used was jammed into the sink, dried egg crusted around its sides. Iris stiffened her arms in front of her. "Shazam," she said. Nothing moved.

There were beds to be made, laundry. But she walked through her house with her hands stuffed deep in the pockets of her robe. She wanted to sit down, but there wasn't one chair in the whole damn house that didn't have ripped upholstery or jabbing springs. She and Jack had said for so long they would get around to new chairs. How many nights had she watched him squirming in the recliner by the door, trying to find a smooth space? She felt her heart open to him as if it took a physical fall, even though she had meant to stay angry.

She wandered into their bedroom, vaguely planning to make the bed, but she stopped at the doorway, looking at the one crucifix in the house. It hung next to the window. Iris hated religious art, and had agreed to put up the crucifix only because it had been a wedding present—she couldn't remember now from whom. Someone who didn't know her very well. She took it off the wall and turned it around in her hand, surprised at its lightness. Cheap construction. Sitting on the bed to relieve her back, supposing she ought to pray, she let her thoughts race away from her. She remembered how, when Jim had been a toddler, he'd sat for hours turning his toy car in tight circles over and over the same patch of floor. It had worried Iris that he'd been so content with the car tracing its own tracks. What had happened to that car? She couldn't remember.

She looked at the crucifix in her hand. The figure of Jesus didn't seem to be in pain. If anything, he looked a little buoyant. She closed her eyes, trying to stop these thoughts, which were probably blasphemous and would bring on swift retribution. She remembered a holy card she had gotten in second grade, showing the Good Shepherd surrounded by dozens of children. His face had been beardless and full of light. Her friend Susan's showed him walking on water, which Iris would have preferred.

"I guess this is your idea of a joke," she said to the crucifix. Two months before she had been closing in on happiness like safe harbor. But now she was right back out in the deep water, and the lights on land were winking out. She got up, hung the crucifix back on the wall and turned away, fighting the habit to touch her lips and murmur "Ad majorem dei gloriam." Old habits, she thought as she left the bedroom.

The local RiteBuy served as the neighborhood town square, and Iris could usually count on running into three neighbors in the cereal section alone. But remarkably, as she hurried through the aisles, she didn't see any familiar faces. Sister must have called the whole town in, she thought. She picked up treats for the kids—cookies that were out of the budget, ice cream. She fingered the oranges, then let them drop back in the bin. She moved past the fish section briskly, but she couldn't help glancing at the glazed eyes of trout, horrible, and beside them neat sets of shad roe.

Jack adored it. On their first anniversary he'd taken her to a restaurant that featured seafood as well as beef; Iris was sure she could stand to look at roe, as long as she wasn't expected to eat it. But when the waiter brought their meals the sight of it, reddish and coiled like intestines, was too much for her, and she'd spent the rest of the night retching, first in the restaurant and then back at home.

Now she stepped back when the butcher told her how much the sets cost. She gazed at them, rich and heart colored. Peerless as a peace offering. After a moment she told the butcher she'd take a single set. She would present it to Jack that night for dinner, and tell him it was a miracle.

In high spirits Iris sped through the store, escaping unnoticed until she made it to the parking lot, where she was unloading groceries—gently, trying to spare her back. The sound of a wheelchair motor burred in her ear; "If it isn't the talk of the town," Kay Wendell said.

Iris let the groceries in her hands drop. "Kay. What a surprise."

"Do you know what people are saying?"

"I feel like I have to go out with a bag over my head." She smiled, but Kay refused to be drawn in.

"The parish is half lunatic about this. Six people have told me that you're performing miracles."

"Well, Kay, you know—people." Kay was squinting, her face twisted and wild, and Iris edged back.

"What really happened?"

"There was more food than we thought. We wound up being able to feed the patients. We were all glad." Iris squeezed her mouth into a smile.

"People are acting like it's the second coming."

"That's not my doing. But it's surprising that one little ham could go so far."

"So you're calling this divine intervention." Kay snickered.

"I'm not calling it anything." Iris stretched out her hand to brush back hair from Kay's eyes, but the other woman turned and began chugging away.

"Don't try to touch me." Kay called over her shoulder. "Do you think I'm waiting for a miracle? I know what to expect from the world."

It occurred to Iris that this was Kay's whole problem, and she was irritated enough to catch up and tell her so. As Iris hurried behind the chair, Kay snapped at her. "Get away from me. I'm not looking for your grubby cures. Get away!" She flapped her hands at Iris, who stopped the chair, caught Kay's frail wrists in one hand, the top of her skull with the other, and bore down.

"I've never known anyone who deserved curing more," Iris said, twisting Kay's wrists a little.

Kay stopped struggling, and in its sudden collapse her body seemed even tinier. "Go on, then," she said. "Make me dance."

"It's not so easy . . ." Iris began.

"I know, walk a mile in your shoes. Well, Mrs. Miracle Worker, I wouldn't mind trading in my shoes for yours."

"Fine," Iris said, and picked Kay up out of her chair before she had any idea what to do with her. The woman was heavier than she looked, and Iris staggered, shoving Kay onto the hood of a sedan before her own legs folded and she dropped into Kay's chair.

"Am I supposed to walk to you? You must have gotten some of the mumbo wrong." Kay pointed to her flaccid legs. "They still don't work."

"Fine," said Iris again, examining the switches on the arm of the chair. "You stay put. I'm just going to put on your shoes here."

"You idiot," Kay snarled. "It's not a Disneyland ride."

But it might as well have been; Iris found the lever to lift the brake, then turned and whirred up the slight incline of the parking lot, away from Kay.

"You'll burn the motor out!" Kay yelled. "Are you planning to take care of me when it's broken?" Iris leaned forward in the chair to urge it along. She felt pleasantly mischievous. When she came to a speed bump she had to take two runs before the chair cleared it, making a harsh, mechanical cough. It stopped on the other side. Kay was squalling from the sedan, attracting attention. To get away, Iris nudged the lever; the engine coughed again but the chair only slid back an inch, settling at the speed bump.

"See?" Kay was shrieking. "See?"

Iris jabbed at the switches, but the little motor whined, the sound all wrong. "Please," Iris muttered, knowing already she was done for. "Damn."

Exhaling unevenly, she tried to stand, to wheel the chair back to Kay and face the music. It was then that her back, dazzling with pain, seized Iris so that she gasped, unable to move. She looked up to see Kay crying and waving her arms. Iris was crying herself; hot blades seemed to be carving channels on either side of her spine. She knew she needed to reach Kay, who would get help for her. But she couldn't move, and had to watch Kay screaming and pointing at her before people finally came out from the store to save them.

❄

Alice Fulton
Missouri Review: Editor's Prize in Fiction

HAPPY DUST

IN the twentieth century I believe there are no saints left, but our farm on Boght Road had not yet entered the twentieth century. At that time, around 1908 it would be, I had a secret I could tell to no one, least of all a saint or an arsenic eater. In my experience, it is better to keep away from saints unless you have business with them. The same backbone that makes them holy virtuosos makes them eager to mind other people's p's and q's. But some of the saints I knew were family, and this made them hard to fend off. Don't think I am speaking of my sister-in-law, Kitty. She was not a saint but a lost soul.

It was through Kitty that I first got wind of the spiritual genius down the road. My sister-in-law had mixed up a batch of French chalk and gumwater colored with Prussian blue and was using this to fashion veins on her face. I was washing the bedroom windows. As she painted, Kitty let it slip that she'd brought some extra milk from our dairy over to St. Kieran's Home. I knew the history of this "extra milk." And I knew only a lost soul would give it to an orphanage. That part of her saga rang true.

While searching for a foundling to take the milk, Kitty said she'd wandered into St. Kieran's garden. It was full of crispy white flowers, and in the midst of these blooms, a nun was standing with her arms outstretched "like an oaken figure on a cross," Kitty said. The nun had her back to Kitty, who was about to vamoose when the sister fell to her knees, kissed the earth, and commenced to speaking Latin.

I put no stock in this at first because Kitty had very re-fined nerves. I'd sized her up the minute I saw her alighting from our dairy wagon in full feather and needle-toed kid shoes. My brother-in-law, Mike Monahan, was holding a parasol dripping fringe like a horse's fly sheet over her head with one hand and steering her around cowflops with the other. My husband Joe tagged behind, lugging her trunks and looking dumbstruck. Oh Mary! I thought, what kind of riga-marole is this? Why would a fine tall man with Mike's black curls and his eyes like bachelor buttons hitch up with such a helplessness?

"Enchanted," Kitty said in that voice you'd need an ear trumpet to capture. She extended her hand in glove to me in my leaky shoes and dress so mended it fell apart in the wash. I shook it thinking this girl's a lost soul.

When we moved to the farm, I was a young woman of twenty, hardy though never comely, with lanky dark hair grabbed back in a bun. They called me Mamie Come Running because if anyone needed help, I was the one that would go and do. Now, at twenty-six, I was chapped and thoroughly sweated from the care of four children and the day-in day-out labor of the place. The washing and mangling, blacking and beating, scrubbing and baking, the making of soap and babies had taken all the calorie out of me. I was thin as a cat's whisker. I had a hacking cough and pallor. My face had taken on shadows. Though I couldn't admit it, I was in a bad state of wilt.

Kitty's delicate ways had me all the more overtasked. She was supposed to do the sewing, but left to herself she'd make only belle-of-the-ball garments and nothing for everyday. And everyday was all there was on the farm. Our little brick house was neat as the Dewey decimal system but meagre and common as could be. We had windows but no curtains, rooms but no closets, walls but no wallpaper. It was mostly brown and coarse, and Kitty shed tears when she saw it. She and Mike lived on the second floor. We took our meals together, and I soon discovered she could make a cup of tea at most. She'd drink it in little sips while Joe and Mike poured their coffee into their saucers and slurped. I don't know what she thought of them. She had that way of soft-soaping a man till he felt he was her all-in-all no matter what was in her head.

Her with her milk baths, saying we were a dairy and could afford the waste. We could not. Two quarts, sufficient for a sponge-down, was what we settled on. Then she wanted to sell the used milk to the poorhouse at a reduction. It doesn't take a wizard to figure what she gave the orphans. She and Mike had a childless marriage. If I was called to help Doc Muswell with a delivery, I'd return to a Bedlam of bawling infants, for Kitty was no good with them.

Now that I was expecting again, I wished we could pack up our home and roll it down Boght Road to Watervliet on a barrow. I would have liked to pull a shade on the past and have this baby in town. I had a superstition that a child's birth predicted the course its life would take. And I was deter-

mined that my fifth would be welcomed in perfect circumstances, without any forceps or cows in the house.

It was this secret intention that led me to take things up
with Katherine Tekakwitha, the Lily of the Mohawks. Kitty
begged to join my pilgrimage, and in early September we
boarded a steamer for Albany, followed by a train bound for
The Shrine of Our Lady of Martyrs in Auriesville. I had baby
Edwardia in my arms, and the three runabout children,
Helen, Dora, and my Joseph, clinging to my skirts.

The train left us off, dusty as coalmen, at the foot of the
Hill of Torture. This long path wound grandly up through
massive gates and meadows toward the sky. I suspected
many pilgrims from the city never knew there could be such
earth on earth. I shaded my eyes and gave the crowd a once-
over but saw no sign of Sister Dorothea or Sister Adelaide.
These relative nuns from New Jersey were meeting us and returning to the farm for their annual home visit.

Kitty put down our market basket and fanned herself
with a holy card. I tried to keep baby Edwardia from grabbing
it. "What are you going to pray for, Mamie?" she asked.

"That the nuns won't stay more than three nights," I told
her. They had requested courtesy at St. Kieran's Home since
their Rule required them to sleep in a convent. But yours truly
would have to feed and entertain them. How to do that was
the puzzle. I only knew they liked looking at the Sears catalogue to see how many things there were in the world they
didn't want.

"You'll never guess what I'm going to pray for." Kitty
gnawed delicately at the holy card. "But do try."

"A magic lantern and a switch of store-bought hair." That
was what she'd told me last night. Feeling a cough coming on,

I set baby Edwardia down and fished a clean handkerchief from my shirtwaist.

"No. Something ever so much more important."

The cough changed its mind and I was grateful. "You wouldn't be wanting a little fountain in your room that shoots perfume before falling back into a marble basin, or white satin slippers, exquisitely fitted, that do not button or lace but are cunningly sewn on in the morning and ripped off at night? You wouldn't be praying that your name become Fannie Well-beloved, Annabel Lee, Clara Lazarus, or Evelyn Friend?" Kitty's pipedreams were famous to me. "Joseph, get over here while I clean your ears." He was a little redheaded dickens of five years. I went after him with my handkerchief. The girls were nicely turned out in their white pinafores and dotted swiss, I thought.

"Dare I speak my heart aloud?" Kitty asked. "I'm praying to be accepted as a non-tuition scholar at The Troy School of Arts and Crafts." She gave me a cow-eyed confiding look.

"That saloon run by teachers excommunicated from The Emma Willard School?"

"Darling Mamie."

It was a sweltering day, and the party next to us had a coverlet fixed to four broomsticks raised above their hats as a canopy. "I wish I'd brought my sundown," Kitty said. Reaching into her purse, she found a little pocket mirror, a jar of finely powdered starch and orris root, and began dusting herself. "This weather is a persecution, is it not? I'm dying, I'm dying, I'm dead."

"You'll be a beautiful corpse," I told her. And she perked up. If she wasn't bleaching her freckles with borax in rosewater, she was applying solutions of corrosive sublimate, prussic acid, and caustic potash to her complexion. There was a tin of Poudre Rajeunissante containing ratsbane in her room, for Kitty had been an arsenic-eater since the age of 17. She stayed pretty nimble despite this habit. But she'd experience the fatal symptoms and be carried off should she stop. Once begun, an arsenic-eater is tied to that unnatural diet all her days. I never let the children visit her upstairs for fear they'd get into her poisons and destroy their lives.

I followed her eyes to six-year-old Dora. She was standing with her arms spread like wings and her head wrenched back toward the sky.

"That's cross prayers," Helen told us. "Sister Honoraria showed her." Helen was my eldest, an independent girl of eight years.

"The nun in the garden, I'll warrant," Kitty whispered. "That child has the most charming buck teeth."

The Hill of Torture was lined with hucksters pitching miraculous medals and phony relics, and I just then spotted our Brides of Christ standing in full poverty by a vendor's cart. Nuns had such dignity and difference, I always thought they should be introduced by a loud gust of trumpets. By the same token, ours were something of a Mutt and Jeff. Sister Dorothea was stately as a steeple, while Adelaide was jolly and stocky. Each had her hand concealed up its opposite bat-wing sleeve, and no peddlars were rushing them. Those men knew better than to pester a nun. I ran over to grab the little black satchels leaning against their hems.

"Good day, my dears. God be with you," Sister Dorothea said. The woman had a voice in her like a velvet counterpane. Adelaide was making an ado over the kiddies.

We saw the procession forming then for the march up the Hill of Torture to the park where Katherine Tekakwitha had been born and saints had been martyred in days of old. We fell in with the other parishioners on the upwards trudge, saying the rosary and singing Ave's aloud. Before long, we were wiping the dust off our eyes with holy water passed hand to hand.

Everyone had been fasting since midnight, and I'd all but lost interest in human sacrifice by the time we got to the top. The nuns were still full of tallyho, of course. The procession followed a dirt path through the Seven Dolors and the Stations of the Cross to the Martyr's Chapel. This was a rough-hewn log pavilion, open on all sides so overflowing pilgrims could hear Mass from the lawn—though being with two Mercy Sisters guaranteed us seats inside. Baby Edwardia was asleep, my Joseph was hoping for a sermon full of tomahawks, and the girls were busy with the pictures in my missal. In 1908, a wasting disease was a blot on the family name. Seeing as I could not confess my health to anyone alive, I roosted on the kneeler, eager to air my secret shame and heart's desire before God's saints.

I knew Katherine Tekakwitha, The Lily of the Mohawks, had recovered from small pox. She had been an orphan. And she had been Godly without being martyred. I respected her for that. My prayer went, "If I was not worn out by the white plague, I would not worry about adding again to our household. But as I am poorly, I am sincerely sorry for it. I cannot go to a resort where the air is Adirondack and sleep on a screened-in porch. But help me be fit enough to give the child its life. Give me gumption. My spirit is gaunt." I told Katherine that if I died, my children would be half-orphans, half-way to St. Kieran's Home. As an orphan herself, she'd know that when a mother goes to bed and dies, her little children stand crying because no one is minding them. The father might try, but he is too discouraged and new to the work to be useful.

Since a feeble mother will have a weak infant, I prayed mine would not be a blue baby or an idiot. *Let it be born modern, a twentieth-century child, with no muck or mire, no caul or purple mother's marks upon it, I prayed. Lily of the Mohawks, I said, let this baby have a decent, not a blind-alley life. I would not mind this baby being a saint, but I would not like it to be a martyr or a lost soul.* A saint wasn't much of a livelihood, but it was better than farming. Farm life was what I did not want for the baby most of all. Last, I prayed it would be an ordinary child and have happy luck all its days.

I got so caught up I hardly noticed the incense and adoration. The next thing I knew, we'd genuflected and were out on the grass again. I spread the cloth and unpacked the bill of fare. I always cooked day and night before the Sisters visited, and then they'd peck away with their puny appetites, selecting a tidbit here, a morsel there. I'd made a round of beef, fricassed chicken, potato salad, picallili, chili sauce, and rhubarb pie, all the same. I knew from last time they would not touch my homemade root beer because of the word "beer."

"Mother, is Sister Dorothea a saint?" Dora asked. She and Helen were braiding each other's brown straight hair. The sky had turned dreary, and the trees looked boisterous.

"A saint has to be dead, I guess." I handed Sister Adelaide a corned beef sandwich and began helping everyone to salad. I didn't know what to say.

"Sister Honoraria is a saint," Dora said. "She was struck twice by lightning, and now if someone sticks pins in her, it doesn't matter, for she don't feel it."

I thought this must be a great gift to a Sister. I knew from washing our relatives' habits that nuns were mostly held together with pins.

"Some religious women fancy they are specially singled out for miracles," Sister Dorothea said, brushing crumbs off her worsted skirt. I'd seen lightning split a crystal dish without a shatter. I'd seen it roll itself up in a ball before exploding. And I believed it could strike twice if it had a mind to. There were but two things I feared: lightning and a dark cellar.

"Sister Honoraria is Dora's teacher," I explained. St. Kieran's was the nearest school. The children went there to be educated with the orphans.

"The Presentation nuns are all very well," Sister Dorothea said. Veils were flapping, and I had to hold on to my hat.

"Their order is enclosed, and a few decades older in the faith than ours," Sister Adelaide allowed.

I told Helen and Dora, who were dandy helpers, to get a move on and find their little brother. He'd gone to watch some boys carve a cross in a tree, and now with a storm brewing, I'd lost sight of him in his everyday blue denim brownie suit.

"Mamie, I couldn't broach this with the children here," Sister Dorothea said, as soon as the girls were gone. "But it is my duty to warn you." She fingered her beads. Kitty leaned forward, egging her on. "It's passing strange how some vowed women believe they're doing God a great favor instead of thinking the world well lost."

"Obedience comes more readily to some than others," Adelaide explained.

"There have been allegations concerning Sister Honoraria," continued Dorothea.

"Concerning her past," said Adelaide.

"Don't be grabbing Sister's spectacles," I told baby Edwardia.

"It is said that Sister Honoraria was called back from a foreign mission, and that she engages in excessive penitential practices." Here Dorothea touched the big black crucifix shoved under her belt. "What's more, this sister's conduct with a priest was deemed—" she paused and puckered her lips. "Familiar. He was observed to impiously venture to touch her hand."

"It is said," Adelaide put in.

"You mean there was a scandal, Maggie?" The shock made me forget and call Sister Dorothea by her Christian name.

Kitty was in her glory. I could feel her nerves shaking next to me. "The nun in the garden," she said.

The girls came skipping over then, dragging my Joseph behind them, and we had to shush. There was no more talk of Sister Honoraria, though Kitty kept trying to sneak up on the subject. The storm held off, and we spent the rest of the afternoon strolling the grounds, greeting old cronies, and telling each other what a grand time we were having in this heaven on earth before the sun got low and the train left for home. The nuns came and went without any uproar, and it must have been a week after their visit that Helen raced home in a great state of emergency. I was putting sheets out to dry on the lines and hedges when she skidded into the yard, out of breath, yelling, "Mother Come Running! Sister Has Fallen!"

"Sister is down?" I said, stopping my work to listen. When I'd heard enough, I left the little ones with Kitty and took off down Boght Road at a good clip.

Once we got to St. Kieran's, Helen led me through the high brick gates into a big garden patch out back. There was Sister lying down in the dirt. A blunt knife and a jar of water were on the ground nearby. She looked dazed but awake.

"Was I struck by lightning?" she said, looking up at me with long gray eyes. I knew I had to get her out of that sun posthaste, but she proved hard to move as a trolley off its track. As I tried to raise her, I noticed an open can of gummy brown perfumey stuff fastened to her belt. When I saw her bare feet, I thought this Sister is a rugged little number—light yet durable, scanty yet galvanized. Once I got her up, Helen wedged herself under one arm, I got under the other, and we limped toward the convent. As we stepped into the cool gloom of the place, I was struck by its smell of starched linen and dusty paraffin. Though it was a hotter-than-blazes Indian summer day, some frosty twilight poured from the high windows. Sister Honoraria (for she was our fallen nun) said the others were at prayers and must not be disturbed on her account.

"Let me take up my cross," she said, "or I will never have my crown." She directed us through waxed amber corridors, up an oak stairway to the nuns' dormitory. The sisters' beds were separated by sheets hung from poles to make cells the size of small box stalls, maybe six feet square. We entered Sister's alcove through a curtain and laid her down on her iron cot. The place was dark as an icehouse. It took a while to make out the white wooden box, straight plain chair, washstand, soap dish, and tin cup that were the furnishings. I told Helen to go rescue the kids from Kitty and ask Papa to fetch Doc Muswell. I then set about pulling the heavy togs off Sister. She spoke of this and that she had to do, but I said the doctor was coming, and she was too listless to argue. When I unfastened the strings of her headpiece, I was surprised to find that the starched bonnet had prickers on its inside. I saw they'd left marks on the skin and stubby scalp of her. Under her habit was a muslin gown big as a croup tent, and as I wrassled with her outer outfit, this undergarment pulled in such a way that I glimpsed a scar, livid and cross-shaped, on her ribs.

"You got a bad cut there, Sister," I said, just to keep the conversation going.

"Here cut and here burn, but spare me in eternity," she said.

"How'd you get a cut like that?" I had lockjaw on my mind.

"No doubt you've heard tales," she said. "People, even good people, are given to falsehood and exaggeration. And yet I would do wrong to say I did no wrong." She asked about the can that had been fastened at her waist, and I said I'd put it out of the way, under the cot. "If I had walked too heavily, or used my eyes with liberty, or kissed an infant for its beauty … for these sins, I might be forgiven," she continued.

"Nobody's perfect," I said.

"Perfection is a nun's purpose," she replied. "She must wash the taste of the world from her mouth with carbolic and sleep on thorns lest she sleep too well. If the chapel is cosy, let her kneel in snow. If for an instant she forgets Christ's suffering, let her take switches to her shoulders, brand herself with faggots, wear an iron chain about her waist." I was beginning to think this Sister was a deep customer.

"The worst sin is shiftlessness," I said. "It's better to shuck your blues and shake a leg."

"Perhaps tales have reached you. Vile accusations have been made," she said, "concerning the orphans. That I had them kneel like dogs and used their backs as writing desks, when in fact they are raised most tenderly."

"That I didn't know," I said.

"I was torn by a confliction of duty—" and she would have gone on but we heard footsteps. There came a light scratching of fingernails on the curtains, and Doc Muswell entered, along with the Mother Superior or some other bigwig, by the look of her. In his single-breasted Prince Albert suit, I'd call Doc Muswell pretty nobby-looking for a country sawbones. Before I married, I'd worked as his housekeeper and assistant, so we were old pals. I knew his wife to be a malingerer, and he knew I had a wasting disease. He had trained me as his nurse, and many times I'd saved him the weary night work of delivering infants. As he saw it, childbirth was long hours for short wages.

"Does Sister suffer from any known disease?" he asked the Superior nun.

"Only the disease of scrupulosity," she answered back. She told him to report to her before he left and excused herself. Once he'd overlooked the situation carefully, Doc asked Sister if she knew the day and place she was.

She said, "I thought I was on the Ganges plain between Patna and Benares, but now I see I'm in Watervliet."

"That's right, Sister," I said, to encourage her. I didn't know where the Ganges plain was located. Somewhere near the road to Damascus most likely.

Doc Muswell took out his stethoscope, and I thought he'd see her scar, but he turned his head to one side and listened without looking, as doctors did in the presence of modesty back then. "You have heatstroke, Sister," he told her. "Forgive me for saying so, but you are chronically overdressed for garden work."

"Your rebuke is well-taken, Doctor. The great discovery is in the heavens above us, not the garden below." She liked to browbeat herself. I'd seen that instantly.

"Well, Doc," I said in her defense, "Sister's skirt, sleeves, and veil were pinned up, under, and back when she had this spell."

"In accordance with Protocol Number 17," said she. The words no sooner left her lips than her breathing told us she was asleep. Doc Muswell asked me to stay awhile and see she drank all of the potion he'd leave. He inquired about my own health, and I told him I was expecting.

"The married woman's disease," he said. When I confessed to coughing blood, he shook his head. "Mamie, it's as I've said. You'll have to get by on one lung the rest of your life." Then he took a packet from his bag and pressed it into my hand. "As a sedative for coughs, this is five times stronger than morphine," he said.

By the lion and globe on the label, I recognized it as Bayer Heroin Powder.

"Use it sparingly, and you won't become habituated. You will have call for it, I think." I was grateful as this medicine was very dear, and the more costly the cure, the more effective. "With your constitution, you'd do well to avoid stimulating food and drink, heat and cold, singing, hallooing, and declamation."

So saying, he donned his hat and took his leave. Sister opened her eyes then, and I fed her the potion he'd left. She was looking more chipper. "I could not but overhear your conversation," she said. "You are in a delicate condition. I have a remedy that will damp the fires of bodily mechanism and shallow the breath, resting your enflamed lung and encouraging the cavities to close."

Nothing could be more powerful than the nostrum of a consecrated virgin. This I knew.

"It is Indian Perfection Medicine. Take it when your time comes, and the pain will not threaten you," she said. Hearing this, my heart soared, for I knew Katherine Tekakwitha had answered my prayer.

I figured Sister got the recipe from a Mohawk maiden with a difficult vocation, and I thanked her feelingly.

"There is no need to thank me," she said. "There is a giving that does not impoverish and a withholding that does not enrich. I have but one request." Nuns always want some little selfless thing in exchange for their favors, I find. God's the same way when you think about it. "Everything in the convent is ours, not mine. To give property without permission is a form of theft. I have been chastised in the past for giving to the indigent. I have been called more of a chemist than a Sister, more nurse than nun. I battle for obedience. Yet Saint Dominic said he would sooner cut up the rule book than let it be a burden to one's conscience. I have taken you into my confidence. I ask only that you hold my words in trust."

"You mean keep mum?"

She nodded, and I didn't stop to dicker. Give me that remedy! was how I felt. She told me the way to the convent's medicine closet, a large room in the cellar that would be open at this hour.

"What if I meet up with one of your sidekicks?" I wondered.

"If questioned, you must tell the truth," she said firmly. "Tell the truth, and say Saint Gregory the Great directed us to dispense to all sufferers that which they need."

I set off for the medicine room on a trail that twisted through corridors of mostly closed doors. The worst of it was windows now and then threw rays on big framed pictures whose sudden faces scared the daylights out of me. All along, I worried some nun would creep up on the balls of her feet in high perfection behind me and ask my business. I had to keep thinking of the baby and of all the cures I'd tried to no avail.

When I got to the convent's depths, which were dim and dank as a root cellar, I wished especially for a lamp. But I remembered "Tekakwitha" meant "she who cuts the way before her" and felt steadier. At long last, I arrived at the third left-hand door of the west wing. In the sincere hope that I had not gone off course, I stopped and turned the knob. My eyes had a tolerance for darkness by now.

I could make out a long table of ledgers and accounts, along with stacks of labels, stamps, and envelopes. It looked like a tidy business for the Sisters, and I wished them well. To my left, I saw shelves holding small white cakes and bottles. Seizing one, I read the Indian Perfection label thrice. I'd already knotted the Bayer Heroin in my apron corner, and now I rolled the remedy in this garment and tucked the hem at my waist. It was high time, too, for a bell was tolling. And since early and provident fear is the mother of safety, and I'd as lief have my wolf teeth pulled as be caught red-handed, I fled.

* * * *

That fall was damp as a gravedigger's skin. By November I'd developed a hectic fever that left pink circles in my cheeks. Before the winter zeros struck, I thought I'd better mend my lacy lung with Sister's remedy. Whether it was her medicine or the disease itself, by some means I was lifted into the high altitudes of hope and held there. I somehow kept my cheer, and in April the last shrouds of snow melted. Though I was large as Jumbo by then, the work of the farm would not allow me to remove myself from view as some think prudent.

One Saturday, having finished the morning chores and served a bountiful hot lunch, I was on my knees scrubbing the kitchen oilcloth and thinking about Kitty. That one isn't one to make love to the corners! I was thinking. Why, I've seen her grab a pair of silk drawers and begin dusting if she heard a neighbor on the steps. When I opened her trunk to get fresh linen, a swarm of moth-millers flew out, and we had to fumigate.

Such were my thoughts when I felt the first pain. I didn't trust it since the baby had been incubating only eight months by my reckoning. And even if it was not a false alarm, it takes time for pain to work itself into a birth. Joe and Mike were leaving for town, but reasoning thus, I said nothing. Every week they went into Watervliet to buy our groceries at Dufrane's Market. While the clerk was making up the order, they'd go across the street to Sherlock's Grill.

Once they'd left, I noticed the pains were coming closer.

Mamie, I said, this baby is going places. I stopped scrubbing the floor and began scouring buckets and bowls. I pumped water for boiling and placed torn strips of cloth in the oven to bake clean. A woman in labor should have plenty fixed for others to eat, yet I was caught short. I could only put a big plate of bread and butter on the table. In our bedroom off the parlor, I set out the spotless containers along with a bar of carbolic. I tied a twisted towel around the headboard rails and fastened two more, like reins, at the foot. Then I covered the room and the bed with old issues of *The Troy Record*. Some expectant mothers put their own laying-out clothes in a bottom drawer, but my warm hopes would not allow this. I was thinking of the here and now, not the always was and will be.

If you go to bed, the infant sleeps and you have to start again. So I kept pacing. After the third birth, things get riskier. I tried to keep my mind on the happy deliveries and forget the poor devils I had seen. I would not think of the abnormal presentations, hemorrhages, obstructions, retained afterbirths, blood poisonings, convulsions, milk legs, and childbed fevers. Working for Doc Muswell, I'd seen prolapsed women full of ironmongery, pessaries to hold their insides in. Childbirth left them wearing these "threshing machines" only hoop skirts could hide.

Such trials swept through my mind in kinetoscopic flashes. Yet those poor devils did not have Sister's remedy. This I knew. The children were outside playing pirate, and I called Helen in.

"You're a young miss now," I told her. She was nearly nine. "You can be your mother's helper." I asked her to go upstairs and alert Kitty, who soon appeared and settled herself on the divan like a brooding hen. When a pain came, I shushed, and when it let up, I started bossing the job again. All along I was trying to gauge the labor's progress, whether I was at the dime, nickel, quarter, half-dollar, or teacup stage. At the teacup stage, I would be "fully delighted," as Doc Muswell said. I figured I was halfway there.

It was twilight, and I was lying down to catch my breath, when Kitty began hollering from the yard. "Mamie Come Running!" she said. "The Team Is Back!"

Rushing out, I saw the wagon and lathered horses but no sign of Joe or Mike. By the ropes of green froth dribbling from their bits, I could see Ned and Susie had grabbed a bite to eat.

"We'll have to unhitch the horses," I told her.

"They are such great brutes, Mamie. Do let's leave them as they are. But what of Michael and Joe? Do you suppose they were thrown and are even now lying in some dark spot?"

"Joe and Mike are skillful whips," I said. "If they got thrown, then they must foot it." I knew those brothers were not brawling or visiting sweethearts. "Nothing ventured, nothing lost," that was the Monahan motto. I watered and un-harnessed the horses without coming to harm, and when I re-turned, Kitty was strewn across my newspapered bed in an attitude of weeping.

"Perhaps the dainty waist and deep full inspirations of some Watervliet wanton have commanded Michael's admira-tion," she said.

I could hear Helen trying to convince my Joseph and baby Edwardia it was bedtime. Dora was singing them a little song. I scrubbed the horse dirt off and lit the oil lamps. Then I laid down on the divan. Now that the pain was mustering, I won-dered out loud if I'd have enough of Sister's remedy.

"Mother, if you needed more, we could have made it our-selves," Helen piped up. Having settled the little ones, she and Dora were giving me big looks. I only half-listened as she prattled about *Papaver somniferum* and lancing the pods so sticky flower milk oozed out. She spoke of scraping, drying, beating, molding, boiling, skimming, and straining, but it wasn't till she mentioned covering the cakes with white poppy petals that I sat up and attended. The word "poppy" had roused me.

"Is this what Sister was doing when she took that bad turn?"

"Yes, and I was helping her," said Helen with a proud little smile.

"You were helping her harvest opium," I said. I got up and stood with arms akimbo, thinking. If Sister's remedy was mostly opium, like Black Drop or Laudanum, I might have become a dope fiend. Hoarding the medicine for tonight's baby was all that saved me. Now I had to weigh the danger of opium against the danger of pain. Most of all, I wanted this baby to be protected by the power of good. And I thought Sister Honoraria was a good woman, even if she was a bad nun.

As I stood thinking, my waters broke. I marched into the bedroom where Kitty was sleeping.

"See here, Clara Lazarus," I said. "It's time to rise from the dead. I need streetcar courtesy. I have to push this baby out."

"Oh, Mamie, I am a wretch. Forgive me," she said. I lay down in a sweat and would have taken Sister's medicine, opium or no, but I could not afford to be dopey until the doctor got here. It must have been near midnight. I sent Joe wireless messages in my mind: come home, come home. Dora brought me a saucer of dark fruit.

"What have we here?" I gasped.

"Kitty says they are little black-coated workers." She looked at me with her bashful, born-yesterday eyes.

I set the prunes down carefully and told her to fetch the blessed candle from the parlor. My mother, Peg Merns, had unfastened every knot or button, door or stall, while I was having baby Edwardia. She supposed so much opening would help the infant enter the world. Thanks to her, baby Edwardia was welcomed into a household of men with their garments falling off and an old bossy in the kitchen. I wanted this child to be born newfangled and free of Irish hoodoo. But I'd kept a copy of a prayer my mother had recited, and I asked

Helen to fetch it from the dresser's depths. It was written on vellum older than Plymouth Rock.

I used the oil lamp to light the candle and read the words to myself: "Anne bore Mary; Mary, Christ Our Savior; Elizabeth, John the Baptist. So may this woman, saved in the name of Our Lord Jesus Christ, bear the child in her womb, be it male or female. Come forth."

That's how it went. It ended with Latin words written so they'd read the same in any direction: S A T O R A R E P O T E N E T O P E R A R O T A S Though she was no scholar, my mother, Peg Merns, said the Latin meant "I creep toward the sower and holder of the workings and the wheels."

I placed the paper on my big belly, and asked Helen if she could see to read it. With a little prompting, she soon had it down pat. I told her I wanted her to recite the list of holy births in a saintly voice while Dora held the candle aloft. My lambs looked scared in the shaky light, but Helen set her balky tongue to the task.

"Anne bore Mary—" she began. She got no further because Dora yelled Papa's home! just then, and the spell was broken. A moment later, Joe was standing at the bedroom door. He had mea culpa written all over him, but I was happy to see him in good health.

"How are you, Mamie?" he said, with hat in hand.

"I am fully delighted," I replied. His face was barn-red, and he looked more at a loss for words than always.

"Where are the groceries, Joe?" I asked.

"I guess we lost track of time in the grill, and the team got tired of waiting for us." He was standing like somebody rusted in place, and I told him he'd better go after Doc Muswell.

"If he's out on a call, don't write 'CHILDBIRTH' on the slate or he'll mosey along. Write 'FULLY DELIGHTED,'" I said. Joe repeated this. "You heard," I said.

After he left, I started to cough. Then, my stars! The pain changed in character. I thought I had a lightning bolt lodged in my spine, though I couldn't let on with the children near. I had been leaning on Sister's remedy to see me through. And if that failed, Doc's Heroin. But how could I bear down if I was doped? I needed all my wits. And what if those medicines fatally depressed the baby?

Once a heavy thought has a grip, it is hard to dispel. I knew labor proceeded at a pace and mine was stalled. I felt my efforts coming to naught. This is the reckoning, I felt. I'm flagging, I'm past repair. I'm at the last gasp. Soon I will not want my body or the breath I breathe. This is the end of the world.

"Go get Kitty," I told Helen, who was standing by. My sister-in-law had been delicately raised, that was evident. She was genteel and artistic, though the man in the moon would make a better midwife. The children could do worse in a godmother, I thought. She came in, and I showed her and Helen the basin on the chair for bathing baby, the penny and binding for its navel, the boiled scissors, baby clothes, and diapers.

"Mamie darling, don't be blue," Kitty said, in her namby-pamby way. "You must use the happy dust the doctor gave you. It is much favored as a stimulant, I've heard."

"You're a good sister, Kit," I told her. "If the baby's a boy, I want him to be called James, after my brother. And if it's a girl, you can call her Annabel Lee."

"Stop it, Mamie," Kitty said. "You're frightening me." Her hands were shaking like a palsy victim's.

"Ma, are you dying?" Helen asked, and Dora started to cry. I'd seen women lose heart and die of exhaustion. I'd seen them die with babies half in and half out. They died because they were frightened. I fully understood it. But seeing those little girls with the solemn waif look already on them, staring at their mother like she was a hobgoblin, I came to my senses. I realized nobody was going to help me. I was it all. And I told myself to get cracking.

"Don't be crying," I said. "Your mother is a fighter. How can I die when there's a baby coming?" Course I can grunt it out, I told myself. God send me a pauper's low Mass funeral with no solemn requiem sung by three priests if I cannot. And I pulled on the towels I'd rigged, and I bore down.

Suddenly it seemed my little shut-in had been cooped up long enough.

Suddenly it wanted liberty. It was coming like a locomotive headlight. It was coming quick as scat. God Almighty! Now this baby was helping. Now this baby wanted to be born.

"Anne bore Mary—" I kept praying, for that was the one phrase I could recall. The pain waxed as it waned, with no pause, and I let the head creep slowly into my hands, though Immaculate Mary, it must be easier to thread camels through needles. The head, the shoulders, then the rest!

I caught the baby and laid it on my stomach. It lay there like a red frog, belly down. I rubbed its back to make it breathe. I held it upside down and patted the soles of its feet. I wiped the blood out of its mouth and blew on its stomach. I dunked it in water. At last I tossed a pinch of Doc's powder over its head and dabbed Sister's soporific of vegetable origin behind its ears.

It gasped and was alive. May God protect the child!

After I'd cut the cord and had the afterbirth, I got up and cleaned the room of gore. Kitty brought in my Joseph and baby Edwardia. "Meet Annabel Lee," she said. I was imagining what Joe would think of this name. Annabel Lee Monahan? Sounds like a lost soul, he'd say.

"You know, Kit, now that I see her, she looks more like she should be called Anne." I had it in mind to name her after

Anne who bore Mary. And Anne Sullivan who taught Helen Keller to read. And Anne of Green Gables, an orphan of renown.

"Anne is the perfect name," Kitty said. "Though I will always think of her as Annabel Lee." She said Mike would take my Joseph fishing later, and I told her to thank him.

"Am I truly a good sister, Mame?" she asked.

"You are one of a kind," I said.

About thirty minutes later, Doc Muswell and Joe arrived. Joe's face lit up like a jack-lantern when he saw the baby. Jiminy Crickets! was all he could say. And he took her to the window to get a better look. Doc Muswell, meanwhile, had walked right past the bedroom door toward Kitty. I figured she must have arranged herself on the divan in a pose she called a "tableau vivant."

"What the deuce is wrong with the girl?" I heard Doc say.

"Oh, Doctor, I'm dying, I'm dying, I'm dead," said Kitty.

"That's impossible, my dear. Mamie would not allow it," said Doc.

Our little bedroom would soon be as full as The St. Louis Exposition with neighbors, nuns, orphans, and my mother, Peg Merns. And I would be unruffled, as if the whole matter had been an everyday affair.

Only to myself would I admit there should be singing crowds and a parade. Like every new mother I thought there should be aerial fascinations—gyrating star mines, electric flowers, and Catherine wheels—to celebrate this birth. For it had been as pretty a fight as any sportsman could wish to see. And since my children now numbered five, I would have liked a display of five balloons from each of which depended a single star that changed its color as it burned.

Just then I heard a bird with a voice so rare it sounded like it had studied at a conservatory. The sun was coaxing the first dusty colors from the ground, and I lay there thinking it had been an ideal birth, after all. Everything went smooth as glycerine, I thought.

I looked at the children dozing on the floor with their stocking feet flung over each other, and our Annie in Joe's arms, and I thought perfection is not what you imagine. Happiness is nothing but God's presence in the silence of the nerves. And though my children were sleeping the sleep of the just, I half believed my unvoiced thoughts would reach them across that room full of twentieth-century light.

❄

Part Two
The Journey Toward Reconciliation

Melanie Rae Thon
One Story

LETTERS IN THE SNOW

for kind strangers and unborn children ~ for the ones lost and most beloved

Sweet Lady in White!

I almost love you. I do love the way your red lipstick matched your little red purse so beautifully. I loved your white fur coat, soft and plush but not real. No creatures died for you. In this, as in all things, you are forever innocent.

We met by chance. Two days ago, I watched you choosing fruit and vegetables. Such bliss! One Fuji apple, green and rosy, one grapefruit blushing pink, one fat orange orange, one small bright banana. You held each piece of fruit as if to weigh it in your hand and heart, as if to see inside, beyond its perfect size and color.

You reminded me of my mother, once upon a time, not so long ago, when she remembered my name and knew me as her daughter, before her lips were cracked and her fingernails broken.

She said, *I remember the important things. I remember that I love you.* She couldn't pull my name from the air, but when I said, *Nicole,* she nodded.

Now I could be anybody: night nurse with her magic meds or cruel cousin Pearl Kane, long dead, long lost, and now returned to mock and tease, pearl divine, this ghost of childhood.

Mother never knows: have I come to ease her pain, or take pleasure in her torment?

Kind Stranger! You left your red purse open in the cart. You turned your back and walked away. The beauty of green beans held you in rapture. I imagined God through you did this on purpose.

You offered a small, good gift with perfect humility. Jesus flooded into your heart. Your mind didn't know what your body was doing.

Dear Lydia, I know your name now, your height and weight, your birthday, all this printed on your driver's license. Five-foot-two and eyes of blue, Lydia Kobell, seventy-six years old last January, hair still blond and full of light. Even in the harsh glare of the grocery store you looked radiant.

I know your children and your children's children. I was tempted to keep them, to stuff their little photographs and all their precious names into my pocket so that I might pretend they were my people. Five siblings, eight nieces, four nephews! Surely one strong brother would see my trouble and let me hide for a month or a year in a dark room in his damp basement.

I didn't keep them. I thought you might be afraid if they were gone too long, that you might imagine some thief with sinister intentions. I left your family in your wallet, in the glove box, all of them safe with your credit cards and license.

Lydia, before I knew your name or loved your grandchildren, I walked swiftly out of Albertson's with your wallet in one pocket of my coat and your car keys in the other. Terrified as I was, I did not scurry. Still, people stared. The throbbing bruise around my eye flared blue and green, a peacock's royal fan of feathers.

Even in the parking lot I did not run. I felt strangely calm: by you and God, silently protected. I punched the lock release on your keys till I saw taillights wink and the trunk of a silver sedan spring open.

I took it as a sign. I took it as a blessing.

Oh Lydia! How grateful I am for your love of vegetables. Your search for the beans most green and glossy gave me time to reach in your little purse, to feel, to find, to take only what I needed. You were in the check-out line and I was thirty-nine miles west before you realized what was missing.

Lydia, I confess. Once I lifted seven dollars from my mother's purse. I bought Kools and Coke. I smoked and drank in the woods by the river with Trina Flynn and Marlee Troyer. We blew smoke into one another's mouths. We coughed and laughed. We never called it kissing.

I entered my new life: ten-year-old thief, prepubescent addict. She knew, of course, my sly detective, my dark-eyed diminutive mother. Why couldn't I be sweet and good like my one and only little sister Lora? If I stole twenty dollars or Mother lost it, what did it matter? In my house, I was always to blame: bridal lace snipped in half, purple grape juice spilled on a pale carpet—china doll dropped on her head, china skull shattered to pieces.

When I was bad enough, Mother said, *You almost killed me once, and you haven't stopped trying.*

My weary father who died too soon said, *Why do you do this?*

It's true. I did borrow Mother's Carmen Miranda Red lipstick and dangling sapphire earrings. Nine years old, Nicole Odair—gloriously, fabulously beautiful. I lost one earring, of course: hanging upside down, skirt flying over my head, careless Nicole exposed on the monkey bars.

Mother charged me ninety-two dollars so that she could buy a new pair. But they were too dear, those sparkling jewels, a great grandmother's last gift, *Here, my darling, be wonderful.* To punish us, Mother never replaced them.

Still, I paid. Ninety-two dollars. I was a child with no piggy bank full of coins, no secret savings, no allowance. *You can pay it off in work,* she said. *Thirty cents an hour.*

Nine, ten, eleven years old, she hoped I'd learned my lesson.

I did learn. I learned my soft-skinned mother who spoke Spanish with a rippling tongue could turn mean in my language, could cling to loss, could hurt as long as memory lasted.

Mother! I can't forgive you. To forgive, some place in the heart has to remain hard, has to hold a stone of blame to cast in silence. I am washed clean by grief and guttered out by the strange sound of merciful laughter.

Mother is a problem at the Sunny Arms Adult Care Center. The three drawers of her little nightstand are full of other people's treasures: a wedding band, a note of sympathy, pine-scented shaving cream, a tiny glass rocking horse, suffering Jesus on a silver cross, two photographs of a thin soldier boy, a box of chocolate cherries, a strand of pearls. If you accuse her of theft, she says, *They're mine,* or, *I don't know how they got there.* She suspects Daisy Lee Valentin, the lady down the hall, the one who shuffles up and down all day, carrying her walker. That eighty-three-pound pixie would walk all night if the aides didn't strap her to the bedrails. Mother says, *She's a witch. She put those things in my drawers while I was sleeping.*

Why speak now?

The bitter child I once was might say she deserved this, to be scolded to tears by two exasperated attendants, to see her drawers emptied on the bed, to have all her wealth redistributed. *Justice divine*, I might say, *justice hilarious*. Now I know: we deserve nothing, neither the blessings nor misfortunes that befall us.

Lydia! I committed crimes worse than theft against my mother. Once, by accident, I saw her naked. Dripping wet, she stepped from the bathtub and I caught her reflection in the mirror, one breast gone and the other one withered. I was in her bedroom, in her closet, tying silky scarves around my throat and ankles. I saw the deep scar from me across her belly, tiny baby Nicole scooped out six weeks early.

My father said, *You were so small we dressed you in doll clothes and you lived in a little doll house and we took you for walks in a little doll carriage.* Nobody ever knew when Daddy was joking! All stories are true. I slept in a doll house. I woke in an incubator. My mother's blood pressure soared and the masked man sliced her open to save us.

Sweet Rose! Your body, not mine, was the first to betray you.

Lydia, bless you for your rosy-cheeked grandchildren. I carry them in my heart though I left them in your wallet. I name one Rose, after my mother. Forgive me for any grief I caused if you thought for a moment your darling ones had fallen into the hands of someone dangerous. The one named Soshana was a special comfort. She'd written a note on the back: *This is me. I'm five. I love you.* One thin blond boy in a group of seven stood apart, leaning toward the edge of the frame as if he wanted to step out of it. I could see from his knobby joints he'd already suffered. Heart murmur or brain tumor, Crohn's disease or juvenile arthritis. He was mine, and I loved him. *Isaac Jerome, far left,* it said on the back, and I thought he might be gone because his was the only name you'd written. I loved him, yes, but I left him in the glove box with Soshana and their cousins.

My mother was sixty-six, my father dead two years, and Doctor Julian said, *Probably Alzheimer's.*

Too young! Lora and I cried out together. But it can start anytime. You might be thirty-five. You might be ninety.

Four years since that day. She no longer knows my name. She does not remember I am her daughter. She no longer asks, *Where's Lora?* She no longer pleads, *Help me break out of here.*

In her fast fingers, in her bedazzled eye, in her search for shiny things that bring brief solace, she is mine, and I am hers, in love at last, beyond all shame, beyond all doubt, the good thieves, right hand, left hand, mother and daughter.

Oh my Rose of all roses, in your closet, I found a lady's red wig, a man's boot and prosthesis. I know I shouldn't be glad. I know I shouldn't find us amusing. But I am and I do when my heart isn't shattered.

Dear Cody,

You looked like a pirate from my high school play: pale scruff of beard and gold rings through pierced earlobes. *Shy Cody, my slender-hipped swashbuckling hero,* when you found me, I'd been shivering in the rain almost two hours. I'd smoked my last cigarette down to the nub and was looking for butts in the ash can. You took pity on me, this stringy-haired wet rag of a woman with a battered face: one eye swollen shut, one wild eye popped too far open.

I told you my husband and I had had a fight, that he'd torn off with the two kids while I was in the ladies room. You believed me. It wasn't such a terrible lie. There was a kind of truth imbedded in it.

I'd ditched Lydia Kobell's car behind a burned-out bar in Big Timber, walked back to the highway and caught a ride with Wyatt Derosa, a trucker hauling ice augers and snow-shoes to Missoula. He was nice enough at first. He said I looked hungry, and *yes*, I was, so Wyatt stopped in Livingston to buy two super-size coffees and six maple doughnuts.

When he got back in the truck, he touched my face, the edge of the bruise. *Cody!* He looked so tender I wanted to love him, to lay my head against his wide chest and hear the valves of his heart opening and closing. But Wyatt Derosa said, *It's almost beautiful.*

I flinched, then laughed. *Beautiful* is a cruel word for a person who's been pummeled. He said, *I mean, a woman so small, a bruise like that, I just want to protect you from everybody.*

Cody, I'm an idiot. I went back to Dixon Spark eleven times after he smacked me. I let him hold me naked in his lap; I listened to the rain; I let him weep; I let him lie, *Never again, baby*. But thick as I am, I've learned one thing in thirty-seven years: there's not much distance between a man who loves to touch a bruise and a man who needs to make one.

I got rid of Wyatt outside of Butte, high on the windy rim of the Continental Divide, bent spine of the earth, at the rest stop where you saved me.

I told him I had a brother down in Wisdom. I pretended to call. I said I'd be fine: Mick was on his way. If I did have a brother, one I could really call, would he be like you, or would he be like my sister and disown me?

Cody, it makes me sick to think I left you, that you might have been scared or cold. I know how that is. You were gen-erous and too kind. We were friends before I betrayed you. You asked about my eye. You thought it was him, of course, the husband I'd invented. I didn't want to lie to you, but the lies had already started. I said, *No, not that, a swing in the park, playing with my kids and my nieces and nephews.* I imagined all the children in Lydia Kobell's photographs. I thought of my sister Lora's girls, Ingrid and Emily, not as they are now, but younger, when I was still allowed to visit.

I loved the story I spun, me in the park with sixteen kids, all of us yelping. *It didn't hurt that much, the swing, because I was happy.*

Later you told me you had a girlfriend named Joy, nineteen and pregnant, the baby not yours. You met her after. You said, *I'd marry her in a minute.* You said, *She laughs at me. My mother hates her.*

You were on your way to Eureka to help your mom clear out your grandfather's house. Last May, he fell off the roof, fractured his jaw and pelvis. He never walked again, never again chewed anything solid. It took him six months to die. With his jaw still wired shut, he scrawled a note to your mother. *Don't let them do this.* That was four months ago, when the doctor put a tube in his stomach.

Grandpa had a Christmas tree farm. He never retired. Once you got lost in the maze of miniature trees. You were four feet tall and they were four inches taller. *But I wasn't afraid. I heard voices like bees and the smell was delicious.*

I hope you weren't afraid after I left you, that the smell of pines was sharp and sweet, that you heard the voices of bees inside you. *Don't be afraid. If there's a way in, there's a way out. You'll find it.* I hope you could always see a light, a farmhouse in the distance. I dropped your bag of Oreos and thermos of hot chocolate at the side of the road. I pray they sustained you.

My thin gypsy, to say I love you is unfair, a burden you shouldn't have to carry. But it's true. I do love you. And it's true. You did save me. You gave me hope—not just for the days ahead, but for the hours and years behind me. Inside your little emerald green Ford Ranger, in the perfect Montana dark, on the cut-off between Avon and Helmville—there, sheltered from snow, sheltered from all things outside us, I was a girl again, fourteen and maybe a little buzzed, stomach empty and just enough wine to be giddy.

I saw you exactly as you are: Cody Weaver, sixteen years old, the faithful son, the benevolent boyfriend, the one not afraid. I saw another life I could have had, another world of possibility.

If it's true time is a circle and not a line, then there might be a way for us to meet on the other sides of our lives, not as thief and child, but as friends or lovers.

I'm sorry for myself, now that I've lost you. It was easy, like the grocery store in Billings, the red purse, Lydia's keys and wallet. You had to take a whiz. You were suddenly shy. You walked deep into the grove of tall pines. You left me alone in the truck with the keys and your trust. I saw my chance, and I took it.

Dear Kirk and Trudie Iyler,

I lived in your elegant cabin above Swan Lake for twenty-eight hours. You were courteous and wise to leave a spare key where I could find it. I busted no locks; I broke no windows. I swear I had a vision: a tall man tipping a clay flowerpot on the porch, a slender red-haired woman sliding a key on a yellow string under it.

I tipped the pot, and there it was, the key and all it promised.

You are clean people, you and your three grown children: Lance, Duncan, Amanda. I saw their names and numbers on the refrigerator and wanted to call them. I thought I'd say, *I'm your cousin, Nicole. I'm at the cabin. Come get me.*

I found the breaker box in the bedroom closet and parted your clothes to flip the switches for your pump and hot water. It took two hours for the water to heat. I heard the hum and groan, the song of pipes expanding. *Trudie!* It was worth the wait, every minute. If it's true God is everywhere in everything, he was the warm water in your bathtub. God the womb. God the mother.

I meant to be considerate, to hang your towels and wash your dishes. I meant to turn your heaters off, and now, I know, your warmth is wasted. Forgive me. The tracks through your house are my confession: *The bad sister of Goldilocks was here. I rumpled your bed. I devoured your porridge.* I ate a whole can of pork & beans. I slurped three bowls of instant oatmeal. If I survive another night, know that your food has become my flesh. Know that you have saved me.

Your towels were rolled, not folded—swirls of green and gold—crimson, copper, burnt sienna—wind through tamarack and pine, the autumn forest. *Trudie*, I imagined you and Lance, your quiet son, peacefully rolling these towels together.

Every corner of your house breathed *hallelujah*, a song of joy in praise of beauty: the towels, a bowl of tiny translucent soaps, a jar of shells, the flagstone mosaic of the fireplace. You and Kirk and your beloved children must have gathered each sea star and slab of rock with gratitude and awe for its singular size and shape and color.

I entered your cabin, your family, your bed. I was one with you, embraced, *holy child*, the long-lost piece of your fabulous puzzle.

Kirk, thank you for the fireplace so carefully laid with logs and kindling. I crumpled paper under the grate, and with your patience in my heart, I torched it. The leather of your couch and the fur of your plush pillows smelled of the animals they once were, and I thought they had sacrificed their lives for me so that I might live one night in heaven.

Oh, merciful strangers! You gave me refuge in the darkest hour, on a night when I wanted to go, but could not go, to my mother, my father, my sister, my children. Your cabin is almost as glorious as my sister's house at the edge of the Rimrocks overlooking the river. My sister's house, from which I have been exiled forever.

Lora, I swear: anything I have could be yours in an instant. When I hammered out the glass of your basement window with a rock and dropped into your house that night three years ago, I didn't think of it as breaking and entering. I thought of it as seeking sanctuary. I was safe at last, *home*, in hiding.

When I drank Stephen's cognac, I didn't think of it as theft, I thought of it as necessary comfort. When I slipped into your bed, I thought, *Soon, so soon, my sister will come home and hold me.* I whispered, *When I wake, I won't be alone and I won't be afraid of anyone.*

I didn't know how badly I'd cut my hand on the glass. I didn't intend to streak your sheets and nightgown. I didn't plan to drink as much as I did. I didn't deliberately drop the goblet. But oh, what a sound as it splintered on tile: bell of joy, bright laughter!

I'm sorry I scared Ingrid and Emily, the children I love beyond all reason. I promise: I didn't come to cause an argument between you and Stephen. And though I see all the trouble I caused, it still seems unnecessary for you to have your own sister arrested, to let her nieces see her hauled away: Aunt Nicole, stumbling drunk, wrists clamped behind her back in handcuffs.

Anybody could have looked at my face—split lip, broken nose—and seen I'd had a bad night already. I could have offered more evidence: bruised wrists and ribs, three fingers fractured. Those fingers healed bent and now cannot be straightened.

I'll say this for what you did: two nights in jail kept me safe from Dixon, and when I got out, he was the one to come, to rock, to kiss, to hold, to love me, and he brought me home, and we took a shower, and the rain came, and I was cold, and we lay together, and I heard the rain on the roof and the leaves and the grass and the windows, the endless rain making everything whole, bringing everything together, and we didn't make love, we just lay there till his skin was cool and mine was warm and it rained all night and it never stopped raining, and the rain was his voice and I knew he was sorry and one of us began to cry or we both did or it was just the rain, and I learned if you go back once, you'll go back forever.

Lora, your good husband Stephen, your brilliant entrepreneurial wonder who was clever enough to invest in land twenty years ago before the movie stars made Montana famous—Stephen, who has earned himself and you a fortune five times over, this man who could so easily afford to be generous, forbids me now and for all time to see your children. And you, my sister, my only one, you have agreed to the terms of Stephen's love, a husband's bitter reconciliation.

Most precious sister, at eight I became a Monarch butterfly; at five you emerged as a Tiger Swallowtail. That Halloween, we disguised our slender bodies in black tights and leotards. We grew lovely wings of colored silk and wire. Lora and Nicole, magically remade by our magical mother. We were luminous. Light glowed through our wings. Our sweet Rose had transformed us.

At nine, I borrowed the sapphire earrings; at ten, I smoked Kools and kissed my girlfriends by the river. Six years later I lost, I gave up, I abandoned my first child. I saw my squalling son whisked away; I never held him! *Too hard,* the Lutheran lady said. *Believe me, this is better.* Now he's twenty-one. I meet him everywhere. He waves to me as I drive through a construction zone. He walks past me in the park holding his wife's hand, carrying their first baby like a kangaroo, in a soft pouch against his chest and belly. Sometimes I find him alone in the merciful light of a roadside bar, and he thinks I'm younger than I am, and he flirts with me and I flirt back—our faces reflect, a natural attraction. Johnny Mathis sings just for us from the jukebox, his voice smoldering so close I think he's really there, in the dark, swaying in the corner of the room where nobody else can see him, and this child of mine, this man, asks me to dance and I do, cheek to cheek, *oh my love*, rib to rib, *my darling*, and I feel him, *I've hungered for your touch*, I swear, *a long, lonely time*, cradled inside me.

At twenty, I let a doctor scoop me out. *Better this way*, I thought. I let a nurse flush me. Gone, this fast, my second child. *You were so small and you slept in a little doll house forever and ever*. My children! One walks the earth and one I carry still: she's a fist in the heart, a pulse in the pelvis. She could be anywhere, any age, her spirit returned in any body. *Be kind*, she says, *you owe me*. And I am kind. When I see a child sobbing in a grocery cart, when his mother walks away and leaves him stranded, I mouth the words, *You're mine; I love you*, and the child sees it's true, and by some miracle stops howling. And God says, *I don't forgive because I never blamed you*. But oh, how he grieves for me and my children.

Lora, repentance is not a single act; repentance is an endless turning, and this is why it broke my heart to hurt Cody— Cody, my child—Cody, the boyfriend who would have married me when we were both children. *Lora*, you have wounded me a thousand times by forbidding me to see your daughters. You can't imagine how Ingrid and Emily heal me with love, theirs for me and mine for them, and oh my darling, the pain of love is sweet and the pain of love is tender.

I would have been a lousy mother at sixteen and even worse at twenty. Every choice was wrong, the ones I made, the ones I didn't.

You think your girls are safe in your house on the hill. Thirteen-year-old Ingrid plays the flute. Eleven-year-old Emily plays the cello. She runs the 400-meter dash faster than any girl or boy in her school. Ingrid does back handsprings in the yard. Ingrid does double somersaults from the high board at the pool. They don't have time to be bad; they don't have time to get in trouble.

But I know this secret. One day last summer I spied on little Emily in the park. She wore a tight white t-shirt and short pink shorts. She was rolling down a hill with a boy, and they kept rolling into each other and bouncing apart, and I heard them laugh, and then I saw them stop, and Emily lay in the grass, and the boy rolled on top of her, and they lay very still and were endlessly silent.

Oh, Children! Perilous are your years.

One day a group of boys circled me in the hallway so each could take his turn sliding up close, unseen, to touch me. Fast hands flicked over all the sweet little girl curves of me. Their twelve hands didn't hurt, but they spoke only Spanish, these white boys, and their quick tongues made it all happen in another country. Five boys scattered when the bell rang, but one lingered long enough to speak my language: *We learned every word from your mother.*

Later that one found me alone. Later: his car, the stars pouring in, the night, the river.

Lora, I'm not saying Emily will end up like me, fifteen and pregnant, sixteen and childless. I'm just saying you never know and nothing in the real world will save us. One false step leads to another. The wrong path may open onto a field of forget-me-nots and poppies.

We do forget in the end. Our mother forgets her mastectomy. It is a grief relived every morning. She forgets the word: *breast*. She forgets: *el cancer del seno*. She lays her hand on the sunken place, *mi corazon*. She says, *What happened here*? She opens her robe to show me.

Oh, our beautiful shape-shifting mother! Sometimes I glimpsed her in the classroom of our high school. I'd hear a silvery sound, her voice a moonlight dance on water. She was a new Rose, a Rose reborn, not the mother I'd seen naked. Our Rose in Spanish rhyme, tempting all the boys with language. Long ago, this Rosa was the first and only child of Presbyterian missionaries—clever Rosa, three years old and already singing Spanish in a Guatemalan village. She learned what her thin parents never learned: she learned to love her body.

Lora, is this punishment or mercy?

My Sister, because I could not come to you, or Rose, or Daddy, I fled, and these strangers—Lydia, Cody, Kirk, Trudie—have saved my life, and so I must believe I have a life worth saving.

Most gracious ones, it was my second night in your cabin. I'd slept eighteen hours the day before, and now, again, was sleeping. The jangling telephone jolted me into panic, three-thirteen, exactly. I thought it must be Dixon. I thought somehow he'd found me. I imagined him a mile up the road, the Window Wizard in his white truck, calling from his cell phone: *Nicole, I'm here. I'm coming.*

Crazy, I know, to leave the safety and solace of this place, to bolt out into the winter night, into the snow, the moonlit woods, to clamor and climb up the ridges above Swan Lake when everything in your cabin said, *You're warm, you're safe, wrong number, don't worry.*

It seemed like another vision. This time, I saw the truck, the snow, his name painted on the side, *Dixon Spark ~ Window Wizard*, Dixon in red letters blazing.

Sweet strangers! I could almost hear your voices. *We are keeping you very safe. We love you.* If only I'd held on to faith! If only I'd believed you.

Father,

Forgive me for my extravagant kisses the day you died. I'd told you to let go when you got too weary. I promised: *Lora and I will take care of Mother.* Liar! I said, *We'll be okay. We'll miss you.*

I thought you would go in the night and make it easy.

But I found you awake another day, alive to see another morning. With your eyes wide but not focused, you saw only light, all your people as shadows. *Daddy,* I covered your face with tears and kisses. *Thank you,* I said. *Thank you, thank you.*

You knew me as a thief then, a betrayer worse than Judas. We were *not* ready! We would never be okay. Lora and I could not take care of your Rose, your love, our mother.

All this you understood, beyond words, beyond your clouded vision. You knew long before we knew, long before we could bear to face it. You were the one to find her lost words, to finish her sentences, to whisper names in her ear, to hold her hand at a party, to match her socks, to wipe the smudge of lipstick from her face when the lips she drew were crooked. *Here, darling, let me help you.* She needed you, only you, partner of thirty-three years, keeper of faith, keeper of memory.

And so you lived another day. And so you struggled to the final hour.

In your suffering, you lived in truth, the pure pain of perfect compassion.

Why, when you loved us like this, did I choose a man like Dixon?

Father, you survived three heart attacks and two strokes, open-heart surgery, one clogged carotid artery. You lived with a cleaved chest and five bypasses. In the end, everything failed you.

I remember your hands, clean and soft. I remember: you wanted me beautiful. If you could see me now, all your loving work destroyed, my thin face realigned by the quick fist of Dixon Spark, you'd weep.

Daddy, I almost hear you.

You and Valerie murmured, *yes*, like Cody's bees, as you mended my teeth, filling the ones gone bad, capping the two I'd chipped, riding fast down the dirt path, flying head over handlebars from my blue bicycle. Ten years old. *Daddy*, I was fearless.

Dear Valerie. My oldest and your youngest cousin, your assistant for twenty-three years. She made you laugh. She'd loved you forever.

Valerie whispered as you worked. It could have been anything: the rain in the night, the new moon after—Troy's accident last winter, his foul moods, the shattered bones that never healed—Miranda in the school play, *Wizard of Oz*, Miranda the star, Miranda the lion.

You said: *pick, drill, gauze, water*.

She said, *I made cheesecake brownies yesterday. I brought you half. They're scrumptious.*

When I let go of words, I heard only love, you and Valerie praying over me.

Father, why have I forsaken you, accepting violence when you showed me the face of love and endless mercy?

Sometimes when you see a man and his family, you know his whole life, not as stories he tells, but as memories, as dreams, as dirt and barking dogs, as light in a window far away, your own burned wrists, your own blood trembling.

Dixon's brothers laugh like twins, erupting for no reason anybody else can fathom. Bald and bearded, Malcolm and Lee, the Spark boys—they even look like twins, though there are eight years, Dixon and Flora and Irene between them.

Dixon's the skinny one, the child lost, the boy in the middle. Dixon, thirty-six years old, and his brothers still tease him about the swish in his hips, the stutter that comes back when he's scared or excited. They love to excite him. They call: *Pretty Girl, Pretty Girl,* their voices high, two twittery parrots. They pat his butt and yip with joy as soon as Dixon's words start tumbling.

They're not mean to be mean. *Boys will be boys,* they say. *We can't help it.* Malcolm's thirty-two, and Lee is pushing forty.

Harmless, their sisters say. *Mush melons.* Irene says, *It's the quiet ones who cause you trouble. Dixon was the one up the tree with his slingshot and pellets, killing little birds, wounding cats and squirrels.* Flora says, *Dixon was the one under my bed with a box of mice or snakes or lizards.*

They're big girls, Irene and Flora. They laugh big laughs. They say, *If he tries anything now, we'll sit on his lap and squish him.*

Daddy, I'm not saying this is why. I'm not offering up excuses.

The laughing Spark brothers go hunting and come back with tall tales of a fourteen-point whitetail buck and a grizzly that almost ate them. They see a field of grass shimmering before a hundred elk rise and run. *Out of range,* Lee says. *Too bad. I'd like an elk head for the office.*

They promise to take Dixon next time, but they forget, or he refuses. Not joking, Dixon says, *If they get me in the woods alone, they'll shoot me.*

Later, drunk on Dixon's Jack Daniels, the three of them sit on the couch, arms looped over shoulders, with Dixon, the favorite tonight, cradled in the middle. Malcolm starts humming *Edelweiss*, and Lee joins him. Dixon's the only one who knows the words, and so he leads, and the three of them get so sad and sweet they're practically weeping.

There are mysteries in every man's life, love and grief beyond all telling.

In a dream, I'm buried in the woods, damp earth packed tight around me. The Spark boys have left only my nose exposed. My eyes and mouth fill with dirt as I struggle. I kick and claw, twist my way free at last, and run toward home as night falls. I hear the brothers, each hard breath, each footfall. They could catch me anytime, but the chase is deeper pleasure. They carry BB guns and little knives, ropes to burn my wrists, a dirty rag to use as blindfold. They toss firecrackers in the trees. Every burst becomes a spark, a laughing boy inside me.

I hear Odile's dogs and nobody's coyotes. When I see the lights of home at last, it's not ours: it's Dixon's double-wide trailer. His father never built a house. Jackson Spark was too busy building kennels. Through little lit windows I see Mother, Father, Irene, Flora. I won't cry. I won't confess. The ones inside will tease or scold if they see me scared and filthy.

I love Dixon like this. I dream his dreams for him.

Dixon's parents breed Rottweilers and travel four states to sell them. A Rottweiler will herd cattle or sheep, goats or children. People with kids need to be careful. Anything that runs is his. His stamina is endless. But when the dog dreams, a cat hissing in the yard is a mountain lion come down to eat him. He whimpers in his sleep, panting hard, legs twitching.

Odile Spark is a tiny woman: four feet, eleven inches—eighty-nine pounds and shrinking. A male Rottweiler weighs thirty pounds more than she does. The whole pack might be snapping and snarling, but when Mama steps into the yard, they shiver with delight and lick her.

My tough guys, Odile says, *my babies*. She sits on Malcolm's lap. He's huge, and she's scrubbed clean, a shiny doll or strange child. *He came from me*, she says. *Can you believe it?* He's her sweet heart, her youngest, *My big boy*, her biggest.

Odile doesn't understand fear. She doesn't believe in unnecessary comfort. She doesn't cook or sew. Jackson Spark, six-foot-three, a thin giant of a man who has to stoop to enter the trailer, mends his own shirts and washes their laundry. He fries the eggs and bakes the chicken. He makes the bed. He washes the dishes. Like all Odile's boys, he's absolutely devoted.

Five kids and seventeen Rottweilers. If one of them cried in the night, nobody whispered, *What's wrong?* Nobody ran to give solace.

I love Dixon like this, as if he is my lost-in-the-middle child, as if I alone can give back what he didn't know was stolen.

Daddy, how could I ever leave him?

But two nights ago, back in Billings, he shot me, and I knew at last, I believed: *Yes*, I said to myself, *this man will kill me.*

Only a toy, Trevor's revolver, metallic gray with a narrow black handle, a perfect grip for a woman or child—small, yes, but its weight felt true, and its silhouette looked convincing. I didn't steal it exactly.

The kid had wounded me all day, puny Trevor, that seven-year-old Jack-in-the-Box, weird wide grin and skinny neck, a vision of Dixon as a child. Trevor popped up from behind my chair. Trevor lay coiled under the bed. Trevor crouched behind the shower curtain. He squealed every time: *You're dead. Fall down. I shot you.* Dixon found the whole thing hopelessly amusing.

So I failed to mention the gun under the sofa when Vanessa picked him up, when lovely lush Vanessa said, *I hope he wasn't any trouble*. She thinks she's better than I am. She has Dixon's kid, but no Dixon. Once she said: *We should talk. Call me*.

I carried the heavy toy for three days. I liked the shape of it, the tug, the weight, the slender grip, the serious intention.

I didn't plan to show it to anybody. Next time Trevor came, I'd leave it somewhere obvious. But two nights ago I got home late from work, four hours late, 9:30. Vince had a hard case, Sean McVey, fifteen years old and up as an adult for murder. I write Vince Kassela's letters, interview witnesses, search the books for precedents. Vince says, *You should have been a lawyer*. Nights like this, we take turns arguing mitigating circumstances.

Sean McVey shot the man who found him sleeping in the back seat of his red Riviera. He was sorry now, just a terrified runaway boy seeking refuge, just a scared shooter with his father's gun, 9mm, stolen from the drawer of Christopher McVey's nightstand.

But the man he killed, Terry Simone, taught sign language to the parents of deaf children, so that they could talk to their kids, so that they could learn to laugh and clap, hands held high above their heads, all ten fingers fluttering. He had three deaf daughters of his own, a pregnant wife, another girl in March coming.

Sorry as he was, the boy was not sympathetic: he'd fired three times; this was a problem. Sean McVey is one of those kids who never looks clean, big for his age and pissed off at the world. His father spoke with his hands too: with a paddle across the butt when Sean was small, with a swift box to the ears when Sean got too strong to bend over a knee and wallop.

That night, before he lay down in the car, I think Sean watched Terry Simone through his living room window. I think he saw the man's delicate hands and wanted to die, or wanted to kill him. Sean made the mistake of revealing Terry's last words: *What is it, son? Can I help you?* I think he hated the man. I think he found kindness unbearable.

But Sean McVey's grief was no consolation to Lily Simone who had to explain it all with her own hands to little Kira and Iris and Natasha. Her fingers became birds. They flew out the window and disappeared. She clutched them in tight fists and held them hard against her chest. No matter how wide she spread her fingers, when she opened her hands again, they were always empty.

Who, besides God, could convince a jury this boy's life—any boy's life—was worth saving? Vince said, *He'll come out of prison in twenty years, and he won't be reformed, he'll be crippled.* Vince said, *I need your brain tonight. We must have missed something.*

So I called Dixon, and I left a message, three messages, and I know he heard, but he didn't believe me. He was always jealous of Vince. He thought he came up short by comparison: *Harvard lawyer, Window Wizard.* He had some wild idea that Vince Kassela might want to jump me. A fantasy, and I thought it was sweet, so I let him keep it.

Vince and his wife and three kids camp together, sleep in one tent, catch forty rainbow trout, then float the river. They're a team: they bike a hundred miles and earn three hundred dollars for kids with spina bifida. Gwen is a hospice nurse. Luke plays the organ for the Methodist choir. Last winter, Janaya and Dorrie built a snow family: five fat happy people who stood in the yard for a month melting. To risk a family like that for a woman like me, a man would have to be delirious.

Three years ago, Vince talked Stephen and Lora into dropping their charges, breaking and entering. Vince said, *I'll help you with Dixon too, whenever you're ready.*

I said, *We're fine.* I touched my face. *Oh this*, I said, *I fell down the basement stairs with a basket of laundry.*

Vince said, *Any time, Nicole. Just tell me.*

Vince, I'm ready now. Help me.

I didn't go to him two days ago. I was too ashamed. Becoming a thief felt familiar. Safer, I thought, for everybody—me and Vince, Gwen and the children—safer, yes, mostly for Dixon.

Dixon Spark, Window Wizard. He repairs cracks and chips in glass doors and windshields. He'll come to your house to lift scars from your windows. He can heal a twenty-inch fracture. It's a wonder, a miracle. In the beginning, I called him Doctor Spark, and he laid his hands on me, and said, *Here, be well again, be healed.* And we laughed and made love, and this was the first time.

The Window Wizard was home when I got home, but I didn't know it. I called his name when I opened the door. He didn't answer. I must have walked right past him. My Jack-in-the-Box sat in the dark, coiled up tight as Trevor.

When I felt him, I was in the bathroom, pantyhose around my knees, squatting on the toilet—a bit of an emergency, so I still wore my coat, and Trevor's gun was there, still in my pocket. I'd left the door half open, no time to spare, bladder bursting.

Then I knew. I smelled him, that dangerous Dixon energy. He sprang into the bathroom, and I reached for the revolver. A reflex, a joke, a stupid mistake. I saw from his face, I wouldn't get out of it.

He grabbed the gun before I could laugh, before I could say, *Trevor's*. He wrenched it from my hand, and with me shackled by my pantyhose, trapped on the toilet, he pulled the trigger. *Daddy!* He shot me.

It was hilarious, really, the ridiculous pop of the toy gun, me squatting there, Dixon furious. But neither he nor I were laughing. He used the gun to hit me hard, my eye; I thought I heard the socket cracking. I can't repeat the words he said, not to you, my father.

He pulled me to the floor, kicked my ribs, my head, my belly. I curled up small and hoped he'd stop before he killed me. I don't know when or why he did. Maybe he got scared too. Maybe he thought he was finished.

Daddy! You came! You and Valerie, murmuring, praying as you fixed my teeth, *only chipped*, you said, *not too bad. Like that other time. You'll be good as new by morning.*

Valerie laid her small hands on my eye and pelvis. She mended the bones; she left the bruises. You told her to bring an ice pack for my face. When I woke, I thought I'd have this as proof: a wet rag, the ice melted. But you or Valerie took it back before you fled. She left a dry towel by the sink. She put the ice in the freezer. I had to take your visit on faith. I had to accept the ice in the freezer as evidence of love and comfort.

I feel you now as I stumble in deep snow. You give me strength. You whisper, *I'm here, baby, right beside you.*

Father, I confess, I tried to take care of your Rose, but I couldn't. Before she lost so many words, she kept her Spanish. Three times I found her with Ana Arredondo, the plump little nurse's aide, a refugee from El Salvador. They giggled like lovers. They spoke as birds sing, their whole hearts spilling out of them.

I tried not to hate the woman, not to wish her back the way she'd come fifteen years before, walking with goats across the Sonoran Desert.

I thought Mother remembered everything from her life in another country: little Rosa playing in the dirt, little Rosa swimming in the river. Rosa speaking Spanish rhyme faster than the village children. *Daddy*, I saw her come alive in a language we never spoke, in a tongue that doesn't include us.

But you saved pretty Rosa's teeth. Twenty-nine years old and she'd never seen a dentist. You were her first, and then you were her husband. Four root canals and two extractions, three white caps and six gold fillings. You'd seen worse, you said. But later confessed: *Not many.*

Rose said you saved her life. Rosa said you saved her Spanish.

Last October, Mother stole Dwight Wilken's yellow sweater. She wouldn't give it up to me or Dwight or Caitlin, the attendant. I felt stupidly joyful. The sweater looked like one of yours, a gift from me, soft cotton. I thought she might remember us, our lives together, some tiny fragment.

Limp with rage and tears, Rose finally surrendered. I helped her then. I found her red sweatshirt, her blue fleece slippers. I expected her to be sad, but when the sweater was gone, it was gone—like you and me, perfectly forgotten.

I took her to the sunporch, and we sat there, warm behind windows. It was cold outside, bright blue, and the last yellow leaves quivered.

To my rescuers in the snow,

I feel you climbing toward me. I give you names—Sam LaRue, Loy Kemmerick, Neville Gaye—men who have been kind to me. Terry Simone appears in camouflage: winter white with tangled branches. He carries his own broken bones. He wears an elk's antlers. His breath hangs in the air. When he opens his mouth, white birds fly out of it.

Last night the phone rattled me from bliss and I ran and I climbed till I fell down, exhausted. As I lay me down to sleep, my father came and said, *Have I told you lately that I love you?*

I finally heard him with my heart. I finally, truly, could believe him. I woke in a bed of snow, the sky clear, the earth glittering. I saw every color spark in white: violet, green, rose, amber. The whole world trembled. I could see each particle of air. I could hear it vibrate. I thought I was dead. I thought, *This is the Kingdom.* I was free of pain and cold and loss and hunger.

I laughed out loud. Nothing hurt me.

Then an angel appeared, a small mule deer. She stepped into the clearing and stood close, barely the length of a body between us. Face in shadow, she seemed dark and her wide eyes even darker, but the fine hairs of her outline caught the sun and burned, a radiant halo.

I wanted to hold her in my arms. I wanted her to step out of her body, so that we might meet in the space between, as light on snow, as blue day breaking. It almost happened. I shivered with the pure joy of it. Then my body began to shake, violent spasms, and this was the end, my jolting return to life in the world. I coughed and my ribs pierced my lungs, and the deer leaped and was gone, and I spat blood in the snow, and the cold was so cold it scorched me.

Later, I crawled, blinded by sun on snow.

I prayed for clouds, and God answered with the wind. Needles of ice cut my face, sharp and invisible.

Now the dark light comes, now the night is falling.

Sweet Saviors, build your fire high and hold on to hope till daybreak. Your faith has made you climb. Your love has pulled you up this mountain.

I have made a bed of boughs. In soft fir, I am cradled.

I might live another night, and wake again tomorrow.
I lie down in my father's arms.
Hush now, precious one.
I hear my father's voice.
Be not afraid, my darling.

Katherine Grace Bond

SAILING TO BABYLON

THE studio was cold today. Helen could feel her nipples hardening against the chill. It seemed immoral to pose with hard nipples. The students rarely spoke to her as they studied every square inch of her skin. Sometimes there would be a chatty beginner. But among the veterans there was an unspoken rule. To speak would be to undress her further, and eye contact was out of the question.

She settled into her pose, going over the verse she was memorizing for Wednesday Bible study. *For this commandment which I command thee this day, it is not hidden from thee, neither is it far off.*

Pastor Schick had included the verse in last week's Comforting Sermon. That was how she liked to think of them, anyway. She didn't know if comfort was what Pastor Schick had in mind as he blazed through them every Sunday, cutting great swaths of righteousness through the fields of the sinful.

There was something in his cadence that caught hold of her every time. "*BE HO*-ly. If you have seen *ME*, you have *SEEN* the Father." The sounds rose and fell like the voice of the Irish tenor her father had listened to when she was a girl.

"I don't know why you go there," Cal said now and again, when he was inclined to talk. "They're a bunch of freaks."

"Yes, but they're my freaks," Helen told him. "It's not something I can explain to you."

And it wasn't.

***

Jilly had been waking up at night again. Sometimes Helen was so tired that she fell asleep in the studio, waking only with the shuffle of palettes and paper.

Today she felt the weight of her calf against the wood, the tabletop flattening her elbows. She had tried for weightlessness when she posed, like an astronaut floating, but she couldn't do it this tired. The flying wouldn't come.

There was a collective sigh as the clock hit four. Students gathered up tubes of ochre and cobalt, drifting out one by one.

"Thanks Helen." Steve began sweeping the floor as she pulled on her robe.

Helen nodded. She would have liked to walk among the easels where a dozen of her hung drying; to see what they saw when they studied her. But she felt shy doing it with Steve still here. She rarely let herself look.

She dressed in the bathroom. The building had once been an elementary school and the stalls only came up to her armpits. Every week she crammed herself into one to get dressed, even though no one ever came into the bathroom then. Dressing behind the little pink door was somehow part of reentry.

It was Susan, her childbirth instructor who had first given Helen Steve's name. Susan, who did yoga and T'ai Chi, which was almost certainly demonic.

"I know he's looking for models," she'd said. "The pay's good. There's nothing sleazy about it. You'd be helping art students. I understand if it's against your religion, but I just thought I'd pass it along, FYI. I know things are tight for you guys."

"No," Helen had said, "it's not against what I believe." She'd taken the slip of paper between her two fingers, looked it over tentatively after leaving Susan's house. She was eight months pregnant. She looked repulsive and the thought of modeling in the nude had a strange appeal.

But she had not called. She'd had her Jilly-babe, dedicated her at the church, dragged Cal around to parenting classes and baby swim lessons, joined the women's Bible study and stopped eating Dove Bars for six months.

Then they'd got broke. Really broke. Cal's Mobile Mechanic business wasn't getting enough jobs and they'd needed to meet the insurance premium and the rent was late. Helen had been inventorying the cupboards the morning she decided: Three cans tomato sauce, one can tuna, eight ounces spaghetti. The two pounds of lentils would get them through a few days if she made soup and there were chicken backs in the freezer. She looked at her Jilly-babe sleeping in her crib in the living room and felt guilty-guilty-guilty that she hadn't gone back to the admissions office. She had meant to go back when her three months were up. Truly she had. But by that time Jilly was smiling real smiles and rolling over and Helen found herself crying for no reason and dropping dishes and the thought of that gray padded cubicle gave her a ridiculous sense of panic.

"Don't go back," Cal had said one morning as she slammed suits into a pile for the dry cleaners. "Stay home with the baby if that's what you want. We'll make do."

She'd loved him then for reading her mind in a way he usually couldn't. And she'd hated herself for saying, "Do you really mean it?" when she knew he didn't and "Yes, let's," when she knew she was piling a burden on him she should have shared.

That was, Helen told herself, why she had fished out the phone number Susan had given her. It was why she could feel noble in offering her body, on Mondays, to the Academy for Realist Art.

She'd told Cal she was a kind of teacher's assistant, reassuring herself that it wasn't really a lie. He never questioned the paychecks she brought home. Why should he question them?

Cal was in the kitchen when Helen got home. Jilly was banging her tray, calling out "YA, YA, YA," while bean halves flew up and stuck to the wall beside her. Cal was eating a bowl of ice cream. Maple nut. He nodded when he saw her and motioned to the freezer with his spoon.

"No thanks." Helen wet a cloth and wiped off Jilly, her tray and the wall. "It was an interesting class," she said. "We're learning about shading. I never thought of darkening something to show light, but it works. You know what I mean?"

"Yeah," said Cal. "Uh huh." He stuck his bowl in the sink. "Guy called from Ottenville while you were gone. Wants me to look at his carburetor." He checked his hands before placing them on her shoulders and running them down her arms.

Helen leaned her head against his chest. He smelled of grass clippings and gasoline. A good smell. She felt her nipples harden again as he pulled away.

Wednesday it was Rahab that got Helen going. Carole was leading the women's Bible study that day — a large pillowy sister in the Lord with rings on all ten fingers. She always crossed her ankles as she sat creaking in the folding chair, and tapped her foot whenever she had a revelation, which was often.

"Would anyone like to share their answer to question six?"

Helen ran her finger down the sheet. She always had to write small on the narrow lines. There was never enough room to say what she needed to, not enough space to write her way to the answers.

"*According to Joshua 2, verse 8, why did Rahab, the prostitute, hide the Israelite spies?*"

"Was she really a prostitute?" asked Helen. "The footnote says she may have been an innkeeper."

"She was a prostitute," said Carole decisively. "But God used her even so."

"Prostitutes are used to being used," Helen quipped.

Marilyn, Vicki and Davis shifted in their chairs.

"The point is," said Carole, "that Rahab feared God and that made her righteous."

"But she betrayed her own people." Helen felt her voice rising and tried to speak more calmly. "She could have warned them the Israelites were coming. She could have turned over the spies. Those were her neighbors, the people she lived with!"

Davis looked horrified. "Well, she saved her family. Remember Helen, the Jerichites were pagans. Rahab was lucky to get out."

Pagans. That's right. Helen didn't know why she was so riled up about this. Rahab and her scarlet cord and her flax stalks. Rahab bringing in strangers in the night. *There goes Rahab again. Children, stay close to your mother.* Rahab didn't draw water at the same time as the other women. Rahab washed her rags out in the stream alone. No wonder two angels of death had moved her with their offer to throw her a rope.

Helen didn't say any of this. She took her pen and drew circles around the numbers on the sheet. Carole was taking prayer requests.

"How is it with Cal?" Vicki turned to her. "Did he listen to the tapes Jim sent?" Helen didn't want to tell her Cal had taped over "God's Call to Manhood" with some Bob Marley.

"He's about the same," she supplied. Vicki nodded sympathetically. "We'll keep praying." She squeezed Helen's shoulder.

Prayer was routine. Helen could spill them out without remembering what she had said five seconds after. "Lord, we just pray that you would just touch Stacy's mother and bring healing to her body and for Carole, Lord that you would grant her rest and refreshment this weekend as she goes to Marriage Enrichment with Dan and that Lord, you would just keep your hand on Davis's son as he resists temptation in the public school."

It occurred to her to wonder why the Lord preferred to be addressed in the subjunctive. She put the thought away, wondering instead why prayer had become so dry. Gannet Road Community Church was a bit more staid than the tent meetings of her teens where she had been saved. She remembered how the prayer team had laid their hot hands on her and shouted the Devil down. She had *felt* something then.

She'd felt as if her lips had been touched with a live coal and the burning was not unpleasant. It had stayed with her a long time. Sometimes it came back when she was alone.

She drifted to the sanctuary with the rest of the ladies. She closed her eyes and tried to let the music wash over her. She tried to leave her body and ascend to the throne of God. It worked sometimes – the gold lampstands, the lapis lazuli, it was all there. But she could never smell God, or hear him and the image lasted only a split second before her feet were back on the carpet between the padded pews.

After that, she tried pondering her unworthiness, but it made her smile too much to think what Carole would say if she saw a painting of her, stretched out nude on someone's living room wall.

She looked at Carole in the front pew, the skin on her arms wobbling in the name of the Lord as she pumped her hands back and forth in the air. "Jesus, oh Jesus." It seemed sacrilegious the way Carole belted it out. Helen confessed these uncharitable thoughts and tried to find a good counterpoint to the melody.

She picked Jilly up in the nursery at the same time Carole was getting her Martha. "Don't forget Friday night," Carole chirped, giving Jilly's cheek a pat. "Dr. Melvin is coming from the Creation Institute to speak on *Debunking Darwinism*. Why don't you bring Cal? It'll really witness to him."

Helen hoisted Jilly onto her hip. "I don't know what's so all-fired evil about Darwinism."

She wouldn't have said it if Carole hadn't mentioned Cal that way. But it had set her off. She regretted it as soon as she saw the hurt look on Carole's face.

"Oh, well Helen, you know," she faltered. "All that evolution they're teaching in the schools – it's confusing. It's an attack on our children." She stopped abruptly and patted

Helen's arm. "You wait 'til they start teaching it to Jilly, then you won't have such warm feelings toward Mr. Darwin."

She gathered up Martha and her bag and departed, calling out, "See you on Friday," with an air of finality that made it so.

Helen left, smarting, through another door. She leaned into the warm spring breeze as she pushed Jilly's stroller up the hill. Her sandals hit the pavement in a steady beat. *Rahab,* they slapped with each step, *Rahab.*

She turned left instead of right at the top, taking the long way home. Jilly chortled and banged her palms on the stroller as it bumped along the dirt path into the woods. Helen savored the feel of earth under her shoes. Cal liked the woods. Long ago, they had made love in the woods near Noblesville. She remembered her guilty longing as she'd clung to him, feeling the moss press into her skin. She'd been eighteen and born-again, much to her parents' Episcopalian chagrin, and was heavy with the knowledge that neither they nor Downey Brook Pentecostal Temple would be pleased with her.

She stopped for a moment and watched a squirrel making an aerial path from cedar to birch and up until it disappeared. She felt lifted by its ascension. If she strained hard enough, she almost felt she'd see over the treetops.

Jilly brought her back to earth, raising up her arms from the stroller, crying, "Ah, ah!" Helen lifted her out and sat down on a log to nurse. Jilly patted Helen's breast and grinned up at her, her mouth full of milk. Helen traced the dimples on the chubby elbows and was alive for the first time that day.

Monday Helen imagined herself a ship. Blue with sails the color of a yolk. She was sailing to Babylon with a cargo of harps and incense.

She shifted to a new pose, sitting, with her chin on one knee, her other leg dangling. Three students put fresh paper on their easels. Steve had a Joni Mitchell tape going, which made her want to dance. David danced naked before the Lord. The thought fluttered through her mind, almost blasphemous. She felt the weight of herself on the table and tried to pray, but all that would come to her was "if I should die before I wake ..."

Cal's eyes this morning were so hungry it frightened her—as if she'd given too much away.

Now she was marooned, shipless and cargoless. She forced herself to let her leg down and leaned back on her palms in a gesture of surrender, listening to the hallway echo of someone climbing the stairs and tramping along the wood floor.

Such high ceilings this building had. Everything always echoed. Helen wondered why they had needed such high ceilings. How had the teachers hung mobiles and crepe paper for parties?

The footsteps stopped at the door. Helen heard the sudden deep intake of breath, so familiar it made her turn her head to the sound. Cal, in mechanic's coveralls, framed in the doorway. Hosea in oil.

In a blurred second he was across the room, looming in front of her like a shield. He reached for her without a word and she let him take her, let him gather her in his greasy arms. He pulled up the sheet she had been posing on and covered her with it as if she was Jilly. Then he strode from the room, leaving her clothes, leaving Steve and his class in a momentary stupor. She heard them gathering at the door as Cal carried her downstairs. They were calling out, "Wait!" and "He can't do that!" and "She has every right –"

She buried her head in Cal's shoulder and did not look back at them. *I should be outraged,* she thought. Outraged. She was being humiliated. Yes, humiliated. No one could own her. Not even Cal.

She could feel the calluses where Cal's hand brushed against her breast. He set her in the truck cab and tucked the sheet around her, his face unreadable.

It wasn't until their driveway that he spoke. "Got a call from the school," he said. "Fan belt. Some guy who's taking a class there. Fixed it. Thought I'd come up and say hi." He sat behind the wheel for a moment, not looking at her. Then he got out of the truck, closed the door carefully and walked into the house.

Helen climbed out of the seat, wrapping the sheet around her like a cape. She stood in the driveway, feeling the gravel cut into her feet, and shivered.

The house was dark still. She watched the front window for Cal but didn't see him. *I should go in and start dinner,* she thought as she walked the path through the side yard, into the grove of alders that stood fifty paces from the back door.

The trees cut off her view of the house entirely. She pressed the balls of her feet into the duff and let the sheet slide from her shoulders. The marks of Cal's hands were on her hips and arms, black and smeared, but not bruising. She touched them, coating her hands with oil, raised up her arms, feeling her nakedness as a kind of strange completion, and sang with the ringing of the alder boughs, "Jesus, oh Jesus!"

❄

Alice Mattison
Glimmer Train

THE BAD JEW

> "I'll eat on a fast day, a bad Jew, exultant,
> happy beyond fear of my maker, my God."
>
> from "A Bad Jew" by Joyce Peseroff

FOR one year, at fourteen, I went to synagogue. I liked a ceremony during which the rabbi carried the Torah up and down the aisles, but on the whole I was restless, vocal with objections. My parents had joined the temple at my request, but didn't go there; presently their membership lapsed. To them religion was a simple matter: we were Jewish, we should always say we were Jewish, we should eat traditional Jewish foods along with our ham and shellfish, and that was enough.

Years later my mother told me that her immigrant parents dressed up on the High Holy Days and went to the movies, letting the neighbors think they were in *shul*. I imagine my grandparents serene as they carried out this deception, but as I grew up, still defiantly irreligious, I never became serene about anything.

"The entire content of Jewish services is 'God's good, we're Jewish, God's good, we're Jewish,'" I'd say to one of my more observant cousins. "And I'm not so sure God's good."

But envy complicated my impatience when, invariably, the cousin would reply, "I follow the laws that make sense and ignore the rest. I just want the children to know they're Jewish." When I married, it was not to a Jew. Children of a Jewish mother are Jewish, but even after my marriage broke up and I was alone with my son and daughter, taking lovers as wild-eyed as possible while soberly working as an editor, I didn't know how to make my Jewish children know what they were.

Eric Teak, a flamboyant man who was not a Jew and not my lover, was the publisher of the Boston environmental magazine *Aqua* when I was its editor. When I worked for him, Eric was in his sixties– ten or fifteen years older than I– with messy gray hair, a belly, and the smooth speaking voice of a younger man. He belonged to the rich Boston family whose foundation paid *Aqua*'s bills. He wasn't married, not then. While interviewing me for the job, Eric offered coffee. I declined, then wondered as he abruptly left the room and returned, hurrying, to set down a glass of water. Confused, I took a sip.

He shook his head, and into the water stuck a long middle finger, which seemed to swell as I stared. He flicked droplets at me. The gesture was all but obscene but I guess it also resembled baptism, because I heard myself say, "I'm Jewish."

"I'm not," he said. Then he said, "Water." The magazine dealt with water pollution, endangered aquatic mammals, depleted fishing grounds, rivers restored to cleanliness. "Can you take water seriously?"

I said I could, and tried to make sense of him.

Nobody worked at *Aqua* but Eric and me. "How's your sex life, Ruth?" he said, passing through the open space in the middle of the office on my third or fourth day.

"None of your business," I replied pleasantly, trying to decide just how much I minded him. (My sex life was all right. For a few years I'd had a lover who lived in New York.) Another time, Eric asked, "Ruth, do you still menstruate?"

One day, downtown, I stopped to look at posters and photographs mounted on a kiosk: students were protesting foreign sweatshops run by American companies. That night I had a dream. Eric stood near me as I proofread galleys at our metal table. The story was about monthly self-examination of the breasts, and I asked him, "What has this to do with water?"

"How often do you examine your breasts, Ruth?" Eric said in the dream, as he might have in life. He stretched an arm across the table and squeezed my left breast through my sweater. "You have cancer," he said, "but it's a good kind of cancer. I'll just cut it out." He took a Swiss army knife from his pocket and opened the blade.

"I'd rather have my doctor do it," I said, and awoke. As I opened my eyes I remembered, from the protest wall I'd glanced at the day before, a photograph of a young woman. Its caption was a quote: "My boss touches my breasts."

A few months after I took that job, Eric and I hired a young man named Tibby to type, answer the phone, and help out. My children's age, Tibby had left college to train dolphins in Florida, then returned home to Boston because his grandmother was dying. Though it was late fall, Tibby wore no coat to his interview at our office; a long green woolen scarf was twisted around his neck. While we spoke, as the three of us sat around the metal table in the office's central room, Tibby seemed to play with something, and then he dropped it and had to scramble to retrieve it: a red wooden yo-yo. Unselfconsciously, he wound the long cord tightly while Eric stared, and only then put the yo-yo into his pocket.

Tibby looked fragile in appearance, like a man on stilts who might fall. He didn't seem impressively efficient, but he was the only applicant we cared to remember after a series of interviews. "How do they capture those dolphins?" Eric demanded of me, as we sat alone, making the decision. "Are they allowed to mate?"

"We need someone *good* here," I said. I admired Tibby's interest in the dolphins and the grandmother.

"Moral or competent?"

"Moral."

"Are we bad?" said Eric. We hired Tibby, who might or might not have been moral but continued to be noticeable, untwisting that green scarf as he arrived, talking, every day. Like my children, Tibby had grown up calling adults by their first names, and sometimes I wished he was slightly in awe of us. He and Eric argued about those dolphins, and the morality of confining any animal. Aging, untrammeled Eric hated zoos and aquariums, however well run, but Tibby believed in the capacity of right-thinking people to do anything right. He did his work, but slowly. His friends visited him at the office, silently watching us or interjecting opinions of their own. Tibby was learning to do tricks with the yo-yo, which looked tiny hanging from his outstretched bony hand, held high above the ground. Occasionally I had to interrupt him with a task as the thing swooped and wobbled. When he wasn't learning tricks, he kept the yo-yo on his lap or on the table, twisting its string on his fingers, or rolling it until it clattered to the floor.

When the three of us were alone one day, Eric paused before entering his office to ask me, "Do Jews believe in original sin?"

"How should I know?" I said. I had an office of my own, but I preferred the light at the metal table, and I was proofreading there.

He said, "You've expressed interest in morality. I'm a Christian, and I believe in original sin. The first thing you ever said to me was 'I'm Jewish'– not that I overhear you praying in Hebrew. Not that a Star of David bounces on your breasts."

"My breasts are my own business," I said. "In what sense are you a Christian? Do you go to church?"

"Yes." He brought his big face close to mine.

"Why haven't they thrown you out for thinking about sex all day long?"

"Sex is part of God's creation," said Eric.

Tibby turned from the copying machine and said, "I'm half Jewish."

"Do Jews believe in original sin?" said Eric, now turning the other way.

"I was raised Episcopalian. My mother's Episcopalian."

It turned out that Tibby's mother went to Eric's church. "Anglo-Catholic," Eric explained to me. "High church. Bells and smells."

"Do they know life is complicated?" I said. "I never found a synagogue where they knew life is complicated."

"That's the main thing Jews know," said Eric. "How hard did you look?"

"I'm not respectable enough for organized religion," I said.

"What an angry lady," said Eric. "Not enough sex. That guy from New York doesn't show up often enough. Or you're resisting him."

"That's a boring assumption," I said. "I'm angry, so it must be sex. Isn't that a Christian idea? Sex is evil? Jews don't think like that."

"Oh, everyone thinks like that," said Eric, disappearing into his office. Then he stuck his head out and called, "Except me." The door closed again.

"Hey, Ruth," Tibby said, pausing at my desk, his arms laden with light, hot pages from the copier, his eyes bright. "Did your parents think sex is evil?"

"No," I said. "They thought it was foolish. But what are we doing to your young mind, sonny?"

"Don't worry about me," said Tibby, and carried off his pile of copies. When Eric next emerged, Tibby hurried to stand just opposite him, raised an index finger, and in the dazzled tone in which Eric himself proposed story ideas, said, "'What Do Walruses Think About Sex?'" He paused. "'What Do Fish Think Of Sex?'" Another pause. "'What Do Algae Think About Sex?'"

"Write 'em up, I'll print 'em," said Eric, and clapped Tibby's thin shoulder.

Tibby took that opportunity to ask for a week off without pay. His grandmother was had not died after all, and he wanted to visit his friends in Florida, to see the dolphins. "I'll find out everything you want to know, Eric," he said. "If I write a story about dolphins, will you pay my plane fare?"

"You're always talking about writing stories. How do I know you'll even come back?"

"I'll come back."

The office was quiet without Tibby, and though I had to do my own filing and copying, I could concentrate more easily without his ebullience and his yo-yo. The day he was to return I came to work a little late. Eric was sitting at the metal table, his head down, and he pointed wordlessly at the answering machine, then stood up, making a strange, alarmed noise, and took me in his arms as I stepped toward it. Tibby had drowned in Florida, swimming in calm water off the end of a friend's boat. The message, which I finally made myself listen to, was from his sister.

Eric and I did slipshod work that week. We hugged often, stopped making jokes and talking about sex. I dreamed about Eric and Tibby and me as if we were a family– the three of us in a car, the three of us walking on a windy sidewalk. Tibby's funeral, in Eric's church, was attended by heartbreaking crowds of young people who looked as if they hardly ever got that dressed up or entered such a building. I looked for the ones who'd come to the office. It turned out Tibby's real name was Theobald.

I didn't like the funeral. I felt rage at the priest who seemed to think that putting on brightly colored vestments and executing stylized movements made a difference, rage at the young people who'd missed seeing Tibby disappear, rage at myself. I could have protested when he asked to go. Our gathering, miles from the scene of Tibby's death, indoors with closed doors, felt misguided, irrelevant, maybe heartless– as if our presence on the shore might have saved him, as if staring out at Eric's complicated ocean could have rescued Tibby.

Eric and I sat close to the front of the church, in a side section. When it was time for communion, he squeezed my shoulder and stood to join the slow procession toward the altar. Suddenly alone, I watched him advance. He looked dignified because he seemed to let himself look foolish– or, rather, unprotected. He let himself be seen doing what he wanted to do. I was reminded of something and then realized, with a smile I couldn't suppress, that it was of the way a good, serious, middle-aged man– like my New York lover– moves toward you when he's decided to take off his clothes and make love to you: dignified in the acknowledgment of the self.

Eric reached the front of the line and knelt to receive the bread. A moment before he had to, he opened his mouth, and I saw his lips and tongue. I watched him receive comfort from the priest, a man his own age. They were like two business-men conferring, except for one man's clothing, except for their postures, except for what they did with their bodies, one feed-ing the other like a parent and a baby, like a bird and a baby.

Without discussion we walked a block or two in the cold. I thought we were venting emotion through aimless roaming, but Eric steered me into a Starbucks. Maybe he always went there after church. "Or we could keep going and find a syna-gogue," he said, as we sat down.

"A synagogue?"

"Tibby was half Jewish. We should pray at a synagogue too. Would that help?"

"Help Tibby? Or help me?"

"Tibby's dead, and I don't see any Jews but you around. The man at the counter doesn't look Jewish."

"It wouldn't help me," I said. Without further remarks, Eric went to the counter and returned with two cups of coffee and a handful of sugar packets and cream containers. We both drank the coffee black, without sugar, and I arranged and re-arranged the containers of sugar and cream as we sat in si-lence.

"Do you believe in heaven?" Eric asked then.

"No."

"That would make it harder."

"Do *you*? Do you believe in heaven?" I didn't know any-body believed in heaven. The optimism of it stunned me.

"Of course, it's impossible to imagine heaven," he said. "I think of clean water, but what does that mean? I would like to believe in heaven."

He spoke so quietly and seriously that I didn't say, "Like to! Well, *like* to!" and indeed he continued, "and maybe I do."

I believed not in heaven, but in the poems I'd read and written in college, in my love for my children– not that I found anything, that long winter, to comfort me for the loss of somebody else's child. I planned to visit his parents but only sent a note, not just out of cowardice. With a magazine to put out and without Tibby's help– we didn't replace him– I worked late most nights.

I didn't go near a synagogue as an adult, I didn't do anything identifiably Jewish, but on every holy day I knew just when sundown decreed candle-lighting and the end of work. I knew what I would have been doing if I had been observant. The religion I didn't practice was not my cousins' comfortable, up-to-date compromise but some unforgiving orthodoxy, the Jewishness that takes over life: defiantly, I did not follow law after law. I didn't follow them so thoroughly that my son grew up apparently unmindful of religion, but somehow my daughter, Laura, learned how to be slightly Jewish, and unlike me, was serenely comfortable as she cheerfully lit the odd Hanukkah candle, attended services now and then, or sent Jewish New Year and Passover cards to my parents, who received them happily. My mother steadfastly cooked on holidays, my daughter was grateful, and both would ignore me when I'd demand "How could God allow Hitler?" looking left and right over my matzo ball soup. But my mother was getting old, and even the matzo ball soup had been omitted lately. The year Tibby died, Laura phoned me early in March to ask, "Is Grandma making a Seder?"

"When did Grandma ever make a Seder?" Soup wasn't a Seder.

"Once, she did." Once, when Laura was about eight, she had. An uncle had read the prayers and the long Exodus story. Other years, the children and I had sometimes been invited to Seders at the houses of the cousins. We took turns reading aloud, we swallowed bits of matzo spread with this and that.

That March I wasn't doing well. Grief for Tibby had dulled but not lessened. I hadn't known him well enough to mourn properly. I didn't miss him, in truth. He'd been in my life so briefly; he was gone and things were as before. I knew no one else who knew him, except Eric, who didn't speak of him. But I didn't feel better. Sometimes I didn't remember why I felt bad. I rarely saw my lover, but had no inclination to spend more time with him, or break up. Later we lived to-gether, then did break up– but that was all to come.

"Do you think you could put on a Seder?" Laura now wanted to know.

"Good God, no."

"I mean the two of us, but in your apartment." Laura was a junior at Brandeis, outside Boston, living in an apartment with several roommates. Brandeis was founded by Jews, and it closes for a week at Passover. "I don't want to feel aban-doned," she said. Some of her friends were traveling home to Seders. "I don't want to go out for pizza that night."

"I'm sorry, honey," I said.

I hung up the phone and looked at the calendar. Passover was in three weeks. I'd heard from no cousins. I couldn't be expected to think about Passover because I was grieving for Tibby, the boy with the yo-yo. Then, of course, I called Laura back– my own child, the child who was safe– and agreed to put on a Seder. The next time we spoke, I asked her, "But who'll conduct it? Who'll be the uncle? Who'll be the Jew?"

"I've been to Seders, and so have some of my friends."

"Doesn't someone have to take charge?" I had already in-vited my friend Annie, but she wasn't Jewish and didn't be-lieve in anything. So I invited Eric. "You're the Jew," I told him. "The believer."

"I'm the Jew."

"I'll meet the bad man," said Annie on the phone.

"Oh, he's not bad."

The Seder was work. Laura had papers to write and no car, so I bought Haggadahs, the books we had to read. I bought what had to go on the Seder plate. I bought matzo and lots of parsley. I bought groceries to Laura's specifications: this was also a dinner party. She promised to cook, along with her friends, and when I came home from work the day of the Seder, three girls were in the apartment, and potfuls of food had been prepared: chicken, rice.

Laura followed me into my bedroom and closed the door. One friend had told her that rice wasn't allowed on Passover, while the other had brought a cake– not a Passover cake, just a chocolate cake.

"If you're going to worry about rules, I'm leaving now," I said. I had brought plenty of wine– not Passover wine, just wine– and in my socks I went back to the kitchen and poured a glass for myself. Laura clutched at her light curls, a habit since babyhood, as she tried to organize my inadequate plates and silverware while her friends washed vegetables. "You're right, the food will be fine," she said then, smiling at me.

Eric, in jacket and tie, was the only man at the Seder. Laura had invited her flute teacher, who met Annie on the front porch. They came upstairs together, looking pleased and expectant, which made me feel like a fraud. As we gathered around the table, I imagined Eric looking at this roomful of women. He'd picture us bare-breasted, I decided. The image in my mind– our varied breasts (and Annie had had a mastectomy) above the mismatched plates– was wholesome, not erotic. Laura lit the candles. She knew the prayer in English.

Crowded around the table, we looked in the book and explained to one another what to do. Laura was bossy but happy. She began the reading, and then we all took turns, joining in for the responses in earnest chorus. I kept forgetting to start at the back of the book and proceed forwards. Some of the Jewishness felt odd, some surprisingly familiar, and I tried to count up just how many Seders the cousins had lured me to. Eric participated loudly and confidently. We blessed the wine and he drained his first glass, while the rest of us sipped. We ate parsley, we broke matzo. The flute teacher– a black woman with long hair coiled behind her head and elegant pewter jewelry– beamed, saying she'd always hoped to attend a Seder. "This is great," said Annie more than once. She, Eric, and the flute teacher seemed like benevolent parents at a school play.

One of Laura's friends wanted to ask the four questions. She knew the beginning in Hebrew. I could see my quick-moving, hair-clutching daughter mind that, and mind the fact that she didn't know a word of Hebrew, which made me briefly regret my life. "Sorry, Jen, it's my house," Laura said then, though it wasn't her house, and she asked the questions in English.

Seders like ours were apparently not unforeseen by who-ever thought up the idea. The ceremony itself was in part about not understanding it. "Why is this night different from all other nights?" asked Laura, who might well ask. It turned out there were no more questions, just elaborations of the first question. "On all other nights we eat vegetables and herbs of all kinds, while on this night we must eat bitter herbs." Chil-dren were supposed to ask these questions, though at Seders I'd attended, self-satisfied children knew more than anyone else present.

Before long the book described more questioning chil-dren, the wise son and the wicked son, the good Jew and the bad. The wicked son asked "What is the meaning of this Pass-over service which God commanded you?" It was my turn to read, and I read that the wicked son was to be abandoned to his wickedness. "You," he says, not "us." The others were to tell him that God had led them out of Egypt. Presumably the wicked son had been elsewhere when this happened, leading his interesting secular life.

"I want to defend the wicked son," Eric announced. "The wicked son's failure is a failure of imagination, nothing more."

"What's worse than a failure of imagination?" I asked. I would never change– I would always be the wicked son– but I would not deny my wickedness. We continued with the simple son and the naive son, and then came the story itself: the Israelites in Egypt, Moses, God. The ten plagues.

"The ten plagues are barbarous," I said. "I don't like God."

"A nice God wouldn't last a week in *this* universe," Eric said from across the table. "That's why the wicked son belongs in the family." He was sitting right at the corner, straddling a leg, and the corner poked into his belly. His napkin was stuck into his belt though we weren't going to get our dinner for several more pages. He smiled benevolently as if he were God's consultant in the matter of hardening Pharaoh's heart so as to require the ten plagues.

"But it's his universe," said the flute teacher. "Couldn't he provide any universe he wanted?"

Eric said, "We picked this one, and we go on preferring it."

"I don't prefer it," I said, thinking of Tibby.

"You wouldn't like a namby-pamby universe," Eric said. "Eve tells the snake, 'No thanks,' – we get a boring world."

"Hasn't our taste just been spoiled by the world we've got?" said the flutist, but her question was unanswered. Laura and her friends were shouting the ten plagues.

To express our moderate sorrow over the sufferings of the Egyptians, we were to dip a finger in our glasses of wine at the mention of each plague– blood, frogs, lice, boils. . . and shake a drop on our plates. Eric stuck all his fingers in, one after another, and flicked extravagant drops, then licked wine off his fingers. "I extend my pleasure over the sufferings of the Egyptians."

"You're a character, aren't you?" said the flute teacher.

The Hebrews fled in a hurry, with unleavened bread, and the Egyptians followed. The Red Sea parted for the Israelites, but drowned the pursuing Egyptians, and we offered thanks for several pages, then finally ate our dinner, with normal conversation. Then, just when I began to think we wouldn't return to the final prayers, Laura proclaimed with good-humored fake surprise, "The *afikomen* is missing!" Half a piece of matzo had been wrapped in a napkin sometime earlier. Laura had hidden it, and the rest of us were supposed to search.

More ritual felt tedious, not just I think to me, but we stood and followed Eric, who joyfully flung open closet doors and even pulled out drawers and peeked ostentatiously into them. On our third trip through the living room, I noticed a book at an unaccustomed angle, and withdrew the blue-and-white checked napkin, which was folded around the piece of matzo.

"You took so long!" Laura exulted, like a little girl. "May I have the *afikomen*, please?"

"No," I said, as the others returned to their places. I was surprised to hear myself. "No, I want something in return." I suppose I'd half-consciously remembered part of another Seder, because the young people assured us that, indeed, the *afikomen* is always redeemed.

"I forgot," said Laura. "I didn't plan a reward. Does anyone have a reward for my mother?"

"You won't give me the reward I want," I blurted out, angry now with the entire evening.

Laura said, "We can't bring Tibby back!" His name hadn't been mentioned, but backs straightened and breath was drawn in; everyone knew the story.

"What made that kid an Egyptian?" I said, in tears. "Why didn't the sea open for him?" I heard myself give a low cry, then lowered the wrapped matzo and crushed it in my folded hands.

The *afikomen* remained unredeemed. After a while I sat down, feeling foolish, and handed the lumpy package to Laura, who distributed bits of matzo around the table. Now we spoke more quickly, thanking God yet again. Then it was time to fill a glass of wine for the prophet Elijah, and to open the house door so as to let him enter.

"The apartment door will do," Laura said. I lived in a second-floor apartment in a two-family house. But I wanted cold air on my face, and a moment alone. I opened the apartment door, then walked down the stairs. Halfway down, I heard a heavy tread and turned to see Eric following me. "We still haven't redeemed the *afikomen*," he said. "I thought what to give you."

"Forget it." The house was old, and tattered rubber mats were nailed to the stairs. Eric tripped and scrambled, recovering himself, and I took his arm. We made our way down the stairs like an elderly couple, the old parents banished from the happy table for bitterness and sorrow. I opened the front door and we stepped onto the little wooden porch. The air was cold and pleasant. Elijah was visiting at the house across the street, too– or else those people just didn't bother to keep their front door closed.

"You can close it now," came a voice from upstairs. "Come back!"

But Eric withdrew something from his jacket pocket: Tibby's red yo-yo.

I gave a cry, then said, "Where did you get it?" I grasped it as if it were holy, an object sacred to my people– as if Eric didn't know what he had– and closed my hand around it.

"He left it in the office. I found it, weeks later, under a pile of papers."

"And you kept it? You carry it around? And you'd give it to me?" I slowly understood that if Eric had it at that moment, he had it all the time.

"Yes."

I kissed him on the lips. Across the street, the house door was still open. I wanted to see someone come and close it. Waiting, in my mind I found a rough map of Greater Boston, with house doors open here and there. Beyond Boston, all through New England, some people opened a door for Elijah. It was an intrinsically good act, I decided, to open a door, now and then, to Elijah. "Everywhere are Jewish people," my grandmother used to say. In New York and New Jersey– my mind moved down the coast, omitting and then restoring Long Island– more open doors. If Elijah or anyone else cared to enter, that was temporarily possible. Eric, who stood behind me, flung an arm over my shoulder and across my body, so his elbow collided with my breast and his hand grasped my arm. "Come on," he said, turning me around. We lingered a moment longer, while the door still stood open to the cold spring air, then climbed the stairs to the noisy dining room, where illicit cake had been served. Eric and I sat down to eat cake and praise God some more– God who could move the ocean aside, but mostly didn't.

❄

Valerie Laken
The Antioch Review

COVENANT

BEFORE you open these notebooks, Mrs. Eronvie, please let me explain a few things. I know you have been tested. I envision you now in that armchair by your front window, opening this box, these notebooks darkened with my pencils, and even from this distance of over a thousand miles, I can picture your face clouding over with surprise, then confusion, hope, and finally, something akin to fear. Maybe you'll open the front door and look out on the street for signs of a delivery person. But I am long gone.

Please understand, I have no wish to frighten you or raise your hopes beyond this meager consolation, so let me say up front that there will be no material evidence here. What's done is irreversible. Lay your hopes to rest, or put them elsewhere. Forgive my cruelty. Hundreds of times I have begun this letter, praying for ways to soften this message, but each time all I am granted is a clearer sense of how terrible these words and pictures will look to you. So I stop. Each time I have stopped, a pathetic failure, and I go to bed nights with this truth, which is your truth, rumbling through me, and I lie awake trying to devise some other way to give it back to you. After losing so much, you are at least entitled to this.

When this started five years ago I was a different man: foul-hearted and confused, swollen with ill wishes for the world. My mother had just died, my mother, not yet fifty, not even gray-haired, left mangled and cold on a hospital gurney on the wrong side of Milwaukee. And only thirteen people at her funeral. Yes, I can say now that perhaps I took it too hard, perhaps I did have trouble *getting over it*, as my girlfriend Sarah kept saying. But surely you can imagine the rage a young man feels when an eighty-year-old half-wit runs his mother into the ditch on a frozen highway and leaves her lying there, expiring, until at dawn a trucker finally finds her? Her temperature was eighty-one when they brought her in. All the doctors' efforts that morning were for naught; she was damaged beyond repair.

I remember the minister at her service telling me, *God has a plan*, as if those words could mop it all up, make sense of it. The only thing I could do at the time was roll my eyes at Sarah: *This guy doesn't know anything.* That was my twenty-two-year-old logic. Ignorant. I couldn't see then, it was not in the plan for me to see it then, that we are mere stewards of His mysteries. I just didn't want that man telling me about my mother. Sarah and I hurried to the car and slandered him all the way home. We noted his foul coffee breath, his moist hands, his way of looking beyond us and through us. And his Bible, his vestments, all his *backward, hollow notions*, we mocked them all the way to my mother's house, which was beginning to smell stale and damp already.

You're thinking that none of this concerns you. But it does, you'll see. Only I have to tell it to you in full, because that's the only way it makes any sense to me.

I used to think I had only done what anyone in my position would do. And then for a while I thought I had done what God's hand moving through me had wanted. But lately, Mrs. Eronvie, even those comforts are fading.

I was dividing my time that spring between the refrigerator room at work and the empty halls of my mother's house. At the grocery store I took milk and yogurt containers out of crates, lining them up along the shelves by date; at my mother's house I stripped the shelves and packaged away the details of her life. I had no idea where the boxes would go in the end, where on earth I would send them. Some nights I called the last number I had ever reached my father at, and though I couldn't tell any more if it was his voice or someone else's on the answering machine, I recorded lists of items for that man, whoever he was: paisley ties, old suits, army watches, albums. *Do you want this, do you want this?* He never claimed any of it; he may have been long gone all over again. At first Sarah would call me when it got late: *Are you coming home soon, baby?* I would sit with stacks of blouses in my lap, folding them carefully to minimize wrinkling, and I would murmur idle lies into the receiver: *I'm almost finished, this is the last of it.*

The first few times I said that, I could hear Sarah's voice melt over with relief: her boyfriend, her possible future spouse, was dutiful, not carried away; he was a responsible son, which was, after all, a good thing. He was grieving. But when she showed up at the door with her carry-out food and found me, time after time, surrounded on the floor by the same piles of photos and papers and clothes, when she began to realize that the boxes and stacks weren't really going anywhere, I'm sure she started to worry. *Honey, I think that some of this will need to be thrown away.*

By May she was done with me. I was *self-destructing*, she said. It was *painful to see.* I had dropped out of MIAD—what good was art school going to do me?—and switched to full time at Rheinlanders Grocery. I was sullen and hate-filled; I shuddered when she touched me. So one night she packed up my things and brought them over to my mother's house, after midnight. *Here,* she said. *Here, move right in. Look how easy it is.* She stood on the front porch, daring me. With her arms still trembling from carrying my things, I could feel her challenging me to see the light.

Rheinlanders is a name you know. Your patience is limited; these notebooks have you curious, so by now maybe you're only scanning this letter. Like a baby hearing its name in a jumble of otherwise useless words, you will perk up now and then, pay attention, try to make some sense of it. And it's Rheinlanders that has you shivering now. The rest of this is just the ranting of a strange man, you think. But we are not strangers, Mrs. Eronvie. We are the same.

I became a watcher of people that spring, and yes, I saw you there at Rheinlanders. Even before the incident, before Katy vanished, when she was just an idea squirming inside your belly. I would put away the morning deliveries and re-stock everything, run the inventory, and then hide out back in the refrigerator room with a radio and a notebook, sketching what I saw. I pushed a pathway through the milk cartons so I could spy through the shelves to the store on the other side. Shoppers do funny things. Scratch themselves, fix their reflections in the glass. I saw a man flash himself at a woman once, and all she did was smile. *Was that staged?* Every minute, despicable thing, and I was there to catch them, to preserve those ugly, nose-picking positions for life. *Hideous,* I would write at the top of the pictures, *Shoplifter.* I scratched furiously through my notebook, tearing back page after page. *Pervert*, if I caught a man turning to ogle a pubescent girl. *Lonely-Heart*. These were my subjects, parading before me, and I in my dim, cold room passed judgment. I'm not proud of it, Mrs. Eronvie. Pride is around my neck like a chain.

I caught you too. Pregnant, first, all bulging, with your hand under your belly as you squatted, knees splayed, mouth hanging, for your gallon of Deans 2%. A cottage cheese eater, you were, and smug, I thought. Married, with a ring, a full cart. *All the Fixings*, I scrawled as I captured you glaring at a can collector who lost his balance and bumped you in the aisle. You jumped and shuddered as if the store were yours, as if you with your burden were a precious commodity that his very touch could contaminate. *Arrogant*, was what I wrote then. I am sorry.

It is so easy, so diabolically effortless to find a reason to hate someone. *There is none righteous, no, not one*, writes Paul. Brother Allen reminds us of this fact each morning at Services. It is a good verse; I have taped it to my cabin door.

But to love, knowing well we are sick, angry people, addled with scars and sores and secrets, that is the tricky part, Mrs. Eronvie, the mystery.

I sketched Katy in your arms once, just one time, before you were parted. Katy all bundled in designer gear with her head rumpled, heavy against your chest in that blue and green strap-on baby holder. Dark hair stood up in tufts at the crown of her head, which was still misshapen slightly from birth. *Wethead*.

I am sending you back these drawings. You must understand that I have suffered too.

I ask myself, after prayers each night, when my heart should be strongest: if I could go back and relive that afternoon Katy was stolen, would I do things differently? Would I interfere with God's plan for you? If I could hide in the thicket as Abraham flashed his wet knife at his only son, would I jump forth and break his covenant, disrupting everything that was to follow? Each time I find only the same answer: the Lord Himself interrupted Abraham. He needed no human hands. To be honest, either way the story has been striking me lately as cruel, evidence not of the Lord's benevolence, but of the fact that we, cruel beasts, are indeed His creation. Like so many other movements of my mind, I keep this thought to myself here.

In any case my actions that day didn't come from faith, because I didn't have it back then. What I did that day stemmed purely from bitter, broken-hearted indifference. I wanted the whole world to suffer as I had.

Outside, the faster youngsters are already returning from their Saturday nature hike. Singing and calling, their voices rise up over the trees and trickle toward me, and already I can see a few of them emerging from the woods and filtering across the valley toward our garden. I will have to hurry. There is less than an hour of Reading Time left, and I haven't yet prepared sufficiently for dinner. Soon the main house will be filled with families, congregants, hungry and eager to celebrate. And you see, it is my turn to work the kitchen. But what does this matter to you? Maybe I am only stalling again, avoiding my task. I have wasted this many pages, this many hours, and what have I accomplished?

By now perhaps you're skimming these sketches anyway, looking in vain for that hideous moment, captured in lead under my smudging thumbs.

It isn't there.

I cannot bring your baby back. This is the best I can do.

I should have had a front row view, there behind the milk containers. The police would ask, and my old boss Theo, and the rest of the staff as well. By then everyone knew about my hiding spot. But what I said to everybody was true on that count, simple and bone-headed as the boy I was: I was out back smoking a cigarette by the dumpsters. There was the smell of rotting produce and approaching rain. The sky was that heavy pink, late-August push of storm clouds driving in. Ninety-five degrees, at least, and windless. I could feel the garbage stench sticking to my skin, so I finished my cigarette, flicked it out at the empty back parking lot, and turned to go inside.

Commotion. Lara Pipkin was coming through the back room, *Have you seen anyone with a baby?*

A baby?

Some lady lost her baby in the store. She's freaking out.

How can someone lose a baby?

I don't know, Lara said. We walked through the back rooms and out into the store.

People are so stupid, I remember saying, so full of bluster, so unaware of how swiftly, how routinely we fail ourselves and fail the world.

And in the store, there you were, up at the service counter next to Theo. You looked so frail next to his girth. Your face was white; you kept shaking your head and pointing your fingers around. *Nightmare,* you said. *Nightmare.* Theo took your elbow and said to me, *Go lock the back door, Jerry. Hurry.* I turned and hustled back through the store. They had shut off the overhead music, and things sounded strangely quiet just then, although clerks and stock boys were rushing through the aisles, and you had left Theo again and joined them. Everyone was calling out *Katy? Katy?* as if she was old enough to know her name. *Katy,* I thought, *nightmare.*

Five or ten minutes I'd been outside smoking, and all of this happened that fast. And for you, that sensation hundred-fold: thirty seconds you turned away, took a few steps, and bent down for that bag of dog food, you told Theo. Hefting it up over your shoulder awkwardly, then standing and turning back to your cart: Nothing. Baby Katy gone. She had been sleeping in her carrying seat, a blanket over her head, inside your cart. And now the whole seat gone, no sign of her anywhere.

I went to the back door and looked around outside. I saw no one, and locked the door from inside. Jingled my keys. Ran my hand through my hair. *Baby snatchers?* This was crazy. This was surely some mistake. A prank, a loophole. Some strange corporate safety drill.

I ducked into the freezer room and looked around, saw nothing unusual. All the crates and boxes in place on the shelves. No babies. I went in the supply closet, moved some buckets and containers around, listened intently for a minute. Nothing. I walked over to the meat department.

What do you think? I said to old Stanley, the butcher.

He shook his head and shrugged. *I got no baby here.*

It's got to be a mistake, right?

Creepy, Stan said, then went back to wrapping cellophane packs, and I walked back to the refrigerator room. My tape deck was on, and Robert Plant was screaming over the bass drum that thumped off the walls, and I thought, *Did I really leave the volume that high?* I crossed the room to turn it down, and when I rounded the corner I saw her. Them. Curled up in my plastic chair.

This dark little woman, so thin, her hair long and black down over her shoulders and resting on her chest. She was all twisted up in the chair, with her knees hugged to her torso, and if it hadn't been for the plastic baby seat on the floor I might not even have noticed Katy right there in her arms, in that warm tight space between her thighs and chest. The woman looked up at me, and in that moment, as her eyes caught the light like stones in the sun underwater, the song changed. Out of all the rough screaming chaos of Led Zeppelin II those first quiet acoustic chords of "Ramble On" came drifting over us. I tell you it was the only beauty I had experienced in months.

No talk, she said, holding her palm up at me. She was trembling.

Tears were streaming down this woman's cheeks, and her chest rippled with the effort of not sobbing, but the baby was fine. She was stroking the back of Katy's head, and Katy gazed up at her, mesmerized, not crying. It was the picture of motherhood. I tell you she knew what she was doing.

She knew the sadness, the misery, sparked in that moment, which would pox our lives forever. She knew it and was burning her way through it. I was stupid. All I saw was beauty.

A minute seven seconds, that part of the song lasts. A minute seven seconds of that quiet, eerie loveliness, before Robert Plant starts screaming again and everything rushes in. We were alone in that minute, with his words washing over us, alone. She stared up at me, shaking her head against my doubts, while I, like a fool, blinked back. I have replayed it all these thousands of times trying to make sense of what rose up between us as I watched her there, turning your child's face to her own breast.

Katy was hers in that moment. Mrs. Eronvie, I do know right from wrong. I am not a madman. What I mean to say is, if a stranger had seen these two together, unknowing, he would have fought to save them, keep them together, a mother and her child. That was the sacred bond they had already entered into. And you see, at that point, I knew her better than I knew you. I knew the kind of bottomed-out emptiness that can draw a person toward such acts. I was motherless, Mrs. Eronvie. These were my people. My kin.

You can't stay here, I said.

And then it all broke free. The music, the moment, the crying. Plant started screaming away, hurling his rage at us, and the woman stood up to plead with me in her broken English. Little Katy, disturbed by it all, started wailing too. They were coming toward me, and I backed away.

In her own language she whispered into Katy's ear.

She seemed to want to stay there in the refrigerator room, and I was telling her there was no way, it was cold, that they would find her soon, were looking for the baby.

There was more crying, and she rocked Katy against her chest and shoulder. I couldn't take it. These were the first people in months who didn't make me tremble with loathing, the first people I couldn't reduce to subjects, the first people to break into my dark little world and shake me. I had to get them out of there.

I thrust the baby seat into her hands. *No. No,* she resisted. She seemed to want nothing to do with it. She clung tight to Katy and turned from the baby seat as I offered it.

No steal, she said, at last remembering the word.

I almost felt her logic in that second, but I pried open her grip anyway and pushed the handle of the seat into her palm, and with my arm around her back I rushed her out of the refrigerator room. The music burst out with us when the door opened, and if we made noise, if there was crying, it may have been covered by this. I looked both ways, I scanned the back room. There was no one. I got out my keys, unlocked the door, and opened it. No one. The rain had come and was hammering down. It splashed off the cement onto our legs.

Go, I said. And then, louder, *Go!*

Her face registered the shock of it all, but she did not hesitate. I wish she had. I like to think that if I'd had even one more second alone with her, with them, I would have changed my mind, come to my senses, seen the moment for what it really was. But she squeezed Katy to her chest and slipped through my arms into the rain, running, with her dress gusting up and that unwanted baby seat banging against her thigh. She was headed for the corn field beyond the back parking lot. I let the heavy steel door slam shut behind her.

It has stayed with me all these years. Sometimes when I sit in our makeshift Sunday school, leading the children through stories of Cain and Abel, and Paul, and Mary Magdalene, I can't help wondering what Brother Allen would say if he knew my past, knew this story as I'm telling it. Would he send me home to Milwaukee, where I have no more mother's house to go to, no more boxes of clothes and papers, no more Sarah waiting to fold me safely into her life? Or would he say in his low, rumbling voice that we are not the sum of our pasts, that Paul himself was once Saul, a fierce persecutor? That the Lord has provided this dark past, so that we may know what light is?

Almost instantaneously, I knew what I had done. I paced the back room for a moment, and then rushed outside after her. Gone. I went back in the refrigerator room, sat down on that chair where she'd been, looked for a trace of her, of Katy. It was cold. There was nothing. I watched the police with their walkie-talkies checking the aisles, and when they came into the back room I cooperated. I opened everything with my keys and watched them look for any sign of foul play. As I answered their questions, my head started pounding with the awareness of how guilty I was, how much I had hurt you, and yet, at the time, I felt there was no going back.

It was the end of my shift. They thought I had helped all I could, so they dismissed me. I sat out in that parking lot a long time though, waiting. They say people come back to the scene of a crime, and I wanted her to. I wanted them to catch her, so I could have it off my back, and two or three times I got out of the car, wanting to go inside and confess my part. I lacked the courage. And then your husband pulled up in his slick car, and you rushed out to him, with your lipstick still bright, your skin unblemished, and I felt allied again to that desperate woman. You had so much, so many things, and I had helped the other side, balanced the score. That was my thinking then. I am not proud of it. But always, my heart has tugged toward the lowly, the ones with nothing, the ones who live beside an abyss they cannot fill. I see now that you are one of them, but at the time you seemed the very opposite. I pictured that woman's first baby, her own baby, dead of cancer or car accident or miscarried, and I thought, who makes these decisions? Who says which babies go to whom, which mothers are taken? If she came back, if I spotted her, I thought for a minute, couldn't I join her? We were married anyway by this transgression, and at least she had the consolation of the child.

She never came back. And though I felt righteous in that moment and for those first few days that followed, I have not managed to shake the matter so easily.

Go to your mirror and look in it, Mrs. Eronvie, if you want to see my face. Every child's wail or laughter turns my head, raises my hair. I look for her everywhere, even here, among our small group, or in the hundreds of towns we have visited on our Missions. I have not found her. My eyes, like yours, are drawn and cloudy from years of sleeplessness. I have grown wrinkles, I do not eat enough. The muscles around my mouth are pulled tight from keeping this story in for so long. And then there are the dreams, Mrs. Eronvie. What I want to know is, do you have the dreams?

Every night she hovers above me. This started almost immediately. At first they were mere flashes of images, cheery and peaceful. She would be sleeping in kangaroo-print pajamas, stretching her little legs every few minutes. I would sit up in bed, flick on the light, try to occupy myself with any other thing, but the images would burn before me, quivering like a slide projected on nothing but air.

I started sketching again, to purge. It was the only way to shake those dreams and tilt toward sleep again. I drew those tufts of dark hair growing, drew her in that mother's arms, with her fingers closed in tight fists around that woman's long dark hair. The bottle to her lips, milk welling around her mouth as she stopped sucking to smile upward, hands entwined. Sitting, with blocks, sucking one fist to her gums, her third tooth. Her first steps, in a field of grass tall enough to quell her fears of falling, her arms splayed, eyes wide with horror and delight. Once I sketched out the vision, put it on paper, she would fade and then vanish, till I was left with nothing but my sweat and guilt. The following night, she would come back, one day older.

I tried drinking, I tried sleeping pills. I tried Nyquil, codeine, pot, Valium.

I tried God. At first it was just that, one more thing to try, so I went through the motions at the back of the Church. I looked around me, wondering what the other people had to hide. The dreams came just as regularly, but faded more quickly. I could sleep for two or three hours sometimes, unhindered. When they did show up though, they became all-out dramas. I sat as a guest at her birthday parties, then went out back and showed her cousin how to wear a baseball mitt. I heard her first word, *perrito*, and saw her rocking her head side to side the first time she understood *music*. You can see for yourself, Mrs. Eronvie. There are seventeen notebooks here. It is a long, cruel catalog of my misstep, I drag it behind me like a body wherever I go. I can do it no longer.

Because I see now *who makes these decisions*, or at least, who ought to. Not man, not me, not a desperate, lonely woman, but God. I know what a terrible weight He carries in His hands, and how easy it is to slip up and let something fall.

But I want you to know the other thing that I know. She is happy, our Katy. She is loved, she is cared for. It is the one thing in my life I have no doubt of. I see her at those parties, with cakes and gifts lined up before her. People crowd the room, singing. She smiles, claps her hands, squeals if ever their attention strays. In school now, first grade I suppose, somewhere, she wears a jumper and keeps her hair in braids. She trips a lot, as you see here in the last drawing. But she lands with her palms out, ready, and though she skins them, she cries little; she is brave and tough in her long-haired way. She dusts the pebbles off, and keeps on running.

I can't be sure, Mrs. Eronvie, but I believe these images are God's way of telling me she is doing just fine without us. That she is uninjured, she is healthy, that the world is one body in Christ, one family, and she is over with her relatives now, drinking the same water as all of us. I don't know, Mrs. Eronvie, if it's a cruelty to share this story, these pictures, or if I should have done it long ago.

I worry that in these years you have become the person I was then, infected with hatred and bitterness and fear. Even before I left Milwaukee to follow the Path, this troubled me. I would drive by your house, seeing your lawn go to seed, watch you curled in that chair by your window, in your robe all day long. I checked the birth announcements every day, Mrs. Eronvie, hoping you would move on and bear another child. I prayed for it at Services, prayed for your life somehow to be restored. And when I saw the moving truck out front, I hoped in earnest that you and your husband were moving away and into a different future. But only he left, alone, in the end. I guess that was two or three years ago. I pictured you inside your empty halls, on the floor with boxes, empty clothes, a mother with no family. And then I left too. In the end not even I was there to drive by and commune.

Covenant

As Brother Allen says, maybe I am only a messenger He uses. Maybe that woman too was a messenger. Maybe these trials are set up by design, to test us and push us into one another, groping, feeble, discovering what is essential. It has taken me five hard years to understand this message, to translate it for you, and here I am hoping again that Katy will leave me when I send this, that the weight will fall away and we will all be lifted up, set free.

Please, Mrs. Eronvie, put these notebooks down and go outside. Don't make a shrine of these pictures. With her giggles and tears and night sneezes she has lived in these books for too long. We should stop staring at her. I hope you will box all this back up and burn it, make of this terrible history nothing more than dust and ashes. Or discard it with less ceremony, throw it out, as I have done with so many versions of this letter. It seems there must be one for every town, every house, every garbage can I pass. Pack this box up, Mrs. Eronvie, leave it out on the curb for any common scavenger to pick up and pilfer and wonder at ignorantly. It would feel good to be that sort of person, Mrs. Eronvie, wouldn't it?

❄

Rose Rappoport Moss
Alaska Quarterly Review

THE PATH OF LIGHTNING

THE stories keep catching in each other like necklaces in a drawer. They tangle in my mind though there's no connection except the scarf in each. It's not the same scarf, though they were probably both bright and cheap and shiny. Eric would have bought something like that. He's French and tight with money though generous in other ways. He was a child during the war, and those years of chaos and hunger mark him still, like granite that rises to the surface in New England fields.

The other was the scarf Vera chose, probably also rayon. Vera's a young journalist after all, in a poor country, and the scarf was not something she would usually wear. She wanted it to distract the guards at the hospital lounging in camouflage and cradling machine guns. They must not notice the small camera she would smuggle into the ward under her curling hair which is full, glossy and black. When she wears it loose, as she did that day, it is easy to dream how it would fan over a pillow or fall over her breasts.

She tied the scarf at her neck with a knot and its red floating points filled the guards with fantasy when they looked at her. They wanted sex and more. Especially the young recruit outside that patient's door. Vera promises what I found with Eric when we brought the rhythms of the world together. Because the new recruit is young he imagines sex and, like a saint's nimbus of light around the longing, a whole day on the beach, among rockpools, in the shelter of a shallow cave. In the long evening, the moon shines ... That he will take her home to his village where his uncle has a farm in the foothills, where there is a meadow at the curve where the riverbank becomes steep. It bends into a copse and makes a place where he used to hide as a child and no one could find him. He will bring a blanket ... By the time Vera comes out of the patient's room he has burrowed so deep in longings, he can hardly see anything in front of his eyes.

Although Vera does not know exactly what fills his heart, she knows that wearing the scarf will gain her admission to the patient and the story. She intends no ill and feels dismay when she hears that after her footage appears on TV the recruit is summoned for punishment, shouted at, hit, and locked up in a cell hardly big enough for the coir mattress and stinking bucket.

But he is a farm boy accustomed to harsh conditions. In his solitary cell, he saves crumbs from the thick slice of bread they bring three times a day, and puts them on the sill between the bars, and, sure enough, a sparrow comes to the sill and accepts his crumbs and looks at him with a bright eye. The bird is accustomed to wooing from lonely prisoners. In this time of isolation and spare rations the recruit resolves to get out of the army as soon as he can, go back to the country and work on his uncle's farm. I don't know whether he does, after all, leave the army as he hopes in prison, or whether, released to daily work and camaraderie, he forgets that this is what he really wants. Many of us have dreams and give them up. Perhaps he was sent to fight guerrillas in the mountains and did not come back.

There is much I don't know. I imagine how a soldier dreams, guessing that our human longings are not that different, though I know that in love the miracle seems that the longing of each requites the other uniquely. Eric and I felt made for each other and that with each other we glimpsed immortality and destiny. Perhaps what soldiers dream is not the same throughout the world. I do not really know what Vera's soldier longed for.

When Eric talked about his years as a soldier, a duty for every young man in France, he did not tell me about longing for women or home. He talked about science. Physics filled his imagination. He signed his letters to me with the loop that in mathematics signifies infinity. Our world rotated on our positive and negative poles. Our meeting and our love felt inevitable though unpredictable, like the course of specific particles in quantum mechanics. In physics, contraries like these coexist as though they can be reconciled. We sustained ourselves for years in paradox and excitement, snatching days and weeks together on both sides of the Atlantic. I believed our storms would smooth out one day into steadiness simple as a blue sky.

I could not understand the physics Eric invoked, though the true language of his heart. described chaos, turbulence, explosions, lightning, wrecks—war rendered into science. He was studying storms on the sun and Jupiter and images of passion and power flooded and flowed like the Gulf Stream in the fierce Atlantic between us. When he called from Paris, icebergs and whales, currents and shipping filled our voices. He said all his work breathed with love. Like the turbulence he studied, that love still leaves a roiling wake in my inward sea and now two scarves float on the surface, flotsam after a wreck.

Since dreams are so particular, I confess I don't know what Vera's recruit dreamed when he allowed her into the ward where she interviewed the woman who had been tortured and focused the camera to show the burn marks on her fingers and soles.

Last week, Vera and José, her anchorman, came to our offices here in Boston looking for help and showed us the footage they aired on TV and some that was cut. The video they played on their news program didn't show the burns on breasts or genitals. People in their country are prudish about sex, and Vera did not want to offend that way. It was bad enough she was showing evidence of torture.

Of course it was not only prudery. The owner of the station and the lawyers knew reasons of state security for forbidding such sights. They did not want to give the authorities too much cause for outrage. Though of course, they also knew that for some, like their Minister of Justice, that is, the Minister of Prisons, torture is aphrodisiac too. He forgets the purpose of his curiosity, becomes engrossed in play and savors cruelty until it becomes tenderness. Hunters speak of the bond they feel with the buck in the crosshairs. I do not know how to predict the contraries people reconcile.

In the end, the Department admitted that the woman Vera had interviewed had done nothing. A typo got her name confused with that of the other woman. Mistakes like that happen every day.

It was really the other woman who was guilty, they said. The one who contacted Vera and José to call attention to certain documents marked Classified and Top Secret. No government can allow such things. Even if it is not a matter of state security. Even if it is money siphoned into private accounts, bribery and kickback, you can't embarrass men in power who hold the lives of others in their hands. It is so obvious that power corrupts I sometimes believe people must condone it, though perhaps they feel they can't change anything. They have to accept and keep quiet. What else can they do?

In countries like Vera's, people who don't condone, don't know what to do about what they know. They feel badly, especially when they hear from a handsome TV anchorman like José.

When Vera told the story on TV, viewers could see the beauty spot over her left eyebrow, near the temple. Then they heard on TV and read on the front page about the woman who arranged to meet Vera and give her the papers. That woman's body was found on a median strip on a main highway. Some people say she was the one who was really guilty, or if not guilty, that she asked for it.

Alive, the dead woman was tall and had deep red hair. Maybe that gave her confidence to do something so brave. They say she was pregnant too. Some viewers felt really bad, and afraid of what can happen to anyone. Others asked, 'How can a woman be so irresponsible? A pregnant woman has no right to mess with confidential papers and TV journalists.'

Anyhow, she's dead, that woman with silky red hair. The TV program shows her father talking about her. He also has that shining hair. After a few sentences, though it is unmanly, he can't help it—his voice breaks. Anyone can see from his face that he has lived through many other troubles in silence. What can anyone do? No one can reach through the glass to wipe the tears from his face – they'd only get blood on their own hands. Even his neighbors and family know it is better not to get carried away. They believe it is God, not us, who wipes the tears from every eye, and God acts only after many catastrophes.

When they see Vera's footage, some feel heavy-hearted, knowing they can't escape splashes of blood. Everything would fall apart without the army and police, and no one wants that. If they must live in the city where they were born they must keep quiet. If Vera came to speak to them, they would know nothing. They would look straight into her eyes like people who look at a camera for a photograph on a license.

Soldiers stand guard outside the hospital ward where one woman moves her hands to show dark burns and the other focuses the camera to record the fingers moving like young birds learning to fly. Wearing that bright scarf, Vera said she was the patient's cousin. She flirted with a recruit a few minutes ago, and the points of her scarf were like a butterfly. With his hand on the hip gun, he stands at the door remembering that meadow by a river where the grass grows tall and you can look up at blue sky and imagine that you are alone in the world, or alone with Vera where no one will see you, where she opens her lips and pulls open the knot of the scarf round her neck, and her fingers slip the buttons of her blouse through the stitching made for it to open.

In this country, working with the Committee, I know how we condone. We say it is not our business. We should not believe only one side of the story. We don't know enough. Though it is impossible to know enough. We have become the center of the world and everyone tells us twelve times more than we understand. What would we know when we know?

When Vera's boss, José, the handsome young anchorman, showed us the video of the woman killed, he said, "I carry her on my conscience." Pain passes from one to other like lightning along branches no one can predict exactly.

I remembered Eric and how he had to tell me that story about the experiment in Japan. He did not say he was carrying it on his conscience, but when I put things together I saw that as soon as the semester ended, he came to me. He never said these things directly, but times when he was lying in bed reflecting, looking at the ceiling, absentmindedly caressing my arm, speaking from memories he did not share with anyone else, he would tell about incidents like the first time he tasted chocolate, a G.I.'s gift, and the afternoon he saw an English and a German plane in a dogfight. He was thrilled.

The year before he went to Japan, Eric talked about fractals in one of those reflective moments after we made love. He would lie there, eyes open, twisting the hairs of an eyebrow, contemplating matters present to his mind's eye. He talked about an equation to describe the pattern that remains similar through the whole coast of Britain, from inlets and peninsulas to nooks and crannies where land and water make love forever.

Afterwards we went out walking in the dawn. The low moon was fading and he started to shout joy to the whole neighborhood. Yelling like that could only make trouble for me in an American suburb, but he did not care. I scolded until he kissed me to keep me quiet and we went into my house where we would not scandalize my neighbors if we made love like starved teenagers. I was the one who would remain. He would go off to France and, if he remembered that exuberance at all, would recall only its pleasure.

Perhaps I condense into one moment the excitement of that whole time. The next time we were together, he broke his journey to Japan for two nights with me. The second night, hunger struck him and I made scrambled eggs. While I was stirring them, he told me about a study of cars showing that traffic never flows in an even stream. Even on roads without obstacles, cars bunch together. At that time, the University of Paris was full of people who wanted to apply fractal theory to sociology.

When he came back from that trip to Japan he was full of wonder over what he had seen – temples, gardens – and stories about how he startled the Japanese men he passed when he went jogging. Perhaps the Japanese jog now, but at that time, it seemed bizarre *gaijin* behavior. Several nights passed before Eric talked about the experiment, and I knew immediately that, though he affected an indifferent tone, it troubled him. One evening while they were all at a table in the restaurant near the university where they used to eat, his group was speculating about fractal patterns in human behavior. They thought the course of a rumor might show patterns like paths of lightning with unpredictable repetitions and branches. They designed an experiment to test their hypothesis.

They didn't think of it as experimentation on human subjects. It was one of those things you can't predict, like that typo the Minister confessed on TV.

That illusion of innocence came to the surface when José talked about the owner of the TV station he worked for. The owner was punished for the story Vera told. His citizenship was revoked, his station was closed and his property was confiscated. He had not just permitted Vera's footage. He had promoted it with teaser questions, you know the kind of thing: What has the department of X got to hide? Why does the Department want to keep this story from you? and so forth.

José showed no sympathy for the owner sitting in an armchair with his hands on his thighs telling what he had suffered before he escaped to another country. Perhaps it is hard for a young journalist caught in the tangle of justice to feel for the sufferings of a millionaire, though the owner is not a millionaire any more. It is too much to expect sympathy if the journalist is young and runs up stairs two at a time without losing breath and the owner is fat and accustomed to having people around who do what he says, and is used to doing what you must, in a country like that, to get a license and a permit to build on this site and another permit to put up an antenna, and so forth until you have fed everyone at the table of the Leader. Now the station owner does not have a country. The Minister kicked him out and told him to go make trouble somewhere else. His exile is not on José's conscience. Instead, José said, "I wonder what he was up to, hiring us and giving us that current affairs program. We are all young. My colleagues are brave. What did he think would happen?" Here too, the line does not go straight but jagged like lightning.

What did Eric's group think would happen? The question did not arise. They just wanted to see the course of a rumor. It seemed innocent enough to their western eyes, and they were theoreticians, proud to be doing research without an eye to its practical outcomes. Eric bought a scarf and gave it to a waitress in the restaurant where everyone could see that he was giving her a gift.

Eric sometimes yelled with joy when he arrived at a new insight, you could hear him braying in the park in Osaka. God knows what the Japanese thought of this crazy *gaijin*. He would not have done it in France. Neither yelling nor the experiment.

She was a young girl from the country, come to Osaka to live with her uncle's family, earn some money by waitressing and learn English part time. She wanted to come to America. She hoped to marry an American and live in a big house like people on TV and have sons who would grow big and healthy. They would run down the beach into the sea shouting and laughing, not afraid to splash each other. Sometimes she looked at the group of scientists who talked loudly and moved with fearless gestures and wrote equations on their arms. What it would be like to live in their countries? What else did she dream, this unassuming young waitress?

She committed suicide when her reputation was ruined. The rumor explained the gift as evidence that she was having an affair with the *gaijin*.

I don't know what that showed about the fractal pattern of rumor. Perhaps that it can strike like lightning out of a blue sky. Like torture after a typo.

The journalists who worked for José have scattered, some into exile, some to other jobs. José says, "I don't know where they are. One came to New York and tried to get work, but the only work he can find is as a waiter." Coming from a poor country, José's reporter feels demeaned. He does not guess that in New York, waiters may be children of millionaires and famous lawyers. He feels that his life has been smashed, he has fallen into a depression and José says, "He is also on my conscience."

José's not really to blame. I'm not really to blame for the waitress in Osaka, though perhaps Eric's exuberance in love had something to do with that experiment. He wanted me to say something to forgive him on her behalf. It didn't make sense, but who else could he turn to except someone who loved him?

When I worked it out, I knew we would never rest on the same shore. I was his wildness, and now I knew where his wildness had struck, it singed me too.

We get so many stories in our office, if not for that detail about Vera smuggling the camera into the hospital room with her distracting scarf, I would hardly have noticed her story. Our boss wants us to know about the cases we're working on, so every week we have a presentation. After all we hear, I feel this remarkable and precious—that no one threatens to arrest me, no one kicks in the door. For myself, I expect to die slowly, not like that woman who has been spared the humiliations of old age. But I expect that when death comes for me too, it will be as though I have been struck by lightning.

Jaimee Wriston Colbert
Climbing The God Tree
The Willa Cather Prize

WAKING UP IN SACRED PLACES

AFTER our cat came back from the dead, I decided it was time to go looking for Jesus. Here's how it went: Last June Alfred got bone cancer, a tumor bulging out one side of his eye, so at first we thought maybe it was another abscess from a late-night fight. "That cat's more of a man than most of *my* men," said my mother. "Probably he's mooning the little Persian next door as we speak," she said. How does a cat moon? I wondered. Though I didn't ask. It's best not to ask my mother about these kinds of things since she'll just make up her own sense anyway. Recently Henri, she's my mother, decided she'd had about enough of the men in her life and she's a little cranky about it too. Said the last straw was Humor Peach, who injected himself in his private part to get it up, Henri said, and then it wouldn't come down.

"Like he was mainlining Stay Puff starch," she said.

We've been talking this way since the day I turned eighteen, or at least Henri talks like this to me. I'm not all that gung ho on guys these days, except sometimes the boat boys in the summer, brown skin and sleek as cats, tending the tourist yachts that bump around in Rock Harbor's harbor like they own it. The boys slip up and down those decks, mopping them, polishing the wood like it's to eat off of instead of sailing to some faraway place; their bleached hair and teeth are as white as salt.

Henri loved our cat. I'm sure she loves us too, her daughters, but human love is a lot more complicated, she's always said. No doubt about it, Henri loved the cat. When the bulge beside Alfred's eye didn't go away and his eyes turned yellow as butter, kind of hollow and wispy and they rolled up into the backs of his eyelids as inch by inch he lowered himself on the tile floor for about the millionth nap of the day, she said, "That's it." And she took him to the vet.

For the rest of the summer Alfred withered away, slipping off pounds easy as removing a sweater. He wouldn't eat much though Henri'd get right down beside him on the floor, chunk of tuna on her finger, stroking the side of his mouth with it, cooing like he's a little bird. "Sweet baby," she said, "my poor sweet little baby." Alfred took to hiding in dark places, closets, under beds, behind the stove that never gets lit in the summer and sometimes not even in the winter until Henri makes a boyfriend chop us some wood. "He knows," my mother whispered, "Alfred knows."

And then Alfred died. And then he came back. It was the night after they cremated him, his box of ashes on the table beside my mother's bed. "For the time being," Henri said. "I've had worse here," she said, "Humor's penile injection kit for one." I thought my mother would never stop bawling. She's generally pretty tough about things, "Harder than a six inch nail" my Aunt Eli once said. I guess not when it came to Alfred. I cried too, but to myself as I always do. "Everything I love quits on me," Henri wailed. Which is mostly true, except, as it turned out, for Alfred. We first heard his mewing from somewhere inside those dark places, the bathroom closet, under Henri's bed. I checked and double-checked looking for a live cat, maybe the little Persian he had those yellow eyes on got in somehow, there were so many possible explanations. And I tried to think of them, I did.

My mother hunkered down in the corner of the living room, bare wood floor, her knees pressed in against her chin, skinny arms curled so tightly around her legs she looked like a double helix, or a couple strands of pasta stuck together, strings of her long blond hair like wheat over her face. "Oh God," she whimpered, "It's my fault. What have I done?" We heard the mewing again, soft but an urgency too, Meow, Meeeooooow, like he needed in out of a long night, or a spot of tuna to get him by.

"Cedra!" Henri moaned, "I think it's because I prayed a threat prayer. My father warned us. You can't do that, he said. You can ask for things within reason, even bargain some, but never threaten. I just didn't think I could bear it. That's what I said, I said Jesus God if you make Alfred die I'll have nothing and I won't stand to live that way, uh uh, no way! After my sister died my father stopped believing. What's the difference? That's what he said."

The mewing came again, this time louder, plaintive, and then a sense of movement in the hall behind us where nothing changes in actuality, but every ion, every electron appears hyped, like that second before a jet breaks the sound barrier or the instant when thunder explodes.

"Oh God!" Henri cried. "My life's come to this, exactly nothing. Divorced, rented house in the middle of Maine, he barely sends enough money to keep his own daughters let alone you, one little sister dead, the other barren and she blames things on me, Jesus! Jesus! How can I take more? To think I had a man who plastered his gold albums on our bathroom walls. Like paint, Cedra. Do you remember? That was our life. He said I went too far, taking his kids out of California, *filching* his girls he called it, 3,000 miles away. Well I don't see him back here claiming them, do you? So don't I at least get to be forgiven?"

"Consider this," I said to my mother. "Maybe Alfred, if it *is* Alfred, just doesn't want to leave you, is all. Maybe this is a good thing. Maybe he just loves you too much." I was about to add that now she could have the benefits of a cat without cleaning the litter box, the vet bills, rabies shots, hair ball vomit, combing out those tangles of fur, but I thought better of it. I wasn't so sure about this whole thing either. It was asking me to believe in the unseen presence of things, fantasies I gave up on when I quit playing house, when I understood there could never be a Santa.

And Alfred or the ghost of Alfred, or some unique blend of wind, rain, tears and spirit, howled. "Jesus, Jesus!" My mother sunk her blond head between her knees and for the rest of the night I patted her like she was my pet, and the ghost cat or Alfred or whatever it was, entered our pores, our flesh, our bones, our hearts, like a wound, raw and begging to be healed.

Finding Jesus is not an easy thing for someone brought up without onramp access. Things I'd overheard through the years ran through my head in one luminous cliché: God is love, Jesus loves you yes he does, Onward Christian soldiers, The meek shall inherit the earth, Do unto others as they do you. My mother used to tell us church was the world on a good day. That from her better moods. Otherwise she'd say things like, "I'm not suggesting there *isn't* a God, but would He let Sunday School kids sell candy bars on his behalf? They're not even Milky Way, for chrissake, no Mars bars, nothing celestial here." Of course, that was before Henri needed to be forgiven. Yesterday she bought herself a rosary though she's hardly a Catholic, and last night when the wailing started from somewhere inside the walls of her bedroom she clutched onto it like the beads were her own mother's necklace, groaning and lamenting, "I believe, I believe, I believe!"

This morning I talked to my friend Scott Barker who's a prison guard and a new convert to some sort of godliness that takes up all of his Sundays. He told me that one day he had a long look around his workplace, and he saw as if for the first time the concrete, the hopelessness, the despair; the men whose chances, if they ever had any were mostly used up. Scott realized there wasn't much separating himself from all of that beyond the gun he was trained to carry. So he took up Jesus, and now it's Jesus who carries him. Scott said, "You should approach Him with a pure heart. Try to be clean as an empty plate. Maybe if you could forgive someone who's done something really bad." Which is how we came to think about Pretty Jimmy, who raped my best friend Heather. "Jesus will listen," Scott said, "but you know it's not a small request, sending a cat to Heaven."

My mother's been inside Rock Harbor Adult Correctional before, threatening some murderer who was harassing her sister. (Aunt Eli taught art in the prison until she rethought her marriage and flew to Hawaii.) Henri told me what to expect. "You don't wear a skirt because they'll hang out under the metal stairs staring up. But even in pants they'll be watching you, like they're on the inside of your skin. If you think you'll find any answers in that place," Henri said, "don't count on it." Then her eyes got that wild look. "He's here!" she hissed. "Can you smell his wet fur smell?" No use pointing out that if Alfred's a ghost, then how is he wet?

In the R.H.A.C. visiting room I examine my outfit while waiting for Jimmy: baggy overalls, plain white tee shirt, not calling much attention to myself yet not some total freak costume either like a lawyer's get-up. A suit of tweedy armor and Jimmy won't talk a word to me. Jimmy's from a family so long in Rock Harbor it's like they grew out of the soil here, like some kind of fungus, mushroom, toadstools, they always come back. He wouldn't trust some lawyer, and since I wasn't *born* into Rock Harbor I'm not so sure what he thinks of me, either. I have no idea what I'm going to say to him. My heart is beating hard, little flashings, a lighthouse under my breast. I can't think of my heart without thinking of my breast, which then makes me conscious of being in a room full of men who all did things bad enough to be here. My face is hot. Nobody's looking at me though, at the people visiting them. It could be an airport without the sense of rush. Time feels stretched out. In the end only half of us get to leave.

When a guard leads him in, the round shells of his shoulders under the grey prison shirt, a lump like a chunk of dirt catches in my throat. I'd forgotten about his looks. Usually when I think of Jimmy I picture him on top of Heather and she's trying desperately to swim up from under him, him pressing her down and she's drowning, drowning. I imagine this now and an open place inside me closes up. Suck in a breath. This isn't a good start, I think, getting to Jesus. But how do I forgive someone who did that to my best friend? I stare at the grey shirt, overwashed, faded; how many others, rapists, robbers, murderers, wore it before Jimmy? Jimmy, Jimmy, Jimmy. Breathe in and out, slowly.

"Why do you come here?" he says, sitting opposite me on a chained-to-the-floor metal chair, diddling and twisting and popping his long hands in his lap, then on top of the formica table between us. Fingernails play a crisp tuneless song.

His speech sounds foreign, like somebody testing the language. I imagine I can hear the ticking of the big wall clock behind Jimmy, dragging the minutes forward. I look at the clock, not directly at him. "Do you need anything?" I ask, feeling dumb. What the hell is the protocol here, visiting someone in prison? I didn't even bring him cookies for chrissake, the newspaper, not even an outdated magazine, though Scott said they don't let much inside these walls that doesn't walk, bleed, and have a social security number.

Jimmy shrugs, green eyes intense. "I need a TV," he says. "Mom was supposed to bring me mine but it wasn't prison safe so they said I have to buy theirs. OK, I told them, but I don't have the money." He lowers his head and I gaze at those brown curls, shorter now, but not so short you couldn't reach out and ease one lightly around the tip of your finger, like a shaving of chocolate.

And then because I have no idea what else to say, I'm telling him about Alfred, rushing the story out like I'm expecting him to laugh at me, scoff, roll his eyes the way guys do at the unbelievable when it comes from the mouth of a girl. "I need to ask Jesus to take back the cat," I say, "Or else my mother's going to have some kind of a breakdown, and I can't exactly think it does my nerves any good to hear Alfred, who's supposed to be ashes in a box the size of a Big Mac, meowing somewhere in our house. You see, now I not only have to believe in Jesus but in ghosts too."

Jimmy nods his head solemnly, stunning eyes and the ridges of his cheek bones like little hills on the tan valley of his face. My God, I remind myself, what the man did to Heather! But I'm supposed to try and forgive him so I concentrate on this. It wasn't his fault anyway, not wholly; probably if I could get to Led Nash who belittled Jimmy into doing it and cheered him on, if I could forgive *him* I could bypass Jesus and go straight to God.

"I knew a fish that came back," Jimmy says. "It happens if you go fishing and you catch them but you don't put them in a bucket, you just let them flop around. My dad and my brothers did that off the dock on Mirror Lake, let the fish flop around. And then one of them stopped flopping so I picked him up. He was dead, eyes wide open, but when I put him in my brother's pail what do you think? He started swimming. At first a kind of a squiggle, then round and round the bucket he went, tail flashing like he was really mad."

I frown, remind myself he's a bit slow, always has been and probably prison isn't going to improve this. Twenty-two, the body of Brad Pitt and the brain drive of an eleven year old I figure, on a good day. "Well Jimmy," I say patiently, "most likely the fish wasn't really dead. Probably it was in shock and the water revived it, is all."

"No," Jimmy shakes his head and a wayward curl slants across a perfectly arched eyebrow. "No Cedra. I know dead. This fish was dead. And then he wasn't."

I leave after the allotted half hour, telling Jimmy I'll be back on his next visitors' day, at the end of the week. I have no idea why. Couldn't I just *say* I forgive him and ask Jesus to take away Alfred and let my mother have some peace? Would He really know I was lying? I'm not sure how to feel about Jimmy. Heather's never been the same since it happened. It's like either a piece of her is missing, or a chunk of someone else was added on. Because we don't connect anymore like we were meant to be best friends, like she's a plug and I'm the socket, that sort of thing. Instead we're lights switching on different rooms. She hangs out with a mostly younger crowd now, skaters, punks if you ask me. But if you look in her eyes there's an old person there, and none too pleased with the way things are. When I look at Jimmy a feeling inside me stirs up. I try not to let it, try to will it down, but there it is, a flopping of something in my gut. Like Jimmy's fish, and it's definitely not dead.

On Sunday Scott takes me to his church. He says he thinks this might be the more direct path, after all. I know church is a very religious place and I expect everyone to be cheerful and loud and maybe doing this in tongues, the language of the truly blessed, because Scott told me they finally have joy in their lives, accepting Jesus as their savior. I'd like Jesus to save my mother. It's more than just the Alfred thing; this is a woman not meant to have to question her own life. We haven't always gotten along, but after I turned eighteen and she told me to call her Henri, things were different. For one, I stopped pestering her about my father who died before I could know him. It's not like I can change any of that, though I'd still like to find out if he was at least smart and maybe tall, and if my mother loved him, just a little. And for another Henri knows I could leave her any time. She's not good about people leaving her. "I'm the one does the leaving," she says. And anyway, where the hell would I go? Most folks who manage to move away from Maine come back again. It's like velcro here, stifling yet awful snug. I like Henri best when she's not going off on some guy, when she's acting sort of like a mother. Lately she's too busy chanting over her rosary to worry about penile injection kits, or who's going to chop her wood in the winter.

So I don't know what it was inside me made me do it, steal the plastic Jesus out of Scott Barker's church. I've never done anything like that before. I'm not saying here that I'm *good*. I've smoked marijuana to relax, inhaled a few beers to get high, done the boat boys occasionally. But I've never been a thief.

What I know is that earlier this morning, bright and hot and filled with what I imagined might be hope, I walked into that church with Scott, expecting to feel different. Holier maybe, or at least safe. I visualized myself in a polished wooden pew even before we sat down on the unpainted bench, imagined sunlight streaking through stained glass windows, blue and godly and significant as a rainbow. In fact the windows were smudged and plain, and flies coated them from the outside, maybe inside too. I thought I'd listen to the singing, the joy, the assurance of people who found themselves in Jesus, Scott said, the Spirit shining through them, becoming the grace and wisdom that eluded me. I figured I'd at least find some answers, if not Jesus Himself.

I waited. All through the minister's sermon, words droning around my ears like insects buzzing, trying to get inside my head but some invisible barrier, a brain cell mosquito net was knocking them out. The heat of the late August morning settled in the church, on people's necks, their breaths, hymns not graceful and uplifting but a little out of tune, it sounded to me, and Scott too close, brushing against me when we knelt to pray so that I couldn't think of things holy, couldn't think of anything at all but his prickly black arm hairs on my naked elbow.

When Pastor Robin invited the "flock" to rise and come forward for the healing service I told Scott I had to go to the bathroom, figuring it would be a while, given the numbers of the afflicted sidling up to the front of the church. I contemplated for a moment if He could heal my thick thighs, but by then I was having trouble breathing and felt itchy and strange inside my skin that kept bumping against Scott's skin, pressed together as we were on that small bench. "Transcend thy body and bathe thy soul in the waters of Jesus's love!" Pastor Robin howled, uplifted hands and arms waving like fleshy white antennae from the dark depths of his frock.

He's a plastic Jesus, not very big, about six inches tall and the color of cream gone bad. He was perched upright on a table in the corridor that stretches through the parish to the bathrooms, beside some pamphlets called *Spread The Word*. Too light to be a paperweight for the pamphlets, he seemed to have no purpose other than simply to be. I lit in on his face, one of those perfect doll faces where all the features are symmetrical, peaceful as a cow's. His eyes won't blink shut, but he's permanently pleasant looking, a kind, doughy-eyed sort of expression. I slipped Jesus into my pack, and then I left Scott's church because now I was a sinner. And if I know anything about church, I know it's not a place for sinners.

At home Henri's in her bedroom, her entire wardrobe strewn about. "What are you doing?" I ask, the plastic Jesus blazing hot as a barbecue tong right through the reinforced nylon against my back, but I can't put my pack down, maybe never again.

Henri shrugs, "I guess we're moving. I have no idea where but I can't sleep anymore with Alfred meowing all the time, I can't live this way!"

"You won't leave Maine," I tell her. "It won't let you." I stare at my mother, she's skinnier than ever, a bruised look around her eyes. "I prayed for you, Henri," I tell her, because I don't know what else to say. That's what Scott said to me when I told him I was having a hard time forgiving Pretty Jimmy because I couldn't concentrate on it, those green eyes of his, that hard chin like he tried to swallow a rock and it got stuck there, that hair.

"You should be praying for Alfred," Henri says, "it's too late for me. I've done the rosary thing, I even meditated to Buddha but I suppose they know I'm not for real. My own father stopped believing. He got Alzheimer's so he's like a child now, about as close to God as you can get." She plops down on her bed in the middle of a pile of clothes. The TV drones from the next room, my little sister Maple hunkered down in front of it, pink thumb planted in her mouth. "It's strange Cedra, I have all these clothes, this furniture, knickknacks that are mine, jewelry, all this stuff associated with *me*, and I don't have a clue. I used to stare at Jumper's gold albums on our bathroom wall, just sit on that high-end San Francisco toilet and look at them while he was who knows where. Is that love? Not a clue."

The next day I visit Pretty Jimmy with Jesus still in my pack. They search my pack at the guards' station as I walk through the metal detector, then they hand it back to me and I'm escorted to the visiting room. Apparently Jesus is not considered contraband. This is my third visit. Each time Jimmy rambles on about things that mean absolutely nothing but it's like he's crooning to me, special notes that make my skin sticky, turn the muscles on the insides of my thighs to jelly.

Again we sit at the formica table opposite each other and Jimmy says, "Do you like snakes? I'm going to have a snake farm when I get out of here. I can sell them to people like me who like snakes, and I'll treat those snakes right. I would," he says. "Some people are mean to snakes because they're afraid.

278

People who believe the Bible blame the bad things in the world on that first snake. But he was actually pretty smart. He didn't eat that apple. did he? I'm not afraid of snakes. Are you, Cedra?"

I shake my head and that's a lie. But at this point would it make any difference?

Jimmy says, "I've been thinking about your cat and here's what I come up with. I don't believe he's a ghost. Things alive have this kind of energy you see, some call it the soul but others say it's atoms, something like that. Whatever you name it, it can't just go away all at once. If you spill a bucket of sand you don't pick up every bit, right? When I was a little kid I dropped a pail of dirt in our front room by mistake. I was making an ant farm and my dad got so mad when I couldn't get it all cleaned up he stuck the bucket on my head, said I had to wear it for the rest of the day. 'A dummy's cap,' he said. Well I think it's the energy of Alfred that's left in your house. He's letting you know the rest of him's gone on, maybe somewhere better."

I study Jimmy's mouth as he speaks, the way his words roll slowly out, hesitating at those full brown lips as if even his language is not sure how it wants to be in this world. I think about what his lips would feel like against mine, and then I know I'm a sinner because not only am I not working on forgiving Pretty Jimmy, making my heart clean as a plate, I'm deliberately forgetting what he did to Heather and picturing him with me.

"So why did you do it?" I ask him. "The thing you're in here for! Could you please tell me why the hell you would do something like that? And don't say it's because your so-called friend Led Nash made you."

Jimmy stares out through the barred window at the other end of the room and I follow his eyes, green like the fields we can barely see. A crow circles, drops, black shadow without

279

voice. Jimmy, his own voice tender, almost a whisper says, "I had a garter snake once. His name was Jim Two. My mom wouldn't let me keep him. Said we had enough mouths, but snakes can last a long time without eating, did you know? And they feel good when you hold them, not slimy like people think." His green eyes lock into my eyes. "Don't you worry about no ghosts, Cedra."

I look at the guard standing at the door, short, a half-in mustache, not much older than me. He doesn't seem too interested in Jimmy or the other inmates with their visitors either. He keeps gazing down at his watch even though the clock would tell him just as well. A wave of voices rises and falls through the room. I lean across the table, a little closer to Jimmy. "Do you want to touch Jesus?" I ask him.

I reach into my pack slowly, pulling a few things out onto the table along with Jesus, a hair brush, a ball-point pen, the portable pack of tissues Henri sticks in sometimes when she's thinking about being my mother. I want the guard to look over and see that these things are OK, they've been checked out, no contraband here.

Probably Jimmy will ask me about Jesus, ask me why I have him in my pack, and then I'll tell him the truth. I'll tell him I stole Jesus from a church, and we'll be almost even. It won't save my mother or help Alfred's energy get to where the rest of him is any sooner, but the sudden need to speak a truth burns inside me so strong I inhale a ragged, steamy breath like breathing dry ice.

Jimmy reaches out a long fingered hand and touches Jesus's head. "Snakes get a whole different skin, did you know? I'd have to sell some of those snakes to make a living but while they're mine I'll take good care of them. You believe I could, right Cedra?" Holding his hand out to me now, like an offering.

I hesitate. My own fingers feel hot and prickly, tingling and foreign and strange, as if maybe I got a bit of that Spirit in me after all. I lift my hand slowly and place it on top of his, lightly at first, cringing, shock of the flesh; then I let it settle in like I mean it, as if all along my hand has been hanging empty just waiting for some fit.

✻

Lee Upton
Antioch Review

You Know You've Made It When They Hate You

Moi and The King: Charity
Performance
Nearly Worth the Ticket

LAST night's opening of *The King & I*, in which costume design trumped character, turned the tables on the painful posing of the original, revealing the sodden colonial politics underpinning the tired enterprise, from the remarkable hoop skirt of Anna to the exciting cummerbund of her countryman. Molly Crane as Anna overwhelmed the role until this reviewer wondered if the production shouldn't have been called *Moi & the King*. She was in mediocre vocal frame and bent on too heavy-handedly stirring the sexual waters between herself and the polygamous Siamese monarch. Generally her role is played with some subtlety and a dose of British rectitude. Or what the British want us to suppose is rectitude Here we have an Anna salivating for her king and ready to flash her knickers every time she executes a turn-about in her hoop skirt, marvelously designed by Mary Achtenberg with delicate hand-embroidered detailing.

The King—one of our newest Korean neighbors in our venerable burg—acquitted himself with dignity in the midst of Anna's incessant bosom-beating innuendoes of sexual congress. One could see that he felt oppressed by the shrewishly seductive manipulations of Anna, a widow who recklessly inspired a romance between one of the king's countless concubines and a shirtless youth.

The surprise of the evening was John Fostergarth, whose hapless portrayal sent laughter to all corners, once the audience realized the joke: the representative of British imperialism was bizarrely at odds with himself and his position. Fostergarth's mimicry of stage fright propelled gales of mirth throughout the otherwise often puzzled audience. His reedy figure, excellently attired in evening clothes of a fit and condition rarely seen locally, slowly became saturated with the self-consuming perspiration of the colonialist frustrated by his own unruly instincts. As with his compatriot Anna, we were led to intuit the venality beneath the skin of civility. Given secrecy and opportunity, the hoop skirt and the dinner jacket are flung aside as impulses from the gutter fly.

Such an unpeeling of the mendacities of xenophobia is nearly worth the price of admission for this chestnut, with musical direction by Timothy Flock. Superb costumes by Mary Achtenburg…

Shampoo, Please!

Can someone wash this musical right out of our hair? We know its message: its flagrant attempt to naturalize the desire of an empire attempting to control far distant real estate, the despoiling and the selling of our own special islands. But what's *South Pacific* without its manic dancing by unrepentant youths? We know the boar's tooth ceremony is a big crowd-pleaser. But call me a cock-eyed pessimist, the mature killer, the mysterious Frenchman in this hare-brained production, is younger than Nellie Forbush, who simply sounds developmentally delayed. The tired, pinched-looking star behind this vehicle is Molly Crane. Are we to find xenophobia charming? No naïve waif is she from Little Rock. Her doubling up preposterously as Bloody Mary might have worked if the audience hadn't been baffled into submission.

John Fostergarth fills the bill as Stew Pot, swallowing the role whole and belching up a more-than-competent performance in what is otherwise a carnival of incompetence—except for costume design, by the delightful and talented....

My Fat Friar

The rain in Spain falls mainly on this musical. With a lil bit of luck you'll miss it. Molly Crane as Eliza Doolittle hardens the heart and then some. Impossible to believe a transformation will take place from filthy flower peddler to stately avatar of elitism. Wilfred Oneff as Henry Higgins takes on a preposterous role with aplomb, despite his sorry voice.

John Fostergarth, still quite new to the stage but certain to be a favorite, pours on the charm as an idle dandy at the horse track.

Molly Crane almost comes to life when she warbles "I Could Have Danced All Night." Here we believe her—and see shining beneath the grease paint a glimmer of what might have been. A tiny ray of sunlight in a chilly production.

Unfortunately, you can't change a tramp into a delicacy, especially one with a backwoods accent. Who wants to see a lady clacking about onstage in a sheath with rope-like sash? In early scenes we might be tempted to call the play *My Fat Friar.* But costume is necessary to suggest the tawdry Doolittle's class-jumping aspirations....

***

Why should Roger Dillingham, the reviewer for *The Pattwell Gazette,* despise Molly Crane? For despise her he did: her artificial gestures, overinflated, unforgettable. Once, halfway through *Oklahoma,* he snuck a detective novel out of his raincoat and began reading by penlight until she came back onstage—her hair stacked on her head so idiotically that he couldn't concentrate on his novel again. Of course she performed without any sense of irony. Of course she floated onstage like a helium-inflated troll.

For at least five musicals and two farces he had reviewed her and suffered.

It was queasy-making just to watch her. No matter where Roger Dillingham sat in the theater, she seemed close to him, and intimate with him, and he felt manipulated. Afterwards, when he got back to his apartment and fired up his word processor, he atomized her faults until the soft fug dissipated.

Why couldn't the theater ever put on a meaningful production for charity—something on the order of *Mother Courage,* or a stage version of *The Battle of Algiers?*

It was no wonder that Roger Dillingham felt compelled to praise John Fostergarth. The rumor was that Fostergarth vomited in a towel before performances. He was the perfect foil for Molly Crane. He was far worse than she could ever be. And the costume designer, the abominable Mary Achtenberg. Well, if Roger Dillingham didn't praise anything in the production his editor would think he was being unfair.

Roger Dillingham rested on a chaise lounge, his legs stretched out before him while the turquoise waters of the swimming pool ricocheted light around him. When he looked up from his novel, he saw Molly Crane.

A boy with a beach ball walked behind her and she turned around. Roger stared at the view of her abnormally large skull on a skinny neck.

Why was she here at the Circle of Health in her pink swimsuit, her hair flattened on the back of her head like a pancake?

Roger himself wouldn't be here if he hadn't been hoodwinked by his aged parents, who agreed to donate to two charities an amount equal to that of a ten-day stay at the Circle of Health. Given that Roger had so little money and was proud of it, they paid for his airfare too. His mother came to his apartment and stepped over the tottering cascades of child welfare brochures. She stood before him in a gypsy peasant dress, a thick, bullish old woman whose long-practiced aversion to anything but her family's physical comfort and aesthetic enjoyment stunned him. Rather than agree to donate out of the goodness of her heart to any number of worthy causes, she struck a deal. "You yourself are a worthwhile cause," she said. "You yourself are a charity case." She and his father were perfectly content to plunge all their energy into interior decoration, long-term upscaling of the arboretum, and the mass-marketing of bonsai. Roger could never make up for his parents' profligate ways, their studious avoidance of reality. They were the products of their own fantasies. They would never let him ignore them. They were two elderly cases of arrested development. And now here he was, sunk in a hub of self-infatuation, of fatuous over-indulgence: a health complex.

But why should Molly Crane be at a health resort, her legs, thicker at the thighs than he expected, laid out on her own chaise lounge? Why should she need to restore her undeniably good health? She could bounce through five matinees and four supper shows a week.

Roger twisted about to get a better view of her, just as her own head snapped around and he was caught staring. The bangs were plastered to her forehead like a Roman centurion's. Her eyes were almost purple, as if dipped in some strange planetary gas. She knew him. He knew she recognized him. He ducked.

Someone must have pointed Roger out to her one night at the theater, and now she had at least two choices: snub him or confront him. She reached into her straw bag and drew out her sunglasses and swung her legs over the side of her chaise lounge and grabbed her straw bag and slung her towel over her arm. He had seen her enough in the theater to know she was about to call out to him. There it was: that grim thrust to her jaw. Her broad mouth opened slightly, gasping with concentration.

Oh God save me, Roger nearly cried aloud. But he could thank his stars: She had a knot of teenagers to make her way around before she could reach him. Roger didn't even bother to pick up his detective novel. He rose, and then, with deep embarrassment, for he hated the thought of Molly Crane seeing him in his swimming trunks, he turned and walked swiftly away from her. He could imagine what he looked like to her from behind: the landslide of his falling-down backside muscles.

He wound his way between metal tables and nearly tripped over one whining toddler as the walkway curved. He passed a stretch of bungalows and a patch of young women who stared at him unselfconsciously.

He knew Molly Crane's type: she wanted to get him alone, out among the banana palms, and give him a very loud piece of her mind.

His chest felt ready to explode, but his hotel room was well beyond the gift shop, and he doubted he could keep up his pace and make it to his room. When his breathing grew even more labored, Roger paused and looked back. At least twenty yards separated him from her, but she was still heading his way, the black ovals of her sunglasses glinting.

A couple in swimsuits and thongs blocked his way. What now? A tiki shed rose to his right, unoccupied. Fronds crisscrossed near him in a Polynesian tableau.

He was practically running when, suddenly, he was sure he was alone. He couldn't see Molly Crane in any direction, and he had come full circle, back to the gate of the pool.

Once more he stretched out on the same chaise lounge he had vacated. He picked up his detective novel. He couldn't remember who the victim was, but the top of his head and his arms were burning, and his breathing wasn't yet under control, and he was staring into the pages of his book trying to make the words stay still when she sat next to him, lowering herself into a chaise lounge.

Molly Crane shifted her weight and took off her sunglasses, and it occurred to Roger that she no longer intended to speak to him but to bully him with her gummy physical presence, her thick thighs and long calves and tiny ankles where he thought—the sweat kept running into his eyes—he could see a pulsebeat. She made his own body look like a burst sausage, like a big useless sack that he was stuck in. He despised himself for hating his body, for allowing himself to feel any concern for his body when there were so many more important things to think about in the world. Virtually anything. Anything was more important.

When he could look up, Roger saw that a couple were stirring themselves into the whirlpool near the tiki shed. Even Molly Crane wouldn't follow him into the close orbit of a pair of lovers in a hot tub. She wouldn't go to that length. She couldn't berate him over the noise of the spray jets. A woman like that demanded to be heard.

And, anyway, if he could catch his breath maybe he would be the one Molly Crane should worry about. Maybe he would be the one to start shouting.

Or maybe she would be the one to be terrorized. Maybe she would be the one who was afraid to be torn apart. He could eviscerate her and pull out her voice box and send all her bodily organs floating in the whirlpool like so much dim sum. He could show her what this world is made of. Because, Molly Crane, I want you to know it's not made of musical romances for unhinged women—and then, his breath catching, he vividly recalled seeing her onstage singing, full-throated, her dreamy eyes gazing upward. What was she so emotional about? She was singing "Hello Young Lovers" to a plank of plywood in the upper balcony.

Molly Crane was sure it was him. Dang! She was practically jogging to keep him in sight after she discovered him at the swimming pool. She had thought she lost him for awhile there. But then she was smart enough to work her way around the pool past the white metal tables with their giant umbrellas, and she trotted right up to his chaise lounge, right up close to him, letting her shadow fall onto his paperback.

Maybe she had only imagined that he was running away. He might not even know who she is—looking like this, out of stage makeup and no longer in one of those ridiculous wigs that Mary kept insisting she wear.

She couldn't believe it: Roger Dillingham. Dang!

Here was the man who made her want to crawl and die after every opening night at the playhouse. Yes. Roger Dillingham, the man John referred to as the MOB—mean old bastard.

If only she could get Roger Dillingham to stop being so harsh. His harshness was inhibiting everyone—Neddy, Alfred, Germaine, Margaret, Barney Kim, John. They were all depressed. Poor John took it hardest. By the end of any opening night he was throwing up air. And John had been through so much. He was the best brother in the world, the sweetest, the kindest. Their father used to joke: any closer and you'd be twins.

But why was Roger Dillingham standing up now? Stay, she wanted to beg him. Stay. If she could only get up the nerve to talk to him, really talk to him, and convince him how hard she tried. She was even going to be taking lessons in Macon from a woman who had worked on two soap operas. You can be put through nearly every emotion in a soap opera: all those funerals and weddings and kidnappings and electrocutions and courts of law. And Molly was going to try so hard to learn how to act. She was. She was the first to admit she couldn't imagine what she was good at on the stage—unless it was playing a woman older than herself. She was twenty-three-years-old and Roger Dillingham kept writing about her as if she were ancient. But she had gone through things, so he must be intuitive. She was a widow, after all. Even if she wasn't good at being a widow. She hardly had begun to love her husband enough—but that was because John was so much in the way. There. She admitted it. John was in the way.

She watched, stiffening with anxiety, as Roger Dillingham padded off—until she saw that he was aiming for the whirlpool. So. He wasn't avoiding her after all. The back of his head gleamed above the pool's rim.

In the name of John, in the name of poor wonderful John, Molly Crane dropped her towel and sprinted after Roger Dillingham. Any musical is no more believable than the contents of a snow globe, but she told herself: you have to believe, you have to give your spirit to it. And she couldn't help but want better things for the playhouse, and for John. She imagined that Roger Dillingham's eyes would harden with dislike if he recognized her. But surely this was because he couldn't see into her heart.

A nice-looking couple were vacating the pool when Molly began to lower herself just two jets away from her reviewer on his side of the curve.

Dang! Infernal whirlpool heat! My loving God! Dang!

Molly breathed steam into her lungs and coughed. What if her skin slid off her bones like a boiled chicken's?

All right. She would live.

And couldn't the heat stimulate a conversation? Surely she could start a conversation with Roger Dillingham about the heat. She could say: Excuse me, do you believe you have any skin that's not parboiled? The suction too—the suction. She had heard of people sucked to the bottom of whirlpools. Years ago someone had warned her: Never duck your head under the water. She could start up a conversation about the suction. She couldn't help but imagine John's comment if he were here: You can tell Roger Dillingham he really sucks.

She took another breath, and another and another, and then the heat didn't feel bad at all. She closed her eyes and leaned backward and felt the sun play against her eyelids. She had a little time to get up her courage. Roger Dillingham wouldn't have submerged himself up to his neck if he didn't intend to stay and get a good soaking. A good soaking could only blanch out bad feelings, and Molly hoped a good soaking would leach away her own faults: my pettiness, she thought, my resentment, my small mindedness. God make me your vessel.

She trained her eyes away from his. It was worse than being in an elevator. You couldn't let your eyes linger. You looked up or out to a tiny point just lower in space than a man's armpit. Otherwise your eyes were violating him. You held yourself back as a courtesy. At most you might make a comment about the weather—language that meant, We won't harm each other. John. John sometimes used an old expression of their mother's: "Don't worry. They can't eat me." Not that John believed in such wisdom.

It would take a little longer and she would loosen up, that was all, and strike up a conversation. She didn't have to accost Roger Dillingham at once. She didn't have to give him the impression that she was stalking him. She could make it look as if the realization of his identity came upon her slowly, here in the churning waters under a sun that was burning her forehead. The recognition shouldn't appear *forced*. She knew her face was as wet as a seal's and flushed, and that even if she introduced herself, it would take him a minute to connect the name with the face.

How bad could Roger Dillingham be? He liked John after all. In his reviews he was always praising John more than anyone else, except for Mary. That was because he understood how remarkable John was. When not even three specialists could figure out what was wrong with John—that's when John wanted to act at the playhouse. And who could say no to him? Everyone thought he was dying—all through *My Fair Lady*, all through *South Pacific*, all through *A Funny Thing Happened on the Way to the Forum*. But then right during the second week of *The Fantasticks* there was the miraculous transformation. But even then he was still dependent on her, afraid of every little thing and of everyone but her. And then he invested his entire inheritance from their parents into the play-house.

"You know you've made it when they hate you," John said about the reviews. But if Molly could get some constructive criticism, if she could find out why she was held in contempt by Roger Dillingham, the only person who had ever reviewed community theater in the county....

Although she feared his answer: He would tell her the truth: She wasn't convincing as a woman falling in love. And she knew why: she couldn't love—not in the normal way. She couldn't initiate the emotional progression. John didn't die, but her husband did, and she wasn't ever there for him. She hadn't been there for him or seen his death and hadn't begun to love him maturely, no, and now she could never love again. Except for John, who was at this hour up in their room napping, because he was so skinny, and he needed so much rest before he met with the acupuncturist. And somehow she was sure Roger Dillingham sensed the truth—sensed how distanced she was from mature love, from the desires of the women she impersonated. And she worried now that her own love for John was harmful. It kept John from a real life, so that he was a dandy at the race track or an ambassador of the British empire every weekend when he could be finding someone to love him now that it looked like he was going to live a lot longer. You can't stop people from wanting love. And Molly knew she had hardly brought her love to bear before Anthony left the house and got into their car and never came back again and then there was his body at the funeral parlor. Unrecognizable because of the accident. Like a dummy body.

She and Anthony had been kids in some ways! Married for less than a year! What she had to give Anthony had only begun to chirp inside her. It was nothing compared to what she would have given him if they had been together for even one more year. Because it takes time, because it's a terrible risk to love someone so much, it's a discipline, and she was weak. She was as miserable at being a wife as she was at being an actress. She was only now beginning to have the heart to admit it, almost to relax into the terrible truth.

John, she thought suddenly, John could learn to relax more too. "You're so anxious," she said to him only this morning right after they checked into the resort. "But anxiety's so funny," he said.

She knows that John doesn't feel like an alien at the resort—already she knows this. She felt a change in him even as they waited for their luggage. He complained about being tired. That was to be expected, but there was something else, some flicker of withheld excitement. She would have to steel herself against the pressure he would put on her to change her life again for him. He couldn't imagine her outside his life any more. Even though they both were young. Young and stunted, she thought.

A weight struck Molly Crane's neck. Roger Dillingham's head nestled into her neck for an instant, and without thinking, with only instinct to guide her she said, "No, you can't stay, Sir" even though she wasn't quite sure what she meant. His body turned heavily and his legs must have folded because he began sliding down her shoulder. She pushed at his shoulder and raised her knees to try to keep the big head from going under the water, and then she shouted and knew she was shouting loudly, more loudly than she had imagined she could before the water stung up high into her nose and the sounds of the bubbling whirlpool jets and the children' voices echoing from the swimming pool came to her distorted curiously as if everything around her was pushing her head down under the water for here Molly was, going under with the mammoth slippery head even while another part of her was calmly considering the situation and gathering one clear thought: Thank you, God, for my vocal training.

She lurched forward and wrapped her arms under Roger's arms, but she too was sliding again and Roger was suckered onto her. The jets were gushing and pulsing into her ears. She was losing her footing again, and foamy water was splashing just as the lifeguard—a muscular, orange-haired woman—ran up blowing a whistle, and another lifeguard ran off blowing a whistle in the opposite direction—and Molly thought of Anna of *The King and I* who whistled a happy tune to disguise fear, and Molly thought it's no good, whistling only annoys people, only annoys people, only annoys people, only annoys people. But then the lifeguard was pulling Roger Dillingham off Molly Crane like he was a great big octopus. And Molly, gasping, said, "I'm okay, I'm okay." She flipped her body onto the cement and told the lifeguard—who at last drew Roger Dillingham's body onto the cement too and worked over his flesh and began flagging—"He's a good man, you can't give up, he couldn't be a better man."

The lifeguard threw her hands in the air and clenched her fists and bent to her task again, bent and pummeled Roger Dillingham's chest with desperate new energy. She pumped at Roger's chest as if she knew, really knew, he couldn't be a better man... as if she could save his life and with it his world, his unforgiving world that had never once satisfied him since he was a boy, never once since the days when he hadn't yet learned to read but liked to sing and do little pretend-magic tricks and even teach a dog how not to snap at a pork chop for a count of three while his mother laughed and said, "You are an imp. You are a pill. You are everything, everything, everything I ever dreamed of."

❅

Melanie Rae Thon
Paris Review

HEAVENLY CREATURES

—for wandering children and their delinquent mother

1. Fathers

DIDI Kinkaid and her three children by three fathers lived in a narrow pink and green trailer at the end of a rutted road in Paradise Hollow. One wintry November night, fifteen days after my father died, eleven days after he was buried, Didi's only son climbed the hill to our house, leaped from our bare maple to a windowsill on the second floor, shattered the glass above my mother's bed, and burst, bleeding, onto her pillows.

The house was dark, all his—Mother and I had gone to town that night to eat dinner by the hot-bellied stove in my brother's kitchen.

Evan Kinkaid helped himself to twenty-two pounds of frozen venison, a bottle of scotch, six jars of sweet peaches. The boy carried away my down comforter, a green sleeping bag, our little black and white television. He found Mother's cashmere scarf, rolled tight and tucked safe in a shoebox full of cedar chips, never worn because it was too precious. Now it was gone, wrapping Evan's throat, a lovely gift, something soft and dear for him to wear home and offer Didi. The starved boy crushed chocolate cookies in a bowl of milk and sugar. He stopped to eat, then slipped his hands in Daddy's gloves: deerskin dyed black, lined with the silky fur of a white rabbit.

In exchange, he left his blood, his dirt, his smell of bonfire smoke everywhere.

On the playground the next day, I saw the little wolf in sheep's clothing: Evan Kinkaid dressed in red wool and green flannel, my father's vest and shirt—both ridiculously loose, two sizes too big for a skinny child from the Hollow.

Why should the hungry repent? Evan Kinkaid wanted me to betray him. I stared, defiant as he was. *Mine*, I thought, *one holy secret*. Mother didn't deserve to know the truth, she who had sent me to school that day, against my will, against what I believed to be my father's deepest wishes. He would have wanted me home, with her, waiting till dawn to fold the clothes Evan tossed and trampled in their bedroom. Daddy wanted me to crawl under their bed, to find every stray sock, to lay my little hands on each one of his tattered undershirts as if cloth, like skin, might still be healed. Neither he nor I wanted to lie in the dark, listening to Mother scour and scurry.

By the mercy of morning light, Daddy hoped I would discover his last words, a note to himself still crumpled in the pocket of his wrinkled trousers: *Don't forget! Honey Walnut.* A loaf of sweet bread for me or a color of stain for a birdhouse?

The dead speak in riddles and leave us to imagine.

Face to face with the righteous thief, I made a vow to keep my silence. I was ten years old that winter day, arrogant enough to feel pity for this failure of a boy, Evan Kinkaid, stooped and pale, a fourteen-year-old sixth grader who had flunked three times, Evan Kinkaid who would never go to high school.

Less than a year later, Didi Kinkaid's pink trailer burned so hot even the refrigerator melted. By then, Didi lived in the Women's Correctional Facility in Billings, and Evan at the Pine Hills School for Boys in Miles City. Meribeth, seventeen, the oldest Kinkaid, a good girl, a girl who might grow up to be useful, lived in Glasgow with foster parents and eight false siblings. Fierce little Holly, just eleven—the dangerous child who once stole my lunch and slammed me to the wall of the girls' bathroom when I accused her—had become the only daughter of a hopeful Pentecostal minister and his barren wife in Polebridge.

So nobody was home the night the Kinkaid's trailer sparked, nobody real, though on any given night there might have been six or ten or twenty-nine tossed-out, worthless, wild kids crashing at Didi's, wishing she would return, their darling delinquent mother, dreaming she would appear in time to cook them breakfast, hoping to hear the roar and grind of her battered baby-blue Apache.

What a truck! Dusty, rusty, too dented to repair—you could squeeze thirty stray kids in the back and whoop all the way to Kalispell—you could pad the bed with leaves or rags or borrowed blankets, sleep out under the stars, warm and safe even in December.

Oh Didi—slim in the hips, tiny at the waist—she might have been one of them, the best one, if you didn't spin her around too fast, if you didn't look too closely. The lost children built shelters of sticks and tarps in the woods behind her trailer. She let them drink beer in her yard. She gave them marshmallows and hot dogs to roast over the bonfire where she burned her garbage.

No wonder they loved her.

Any day now, Didi might honk her horn and rev the engine hard to wake them. *Sweet Mother of God!* Didi, home at last with four loaves of soft white bread and a five-pound tub of creamy peanut butter.

In half-sleep, the throwaway children kept their faith, but when they woke, they remembered: Mother in chains, Didi in prison. Of her seventeen known accomplices, three were willing to testify against her. *Three of them!* Sheree, Vince, Travis. *Traitors, snitches.* Three who still believed in real homes: mothers, fathers, feather pillows, fleece blankets.

Every night, these three lay alone between clean sheets, trying to be good, trying to be quiet, taking shallow breaths, hoping their clean and perfect mothers might slip into their rooms, kneel by their beds, and with tender mouths kiss them, kiss them, kiss them.

But only Didi came, in dreams, to mock and then forgive them.

Didi Kinkaid was made for trouble, slender but round, lovely to touch, lovely to hold, and mostly she liked it. To Didi Kinkaid, any roadside motel seemed luxurious.

What she liked best was the bath after, when the man, whoever he might be that night, was drowned in sleep on the bed and she was alone, almost floating, warm in the warm water, one with the water—not like the trailer where there was only a cramped closet with a spitting shower, three kids and twelve minutes of scalding water to share between them.

Any night of the week Didi might be lucky or unlucky enough to glimpse the father of one of her children—one good ole boy pumping quarters in the jukebox to conjure Elvis—one sweet, sorry sight for sore eyes slumped on a bar stool—and a feeling long lost might rise up: pity, fear, hope, desire.

There was Billy Hayes, Meribeth's father, and she'd loved him best, and she might have married him. But Billy was too young for Didi even when she was young—just sixteen when she was twenty—a skinny golden boy with a fuzz of beard and long flowing hair. Billy got sad when he drank and started looking like Jesus. She didn't have a chance with Billy Hayes, a boy still in high school, a child living with his parents. Didi knew from the start a woman from the Hollow could never keep him.

Now, the taxidermist Billy Hayes was old enough, and the years between them made no difference; his hair was thin and short; he had four kids and a wife named Mary. Mary Patrillo's patient parents had taught Billy Hayes to stuff the bodies of the dead and make the mouths of bobcats and badgers look ferocious, but the place he'd opened in Didi Kinkaid stayed empty forever.

When she told him she was pregnant, he never seemed to imagine any choice for them but having the baby—*I'll help you*, he said. And so it was: Meribeth came to be; and though Didi thought she'd loved Billy as much as she could love anybody, the child was her first true love, her first true blessing.

Billy helped her steal a crib and a high chair, booties and bibs, disposable diapers. *Shopping*, he called it. One night, their last night, he came to the trailer with a blue rubber duck and seven white rubber ducklings, toys to float in the tub Didi didn't have, so they put Meribeth in the kitchen sink with her eight ducks, and Billy, Sweet Billy Boy, hummed lullabies while he washed her.

Evan's dad was a different story, a mean sonuvabitch if ever there was one—Rick McQueen, Mister Critter Control, who was kind enough in the beginning, who rescued her at two-thirty one morning when she came home to discover pack rats had invaded the trailer. It didn't occur to her that a man willing to drown rats and feed cyanide to coyotes might harbor similar attitudes toward his own child. Evan swore to this day that he remembered his first beating. *Before I was born, when I was inside you.*

He banged his head and bruised his eye. Even now, when he's tired or mad or hungry, that place around the socket still hurts him. He traces the bone. *You have hard hips*, he says, and this much is true, so what about the rest of it?

Didi remembers how Evan kicked and punched, twisting inside her womb for days after the pummeling. She thought he'd choke, furious and desperate enough to strangle himself with his own umbilical cord. Maybe Evan truly remembers the beating, and maybe he's only heard Didi's story. Truth or tale—what does it matter in the end if a boy believes he felt his father's fists hammering?

You saved me, Didi says, and this is fact. The baby fought the man. If she'd had any inclination to forget, if she'd been tempted by Rick McQueen's tears, scared by his threats, or lulled by his promises, the baby unknown and unnamed reminded her night and day: *You let him stay, I'll kill him.*

Holly's father could have been any one of three people—it was a long winter, too cold, so it was hard to keep track of who was when, what might be possible. There was her cousin, Harlan Dekker, and a fat man by the river whose name she's blissfully forgotten, and a third man too thin, like a freak, like the Emaciated Marvel in a cage at the carnival. *Half my life behind bars*, he said, *a guard, not a prisoner*. Now he lived on the road, *free*, he said, in his rust-riddled Mustang.

The man who could suck his belly back to his spine didn't have the cash for even one night at a motel, so Didi, in her kindness, in her mercy, brought him back to the trailer, and they made love right there with three-year-old Evan and five-year-old Meribeth wide awake, no doubt, and listening. He had a pretty name, *Aidan Cordeaux*. The last part meant fuse, and the first was the fire, so maybe the flickering man did spark inside her.

Strange as it was, she often hoped the starved prison guard was Holly's father, that the night she'd conceived her youngest child, Evan and Meribeth had been there with her. *Little angels!* She felt them hovering all night, close and conscious, her darlings lying together in the narrow bunk above the bed where she and the Living Skeleton made love, where she touched the man's sharp ribs and knotted vertebrae, where she prayed, *yes, prayed*, for God to give him flesh, to restore him.

She heard her two children breathing slowly afterward, asleep at last, and the man was asleep too, up in smoke, and so she was alone, yes, but safe unto herself, blessed by her children, and the sound of their quiet breath was so sweet and familiar that she felt them as breath in her own body, as wings of sparrows softly fluttering. *God*, she thought, *his messengers*.

She was drunk enough to pretend, drunk enough to imagine. Later, the cries of feral cats in the woods sounded half-human, and she had to laugh at herself. What a hoot to think God might send angels to Didi Kinkaid in her trailer. *Just my own damn kids, but Christ, it was comforting.*

Her cousin Harlan was probably Holly's dad. It made the most sense: Holly and Harlan with that bright blond hair, those weird white eyelashes. Harlan's wife lived in Winnipeg all that winter, following her senile mother out in the snow, lifting her crippled father onto the toilet. Harlan and Didi met four times at the Kozy Kabins: twice to make love, once to watch television, once to be sorry.

More than anything, Didi wanted to believe Holly's father wasn't the fat man in his truck who passed out on top of her. She'd escaped inch by inch, hoping his cold sweat wouldn't freeze them together. She walked back to the Deerlick Saloon, to her own car, a yellow Dodge Dart that year, lemon yellow, a tin heap destined for the junkyard. She thought she should tell somebody he was out there alone at the edge of the river. She pictured him rolling off the seat to the floor, pants pulled down to his ankles, ripe body wedged underneath the dashboard. He could die tonight, numb despite all that flesh, and Didi Kinkaid would be his killer.

But the bar had been closed for hours, and her fingers were so stiff she could barely turn the key in the lock of her car door, arms so sore she could barely grip the wheel. Didi didn't feel sorry for anybody but herself by then, so she didn't stop at the all-night gas station, and she didn't call the police when she got home—she didn't even tell Aleta LaCroix, her neighbor, the babysitter—she just dropped into bed, shivering, and the truth was she was so damn cold she forgot the man, his flesh and sweat, his terrible whinny of high laughter.

In the morning, she smelled his skin on her skin and she used every drop of hot water in the shower, all twelve minutes, and she drank bright green mouthwash straight from the bottle and she listened to the news on the radio. There was no report of a dead man gone blue as ice by the river. She figured he'd been spared and so had she, but when she thought of it now, she hoped to God she hadn't been cruel or stupid enough to abandon the one who was Holly's true father.

When Didi Kinkaid's child splintered the window above my mother's bed and entered our lives, her story became my story—her only son burst in my heart, her bad boy broke me open. My father was dead. Eleven months later, the second night of November, the night Didi's pink and green trailer burned and melted, I knew my mother was dying.

Didi had been in prison since August. When I imagined her children—the desperate ones she'd borne and the wild ones she'd rescued, when I imagined all the sooty-faced, tossed-up runaways left to wander—I understood there are three hundred ways for a family to be shattered.

Soon, so soon, I too would be an orphan.

2. Fire

The fire was revenge, intimate and tribal. We came to witness, we people of the hills and hollows, lured up Didi's road by smoke and sirens. Through the flames, I saw the glowing faces of Didi's closest neighbors: Nellie Rydell and Doris Kelso, Lorna Coake and Ruby Whipple. I thought that one of them must have sparked this blaze—with her own two hands and the holy heat of her desire.

Who poured the stream of gasoline, who struck the match, who lit the torch of wood and paper? *Tell me now. I keep all secrets.* Was it one of you alone, or did all four conspire together?

For the small crime of arson, no respectable woman ever stood trial. The trailer was a temptation and an eyesore, a refuge for feral cats, a sanctuary for wayward children. Now Didi's home could be hauled away, a heap of melted rubble. *An accident,* Ruby said. *A blessing,* Lorna whispered.

Who can know for sure? Maybe the small boy called Rooster lit a pile of sticks to warm the fingers of his twelve-year-old girlfriend Simone so that it wouldn't hurt where she touched him. Maybe cross-eyed Georgia squirted loops of lighter fluid into the blaze just to see what would happen, and all the children danced in the dark, hot at last, giddy as the fire spread, too joyful now to try to smother it.

But I will always believe those four women in their righteous rage burned Didi out forever.

Didi Kinkaid trespassed against us: she harbored fugitives; she tempted boys; she tempted husbands. She slept with strangers and her own cousin—and despite all this generous love, Didi Kinkaid still failed to marry the father of even one of her children.

Compared with these transgressions, the crimes named by County Prosecutor Marvin Beloit—the violations for which Didi Kinkaid was shackled, chained, and dumped in prison—seemed almost trivial: receiving and selling stolen goods, felony offenses, theft of property far exceeding $1000. To be precise: forty-one bicycles snatched by children and fenced by Didi over a thirteen-month period.

Forty-one, including the three treasures in her last load: a black and yellow 1947 Schwinn Hornet Deluxe with its original headlight, worth an astonishing $3700; the 1959 Radiant Red Phantom, a three-speed wonder with lavish chrome, almost a motorcycle—and radiant, yes—worth $59.95 new, and now, lovingly restored by Merle Tremble's huge but delicate hands, worth $3250; finally, the lovely 1951 Starlet painted in its original Summer Cloud White with Holiday Rose trim and pink streamers, worth only $1900, but polished inch by inch for the daughter Merle never had. To him, priceless.

In court, Merle Tremble confessed: the jeweled reflector for the Phantom cost him $107. *A perfect prism of light, worth every penny.* He found a seat for the Hornet, smooth leather with a patina like an antique baseball glove, worn shiny by one particular boy's bones and muscles. *No man can buy such joy with money.*

For six years, Merle Tremble had haunted thrift stores and junkyards, digging through steaming heaps of trash to re-cover donor bikes with any precious piece that might be salvageable. Under oath, Merle Tremble swore to God he loved his bikes like children.

No wonder Didi laughed out loud, a snort that filled the courtroom. A man who believes he loves twisted chrome as much as he might love a human child deserves to lose everything he has, deserves fire and flood and swarms of locusts. But Didi's lack of remorse, her justifiable scorn, didn't help her.

For crimes named and trespasses unspoken, Didi Kinkaid received ten years, the maximum sentence.

Ten years. More than any man gets for beating his wife or stabbing his brother. More years than a man with drunken rage as his excuse might serve for barroom brawl and murder.

Didi's transgressions wounded our spirits. She fed the children no mother could tame. She loved them for a night or for an hour, just as she loved the men who shared all her beds in all those motel rooms, and this terrifying, transient love, this passion without faith that tomorrow will be the same or ever come, this endless offering of the body and the soul and the self was dangerous, dangerous, dangerous.

If she was good, then we were guilty. Exile wasn't enough. We had to burn her. When Didi heard about the fire, she knew. *Busy-body do-gooders*, she said, *always coming to my door with their greasy casseroles and stale muffins, acting all high and holy when all they really wanted was to get a peek inside, see if I had some tattooed cowboy sprawled on my bed, find out how many kids were crashing at my place and if my own three were running naked. Kindhearted ladies benevolent as that did the same damn thing to my mother. Ran her out of Riverton in the end. Killed her with their mercy.*

The bikes were just an excuse. *It could have been anything,* she said, *but in the end, I made it easy.*

3. Bicycle Bandits

Didi never asked the stray children for anything. Rooster and Simone brought the first bike to her doorstep, a silver mountain bike with gloriously fat tires, tires nubbed and tough enough to ride through snow and slush and mud and rivers, a bike sturdy enough to carry two riders down ditches and up the rocky road to Didi's trailer. A small gift, for all the times she'd fed them. Rooster said, *I've got a number and a name, a guy willing to travel for a truckload.*

Stealing bikes was a good job, one the children could keep, without bosses or customers, time clocks or hair nets. They loved mountain bikes best—so many gears to grind, so many colors: black as a black hole black, metallic blue, fool's gold, one green so bright it looked radioactive. Rooster had to ride that bike alone: his Kootenai girlfriend was afraid to touch it.

There was a dump in the ravine behind Didi's trailer, *the Child Dump,* she called it, because sometimes it seemed the children just kept crawling out of it. They glued themselves together from broken sleds and headless dolls and bits of fur and scraps of plastic. Their bones were splintered wood. Their hearts were chicken hearts. Their little hands were rubber.

She expected them to stop one day—she thought there might be nine or ten or even forty—but they just kept rising out of the pit. In court, the day three testified against her, County Prosecutor Marvin Beloit said he had reason to believe more than three hundred homeless children roamed the woods surrounding Kalispell.

They slept in abandoned cars and culverts. Busted the locks of sheds. Shattered the windows of cabins. Desperate in a blizzard last winter, two cousins with sharp knives stabbed Leo Henry's cow in the throat, split her gut with a hatchet and pulled her entrails out so that they could sleep curled up safe in the cave of her body.

Three hundred homeless children.

Sleep was good, was God, their only comfort.

Nobody in court wanted to believe Marvin Beloit. *Not in our little town.* Didi pitied him—her brother, her prosecutor— a man alone, besieged by visions. She knew the truth, but couldn't help him.

Ferris, Cate, Luke, Scarla—Hansel, Heidi, Micah, LaFlora— Dawn, Daisy, Duncan, Mirinda. These children offered themselves to Didi in humility and gratitude. Joyfully and by design, they became thieves. They'd found their purpose.

Sometimes when a child stole a bike, he stole a whole family, and they lived in his mind, a vision of the life he couldn't have: they pestered, they poked him. Nuke was sorry after he took the candy-striped tandem with a babyseat and a rack to carry tent and camp stove. That night he dreamed he was the smiling infant who had no words, who knew only the bliss of pure sensation. Wind in his face carried the scent of his mother: sweet milk and clean cotton, white powder patted soft on his own bare bottom. Daddy peddled hard in front, and the sun seemed so close and hot the baby believed he could touch it.

But Nuke woke on the hard dirt to the spit of his real name, *Peter Petrosky*, his mother's curse: *Not in my house, you little fucker.* Then he was an only child caught smoking weed laced with crack in his mother's house, in his father's shower. Doctor Robert Petrosky was a genius, an artist with a scapel who could scoop a pacemaker from a dead man and set it humming inside the chest of a black Labrador. Peter didn't wait to receive his clever father's pity or redemption. Sick with sound and light, the boy lay under his bed for an hour then climbed out the window. Now he was Nuke the nuke, a walking holocaust, sending up mushroom clouds with every footstep.

Wendy, Wanda, Bix, Griffin.

Tianna found a smoked chrome BMX with a gussetted frame and scrambler tires. She could fly on this bike, airborne off every mogul. Indestructible. *Tianna!* Thirteen years old and four fingers gone to frostbite last winter. *No more piano lessons*, she said, *no flute, no cello.* Tianna imagined sitting at the polished mahogany piano in her parents' cedar house, high on a hill, overlooking the valley. Oh! How strange and lovely the music would sound, true at last, with so many of the notes missing.

She might lie down, *just for a moment*, and fall asleep on her mother's creamy white leather sofa. Sleeping outside was torture. Tianna sucked and bit her stumps. The fingers she'd lost itched in the heat and stung in the cold. *They're still there*, she said, *but I can't see them.*

Naomi, Rose, Garth, Devon.

Angel Donner bashed into his own basement and stole his own bike, a black and orange Diablo Dynamo that any kid could see was just a pitiful imitation of a Sting-Ray, worth less than fifty dollars new and now worth nothing. He remembered it under the Christmas tree, his father's grin, his mother's joy, his pit of disappointment.

Laurel, Grace, Logan, Nikos.

There was the one who called herself Trace because she'd vanished without one. *Idaho, Craters of the Moon, family vacation.* Cleo Kruse climbed out the bathroom window while Daddy and his new wife and Cleo's two baby stepsisters lay sweetly sleeping. *Knew I was gone before it was light, but didn't start looking till sunset. I read about me in the paper. Daddy thought it was just my way—doing all I could to cause him trouble.*

Trace was the little thief who jimmied the lock of the garage where Merle Tremble had laced each spoke of his Hornet Deluxe, his Starlet, his Phantom. Cleo disappeared at eight, and now the girl gone without a trace was barely eleven. *Too big for your britches*, Daddy always said, but anybody could see she was puny. She wore loose t-shirts and baggy jeans, chopped her hair short, turned her baseball cap backwards. *I'm a boy*, she said, *half-way. That's the real problem*. She could never mind her P's & Q's, never cross her legs in church, never sit still like a lady. Cleo Kruse was a six-year-year-old bully, suspended from first grade—two months for pinning and pounding a third-grade boy who called her *Little It*, who pulled her from the monkey bars, flipped up her skirt and said, *If you're a real girl, show me.*

Boy or girl, what did it matter now? Out here in the woods, down in the Child Dump, everybody was half-human. If you stole groceries to eat in Depot Park, you could convince yourself you might go home someday, scrub yourself clean, eat at your mother's table. But if one day in August you got so hungry you ate crackling bugs rolled in leaves, you had to believe you'd turned part lizard and grown the nub of a tail. Cleo had eaten bugs in leaves so many times she decided she liked them.

Jodie, Van, Kane, Kristian—Faith, Finn, Trevor, Nova. They broke Didi's heart with their gifts and their hunger.

Sufi wanted to twirl like a dervish, spin herself into a blur, turn so fast the back became the front, the air the breath, the girl nothing. She wanted to stop eating forever, to grow crisp and thin, to see through herself like paper.

She didn't believe in theft. If nothing belonged to anybody, how could anything be stolen? Objects passed, one hand to another, and this was good, what God wanted, so she was glad to ride the Starlet out of Merle Tremble's garage, grateful to be God's vessel, perfectly at peace as she watched Cleo buzz ahead on the Hornet, and Nuke disappear on the Phantom.

Caspar, Skeeter, Dillon, Crystal—Renee, Rhonda, Bird, JoJo— Margot, Madeleine, Quinn, Ezekiel. Swaddled in her narrow prison bed, Didi counts the lost children as she tries to fall asleep—so many came to her door, and now she wants to remember. *Cody, Kira, Joyce, Jewell.* If ninety-nine were found and one missing, she wouldn't sleep: she'd search the woods all night, calling. Nate carved his own name into his own white belly, a jagged purple wound that kept opening. *If my head's smashed flat, my mother will still know me.* Ray taught the others to make beds of boughs. Cedar is soft enough, and young fir with blistered bark smells of balsam, but spruce will stab your hands and back: a bed of spruce is a bed of nails.

Didi tries to rock herself to sleep, but the rocking brings the children close, and she sees their lives, so quick and sharp, one dark cradle to another.

Dustin, Sam, Chloe, Lulu—Betsy, Bliss, Malcolm, Neville. Oh Didi, you sing their names. Mercy, Po, Hope, Isaac. Let them all join hands. Here is your ring of thieves. Let them dance like fire around us.

4. The Lover

When Didi Kinkaid was good, she was very very good. She fed the poor. She sheltered the homeless. She lived as Jesus asks us to live: turned only by love, purely selfless.

But when Didi Kinkaid was bad, she abandoned her own three children, deserted Evan and Holly and Meribeth for nine days one January while she lived with Daniel Lute in his

311

log cabin, perched high on a snow-blown ridge above Lake Koocanusa. Later, she swore she didn't understand how far it was, how deep the snow, how difficult it might be to find a road in the grip of winter.

She slept fourteen, sixteen, twenty hours. She woke not knowing if it was morning or evening, November or April. Daniel Lute's cabin whistled in the wind at the edge of outer darkness.

He fed her glistening orange eggs, the fruit of the salmon, its smoked pink flesh, his Russian vodka. Ten words could fill a day, a hundred might describe a lifetime.

They made love under a bearskin, *a Kodiak from Kodiak*, and the bed rocked like a boat, like a cradle, and the cradle was a box, sealed tight, sinking to the bottom of the lake far below them.

Daniel was a bear himself, tall but oddly hunched, black hair and black beard tipped silver, a man trapped in his own skin, condemned to live in constant hunger until a virgin loved him. Didi couldn't break that spell, and for this she was truly sorry.

On the seventh day, Daniel dressed in winter camouflage and left her alone while he stalked the white fox and the white weasel.

In utter silence, all the skinned Kodiaks walked the earth, bare and pink, like giant humans. Didi woke drenched in sweat, the skin of Daniel's bear stuck to her.

His fire flickered out. She'd never been so cold. She thought she'd die here, the stranger's captive bride, her face becalmed by hypothermia. But her children came to drag her home. Their muttering voices surged, soft at first, then angry. She tasted Holly's black licorice breath and smelled Evan's wet wool socks. Meribeth said, *It's time, Mom. Get up.*

The children sat on the bed. Didi felt their weight, but never saw them. Tiny fingers pinched her legs like claws. Two little hands gripped her wrists and tugged. Six tight fists pressed hard: chest, ribcage, pelvis, throat.

The basin by the bed was full. It took all her strength and all her will to rise from this bed of death and go outside to piss in the snow. Her clamoring children had grown furiously still, unwilling to touch, unwilling to help. She ate pickled herrings from a tiny tin. They tasted terrible; they filled her up. She pulled Daniel Lute's wool pants over her own denim jeans and cinched them tight with his leather belt. Though the bearskin was heavy, she took it too, just in case she couldn't make it off the mountain, just in case she needed to lie down and sleep inside the animal.

She returned with gifts to appease her children: $309 in cash, two pounds of smoked salmon, a silver flask with a Celtic cross, still miraculously full of Daniel's brandy.

She came with a preposterous tale, the truth of sinking thigh-deep in the snow as she climbed down the ridge, the luck of finding the road around the lake before dark, the blessing of hitching a ride with an old woman driving herself to the hospital in Libby. Adela Odegard had crackers in the car, five hand-rolled cigarettes, half a thermos of coffee. *The gifts of God for the people of God: Body, Blood, Holy Ghost.* Didi ate and drank and smoked in humble gratitude.

Adela Odegard looked shriveled up dark as an old potato, a woman so yellow, so thin, Didi thought she might be dead already, but her wild, white hair glowed and made her weirdly beautiful.

In Libby, Adela delivered Didi to her nephew, Milo Kovash, and Didi slept on his couch that night. In the morning, Milo gave her ten dollars and dropped her at the truck-stop diner. He knew a waitress there named Madrigal, and the waitress had a friend named Fawn who had a little brother named Gabriel, *Gabe Lofgren,* sixteen years old and glad to skip school to drive Didi Kinkaid down to Kalispell.

A story like that could turn the hard of heart into believers, or the most trusting souls into cynics.

5. Home

Didi's children chose to believe. *Mercy,* she thought, *who deserves it?* She smelled of creosote and pine, pickled herring, her own cold sweat gone rancid. She had Daniel's pants and belt as proof—so yes, some of what she remembered must have happened.

After her shower, Didi wore the bearskin around her naked self, his head above her head, and her children stroked her fur: their own mother, so soft everywhere. The Kodiak had a face like a dog's. He might be your best friend. *From a distance.*

Didi told her children that the cabin above the lake was dark as the inside of a bear's belly. *Swallowed alive,* she said, *but I had a silver fishing knife; I stole it from the trapper.* She showed them the jagged blade. *I cut myself out when the bear got sleepy.*

Now the Kodiak's skin was her skin, the gift of the father she never had, Daniel Lute: she could wear him like a coat, pin him to the wall, use him as her blanket.

Didi and her children drank Daniel's brandy, and the ones who wanted to forget almost did forget how they'd lived without her.

Two nights before Didi returned, little mother Meribeth, not yet thirteen, had made soup with ketchup and boiled water, crushed saltines and a shot of Tabasco. Every morning of the week, she got her ten-year-old brother and six-year-old sister to the bus on time—so nobody would know, so nobody would come to take them.

Though Evan might pull Holly from her swing, though Holly might bite him, though Meribeth might scold them both—*You little shits*, might cuss them down, *I'm so damn tired*—they belonged to one another in ways that children who live in real houses never belong to their brothers and sisters.

Only Holly stayed hard now, refusing to eat Daniel's fish, loving the pang of her hunger, the fishing knife stuck sharp in her belly. Brandy burned her throat and stomach, and she loved that too, the way it hurt at first, then soothed her. *Mother in a bottle, the slap before the kiss, the incredible peace that comes after.*

What do I know of Didi's grief? Who am I to judge her?

The day I became a twenty-two-year-old widow, the day my husband who was a fireman died by fire—not in a trailer or a house, not as a hero saving a child, but as a father driving home, as a husband who dozed, as a man too weary to turn the wheel— that day when my husband's silver truck skidded and rolled to the bottom of the gully— when three men came to my door to tell me there was no body for me to identify— only a man's teeth, only dental records—that impossibly blue October day, I began to understand why a woman might refuse to dress and forget to wash, how a mother might fail to rise, fail to love, fail to wake and feed her children.

Didi, I know what it means to melt away, to repent forever in dust and ashes. My daughters lived because my brother found us. My children ate because my brother in his bitter mercy stole them.

Lilla, Faye, Isabelle—most darling ones, most beloved—though I lay in my own bed, I deserted them in spirit.

In the days after the trailer burned, in the months after Didi Kinkaid went to prison, people said she got what she deserved. *But Didi, what about your children?*

One Friday night, as Didi lay rocking in the cradle of Daniel Lute's bed, Meribeth and Holly dressed up in her best clothes—a slinky green dress, a sparkly black sweater. The little girls teetered on their mother's spiked heels. Evan let Meribeth paint his nails pink and glossy. Holly rouged his cheeks and smeared his mouth red while he was sleeping. In the morning, the boy glimpsed the reflection of his own flushed face and soft lips, and before it occurred to him to be ashamed, he thought, *Look at me! I'm pretty.*

Didi, no matter what we deserved, our children deserved to stay together.

6. Mother

After her nights under the bearskin, Didi made a promise to always get herself home before dawn, to never again let her children wake alone in daylight.

She vowed to love her work. That's where the trouble started. She'd spent the whole dark day hunched over her sewing machine, drinking and weeping like her own pitiful mother. *Oh, Daphne!* Seven years gone, ashes scattered to the wind from a high peak in Wyoming, and still, after all this time, she could blow through a crack under the door and make her daughter miserable.

They were ashamed together, mending clothes for the dead who can't complain and don't judge you. Didi saw Daphne's crippled hands, each joint twisted by arthritis. Mother needed her Whiskey Sours, her Winston Lights, her amber bottle of crushed pills—though the killers of pain made it hard to sew, and the smoke made her bad eyes blurry.

Seeing her mother like this made Didi wish for the father she didn't have. Murmuring beekeeper, Jehovah's Witness, busted-up rodeo rider with a broken clavicle—who was he?

Be kind, Daphne said, *any man you meet might be your daddy.*

Didi's real father was probably the hypnotist at Lola Fiori's eighteenth birthday party, the Amazing Quintero, who chose Daphne because, he said, *Pretty girls with red hair are the most susceptible.*

Under his spell, Daphne was an owl perched on a stool, a wolf on all fours, a skunk, a snake, a jackrabbit, a burro. She hooted and howled. Quintero made her ridiculous.

Alone, in Quintero's room, the hypnotist blindfolded her with a silky cloth, its violet so deep she felt it bleeding into her.

Didi imagined her mother on her hands and knees again, not hypnotized, the scarf tied around her head like a halter. If this was the night, if Quintero was the father, if her mother hooted and howled and bucked and brayed the night Didi was conceived, the whole world was horrible.

As Didi sewed, as Didi drank whiskey and water, as her own fingers ached, as her own seams grew crooked, she thought, *There you are, Mama. I'm just like you.*

At dusk, she delivered the pressed clothes to Devlin Slade's Funeral Home: a gray suit for a handsome young man and a white christening dress for a newborn baby.

She meant to drive straight home. Rain had turned to sleet, and all the dead were with her. She was almost to the Hollow, almost safe with her children in the trailer, and the sleet softly became snow, and she thought God must love her even now, despite her fear, despite her sorrow. In the beams of her headlights, He showed her the secret of snow: each flake illuminated.

Each one of them, each one of us, is precious.

Mesmerized by snow, Didi didn't see the deer until the animal leaped, with astonishing grace, as if to die on purpose. The doe bounced onto the hood and crumpled on the slick pavement, but she didn't die, and Didi stopped and got out of the truck and walked back down the road to witness the creature's suffering. The animal lay on her side, panting hard, legs still running. Frenzied, she tried to stand on fractured bones. They'd done this to each other.

A man appeared, walking out of the snow, a ghost at first, then human. He'd seen it all, before it happened. The stranger had a gun in his glovebox to put Didi and the deer out of their misery. The blast of the bullet through the doe's skull made Didi's bones vibrate. She felt snowflakes melting on her cheeks and was amazed again: this mercy in the midst of sorrow.

The man dragged the limp animal toward the woods, then knelt to wipe his hands in the snow. She would have gone anywhere with him. That January night, Didi Kinkaid considered Daniel Lute her personal savior. *Heading to town*, he said. *Need some medicine.*

She ditched the Apache less than a mile from the trailer, and slid into Daniel's El Camino. She told him: *One drink, that's all, three kids home alone*; and Daniel said, *No problem.*

If Didi learned to work with love, nothing like this could ever happen again. She had small hands and a good eye for the eye of the needle, a mother's gifts, both curse and blessing. Self-pity led to betrayal. Any work done with dignity might become holy. Sometimes, as you sewed a frail woman into her favorite lavender dress, as you stitched the seams to fit close where she'd shrunken, you touched her skin and felt all the hands of all the people who had ever loved her.

After Didi Kinkaid came home to the children she'd abandoned, she saw every filthy, furious, half-starved stray who rose out of the Child Dump as her own. Their mothers had failed to love them enough, and now they hated themselves with bitter vengeance.

Mine, she thought, *each one. I was that careless.*

When she cut gum out of Holly's hair, or bandaged Meribeth's thin wrist, or touched the sharp blades of Evan's narrow shoulders, she couldn't believe she'd done what she had done; she didn't know how she'd survived one day without them. No man could save her now. No tub was deep enough to tempt her. She sewed with faith. She loved her children. She never stayed out till dawn. She kept these promises. She offered herself to the strays, and the ritual of love made her really love them.

7. The Road to Prison

Between March 1989 and early April 1990, Didi borrowed her cousin Harlan Dekker's white van three times to deliver bicycles to Beau Cryder who agreed to meet her just south of Evaro. For testimony against her, Beau walked free. *Flesh peddling*, the lawyers called it, not in court but to each other.

Nobody wanted Cryder, twenty-five and still a kid, a bad luck boy, out of work seven months, with a pregnant eighteen-year-old wife and a two-year-old son. Nobody wanted to trace the bikes to Liam Jolley, Beau's uncle, a once-upon-a-time hero in Vietnam and now just a crippled ex-cop in Missoula. Nobody ever wanted to hear how Liam's devoted daughter Gwyneth had ferried the bikes—sometimes whole and sometimes in pieces—to dealers in Butte, Boise, Anaconda, and Bozeman.

They were the victims of Didi's crimes. Her body could be exchanged for theirs, her breath for their freedom. Nobody in or out of court objected.

When Didi learned the value of Merle Tremble's bikes, she understood she'd been both betrayed and cheated. Beau paid two hundred for the set, three-twenty for the load: at the time, it seemed a fortune. Didi planned to stop in Kalispell on her way home. She wanted to buy her raggedy band of thieves two buckets of fried chicken and a tub of buttery mashed potatoes. They needed brushes and toothpaste, calamine for poison ivy, gauze to wrap their cuts and burns, arnica for bruises. She intended to bring gallons of ice cream: *Fudge Ecstasy, Banana Blast, Strawberry Heaven*. She wanted the children to know there was enough: they could eat themselves sick tonight and still eat again tomorrow. Sooner or later, she'd spend everything she'd earned on them. She didn't care about her profit.

Didi took Evan on her last trip, to help her load the bikes, to help her deal with Cryder. She promised to pay him fifty. *My best boyfriend*, she said, *my partner*. In truth, she'd made him her accomplice.

They might have gone free for lack of evidence, but Beau Cryder refused to take Angel Donner's Dynamo and a cheap BMX with popped spokes and a bent axle. Didi headed back across reservation land, through Ravalli, Dixon, Perma. She thought she was safe here, outside whiteman's law, protected by the Kootenai and Salish. She planned to dump the bikes before she got to Elmo.

They stopped at Wild Horse Hot Springs, *to celebrate*, she said, and they left the bikes in the van while they soaked for an hour, naked together in one room, immersed in hot mineral water.

She never figured on a raid. Never contemplated the possibility that Travis Poole might become a snitch, might want to go home, might tell his father, who would tell the police, who would tip bounty hunters—two trackers who lived outside the laws of any nation, who were free to bust down the

door of a private room and drag a kicking woman and her biting boy from sacred water. The men shoved Didi and Evan
out the door barefoot and naked, wrapped them in stiff wool
blankets, bound them, gagged them, and stuffed them face
down in the backseat of their beat-to-hell black Cadillac.

At precisely three-twenty-six, back on whiteman's time,
the fearless hunters delivered two fugitives and their stolen
bicycles to the proper authorities in Kalispell.

8. The Kingdom on Earth

Didi never caught a break for good behavior. If a guard
spit words, she spit back. She was disrespectful. She stashed
contraband: twenty-seven unauthorized aspirin, ten nips of
tequila, and one shiny gold tube of coral lame lipstick. Lipstick inspired vanity and theft, dangerous trades and retribution. Twice denied parole, Didi Kinkaid served every minute
of her three-thousand-six-hundred and fifty-three-day sentence.

Now, four years free, she sews clothes for the living and
the dead in Helena. She could start a new life with a new
name and a grateful lover in Vermont or Texas. But she stays
here, close enough to visit Evan once a week in Deer Lodge.
Her boy lives in a cell, down for fifty-five, hard time, attempted murder.

Evan was twenty years old and out of the Pine Hills
School for Boys just thirteen months when he hit the head-
lines. A weird tale: hunting with a forbidden friend, Gil Ransom, thirty-nine and on parole, a known felon—dusk, out of
season—Gil's idea—*just a little adventure*. They fired from the
windows of the car—dumb beyond dumb and highly illegal.
Any shadow that moved was fair game: deer, dog, rat,

chicken. They smoked some weed. They split a six-pack. Evan saw trees walk like men through the forest.

An off-duty cop who recognized the roar of Gil's Wrangler followed them up a logging road, bumped them into the ditch, and tried to arrest them. Gil shot Tobias Revell three times: *Just to slow him down, nothing serious.* They left him crawling in the snow, wounded in the leg and neck and shoulder. He could have bled to death. He could have died of shock or hypothermia. But he was too pissed off to die. He lived to speak. He lived to bring those men to justice.

Justice? Evan learned that it didn't matter who pulled the trigger. For the abandonment of Tobias Revell, for the failure to send someone out that night to save him, Evan Kinkaid shared Gil's crime: the gun, the hand, the thought, the bullets.

Meribeth does not visit her brother. She teaches in a three-room school and lives without husband or children in a two-room shack up a canyon west of Lolo. I picture her as she was: flat-chested and gangly. She speaks softly. She walks swiftly. She never looks anybody straight in the eyes, but she never looks away either. She seems humble and kind, dignified even when she wears a dress sewn from an old checkered tablecloth. Meribeth Kinkaid, a princess in rags, mysteriously moving among peasants who scorn her.

Meribeth's worst fear is that one day her mother and brother and sister will knock at the door of her secret cottage in the canyon. Meribeth's deepest desire is that Evan and Holly and Didi will one day sit at her table to share a meal of bread and fish and wine and olives, that they will all sleep that night and every night thereafter in one bed in the living room, on three mattresses laid out on the floor and pushed close together, breathing as one body breathes, heart inside of heart, holy and whole, miraculously healed.

Eight months after she was adopted, Holly Kinkaid escaped Reverend Cassolay and his good wife Alicia. She didn't want to be saved. She'd been baptized by fire. If she couldn't live with her brother and sister, if the trailer was burned to rubble and gone forever, Holly wanted to live alone in a junked car or a tree or a culvert.

I am a mother now, an orphan, and a widow.

Sometimes in the early dark of winter I feel Holly at my window watching my daughters and me as we eat our dinner. She won't come in. The cold no longer feels cold to her. The cold to her is familiar.

This morning—a deep gray November morning, woods full of damp snow, light drizzle falling—I followed the school bus to town, twenty-three miles. My daughters Lilla and Faye, nine and six, sat in the far back seat of the bus to flap their hands and wave furiously, to smash their lips and noses flat against smudged glass. Their terrible faces scared me.

Isabelle, my youngest, my baby, slept in her carseat. I heard every wet sound: wipers in the rain, melting snow, dripping trees, the murmuring woods closing around us.

I saw flowers in the rain: boys in blue and girls in yellow, a tiny child in a pink fur coat, and another dressed in bright red stockings—all the pretty children waiting for the bus in bright pairs and shimmering clusters. Sometimes a mother stood in the center to shelter them beneath her wide umbrella.

In this rain, in this dark becoming light, I began to see the ones who won't come out of the woods. *Griffin, Bix, Wanda, Wendy.* They wear olive green and brown and khaki, coats the color of fallen leaves, jeans stained with blood, boots always muddy. They steal the skins of wolves and wings of falcons. The red fur of the fox swirls down Tianna's spine, and her teeth are long but broken.

Hansel, Heidi, Micah, LaFlora. They never grow up or old. They starve forever. Cleo Kruse who vanished without a trace, who could never be just one thing or another, has the body of a lynx and the eyes of a hoot owl, the legs of a mule deer, and the hands of a child.

Faith, Bliss, Trevor, Nova.

Vince Lavadour who betrayed Didi Kinkaid, who testified against her, has lost his arms and legs, has found instead his fins and tail. The boy slips free at last, a rainbow trout, gloriously striped and speckled.

Nate, Ray, Grace, Laurel.

Angel's skin bursts with thirty-thousand barbed quills. Bold in his new body, Angel says, *Only fire will kill me.*

Dustin, Rose, Lulu, Chloe—Georgia, Sheree, Travis, Devon.

Rooster knows that if he eats as the coyote eats, he will live forever. And so he does eat: snakes, eggs, plastic, rubber, sheep, tomatoes, rusted metal, dead horses by the road, dead salmon at the river.

Simone, Nuke, Duncan, Daisy.

Last summer, Sufi flung herself fifty feet into the air at twilight. Flying heart, Vesper Sparrow, she sang as if one ecstatic cry could save the world. Now she lies broken under dead leaves. She smells only of the woods—pine under snow, damp moss, a swirl of gold tamarack needles. Her wish comes true at last: she is one with God, one with mud and air and water. But if Didi called her name tonight, from death to life she might recover.

Naomi, Quinn, Madeleine, Skeeter—Rhonda, JoJo, Neville, Ezekiel—Finn, Scarla, Luke, Jewel.

How quickly the night comes!

I am home at dusk, so many hours later, my three girls safe this night in the house their father built before he left us. Birds cry from the yard, and I go to them, a mother alone in the gathering dark. A flock of crows whirls into the gray sky. *Didi, there must be ninety-nine, there must be three hundred dark birds rising on their dark wings.* When they land, the crows fill a single tree, every branch of a stripped maple.

Your children are my children. They are dangerous. They are in danger.

One by one, each black-eyed bird falls to the ground, brittle and breakable, terrible and human.

Oh my children, all my little children, I knew you before you were in the womb. Love is the Kingdom on Earth. As we fall to earth this day, let us love, let us love one another.

❄

Julie Rose
The Antioch Review

STUNT FOR TWO

HE was up on the stilts, sweat and white paint creating a soup upon his face, but he held the smile, orange lips forced upward in a pantomime of idiotic joy. Juggling the batons, he stalked through the crowd collected in town at the mouth of the covered bridge for the annual Bridge Dance. Town was a post office, a fly shop, a diner, and a sign that said Hank's Meats Dressed Here. Town was the two hundred odd people who lived in the turretted, cupolaed old houses perched along the banks of the river and on the low, sloping mountains rising out of the river valley; town was who whittled and canned jellies and fly-tied during the winter months in expectation of the influx of spring and summer hikers and fishermen; town was who waited out those bountiful months in the valley—filled with cyclists and kayakers in neon-colored ly-cra, garrulous men in waders, and trail-beaten Appalachian hikers in search of a shower—for the contraction of the valley back into the alcoholically quiet winter months, whose blanket of stupor and silence was punctuated only by infrequent, random acts of self-destruction.

The families amongst whom he'd grown up, those who lived in the shacks, cabins, and trailers along the river or in the wooded ridges overlooking the river valley, sat on red and blue coolers in the middle of Main Street, drinking beer. They visited each other's coolers, squatting. An Irish band from The Lantern was playing, and the boys from the West Hope fire station were tending charcoal grills in the apron of park by the river. In the oppressive stillness of the late afternoon, clouds gathering above, the charcoal smoke clung in the air without moving.

Luke singled people out one at a time, first making eye contact, then a series of faces: happy, joyous, sad, weeping, then quizzical, then happy again, and they would make them back at him, mimicking his mimed faces like an infant in a bassinet. At first he had been surprised and disappointed by it, how easily manipulated they were by his faces, how foolish they were prepared to be.

They were the same faces he had made for Sun when she was little, as she lay on a blanket on the lawn while he practiced fire-eating or a new stunt. He'd go over in between stunts and run through the face series and she'd shriek with gratification as if he had just told her the secret meaning of the universe. Her chubby legs would flail in the air and she'd be shrieking, howling, with delight. "Your mother's not coming back," he'd say, still smiling furiously. "So you're stuck with me. Unless you have a better idea," he went on, producing a bottle filled with milk from his sleeve. Her mouth clamped on to the nipple hungrily.

Now he grimaced broadly and scratched his head and lit his clown hair on fire and put it out again. An attractive dark-haired woman in riding breeches whom he didn't recognize squealed in delight and grimaced back at him. "Look out, your hair," she called up at him. "Look Ian, look at his hair," she said, tugging at her paunchy husband. He obligingly lit his hair on fire for the husband. As he went through his faces and waited for the man's attempts to match them, he tried to dredge up compassion and fondness for humanity, for the man and his wife, but they had the glossy, sleek, complacent look of people to whom nothing of depth or urgency had ever happened, beyond the inconvenience of turned milk in the fridge or too much chlorine in the pool, and surely such people existed: those that glided over the surface of their lives without incident, didn't they? He went through each face, all of the sad and angry and questioning ones, until he got full circle back to the joyful face. He made it even though summoning joy felt like approaching a stranger and hugging him.

At first he hadn't seen how he could smile and clown and play the fool, the court jester, in all the grimness of the past month, but then he had discovered that up in his aerie on the stilts, or on stage swallowing fire, or outdoors driving a motorcycle through a false wall that burst into flames behind him, he was at a pleasant remove not only from other people, but the part of himself that lay awake at night, thinking unquiet self-hating thoughts, the purely hateful part that wanted to lash out and strike a man in a grocery store for yelling at his son, or tell the woman who was no longer his wife that he had never loved her and had cheated on her repeatedly (both lies), or in some other way match another's cruelty with his own. Then he went through his routine on the dark narrow lawn beside the cabin: fire eating, juggling, handkerchiefs and other objects appearing out of improbable places, and it kept him from himself, or at least, the part of himself that he dreaded and loathed, the part that was always asking *Why?* and *If only I hadn't* and *If only she had* ... which he knew to be a thankless revolution of the mind and not really thought at all.

Painting up with the pot of white earlier that afternoon, he had reminded himself that the expectations upon a clown were merely these: that he light parts of himself on fire; that he routinely wet his pants; that he fail to anticipate falling objects and full buckets of water and snakes sprung from cans; that he stumble and trip and fall on his duff with frequency; and that, amidst all such self-abuse, he retain his equanimity. At forty-one, the foolishness and self-flagellation of his clown self seemed to him to match his real personality more closely than did the intelligent dark features that reemerged under the washcloth at the end of each gig. They worked against him, he knew. What he said and did were disappointing in comparison. In his affections, he was urgent and puppyish, a face licker. *I love you this much,* arms spread wide, he would say to Sun as the school bus pulled up on the dirt road outside the cabin. At fourteen, his daughter's nose would be snarled in embarrassment, her hands jammed into her pockets to forestall any hugging intentions he might have had. To the few friends that were still stuck in the town of West Hope like him, he told many self-deprecating narratives about "the clown's life," as if it were happening to someone else. Far better to mock oneself, to render oneself ludicrous, than to be an object of pity.

The first two kayakers appeared at the northern bend of the river. From those stationed on the banks came cries of encouragement as they hit the riffles, shot under the covered bridge, and disappeared around the southern bend. Beyond, on the far side of the river, they were parking cars in a field. The sun was setting across the metal hoods of the parked cars. The river was coming down now after the spring run-off; in the middle large rocks jutted out and a blue heron stood motionless upon them, then the riffles flowed away under the covered bridge girders where it turned deep and wide and fast and where the camp sites and showers for the Appalachian Trail hikers were. Farther down river was his place, the old fishing cabin with the screen porch he had built for Chloe to use as a studio when he and Chloe and Sun had first moved in.

From across the river in the parking field he heard the thudding of car doors and squiggles of laughter of women when there are more than two. The latecomers traipsed across the field to the road. Through the covered bridge came three tall figures and behind them tagged a small one, whom he presumed was a child. She wore a long t-shirt—a dress?—and as she emerged from the tunnel, the other three going on without her, the child looked up at him with the unmistakable smile of a seductive, horny woman who had spent too long on the Appalachian Trail by herself, and said "Well, *do* something." She had a tiny foxlike face that ended in a pointy chin, and dark predator-like eyes. She was nineteen or twenty, at most. From the glow in her face and eyes, it was almost a litness from within; he could tell that she had not yet ceased to be bewildered by and in thrall to her life in the way of children. She had not yet experienced her first real disappointment in life. She did not know to be afraid. *Do* something, she repeated in that brash, bossy, tough girl kind of voice which he had heard his daughter Sun adopt around boys. The girl's ripe scent was camouflaged with bug spray, and he guessed immediately that she was staying at the campground. He tooted and lit his nose for her and made it blink in an urgent flashing. She glanced once over her shoulder at him and fled into the crowd toward the bandstand.

He scanned the crowd for the fox-girl. She struck up conversations with the band members, and then with two of the boys from Sun's high school who were known to have set the fire that had burned down The Lantern. He watched her anxiously, with the growing urge to protect or at least caution her, give her fair warning about the world. When she disappeared from view he wove through the crowd with the idiotic smile plastered across his face looking for her. She had sleek hair pulled back in a pony tail and as the night fell and the street lights came on she looked like an otter, emerging into a pool of evening light, with her pointy white face and bright twitching eyes, and the hand holding the cigarette like a little paw she kept scritching up to her face and dropping down again in an anxious gesture as she talked to the band. She used tough language; he overheard that much, and it made him grin, along with which arrived a sharp, twisting, visceral pain, as of a boa winding through his innards; grinning and twisting up inside, he looked at the girl and was reminded of nothing so much as of Sun coming down from her room in an Evil Knievel Halloween costume he had once bought her, and, at twelve, announcing that she was going on the F-ing job with him. She had refused to wear a top that summer, running around in cutoffs and barefeet with her flat washboard chest bare as well, saying she didn't care, the boys got to. She made up a series of stunts for two to lure him into taking her with him on jobs.

Last month, when she was nearly fifteen, he had at last agreed to demo the best one. She drove the pickup forward very slowly. Attached to the fender by a retractable leash line, a collar around his neck, he was to chase behind, attempting to climb into the bed of the truck, failing, and, ultimately, permitting himself to be towed across the grass. They had started out, and her face glowed with pleasure as she turned back from the driver's seat to look at him.

The girl's face glowed like that. She did a subdued, little dance by herself off to the side of the bandstand. He followed the glow and felt the twisting.

When it started to rain, the drops hitting the river first in little spats, he twisted up his face in gratitude. The girl had gone into Sal's. She sat in a booth looking out at the rain. Through the distortion of the old glass she looked at him, he thought, as if she wanted something. He took his time. He knew exactly what he would do. The band broke down their set, the firemen covered their grills, and, as the rain came down more heavily, people ran under the bridge. When it cleared to a slow drizzle, everyone ran for their cars, lugging coolers and children. He took his time getting off the stilts, and he walked slowly toward his truck in the parking field.

He squinted at the wet road, the river running on one side, the rock face out of which the road had been carved jutting up on the other. A quarter mile from the covered bridge he spotted her. She was walking in the dress, no rain jacket, no black garbage bag as some of the hikers wore, back toward the campground. He slowed.

"Need a lift? Campground shuttle going your way," he said.

"Great," she said and as he heard her tough little twang something akin to heartburn began seething in his chest.

She jumped into the front seat, wet and ripe smelling and yes, there was that brightness in her eyes and even in her wet skin, nothing ethereal about it, just vitally alive, and acutely conscious of that fact. She kept glancing over at him and snickering quietly, as if she found it extremely amusing that she was being driven to her site by a clown.

"What?" he said.

"Nothing." She shrugged. The road under the pines through the campground snaked around toward the river sites and then looped back onto the main road.

"You know you really shouldn't assume that everyone you meet is going to have your best interests at heart," he said. A yellow dome tent came into view. He slowed and waited.

"I don't," she said. Then she propped her knees on the dash and continued telling him about the Blue Ridge Mountains and how she had gotten lost in them.

"Alright, keep going," he said and drove out of the campground toward his cabin.

At the kitchen sink, he scrubbed the face paint off with a dish towel. He mopped under his arms with the towel, wrung it out, put water on for tea and listened for the running water of the shower to stop. He scooped a clutch of postcards that lay face up on the table into an overturned pile and went into the bedroom to change into a clean shirt. The postcards were all from Chloe.

Last month he had been working in the growing darkness with the batons, not noticing the fading light it had happened so gradually, when she had called, sounding drunk.

"Remember that first summer in the cabin, just the three of us?" she had said without salutation. "I would be touching up a canvas on the porch, looking out the window and listening for her. One day, I saw you standing out in the middle of the river casting. You had her rigged up in a rucksack on your back. That's when I knew it would be alright."

"What do you want?" he said. After fourteen years, still the old anger.

Chloe in a sleeveless summer dress and bare feet, her pale blonde hair dark and wet from the shower, saying, inanely, "There's tuna salad in the fridge. Don't forget to call Phil and Joanne and tell them we're not coming," and then standing awkwardly at the front door, like a stranger waiting to be escorted out.

"The diptych paintings are going better than I expected," she said. "I'm calling them 'Mirrors of Self.'"

"If you're calling for Sun she's not here."

Hurt silence from Chloe. He could picture her, sitting in the big armchair she used to have on the porch. She would be staring out the warehouse windows of her now much larger studio in Miami, and looking from painting to painting, and feeling the deep satisfaction brimming over, and yet having the whole night stretching before her, and with the sun setting pink and flamboyant and a wine glass on the floor by the chair and her ashtray all poised to enjoy the pleasure of unwinding and talking about her most recent show and the new one in progress in modest, self-effacing terms, she would lift up the phone and call, and how like a cat slinking up on your chest on a cold night, rumbling away under your chin, to satisfy its fleeting and undiscriminating need for warmth and companionship, not to be mistaken for fondness.

"You didn't want this, remember? 'A life of quiet desperation,' was the exact quote, I think," he said.

"Tell Sun I called," she said, "If you can rouse yourself out of your self-pity long enough."

He had stood with the phone in his hand. He had thought he could feel the dull ache spread through each entrail and organ of his body. Outside the river was blanketed in fog. The skid marks in the grass were healing over, and the schoolbus driver had only once forgotten that week and stopped along the road by his cabin.

He had dragged his mattress out onto the screen porch to hear the river that night. Lying awake, listening to its drone, he had jumped up, relit the kerosene wick, and began rummaging through the house room by room, piling essential things you would need to survive in the wilderness—waterproof matches, water jug, blankets, food tins, rods, reels, hunting knife—on an empty chair on the porch. He sat back down, and lit a cigarette, and looked at it, calmer now. If need be, he could do that. Drive to the Canadian interior and let the wilderness take him when and how it wanted. In the morning, waking and taking his first mug of coffee out onto the porch, glancing at the pile, he'd felt foolish.

"She had plans I told you," he had said the next time Chloe called. "She's with a friend."

What friend, Chloe wanted to know. She wanted the name of the friend and the phone number. She wanted to talk to Sun. Give her the number.

"I'm not giving you the goddamn number so you can forget it," he burst out. He pounded his fist against the kitchen cabinet. The china rattled inside. "She's not here, goddamnit. Don't you listen?"

Where had she gone? the voice wanted to know. The voice no longer belonged to his ex-wife, nor to anything but the implacable. He told it, dismally, that she had gone, that she had *cut her tether, gone AWOL, flown the coop,* did it get the idea? He spoke from the mesmerized deep sleeping place within himself, the part of himself that was in hibernation.

The voice suggested that she might be somewhere in San Francisco, acquiring more body piercings. He was silent. When the voice had said that perhaps she was in Maine, somewhere with a rocky shore (she loved to swim), he had said he thought that more probable. He pictured her there. She was leaping from rock to rock on a jetty that stretched to the sea's horizon. She leapt, getting smaller and smaller, until she disappeared.

The shower stopped running and the girl poked her head around the bathroom door to ask for an old shirt and a pair of sweatpants. "If it's not too much trouble," she apologized.

"Not at all. I have a daughter about your size," he said, and rummaged around in Sun's drawers in the living room, his fingers stiff and fumbly and unresponsive all of a sudden as he herded through the jumbled clothes and came away with her old blue sweatshirt with the hood and a pair of jeans with holes in the knees. He handed them to the girl in the bathroom, looking the other way.

"What's your name, anyway?" he said to the rain dripping down the screens on the porch and the empty living room.

"My trail name's Marigold. You're a saint," said the girl, stepping up behind him, and draping her arms over his shoulders the way Sun used to when she wanted to ride on his shoulders and like a reflex, he pulled the girl up and over his shoulders, cradled her in his arms, and deposited her on the mattress on the screen porch. She grabbed at his ankle and pulled him onto her and stuck her hands under his arms and then ran them down his sides first outside then under his shirt trying to get him to laugh, and saying Oh no you don't mister, and it was as if they were two creatures denned together in a storm by chance, and with two creatures, say wolverines, playful and feeling each other out, both, it didn't matter that they knew nothing about each other. They found it out the fast way.

She wanted to wrestle and tussle at him and show him she was swifter than he was for all his strength, and he let her slip out when he effortlessly pinned her, the way he had always let Sun, and he felt that he knew the essence of her, the girl-core cat fighter in her and in all girls until they truly become women, and even then sometimes they let themselves remember it, he thought as she pulled him onto her and then pretended to fight him off. She made it clear that she desired him, and desired that he admire her, and submit to her, as she snarled and clawed and ran her hands everywhere, fingers in his mouth, a hand behind his neck, bringing his head down and opening her mouth to his and brushing her hand over the hillock and he felt himself cut loose from the grim mooring he'd hooked himself on and was drifting on a fast joyful current with this girl whose neck he plunged under to kiss and as he nosed down from her throat toward her breasts it was Sun's scent, unmistakably, the sweet chamomile milky smell of her skin still in her sweatshirt, and she was looking proudly out of the cab of the truck, looking back at him and grinding the gears so that he cursed and motioned her out of the truck.

"Like this," he had said, and jerked the truck into first, revved the engine, pulled to the edge of the lawn where she'd ripped up the grass, his eyes burning furiously looking at that grass where the brown slashes were and which would turn yellow and stale, and he tossed it into reverse and backed angrily across the lawn in a zig zag making a hideous thump as he backed into her where she must have been squatting. He heard the thump and pulled forward. When the tires thudded over what felt like a hillock in that same instant, he bowed his head on the wheel and, after pausing, slammed his forehead repeated against the steering wheel as hard as he could, and now he was slamming the girl back against the pillows piled at one end of the mattress, saying Your real name. Tell me your real name, and she told him and he said, No it's not. You never mind what your name is. You call me Daddy, say it. Say it. She held still beneath him as he pushed himself into a pushup position, one arm on either side of her, and just stared at her, she would later say, with the look of a bear who's had his leg bitten off in a trap and who is still dragging the trap with him.

She lay on the couch inside with the blanket he'd given her. Her ankle throbbed. The kerosene lamp flickered on the table, keeping her safe. His breathing slowed and deepened and he stopped moving around out on the mattress on the porch. She stole one of his cigarettes and sat at the table to smoke. The top postcard showed a lobster boat going out at dawn. She intended to smoke the cigarette, make sure he was asleep, and then slip out. She would get back on the trail and back into the business of trying to find herself. She would look at the mountains, the leaves glistening with dew, the small lakes and valleys, and ask herself *And how do I feel about that? What is important to me? How can I go toward it if I don't know?* She remembered the urgency in the man's eyes and fingered the top card.

> *May 17*
> *Ramblin' Rose Guest House*
> *Bar Harbor, ME*

Dear Luke,

A sunswept windy day. Out by the dunes to paint early before the Touristas took over the beach. Think I got the grasses exactly right. It's the small victories. No sign of her at the three major hotels. Not on the books at any of them. Will check the smaller places and start hitting the restaurants and bars this afternoon. Are you sure you didn't yell (what you call lecture) at her about the tattoo again?

> *Chloe*

P.S Am wiring $100. Get your phone reconnected immediately.

Stunt for Two

May 27
Thundering Shore Motel
Kennebunk, ME

Luke,

Give me a break the phone company wouldn't reconnect your service for six weeks. Did you tell them your daughter is missing and for all we know could have been inducted into the white slave trade? She's not in Bar Harbor, at least not that I can find. I did find a great little gallery that has some interest. I'm to send slides. She hasn't called? You may have to cancel those gigs and get out here. Didn't you and she once go camping via mail boat to that remote little island that's a part of Acadia? I'm going to drive up the coast toward there. I'm going to whip her little fanny when I get hold of her.

Chloe

June 2
Cranberry Isle Inn
Cranberry Isle, ME

Luke : If you thought she wouldn't have the guts to camp by herself on Sheep Island why didn't you say so? I was freaking petrified when the wild boar came snuffling around the site and I couldn't find my glasses, even. She could just as easily be in San Francisco. This is pointless. I've lost an entire month of beachscapes, and my goddamn daughter <u>who was under your care</u> is god knows where. Have you even alerted the police? The news station? They could at least post her picture on the six o'clock news. Jesus Christ Luke, <u>do something</u>. -- c.

The girl, whose real name was Elise Bottorf Schwartz, who had left her small reform Jewish suburban community of New Rochelle, taken the trail name Marigold, lost a pair of nail clippers, one hiking boot, and her virginity on the trail, read the post cards, fingered her crystal amulet. "I am exactly where I am supposed to be," she whispered.

***

To him, Elise Bottorf Schwartz, self-christened Marigold, whom he likes, has no name. Only Sun has a name now. Everything else is Not-Sun. The girl is in the kitchen when he returns, several days later, from a stupid job tugging spoiled children around on ponies. He is a mime, a performer, not a stable hand. He considers his work to be an ancient tradition, a craft. Chloe has always patronized this. He hears, as he is scrubbing his paint off in the bathroom:

"... a lost, searching quality."

"... as if he never fully realized his potential."

"... a trapped little boy waving helplessly from the bottom of a well ..."

He scrubs up into his scalp with the washcloth. His eyes stare out of bruise-colored sockets. They look small, beady, and untrustworthy. He thrusts his head under the faucet, towels and combs his hair.

Chloe, for it is she, of course, who has parked the rental car out front, is in the kitchen, talking to the girl. The white rental car is parked on a diagonal across the front driveway, pinioning the house against the river. Now that Chloe has arrived, he knows that she will take over the cabin, announcing meals and making phone calls to the highway police, involving him in the putative search for their daughter, who lies in chips, shards, and wands of bone and ash in a small granite box with a clasp in his sock drawer. Underneath the box is a certificate. What words there are, are italicized, as if the scrivener had felt the need for either emphasis or formality.

He feels he has temporarily misplaced her; that part is not a lie. The sense of having gone to the ticket counter in Grand Central, and heading back to the bench where he stashed her, and her not being there, having wandered over to the water fountain leaving their bags unattended, it feels more like that. Her death is more of an unmooring—a boat that has floated off *but surely can be found again, a tippy sampan easing off just out of sight on the horizon*—than a finality, and ever since he has been wandering around a sort of vast Grand Central in his mind, looking here, then here, then in the less obvious places, then finally with increasing panic and franticness, in the dark sooty corners, the cavernous, poorly lit tunnels and chambers leading into and out of the frenetic, well-lit hive of the station. It feels more real that he has absentmindedly misplaced her than did the sickening thud, for that was all there was, really, of her loss.

He is not a cruel man. If he can defer, for even a few more moments, for Chloe, the sickening thud, that crudely simple antechamber into a labyrinthine grief, he will. He is a truthful man in an untruthful situation, he thinks. He is more generous than truthful, he supposes. He imagines Chloe engaged in the search, taking in the seascapes, the rocky pinnacles alit with sea fowl, full of the sense that her daughter is just one pinnacle before or behind her, and at first he can only see it as a gift, a kindness. What he wouldn't give to have that for just one day. The cruelty of letting her believe her search might lead her to anything other than the deadening blow has occurred to him, of course. But there is need involved. In the postcards Chloe has written Sun is still alive!

Chloe and the girl talk on in conspiring tones in the kitchen. He opens the mirrored door of the bathroom cabinet and removes the pot of white once again. He unscrews the lid and daubs the white back onto his cheeks, smoothing it across his cheekbones toward his hairline. Chloe will later tell him, he knows, that the girl ought to shave her legs, figure out her hair, and what is he doing shacked up with a twenty-year-old hiking mistress. Let Chloe think he is doing it with the girl.

"She feels she is needed here. Karmically," he will explain. He himself is dubious about what this means. "Also, there is a sprained ankle involved."

He pictures the girl returning to the Trail. She is a ghostly white figure silhouetted with the others against a misty mountain backdrop. They are climbing the hills into the north, out of the clutch of this river valley, with walking poles in either hand, and, planting them just next to each footfall, they look like mystical, four-legged creatures on an unearthly journey. Is there so much difference between them and the religious pilgrims of yore who jettisoned all their earthly possessions in order to shepherd their souls into the eternal ethereal? he wonders. He imagines placing the small granite box in the bottom of the girl's backpack so that he would not have to choose the final moment, the final place, where his daughter's journey will end. In orange paint, he outlines a vast, rubbery smile around his own lips. The smile stretches almost to the perimeter of his jaws and stops at the lobes of his ears. When he wiggles his ears, the smile twitches upward at either corner.

In the kitchen, where she is still alive, Chloe and the girl are looking at maps. Chloe's gleaming hair is pulled back to her nape. Diamond earrings glint in her ears. She looks like a stone that has been polished against the shore. They are so engrossed that they do not hear him come in. The girl shows Chloe the starting point of the Trail, down in Georgia. With the smudged tip of a pencil, Chloe traces on the map all the places Sun is not. All the places the girl will go, may go, could go. He shuffles across the linoleum kitchen floor toward them in his socks, holding his hands outstretched, palms up, as if feeling for rain. He sits on the table and wiggles his ears. His smile twitches and twitches so that even as he is telling her she does not have to believe it either.

Part Three
The Search for Transcendence

Mary Kenagy
Georgia Review

MEETING THE FAMILY

JD and I met by walking someone else's dog, all three of us truant from the same party, one of those Venice Beach parties. My housemates put it on for my twenty-fifth birthday. We walked away from the house, up the streets toward the beach in the dark. JD was more interested in Valentine, the pit bull, than in me, and I was glad not to talk. I find parties difficult.

The sky was hazy and pale with scattered light from the city, and the air was warm. Valentine dragged us to the empty boardwalk, and we walked between the bare pipe-metal frames of the vacant stalls. Far away in the dark, we could hear the waves. Though I live three blocks from the beach, I hardly ever see the ocean. It's sometimes on the horizon, always hazed over. From a distance, in the sun, the water looks like blacktop. At night, the beach is a place to get mugged.

The dog, who weighed more than I did, pulled us into the dark, across the difficult sand and sharp, dangerous objects of the beach, onto the hard shore where the little night waves churn up ocean particles. I'd lived in the city for a long time, but I'd never known this: the LA ocean glows.

The shallows had a ghost green, animal light: the ocean's grain clashing and separating, its tiny phosphorescent creatures riding the surge. JD and I stood watching, ten steps apart, while water seeped into our good shoes and the dog rolled in the surf. At the swirling edge of each wave, the light was brightest.

The next day at the office—I work in advertising—it was hard to believe what I'd seen. I was glad I had a witness, even only a friend of a friend. When I got home, JD had phoned. "The water," he said. "It was really glowing, wasn't it?"

That started us, as a couple. It was June then, and this is October. I'm a rotten flyer, and I told him so, but he asked me to come to Oregon anyway, to where he's from. His aunt has cancer.

We fly in a tiny plane from Portland to Redmond, a town in the middle of the state. I refrain from throwing up, and am proud. From Redmond, we rent a car and take turns at the wheel. While JD drives, I practice smiling in the passenger side mirror. People will like me better if I smile more, my mom tells me. We pass a gas station with chain-saw art out front, giant, brightly painted figurines with many-planed surfaces. Half an hour later, at a break in the trees, we pass a bar surrounded by more of the same. "We're close now," JD says.

When we arrive at his aunt and uncle's house, a building the size of an airplane hangar and made of logs, no one is home, so we drive to a nearby pond where the family often fishes. We park behind a low rise, intending to sneak up on them all. As I step from the car, my breath is a cloud of vapor.

Shaggy, iron gray dogs, too many to count and tall as horses, come bounding through the trees. I see them, and then they're on top of me. "Molly! Reba!" yells JD, and then I'm lying in the mud looking up at the silver undersides of branches, and someone is wiping my face with a piece of lunchmeat. I keep smiling, though my leg feels partially detached. "This is Evan," JD says.

"How do you feel?" someone asks.

"Overdressed," I say.

Everybody laughs. The dogs are licking my face, I think I've hurt myself, and JD's relatives are standing around me in a ring. They think I'm a good sport. I decide my leg is okay. Someone helps me up, and everyone is hugging JD. The dogs are as tall as I am, practically.

The women fish in the irrigation pond a while longer before we go back to the house, identically whisking their lines over the black surface. Their men are elsewhere. Naomi, the dying one, flicks her line upward and pauses. The long, yellow S unrolls vastly behind her. I wrap JD's coat around my waist because my skirt is torn, and sit down on a log. It hurts to sit, so I stand, and when I touch the tear in my skirt, my fingers come away wet and red.

From time to time, the others ask Naomi if she needs to sit down, and she keeps saying she's fine. The trees are silver with lichens, and the sky is white. The cold makes JD's family all look rosy and healthful, or maybe it's just them. I ask JD if he thinks about moving back. Of all his relatives, only he does not live in Oregon. In LA, he works for an engineering firm specializing in zoo exhibits. "When I'm old," he says, waving his hand vaguely, as if old age exists in a distant and uncertain location. The future is a topic we mostly avoid.

"What do they do for jobs out here?" I ask.

"Ranching," he says. "Some timber." We laugh, imagining ourselves as lumberjacks.

I am five feet, two inches tall. In LA I wear platform heels always, to work and on the weekends, but not here, because I wanted to blend. The angle between our faces is different. "This is a good place," JD says. He looks around, as if for evidence, as if he expects me to doubt this. "They're talking about a museum."

"Of chainsaw sculpture?"

He looks into the distance. "A historical museum. On the Oregon Trail."

"Blue Sasquatch number five. Nude with Beer," I say, determined to sell my joke. These are actual statues I saw from the car, each nine feet tall, the nude's nipples like pink dinner plates. In LA, in our normal lives, he would have laughed. I keep forgetting this is where he's from. "I'm sorry. I'm nervous," I say.

Somebody's fly rod bends: a fish is on. Naomi hurries from rock to rock toward the woman, who is her sister or cousin or niece, waving a green nylon net and yelling to keep reeling. Everyone shouts cheerfully, and the lanky dogs follow Naomi. The rocks are mossy and wet, and I worry she'll fall, but only an outlander in the wrong shoes would slip here. Naomi wears tall black rubber boots, tight jeans, and a gauzy pink scarf tied around an Elmer Fudd hat. "She doesn't look sick," I whisper to JD. "Maybe she'll beat this."

He tells me that when Naomi found out her time was up, she stopped chemotherapy so she could get out of bed and try to have fun for a while. So far, her plan is working. "Because she's stubborn," he says. Everyone watches Naomi lean over the water. Someone holds her free hand as she swishes the net. We're all measuring her breathing and complexion. The fish flexes and shakes, heavy and silver in the nylon strands.

"The tumors are growing like crazy now. I think she hurts pretty bad," says JD.

The fish's name is Homer. Once netted, he is unhooked and swims away into the black water: a flash, then darkness. "Say hi to Marge," someone says. Even the fish are old friends. I can feel the pulse in my cut, discrete beads of pain which I have every intention of keeping to myself.

When we get back to the house, I'm still bleeding. I quietly tell JD, who turns me in to the authorities immediately. Naomi was a nurse. She takes me into the bathroom. "Pull that skirt up," she says. She has an ashy spot on her cheek. She's dying. Do what she says, I think. "Stand still and try not to flinch." She clicks her tongue. "They got you good."

I try to twist around to see in the mirror, but I can't. I'd planned to be a great help to the grieving family on this visit, to show JD a whole new good-in-a-crisis side of my personality. "I have some suture strips," says Naomi.

I feel I need to apologize for getting hurt. "I fell on a pointy rock," I say. I sound like a little kid. She sterilizes the cut with a clear, searing liquid and sutures the welt. I try to concentrate on other things. I see that JD, who in real life is tall, is of medium height for his family. I feel that even my most rugged shoes are too urban, and that his family will never like me. Even JD's checked wool coat is too new, the colors too sharp. We're both outsiders. So far, his mom has not said anything to me but hello. He warned me that she's quiet, but I'm scared of her.

Naomi presses each adhesive suture strip into place with cool, expert, former-RN hands, talking continuously. "The scar will last a long time, but not forever," she says. "Butts heal slow. Try to stay off it." Maybe on the plane home the flight attendants can just strap me to the wall. I pick up my bloody skirt and look behind me in the mirror. Naomi is smiling, waiting for me to get that she's kidding about staying off it. When I look at her, she laughs. "Just do what's comfort-able," she says. My family didn't joke much even before my father died, and afterward, when it was just Mom and me, not at all.

Naomi and I kneel to pick up the wrappers for the suture strips, which I've knocked off the sink. I can smell her breath and her lotion. I try to sniff out death. I smell animals and laundry mostly, but there's something underneath, the begin-ning of decay, skin cells floating away and not being replaced, the body giving the last of itself up. I've never been this close a dying person. My dad was buried in a closed casket. I was twelve, and I never saw the body. Naomi catches me staring at her hand. Her fingernails are a shimmering ocean green. "They stopped growing," she says. "Missy keeps right on painting them for me." Missy is her daughter, twelve. JD has told me all about her.

Before dinner we all stand around in the kitchen eating mixed nuts, and some of the family ask me where I'm from, and where my family is from, and I ask them about fishing. I think they feel sorry for me, having no siblings, though they try not to let on. I like that they don't avoid the topic of my family, though JD has told them about my dad. JD's uncle Mitch is reporting philosophically on the steelhead season when JD interrupts to explain to me that steelhead are land-locked salmon. "It's not like I've never fished," I say, which is technically not a lie. I have fished from the pier at Santa Monica.

"You fish?" says Mitch, delighted.

"You *fish*?" says JD, incredulous. I wonder what else he's told his relatives about me.

After a quick prayer for health, we sit down in the dining room and at various card tables in other rooms. The family eats quickly and seriously without much talk—men, women, and children consuming six enormous chicken tortilla casseroles one of the sisters has brought from home. The food is monochromatic and very good. I count fourteen adults and seventeen children, though I don't think all of them are sleeping here.

After dinner, Naomi insists on helping wash up. "We know where stuff goes," says her sister Beth, but Naomi waves her to a stool. Sisters are mysterious and fascinating to me. JD's mom is the oldest, but quiet. She brings things to the sink to be washed. Lena prerinses, Marnie washes, Rebekah dries, and Naomi, the alpha female, puts away. Beth and Lila, the youngest, sit on the counter and tell a story about a woman from their church who put dishwashing detergent in her clothes washer. The bubbles came right up the stairs. I'd like to help wash up, but there's no job for me. I stand enviously by the refrigerator and alphabetize the magnetic letters, thinking about Monday, how I'll describe this at the office. Advertising is a hardening business, since most market research indicates that taken as a whole, people are vain and foolish. Eventually, this belief begins to creep into an advertiser's heart.

The dishes are nearly finished, and I have discovered the job of wiping down counters and tables, when Naomi brings her hand down hard on the counter beside the stove, angrily, as if she were squashing a bug or cutting off an unbearable conversation. Her eyes are closed. Lila stops talking. Naomi leans on the counter and brings her hand to her temple. We stare at the ashy spot on her cheek, at the too-springy bangs of her obvious wig. JD's mom slips her arm around Naomi's back and leads her to the couch in the next room.

In the kitchen, Lila begins to cry. Marnie pulls off her wet, yellow gloves and hands them to Rebekah, then goes to Lila and begins to rub her shoulder. "Cut it out, sweetheart," Marnie whispers. Someone takes my hand. It is Beth, right beside me.

Missy is sharing her room with me. She offers to teach me a coded language she has invented, a complicated sort of pig latin, but she gives up after half an hour, annoyed at my slowness. JD thinks Missy will grow up to be a black sheep. I asked if he was a black sheep too, and he said no.

Missy is on her bed, I'm on the floor in my sleeping bag, and the lights are out. She has already gone through my luggage and tried on my makeup and asked me questions about California. Have I eaten at Planet Hollywood? Yes. Do I live near any famous people? No, though I once saw Lou Diamond Philips in a pet store at the Galleria. He had come in by a secret entrance to look at chinchillas. "Who's that?" she said, and I felt old. After dinner Missy and I stood in the backyard and she phoned her best friend on my Nokia. "I'm calling you from a pink cell phone!" she yelled. Distracting Missy is something helpful I can do. I don't tell her about my lost parent, what we have in common—not yet. Twelve-year-olds are not that interested in other people's losses. I remember that.

Before she goes to sleep, Missy asks if I'll hear her pray. She recites a long string of blessings. She blesses her aunts and uncles and cousins, the seven wolfhounds by name, her friends at school, her teacher Mrs. Rush, the police, the president, the AA baseball team, and the fish in the irrigation pond. I lie on my stomach, half awake, and watch the colors turn on the ceiling. The pain in my behind has turned to a dull ache. Missy's nightlight is a stained-glass wheel that turns in front of a tiny bulb, casting colored shadows that advance across the walls and ceiling. When she was afraid of the dark, her mom found this, she says.

She blesses me and then blesses JD a second time. She is getting near the end of the list, her voice slowing down. "Should I ask for Mom not to die?" she says.

I open my eyes wide to catch the light. Green and glowing indigo pools slip across the surfaces of the things in the room.

I've never prayed in an organized way. I've never thought about whether or not I should ask something.

"What do you think?" she says. This is a kid's room with aspirations. There are giraffes on the bedspread and a poster of one of those boy bands on the back of the door. The blinds are open to the night sky, which out here in the middle of nowhere is spangled. As soon as her mother tucked us in and closed the blinds and the door, Missy opened the blinds again. She likes to look out while she falls asleep, she said. The doctors have said Naomi will live six weeks more. I don't want Missy to know what I know about prayers.

"What if you ask and she still dies?" I say.

The colors wheel by, purple and ivory and dark red. "What if I don't ask and she dies?"

"Did you ask your mom about it?" I say, because I am stumped.

"She says the Spirit teaches you how to pray."

"That's good," I say.

"It's just to keep me from asking more."

I hear her flop back onto her mattress, and we watch the vivid stars. Living out here could be difficult. Missy's best friend, the one she phoned, lives thirty miles away. I'm afraid Missy will not be cool when she gets to high school, that she's too smart, and there will be girls from the town and she'll be from the country. She'll have no mom or older sisters to show her the ropes, and she'll have to care for her younger brothers. I wish I could give this girl an easy time in life.

"We hardly ever talk about that," Missy says. "You know how some stuff is weird to talk about with your parents."

"Sure." I'm already fantasizing about being her cool Aunt Evan. Missy has a dozen aunts already, but I know she needs me. She needs someone who is not from here to like her. "Ask it. About your mom. While you're on the line," I say, because I believe she really does want to know what I think. I used to pray for my dad to be safe whenever he flew on business. It never cost anything to ask.

I can't resist adding some advice. "Talk to your mom as much as you can. Ask her about everything you can think of, even if it's weird." This is my own regret, all the things I never found out about my dad. Missy is quiet, and I don't add any more, though now my mind is blooming with good advice. Back then, people didn't leave me nearly enough room to think.

I hear deep, even breathing from the bed. I'm completely awake, and I don't know at what point Missy fell asleep, or whether she heard anything I said. The nightlight turns. I whisper, "Don't let Naomi die." I believe in God, but I have no expectation that God will step between Naomi and her rioting cells. It's a cheap prayer. By now, there is a moon. I imagine what I might look like from on high: a very small half believer with a sutured welt on her backside, lying on her stomach on the floor of a big, full house, asking for things. Maybe asking does cost. If you ask too many times for something you won't get, your belief erodes.

Down the hall, JD is sharing a room with his nephews. We've talked clumsily about prayer, and I know JD prays every day, but I'm not sure what that means. I imagine, in a purely hypothetical way, us having children, people who would look to us for answers, a little island of humans shaping each other.

The bedroom door opens. It's JD, still dressed but shoeless. The house is dark except for the various nightlights. He tiptoes around Missy's bed, lies down beside my sleeping bag, and we kiss, listening to her breathe. From the floor we can't see her, and the colored light from her bedside table doesn't touch us. We are underground, in a sunken pond, a secret compartment. JD starts to unzip my sleeping bag, and the sound, isolated in the dark, is so loud. I put my hand on his to stop him. "Missy," I whisper. We listen. Her breathing has gone quiet. For minutes we don't move, breathe shallowly through our mouths. JD is her favorite topic of conversation. She loves him. Seeing this would hurt her, and she would immediately and permanently dislike me.

When JD is gone, I fall asleep without turning off the nightlight. In the morning the wheel is still turning, though the daylight obliterates the colors from the walls.

I watch JD among his family. He's odd with them. His outdoor clothes look very new, his haircut very precise, and I like these things. He hangs around the men and doesn't talk much. Occasionally they tease him. He says creek instead of crick, and they discover he has paid too much for his truck. He looks at me when this happens, and is glad I'm there. Their laughter sounds almost angry, and for a moment I wonder if they wish they'd been the ones to move away and overpay for things.

I sit down with one hip cocked because of the cut, which makes JD's high school cousins EK and Tyler smirk, and I wish I'd brought another skirt. I have a slight fever from the cut, which Naomi says is a defense against infection. JD sits on the arm of my chair and rubs my back, which he hasn't done in front of other people before. His mom and I discover that we've both been to Victoria, British Columbia, and have drunk tea in the same shop there, and that we like each other. I stand as much as possible. I figure out that I can help with the dishes by collecting things and putting them on the counter in reach of JD's mom, where she can organize a staging area for the prerinse. I set the table. To prove that I have no hard feelings, I feed the wolfhounds.

The men plan to hunt deer, a scenario which I'm sure will be fraught with opportunities for JD to prove to his family that he is indeed an utter alien, but he turns out to speak their gun language fluently. He has hunted as a boy. JD is a person who can't stand to see animals in cages, only in ecologically accurate habitats. He doesn't even like the word *cage*.

"You never told me," I say, as we drive to Wal-Mart for what everyone is calling ammo. His uncles and cousins have entrusted him with this job. Our errand becomes a fight somehow, our first. I pretend to be put off by the idea of killing animals for sport, but really I'm only foolishly disappointed that I didn't already know this about him. Jealous, actually.

He turns off the car radio and tells me that I think I'm cosmopolitan, but really I'm sheltered, and I manage to twist the conversation around so I can taunt him about the hypocrisy of zoos and the arrogance of trying to re-create habitat, which I know are sore spots because he taught me these arguments himself. He slows the car way down on the main thoroughfare. We're moving so slowly that other drivers blare their horns at us as they roar past, and he says that captive populations have been used to restore many threatened species, such as the California condor, and that I am a princess, and I say fine, I'm a princess then, and I pout and ignore him while he tries to apologize. He has his pride, and after a while we're both quiet. The strip is wide and brightly lit, and other twenty-five-year-olds are out cruising together. My dad used to call me princess.

I've never fought with a man before, only with my mom. We've always fought dirty, crying and slamming things. I used to accuse her of not missing Dad, and sometimes she'll say it's no wonder I can't keep a boyfriend. Right at this moment she is salsa dancing at her retirement community in Palm Springs. She's sixty-five. (She had me late, risking her life, she has pointed out.) Since moving there four years ago, she has instituted Friday salsa nights at what residents call the clubhouse, as if they were all becoming kids again.

JD's and my fight is a clean one, I guess, and it ends when he pulls into a 7-Eleven and comes back to the car with Slurpees, which we both like, and we sit on the curb and drink them without talking. There are some things you can buy anywhere in America. There are some universals.

But at Wal-Mart, I'm afraid that he'll get the wrong kind of bullets. I've memorized his uncle's order, and I remind him, which is unnecessary.

"Shells," he corrects me. It's nearly midnight. From this new angle he looks like a stranger, me being shorter in my low-heeled running shoes. Not that I run.

"Whatever," I say. I walk away, into a different part of the store. I pass what seems like a quarter mile of laden shelves, twenty feet high, extra stock piled overhead: linens, lamps, tires, stereos, lawn furniture, denim coveralls, sporting equipment. With each step, my foot seals itself against the linoleum, secure and well-supported in the arch. The steadiness is wonderful. As I walk I decide that from now on, I'll wear running shoes every day. I'll wear them to the office. I stop in Clearance between bins of flannel sheets and sea-green jelly shoes. My head feels light and hot, and my cut has started to hurt again. The idea of work gives me a nervy twinge of angst, and my spine hunches automatically.

I pick out a gift for Missy, a headlamp on an adjustable elastic strap, because I want one friend in his family. JD finds me at the checkout and tries to pay. "It's just from me," I say, pulling my credit card. The fight is back on, and this time he drives right past the 7-Eleven. Everybody says your first fight is such an important milestone, but the truth is, it just feels bad.

Late the following morning, the men have returned from hunting and things have changed. Missy, JD, and I sit cross-legged on her bedroom floor. Or, they sit cross-legged and I kind of twist up on one hip. JD has done something so bad that no one mentioned it at breakfast. Now, in Missy's room with the door closed, he talks. "I shot a doe," he says. He closes his eyes and lets his head fall back against the wall, as if he's just confessed to a murder. I look at the hundreds of dark points on his throat. It has been explained to me that one does not shower or shave or use any sort of chemical products on one's body before hunting, because deer can smell this.

Missy tells me the rules: The doe is always protected. Only bucks are hunted. JD says he was nervous, trigger happy. The doe was standing in a thicket. He mistook the crossing branches for antlers; he feels terrible; he should have waited until he was sure—another rule. I remember breakfast, how none of the men spoke, how Naomi and I dragged along a conversation about why the winter biathlon is the way it is while everyone else chewed. All were mortified for JD's sake, it turns out. Not even JD's mom could help Naomi and me, though I think she wanted to. I'd assumed the rest of them weren't morning people.

Missy sighs and pats JD's hand. "It's okay, JD." Here is a girl who'll stand by a guy. He looks down at her. "I'm sure she didn't suffer," she says. I should be the one saying this.

He looks out the window at the late morning clouds. "I hit her in the belly. She was torn up but not killed. She ran off trailing her guts." Missy holds JD's hand and starts to cry, and JD looks at me for help. From Missy's bookshelf, I know she's a girl who believes in talking animals. "We tried to find her, but she went into the creek," JD says.

"The crick," Missy says thickly. She tries to pull her hand away, but he won't let her. "You could have found her. If you'd spread out," she says.

"We tried. I wanted to stay, but we had to come eat."

Missy withdraws from the floor to sit alone on her bed. JD stands. I can see that he wants to sit beside her, but he's afraid she'll push him away. He looks at me. His hands hang at his sides, waiting to know the right thing to touch.

"Maybe she found some other deer," I say.

They both turn. I have said something asinine. "Other deer won't let her near them. Predators could follow her blood," Missy says patiently. JD moves toward her.

"I am sorry," he says.

"It's okay," Missy lies. She runs her thumb along the edge of a shelf, pulls down a book, and pretends to read. It's *Watership Down*, and JD is helpless. He looks at me again, where I'm still sitting on one hip on the floor, still trying to figure out what I feel about the doe. I look into the mild eyes of the giraffes on Missy's bedspread. They float as if in zero gravity, their long legs and necks curved in the white space, manes and tails streaming behind them.

We are leaving tomorrow, and none of the men are speaking to JD, including his dad. I don't think they mean to punish him, but they're horrified at his blunder. No one wants him to have changed. His mom watches him sadly. She keeps fussing over him, trying to bring him things and arranging his collar, until finally he ducks out from under her hand and walks from the room. Bewilderingly, the previously stolid hunters have become positively chatty with me. I'd been braced to take the blame, the silent treatment, even open hostility. Instead, they ask about our flight out, and how I slept, and what exactly my job is. When I come clean about working in advertising, they ask whether I know the person who thought up those Old Navy commercials with The Jeffersons. They ask shyly about JD's job, if I know what it is, exactly, and what his house looks like, and whether he has nice friends. They also ask, over and over, about how my famous cut is healing. They've known about it all along, it turns out. In the kitchen, JD's uncle Mitch, Naomi's husband, pretends to swat me with a twisted-up rag, and they all apologize for the dogs, which they hadn't done before. It's okay, I keep telling them. I try to be especially nice to the dogs so the men will believe me.

When I am swatted with the rag, JD pretends not to see, and Mitch does it again later, right in front of JD, the towel twisted tight so it pops but doesn't hurt. "What you going to do?" Mitch says to JD. He whips the towel again, this time a direct hit on the wound. Mitch, I think, wants everybody to laugh and forget all about the doe and go back to normal. JD, I know, isn't good at laughing at his mistakes, but he hates being on the outside of his family. I'm between them, blocked in by counters, and we've drawn an audience. Young EK, holding a dog-chewed foam-rubber soccer ball, stands in the kitchen doorway, through which a gaggle of kids watch.

Missy is there, and looks worried. "Dad, cut it out," she says.

From the living room the women watch, too. "Leave her alone, you bully," says Beth. There is a long silence, and some of the women look toward the stairs. Naomi would normally be the one to smooth this over. She could make JD laugh, and Mitch laugh, and the kids would run off with the ball, dogs following, but Naomi has just had another spell and has gone upstairs to lie down.

Mitch looks at the towel in his hands as if he doesn't know how it got there. Soon Naomi will be gone, and they'll be on their own, all of them. He presses the heels of his hands to his eyes. "Sorry, Evan," he says.

"It's all right," I say.

His sadness makes him huge. He is a wall of soft, checked wool, and I want to put my arms around him. JD takes the towel from his uncle, folds it in four and hangs it over the oven door. He takes my hand, and we interlock our fingers without looking at each other, palm to palm, the way we did walking back from the beach on the day after my birthday at the very beginning.

The family knot loosens. People pour more coffee from the thermos on the counter and wander into other rooms. I sit on the sofa, and JD sits on the floor while I rub his neck.

"What are you thinking about?" I ask.

"The future," he says.

"It'll be so strange without Naomi," I say.

"That's true," he says, as if he'd been thinking of something else.

In the future that I would choose, he and I will be together. I want to ask about his version, but this is not the time, and it would be tricky even without relatives in earshot.

Naomi has invited the entire neighborhood over for a potluck. Before her spell, she spent the morning suspending tiny plastic animals in a Jell-O salad, and by afternoon the house is full of people holding paper plates. EK chases Missy from room to room, trying to put plastic pigs in her ears. JD and I eat lasagna in a corner with some young cousins. Naomi approaches us. "I'd like to talk to you, JD," she says. Missy has done Naomi's hair, and her wig is full of tiny, glittering barrettes shaped like butterflies and ladybugs.

They go outside together. From the dining room window, I watch as JD supports her arm in the driveway. The party has tired her more than she lets on. She puts her hand to her temple, into the insect cloud of her wig. I try to read their lips. Missy runs by, threading between diners, EK in pursuit. "Don't touch me don't touch me!" she yells.

"Oh, grow up!" he yells after her, brandishing a tiny pig.

Outside, Naomi sits right down on the wet concrete drive, her legs straight out in front of her, like a child. JD kneels beside her. He gestures toward the house, but she waves him off. She's fine, she's saying. She pats the concrete, and JD, in his dress pants, sits. He's good. I want to be alone with him. Naomi talks and he listens, and I watch, glad he's mine. I smile at family members and neighbors and drink tomato juice after tomato juice.

After the potluck, JD's mom, with uncharacteristic authority, orders Naomi to take a nap. I collect dishes and bring them to be washed. Beth hands me an apron that says, YOUR MOTHER DOESN'T WORK HERE.

In the garage, the men are nailing up a piece of plywood, JD with them. The laundry room door is open, and they are laughing. We hear parts of sentences between hammer strokes.

"—so Dad goes forward to check it out—"

"—forty yards. Eight point buck, all by his lonesome—"

"Out near Madras with Rick Metzger. This was in '65, '66—"

More hammering. "—woke up the emergency room doc—" There is laughter, and Mitch's voice rises above it.

"It was a shame. Ruined a damn fine dog. Pointer."

I hear JD's voice. "Give me two more eight-pennies," he says.

"Here you go, champ," says Mitch. More hammering. Naomi has made this peace.

Missy shows me her collection of beaded bracelets, gifts from JD in the past, one for each visit. I tell her they probably came from a store on Melrose Avenue, and she is impressed. We try them on ritually, in chronological order. "But this time he forgot. He brought you instead," she says. She means it to sound sweet, but I know better. She pays a lot of attention to how small my wrists are. That she will be a big person, like her mother and aunts, already bothers her.

We undress, brush our teeth, and wash our faces without talking, Missy ignoring me strictly, but I know how to win at the silent game. You just wait. We get into bed. Missy lies on her back, and her headlamp makes a pool of light on the ceiling. She turns over and touches her pillow. "In the morning, you could go like this on my mom's pillow and you'd have a big bunch of hair," she says. She takes off her headlamp and holds it in her hands, and her fingers glow red. I know she thinks they are fat. She says, "JD told me your dad died when you were twelve. How come you didn't say anything?"

"I was going to."

"JD brought you because of your dad." She turns off her lamp and sets it on her bedside table. "He never brought anybody before."

I can feel a vast, all-swallowing wall of anger where she is. She's too young to separate her grief at losing her mother from her grief at losing JD from her hatred of her fingers and her hatred of me for having small hands. But are any of us old enough to separate real griefs from petty ones? I can't think of anything to say that the angry silence wouldn't gulp down whole.

I think of my mom. In Palm Springs it's past midnight, and she is in bed in her condominium, in her pink bed jacket with her hair in rollers and night cream on her face, with the air conditioner running and the pool lapping in the dark outside. When I see her nowadays, she wants to talk about Dad, but I don't let her, because back when I wanted to, she never would. She's too proud to talk about him with anyone else. The people she lives with think she's always happy. They forget she's a widow, and she's a bit of a scandal because of her boyfriends. Next weekend I'll drive out there. Mom isn't tough. She needs someone to talk to.

The bedroom door opens. It's JD. "No boys allowed," I say. "We're having negotiations."

He looks toward Missy's bed. Tonight, Naomi has come back a second time and closed the blinds, and I can see by how he moves that his eyes haven't adjusted to the dark. "Where are you? Is she asleep?"

"No!" says Missy.

"Down here," I say.

He had almost stepped on my head, and he moves back, stumbling over my suitcase. "How's it going?" This is what JD says when he wants to talk. He stands beside my pillow, our bodies in separate planes.

"All right," I say.

"Want to go for a walk?"

"It's ten fifty-two!" says Missy.

"Hi, Missy. Can I borrow Evan?"

"You can have her." Missy's voice is muffled by her pillow.

A walk means JD has something to say. I knew before we left LA that he was nervous about my meeting his family—for good reason, since he loves them. There have been rough spots, but everybody is speaking to everybody else again. I didn't get to be as steady and useful and comforting as I'd hoped, but we've come through our first fight. We've passed two milestones in two days. All in all things have gone pretty well.

Or else he's going to break up with me. I sit up in my sleeping bag. Maybe I've completely misread the signs all weekend. Maybe he's still mad about Wal-Mart, realizing he needs to be with someone who is his people, and he's trying to figure out a way to let me down easy. When he was holding my hand in the kitchen, he was feeling sorry for me.

Maybe the men were being nice to me because they knew suddenly, instinctively, that I didn't matter anymore. In the driveway Naomi was telling him that if he wasn't sure the best thing was to call it off. I suddenly hate Naomi. And Missy. All these female relatives of his, these bald, Jell-O-making fisherwomen. My cut begins to ache, and I realize I'm sitting with my back hunched, pain needling the junction of my neck and shoulder. When JD said he was thinking about the future, he meant he was thinking about how to get rid of me.

I straighten up, take two deep breaths, and regain a grip.

"Now it's ten fifty-three," Missy says.

All Missy knows is that we're leaving tomorrow, and we're leaving together, and she won't see JD again until Christmas. She is more like my mom and me than Naomi or JD. She needs help. She'll carry a grudge. If we walk out now, she'll hate us both forever.

I reach up for JD's hand and pull him down to the carpet. The boxsprings squeak as Missy rearranges herself. She lies on her back and hangs her head over the edge of the bed, up-side down, her blonde hair huge in the faint light from the hall.

"How's it going, Missy?" JD says. She doesn't answer.

He leans close to me. "Anything wrong?" I say.

He makes a non-specific noise in his throat.

"What?" I say.

He leans closer and whispers, barely audibly, "Come for a walk."

"Oh, just say it here. It doesn't matter," I say. If he's going to break up with me, Missy might as well hear. I'll never see her again after tomorrow.

"I don't care either," Missy says, still upside down, and she folds her arms fiercely across the narrow front of her nightie. Then she says something else, in her secret pig-latinate language. I recognize one word, *tomorrow*.

JD answers in the same language. They worked out this code together long ago, of course. A twelve-year-old could not invent such a thing alone. No wonder she loves him. He gets up and sits on the edge of her bed. "We have to go back to our jobs," he says. "I'll miss you a lot. Only two months till Christmas."

She rests her head on the pillow, near him. "You won't see Mom again," she says.

"I don't know ..." His voice fails him. He knows she's right. This was what he didn't want to say in front of her. Nothing about us, about me.

I am a self-centered woman.

I think of the people who were still at my birthday party after JD and I left with the dog. My housemates were drunk, but they had wanted to present me with the cake they'd made in the shape of a porcupine, and have me blow out the candles, and give me some shirts they had painted and throw a barrel of Gatorade on me. When I left, they were smoking on the balcony and having a shouting match with someone in the alley below. They work in advertising too. The next morning, after the Gatorade had been knocked over and the cake stepped on, they told me, sadly, hung over, that the shirts had been stolen. "You met someone," they said, trying not to show their disappointment. "Good for you." They all knew how much I had wanted a boyfriend. It was something we used to talk about.

JD and I don't leave Missy. We sit at either end of her bed until she has cried herself to sleep, JD rubbing her head and me rubbing her feet. Even after that, we don't go far. He takes my hand and we stand outside the room, the door ajar so we can hear her if she stirs, as if she is our own child. We stand in the hall, holding each other and listening to the house. Mitch is lying awake, I think, counting Naomi's breaths, willing her to live. The big bodies of the logs in the walls are settling, creaking and groaning below the range of hearing. Love is not light. Downstairs, someone opens a door and stumbles to the bathroom. The wolfhounds move in their kennels, their long, thin limbs crossed and lax, never quite asleep the way humans sleep.

There's church on Sunday, and the congregation prays for Naomi. The minister covers his bases. He asks for everything—death and no death, no grief and good grief and comfort. Naomi nods to herself, her wig tied on with the same pink scarf—Missy's, it turns out—that she was wearing when I first saw her. She smiles, trying not to. She knows what the minister is up to. Missy's eyes are screwed shut, and she holds her mother's hand, her face puffy. This morning she cried and held on tight to my hair and said I couldn't leave. We've traded bracelets, and she has recorded my address in her scented book.

I look at JD. His hair will thin from the back, like his maternal uncles' hair. His eyes will be remarkable, full of lines. We will try not to be selfish. For example, we will drive to Palm Springs together so my mother can stop worrying about whether I'll ever have a boyfriend. In the past I've enjoyed exaggerating my failures to her because I know she believes they must be, somehow, her fault. Seeing JD and me together will be a load off her mind.

At some point in the service someone has said the word *resurrection*, and that's all I'm thinking about, the body rising, leaving the shadow of its hair and floating, bald and weightless. I imagine standing on vapor. I don't feel God here any more than I did the time JD and I went to church in LA, in a big glass and steel building. God is like the ocean on the other side of the beach in the bright smog, nearby but not in your day. I might as well ask again. *Let Naomi live.* I look up and down the row of bowed heads. This is a small church, and everyone knows JD's family. I get the idea that we're all waiting, row upon row of us, leaning forward, listening for an approach. Even after we divide and walk out, we'll go on waiting separately, counting particular deaths, listening for particular resurrections—which is to say, we believe. Naomi's resurrection is all around us, filling the spaces between us, more solid than what is solid looking.

Kathy J. Karlson
SNReview

CLEOPATRA AND THE GREAT APES

WE were all together just a few months ago at the lake, the four of us, sitting at evening, talking, Dr. Dahlberg's aged children. When we all sit together, we do not exactly look alike, except for the slight extra bulk of all the Dahlbergs and the really handsome, large heads. We all resemble our father in some way, by hair color (he was a dark Swede) or by those short fingers and broad hands. Of our mother we have the light blue eyes.

Ben told a story about some kid saying to him, "Shut up or I'll tear you another one."

"Oh, the poor kid," I said.

And Cappie said, "The poor kid? That a child...well, the utterance horrifies." And then he leaned his white head forward and summed up, "It represents the falling away of all civility." Then Cappie leaned back in his wooden chair, embarrassed to be exposing any sort of opinion that might not fit a family code of openness and liberality.

Hurt and sex. We hushed up. The island across from our dock receded into shadow. It was beautiful that evening, beautiful in the contrast between the still water and the pine trees that massed down to the shore. After we were quiet for a while, we went to our other usual topics—death, our families, our mother and father. I introduced the topic of our deaths. I said that when I thought about it, I supposed my brothers and sister and I would die in the order of our births—Cappie, Ben, then me, and finally Lally. We would follow this order of things, live until some vague time ahead when age would lower us into death, perhaps when we were all in our eighties or nineties. Cappie was not amused by the idea he would die first. "Really, Astrid," he said to me, "I'd prefer not to think of it."

"Oh, Cappie," said Ben and began to say something probably about how stuffy Cappie is and so on, but thought better of it.

Because our father had died young, and had died when we were only partly grown, I said that I believed that we would be compensated for the untimeliness of his death, compensated by an order to our own dying. Our lives would pass like merchandise moving on and off the shelf, with more or less handling, with interesting ups and downs, with no real stories—no battles against evil or with our own flawed characters. We had already suffered.

Our mother lived long, well into her nineties. But our father died in 1951, just two days after his fiftieth birthday, died in surgery as he was taking out Mrs. Boyd's gall bladder. Lally was only five years old; I was fifteen. We lost him in the dark Iowa winter, and we all agree—winters still keep that reminder of grief. Winters are the dark time, sometimes relieved by the heart-sensed brilliance of sun on snow, but we felt ourselves looking for our father years and years, long and long.

Before he died, our lives were lived under his; the house was organized around his coming and going. Father was said to be the best surgeon in the state. He could repair tendons, delete a bad appendix and then scrub away infection. He could recast badly mended legs or cut out a festering tooth. He could clip out breast tissue and leave only tiny marks like a delicate ladder, marks that would fade from their pink into a fine white. Lally told me that Mother described this sewing of the breast. Lally didn't remember why: "Maybe I saw Mrs. Seligman without the bumps that should be on her blouse and wanted to know 'what happened to her front?'" (I noticed last year at the doctor's that my own breasts looked just like my mother's. As I stood there in the little office, I had one of those shocks that time gives you sometimes; I raised my arms to put on the gown and thought, "Why is my mother here, naked like this?")

Before the war, being around Father was mostly a boon. He was very busy, often away from home, and when he was around the house he could be merry as Micawber. He punned, waved around a wooden spoon like a wand, told mystery and ghost stories, and spent a little time in kindness if need be. We loved to be in his presence. As other doctors were, Father was often paid in chickens and pigs and brought home these animals after the farmer had butchered them. Once, for saving a choking child, he was paid with a wonderful milk cow named Lindy. Father told us that Lindy was ours even though she still boarded at the farmer's house. We went to see our Lindy on trips into the countryside. Mother asked to stop at a few places for eggs and fresh white butter, and the farmers' wives propped their elbows on the car window, chatted, gave us pansies and primroses. When they leaned in, they smiled at us. At Lindy's, the farmwoman, Mrs. Peterson, always gave us a pie of the season, apple or pumpkin or plum or gooseberry. When I was very little, before Lally was born, I was sometimes called to come out of the car to sit on Mrs. Peterson's ample lap, and I recall the faded patterns in the soft cotton of her dresses and aprons. The checks or roses on trellis or ribbon stripes lay across the fabric and the fabric smelled like the ironing down in our basement at home. I remember leaning my face against Mrs. Peterson's bosom and gazing at her plump arms, her forearms speckled red by the sun.

Before the war, our father was plainly happy to be driving out, to be carrying my brothers and me with him all around the county. Lally hadn't been born; we just went day to day in the order of things.

But after the war he was changed. His enthusiasm was gone. He was subdued, or when he did break out of his low mood, he was reckless and angry. During the war, he was a medic, a Captain with Patton's Army. His job was a bloody mirror of what he did at home—in Italy he ran a plasma and blood bank, shot horses, amputated arms and toes, sewed up groin injuries, gave morphine to soldiers, nurses, or the Italians who met the medics on the roads. He gave these people morphine when they were on their way to dying. He did the postmortem autopsies on soldiers when sepsis had set in or when the dead man seemed perfectly sound on the outside. When he got home, he never talked about the war. He said he couldn't understand why men would get together to talk about the war. Mother said later that he had got mangled in his heart.

After he got home, sometimes he spoke to us, even to our mother, with a grinding sarcasm that was odd and new to us and frightening. Cappie said he brought something home from there. He was mean sometimes. After the war, if we were in the car, and Father lost his temper, Mother would turn away to look out the window.

"Get that pain off your face," he said to her once. When she didn't answer, he got madder, and stopped the car and just marched ahead on the gravel road. And we sat silent in the car. If we were at home he might suddenly beat the arms of chairs or throw books across the room. Sometimes he would strike us and then run away up to his room and fling books around. The temper seemed to be triggered by the boys especially, if Cappie dropped his spoon or Ben got smart. But the blast could happen to me, too, on a placid afternoon when the sunlight lay flat and serene along the clipped lawn and we all were quiet and innocent. We started to get sullen with him, to stay away from him if we could, while Mother kept telling us that he was good.

Then Mother got pregnant, and she, too, became distant. She sat and cuddled her lap. As Lally grew in her, Mother was quiet, rocking and rocking, her self seemed absent. She was forty-two years old. I was ten and I was put off by the pregnancy. Mother gave me less attention—her body was remote, her face often turned away, and sometimes she cried when she stood washing bowls in the sink.

Then Lally was born and the whole world flipped. She was like this human angel baby, the bringer of glad tidings. One of Father's friends, a doctor from the University of Iowa, said that Lally was born with all the good genes from both families. She was a round and pink and perfect baby with huge, beautiful blue eyes and white-fluff hair that became blond when she got older. Our father was suddenly happier; he played with her little toes and talked low with her and was happy, once again, to bring us apples or interesting stones he found while walking to work and back. His outbursts stopped suddenly. It was as if there were no more yell or scorn in him.

It settled, the family silt just settled—back into the pre-war, happier plains. Father walked to the office; Mother went to meetings and gardened and cooked. Lally toddled, Cappie was gone from the house, into business, and Ben went to college. I played flute in the band, collected leaves and pressed them in my diary, and rode around on my bike with Meredith and Kenny, my best friends. But then I started to change in my body and I stayed home more, reading and wondering about my sore breasts, or slinking around school, wishing for I don't know what. Wishing for calm. Wishing Lally weren't so perfect. Wishing everybody would just drop dead, or drop into the ground, or drop off a high building. Wishing that winter could be warm instead of so bleak, could have in it palm trees and a beautiful brown-eyed boy near the trees, just for me, a boy just for me.

Then the death came. I was fifteen when Father died. Mother came to school and got me out of the 10th grade where Mr. Soder was droning on about sine and cosine while I looked out the window and envisioned a better world where I was queen and handmaidens came behind me. Into that world came the principal, Mrs. Whittier, whose face looked like the face of Jesus in our Universalist Church—so sad, so full of compassion, with her arm stretched out like his, her arm stretched out to me, as I turned in my yellow desk to see what the little knocking meant. Saw the principal, saw my mother, looked out into the aqua sky of early spring, then looked back at them.

While Father was operating, he was simply felled, as if God bent down and jerked his heart to get his attention. The operating nurse pulled him off Mrs. Boyd's anesthetized body, rested him on the floor, called out for help, and got the scalpel out of Mrs. Boyd's gut. As others bent down to him and saw that he was dead, the operating nurse calmly tied off the lines binding the wound in Mrs. Boyd's belly, making tiny stitches: she stanched the blood, took out the cotton, cauterized the loops of extra tissue, and closed up. Mrs. Boyd could never really tell by the scar that Dr. Dahlberg had died across her abdomen before he sewed her up. The nurse's stitches were perfect. But of course she knew what had happened and dined off the story for years in our little town. "You know, that lovely Dr. Dahlberg died right on my body. "

I can remember going out on the porch at the lake house a couple of nights after he died. We were out at the lake house just to get away for the evening, and a big wind came off the lake, and then all the gnats and mosquitoes blew away, far away, it seemed. I stood and felt frozen there and felt that I was waiting for the monster from the lake, for the long reach out of the suddenly broken water. I gripped my head, my chin, to make myself look. Mother found me.

"Astrid," she said. She stood behind me and put her hand on my head, standing calm and still, holding on. She turned and picked up the towels, the sand spoons, the hats, and when I could finally speak, and I told her about the lake monster, she said, "Well, darling, if there's a monster, it won't get us."

She said, "Your father would have wanted..." but she said no more. Later, when she came to sit by my bed, she said, "All will fall away to love, even though people are captured. Even though people fall, even though they are eaten by monsters. Even so."

She plumped the pillow under my arm. "We have so many things. Don't cry so hard," she said.

So Mother was left with no husband, with four children, one working, one at college, one in high school and one just five years old.

Before the funeral, Mother tried to teach Lally about death. But at the church Lally saw him in the coffin and called to him, "Are you there? Are you there? Get up! It's time to get up."

Lally wouldn't accept. Even though people told my mother that Lally was old enough to understand the finality of death, it seemed that they were wrong because she kept asking about him, especially on the day he was buried, about why he was all dressed up, about why he was asleep in such a fearful shiny box, about the handles on the coffin. In the church, Lally went up to where Mother was saying her last goodbye, and then I followed to bring her away. Mother said to her, "Lally, he can't get up. He died. We're going to be in church now. Then we're going to go to bury him."

"No," said Lally, "he won't like it." The hair near her face was covered with mucous and tears.

"Lally," said our mother, "we don't know what he likes, now. Except, he likes you. He just can't tell you. He's here but he just can't answer if we ask him."

Then Mother began to cry and it looked like her body made a stream of life down her face, water rushed as if she'd been saving tears all her life, and Lally, seeing the tears and the face of grief, stopped her questions. Lally went back to the first pew in the rows of pews that curved around in the church like ribs of a giant fish, and then she sat on the hard wool cushion and kept still while our mother kissed our father's face. Then Mother stooped over and took off her wedding ring and lifted the tip of his baby finger to leave the ring with him.

Mrs. Tauber stood up and sang "Steal Away" and then "For the Beauty of the Earth," and then Reverend Lee Holdt talked about the saintliness of Dr. Dahlberg and called him so many good names. I remember feeling a horror coming on that this was really the end of him. I was afraid I was going to throw up. Then the funeral was over and we walked out while Orvis the choirmaster played "My Lord, What a Morning," our father's favorite church song. Outside, the air was fragrant with grass new mown and with fresh spring sun. People drifted around us, kissing us sometimes, or standing back with down-turned faces, and then we all drifted to the cars and followed the black car out to the Red Oak cemetery where we watched him be buried. Lally had dribbled tears all over her lavender dress; the boys were solemn. Cappie didn't cry but Ben cried so hard he got the hiccups and then we began to laugh and cry all together. I remember thinking that Father would rather have been in his own garden, even buried there, than to be left out on the edge of town with all the other dead people.

The boys decided to stay home for a while until the money was sorted out. Cappie at 25 had already started and gotten settled in the biggest bank in Des Moines. The bank president let him off for two months because he really wanted Cappie to stay at the bank. Ben was at his first year at Ames; he came home for a couple of weeks and went off again when Mother made him go. But after he finished that first year, Ben got a job in the Red Oak Pharmacy and waited a whole year with us before he went back. I was glad. Ben made Mother happy in some way that I could not—and everybody knew we had to make things better for her, but mostly better for Lally.

Dr. Dahlberg was dead. Father was dead.

Lally was dazed all the time. Lally seemed unaware at first. She asked for her Dad over and over and then was heard to explain to her little girl friend, Annie, that her Dad had gone to Heaven. But Lally said that she didn't know where Heaven was or when her Dad would come back. She was waiting for him. I wonder if in her mind he walked over and over again down our broken walk, up the wrap-around porch, through the big red front doors, and into the hall where he would sweep her up in his capable arms and carry her off to continue their domestic life. It was as if the sun had moved into arctic night; her life was shaded and darkened by the lack of her father. She never saw him angry and undone the way we had seen him. She had only the good of him. Sometimes she would get in bed with me and I would wake up to find her crying. Mostly, I was nice to her and tucked her in to me, but once, I said, "For God's sake, shut up. I have to go to school. We have to get up in the morning."

She only said, "Huh-uh," her quiet no. So then I felt bad and took her down to the kitchen for a little milk. I carried her, and I can still remember the smell of her damp head, a plant smell, a sour leaf smell. And I thought, oh this is what pity is. I felt pity for her.

Ben saved her. He showed Lally how to hold a lot of cards, how to play fish and hearts. He tried to teach her bridge, too. He took her on walks to learn the names of trees, and the two of them made up a story about how Cleopatra saved the great apes of Africa. Ben said that Cleopatra sailed down the Nile and crossed into the Congo and made a whole land where people took care of the great apes by planting bananas. Ben said that though some people said Cleopatra died when she was bitten by a snake, in fact that she had held the snake to her own chest. But Cleopatra had fooled everyone and instead gone on this great adventure to save our hairy monkey kin. He kept up this tale of Cleopatra and then Lally made a world of it. She had a troop of monkeys who dodged the white man, the lion, and the Pygmies. The monkeys loved her and stayed with her and beckoned to her. "Leave your tears with us," they said.

Slowly Lally came out from behind her feeling of night. Mother got a job and kept our house going and in the fall I went to Ames a year early with Ben. The world got some order. But once in my chemistry class, I said to myself, Dr. Dahlberg is dead and he was my father. And I felt that somehow I would never recover from this, that somehow I had lost my true self.

We went our ways, we Dahlbergs, but we were mindful of the early days, mindful of our father. If you have lost someone to death, the dead person can become a shadow over your life. But then years pass and the shadow is less dark, the feeling of loss less piercing. Death itself seems to move away as if moved to an outer planet. Acquaintances die and you read the obituary page but you still have the other ones who were close with you in childhood.

For Lally at five, the world enlarged and grouped during the funeral. She told me once that all she could remember was people moving, women's dresses, an ebb and flow of sound in the house, not chaos but not the usual order, not the normal sun coming through her window, not her father calling her to breakfast and kissing her goodbye before he walked to town, not the slow breakfast in the wooden booths of the kitchen after the rest of us had left for school, not the walk out to the sidewalk with him, not the greeting when he came home. Lally says she remembers confusion and then the blank of white sheets at night on her bed and then too much quiet in the house, and that feeling of being not the same person. But she got over it, she said.

As I said, Cappie was already gone from home when our father died. He had already started to become the most successful of us. He knows something about the American world of business and assertion, too, compromising things that he can accept and that don't frighten him. He has made a lot of money for the Des Moines bank, and for himself and his family, too. His wife Marsha gave him two boys, a kind of planned present as if for an elaborate birthday, and then she loved the boys and attended to their every step and when they went off to school, she turned to Cappie. Most people like them seem to have some kind of bump or maybe a canyon or abyss in their married lives, something to bend the marriage. Marsha got uterine cancer, but she got through it; now they are fine. Cappie and Marsha like one another. When Marsha was sick, Cappie's eyes took on a look, a fear I had never seen. But, as I say, they are all right.

Then Lally got sick. She told us last year when we got all our families together at the lake in August, told us her biopsy news. She made a joke of it and swatted away the mosquitoes.

"Remember," she said, "when we heard the crop dusters or when they sprayed for mosquitoes, I ran out to see them? I loved that stuff lowering over the elms."

"DDT for breakfast," said Ben. "Death for dinner."

"Jesus," said Cappie, "Jesus, Ben."

Lally said, "Well, I am not going to die."

"You have to go up to Mayo," I said.

"Already did," said Lally.

"Well, next time, I'll go with you," I said and this dread came back, a dread so deep that I thought my heart would cave in and I would be pressed into the dirt.

"Rats," said Ben to Lally, "I was just about to borrow money from you."

Cappie gave him the look. Some kids from next door were running up and down our dock and Cappie got up to shoo them away so that we could talk to Lally and watch the lake in peace.

"You'll get over it," I said. "They can cut it all out."

"Well, Mrs. Donaldson got breast cancer and then she got it in her brain. She got breast cancer in her brain. I heard mother telling Mrs. Jones. She thought I was listening to the radio. And that farmer, the one on past the water tower, he got breast cancer, too. He died. Mrs. Donaldson didn't die, not for a long time. I have one large tumor in my left breast, a big, old lump."

Ben stood up and placed his hand on her still golden head. "I am making a ring of fairies to hold in all your cancer cells and flush them down into the woods where goblins will get them. And then I'll make a ring."

Cappie started to interrupt. Lally said, to Ben, "And then?"

"I'll say, 'You will not come across this fairy ring, Mr. Cancer. You will go this far if you want to, but that's all. Or, oh! I will get Cleopatra!"

"Oh very helpful," said Cappie. "Shit," he said, a word I had never heard from him.

Of course, Cappie was the one most afraid because of his wife, what she went through, otherwise he never swore. Radiation. Lally said it was like taking in the Strontium 90, all the hooha about strontium 90 and the mothers' milk.

"That milk passed through someone's breast," she said.

"Yeah," said Ben. "A cow's breast."

"Ben," said Cappie, "you are making me mad."

It seems that those beautiful fields of wheat and corn, the rivers and the lakes, carried and stored bug and weed killers, and people killers, as it turns out. I told my friend Darleen at work that pesticides are leukemia makers. I had to blame something. Darleen said it would be fine, that we were all here anyway at the very beginning of the earth, of the galaxies, when the stars were made. Not me, I said. I'm too much of a mammal.

"I became present, stepping out of the sea," I told Darleen. "I became a fur bearer and sat deep in the fronds."

"Astrid," she said. "You beat all."

"You know, Darleen," I said, "we are most apt to get cancer, we mammals, so fecund, so alarmingly multiplying all the time, in every part, in the marrow. Remember the marrow? Remember? Didn't you crack chicken bones?"

"My mother made lamb stew; we did break those bones. Only you could remind me."

"Our father told us how rich that marrow was, like a constantly brimming cup, a blossoming rose, making our blood."

"Jesus. Okay, okay. Enough already," said Darleen.

So the doctors gave Lally chemicals that made her puke when she rinsed out her mouth, that made her feel as if her own heart was attacking her, her lungs were shrinking, her skin was turning to ash. I just drove to work and called people fucking assholes and yelled at them in their shiny black cars and their hot red tail lights with the battered chrome and the stuffed animals in the back windows and road dust all over the hoods of all the cars. I even yelled at my neighbor who instantly forgave me because she had seen Lally in town with a red wig and that pale, pale face.

I made Lally chicken with lemon every day so I could do something. Since I had never married, I made Lally my child. I did not want to be left alone with my dogs. I tried to push protein on her almost every night until her husband, Bill, let it be known that I was coming over too much. So I sat alone in my lounger and then Lally got better. All those treatments up at Mayo, all our prayers, or what? Genetics? Early childhood love? At any rate, now all she has to show is a faint blue shadow near her nipple and a tiny line. And this fact of her being better was what we all celebrated at the lake a few months ago.

But now I have my own troubles. Here, my friend Andy sits with me every day for a few hours up near the lake now so I can look over the lake valley. Andy brought me one of those special chairs that tilt back so you can be reclining with your feet up, your legs partly bent. Lally says I look as though I am nursing the sky.

This is the best time to see the skies—the trees not quite fully leafed, the wind up so it pushes the clouds all up and down. When father used to take us out in the car, I loved to watch the sky, to see the big faces in the thunderheads, or make believe that I could be on the outer tip of the cloud's throne, commanding the whole world, sitting up so high to see the East rushing to meet me. I thought it would be lucky to be buried just in the line between two climate zones so you could be always there in two worlds. It would be mysterious to be in those two worlds and I also wanted ravens to be standing in their Norway pines like Gods, holding secrets.

My sense of the order of our dying was almost right, at least probably, but I will never know. And so I want to say some things before I have to go, before we meet at the lake again and I tell news that may mean that this is not the easy leukemia. It's just this:

Do not hit your children, do not hit your children, do not hit your children. Do not be sarcastic with them, or fly from them, or think that they are your property or that they belong to you. No matter how you have suffered, do not hurt them.

And if you think you have no place to go, except for joining some discontented group, then look around only for beauty because it will be short. And the dream I have of dancing in the snow, with my brothers and sister, the dream of being together after we are dead, now seems foolish, and I remember that our mother told Lally that Father was there but couldn't speak. Or be seen. But I want to be seen. I want to have done more. I do not want to be the first one to die; I do not want to go where I may not be seen or where I may not be able to talk to them again, talk to them over and over about our father. I wanted an order, anyway, or a better story, but I am afraid I will not get it. I wish that Ben's Cleopatra story could be true; that I could go with Cleopatra and wait for the others, go be with the monkeys. I wish that story could be true. Or that I would be Cleopatra. Or that our father had never died so young.

Robyn Parnell

COEUR D'EVELYN

"AND Je-sus said come to the waaa-aaah-ter/rest by my side ... sit by my side—stand by my side? Ah, shit."

True to its mercurial, undergraduate nature, Anna D'Onofrio's long-term memory took a sabbatical at the precise moment when a reminiscence might have provided reassurance. She could not recall the lyrics to her once-favorite camp song.

Anna stood on a knoll overlooking Coeur d'Alene Lake. She kicked at pebbles scattered amid tufts of grass and gazed at the lake's cobalt blue waters. The two women were precisely where the Resident Manager said they'd be: directly below the knoll, on the pebble-sand beach. The diminutive pastor, whose name Anna had already forgotten, leaned back against an ottoman-sized gray boulder; to her right was an elderly woman in a wheelchair.

The Ladies of the Lake.

Anna fingered the frayed spine of the book she kept in her parka's pocket, wondering whether she should offer assistance. It's one thing to push a wheelchair down a hill...

***

"An intern? Anyone paying attention down there in Boise?" The stout, dog-eyed Resident Manager tugged at the collar of her blouse, scooted back in her roller chair and patted a once-white coffeemaker on the typing table behind her desk. "I'd offer you a cup if I had any. Jayson constantly complains that it's not an espresso thingy, which doesn't stop him from draining the pot.

"Wish I could offer more enthusiasm, Miss Dono ..." the woman glanced at the papers Anna had given her, "Ms. Anna D'Onofrio. I forgot to introduce myself the first time; our clientele has that effect on me—ha! Claire Dawes, Resident Manager-slash-Grand Poobah of CDM-ALC, Coeur de Marie Assisted Living Center. Sooner or later everyone asks, but no, I don't know why they didn't just name it after the lake. Guess 'Heart of Mary' sounded better for soliciting donations from the parishes—you know how Catholics go for anything having to do with Mary. No offense; they knew I wasn't Catholic when they hired me. Seeing as how we're closing, what if they did take offense? What'll they do, fire me?"

Claire Dawes' eyes contracted into slits when she chuckled. Her chair squealed in protest as she shifted forward and rested her ample forearms on her desk blotter. "Sorry I didn't get into this when you first arrived yesterday, but you seemed tired after your long drive. I'd have called your advisor had I received the papers earlier, but the fax came only ... well. It was yesterday morning before anyone checked the machine and you were already on the road by then, weren't you?"

"That would be yes." Anna resisted the urge to tug at her nose ring. "I left early. Excuse me, did you say 'closing?'"

"Nice drive, isn't it?"

"Yes, it is—was. Scenic. Lots of ... scenery."

"Closing. As in, closing. No new residents for ten months now, and for the past six we've been finding new situations for those who haven't yet transferred out. And St. Stephens College still thinks we need interns? Now, this is your advisor's screw-up; don't take it personally. You're welcome to show up every other day or so. I won't keep tabs."

Anna interlaced her fingers behind her back and hoped that Mrs. Dawes wouldn't offer her a seat.

"You sleep all right? I never got around to canceling the intern's room at the Econotel; that's yours if you stay. You make your decision and let me know. If you stay you can work out a schedule with Pastor Lee. You missed her yesterday; she comes over from Spokane on Mondays, Wednesdays and Fridays."

"Actually, I did see her yesterday," Anna said.

"You met her, eh?"

"Well, it wasn't much of a meeting. She was ..."

"I should've warned you. First off, don't take anything she says personally, even if it's about you."

"I think I know what you mean." Anna stifled a grin.

"You know she sued her former church." Mrs. Dawes lowered her voice. "She's been at several; it was confusing when I checked her references. A disability or discrimination lawsuit, on account of her being a recovering ... I don't know, alcoholic or something. You can sue a church for that, these days. You can also be divorced and be a Presbyterian minister. I'm a Baptist, or so my husband says. They do what they like—Presbyterians, the Catholics—it doesn't bother me."

Mrs. Dawes cracked her knuckles and raised her voice. "With the Rev. Lee, take what she says with every grain in the salt shaker. I think she tries to offend; she's bucking to get fired, so she can file a lawsuit. You can tell, with some people. Anyway, they pay her salary, her current church. She's part of an ecumenical exchange program, going to be in charge of ... come to think of it, she hasn't told me what her plans are. Guess I need answers from the both of you, eh? If you stay, fine. Just give me the evaluation form at – how many weeks is it? I'll fill out whatever you want."

***

Assisted Living Center, feigning purpose of direction and wondering if it was the stillness of the nearby lake that made everyone talk nonstop. She sensed a dreadful, garrulous trend, starting yesterday afternoon, when she'd arrived. Fresh out of her car, she'd approached the only person she'd spotted in CDM's parking lot. Judging from the staff profile Anna had received in her internship packet, that person was the Rev. Evelyn Lee, Presbyterian minister and Interim Chaplain to CDM Assisted Living Center.

Anna intended to introduce herself, then ask directions to the restroom.

"So, you've found us! Of course, the real question will be, how will you find us? I'll not go there; let Claire earn her manager's title." The woman offered a handshake. "For what it's worth, welcome to Coeur d'Alene, lake and the town, and to Coeur de Marie Assisted Living Center."

Anna wondered how a hand so small could be at once so firm and cold. "Thanks. I'm Anna. You must be ... ?"

"You were heading the wrong way." The woman jabbed her thin finger behind Anna's head. "The entrance is there. Come with me, back to my van. You can help with the props. It's best in any new situation to dive right in. First thing to remember: CDM-ALC, Coeur de Marie Assisted Living Center." The woman repeated the phrase slowly, as if English was not Anna's first language. "C-D-M, A-L-C. Remember the latter acronym: Assisted Living Center—not a nursing home; they're insistent about that. Your Mother Church wished to lighten her institutional baggage and sold off her Old Folks homes to HMOs. Privatization is to be her new savior. How many can you carry?" The woman pointed at the rear window of a dusty minivan. The van's cargo hold was laden with wall banners.

"I could carry a lot, after I find a bathroom."

"I noticed your eyebrow rise," the woman said. "Giving you the facts is not an indictment of Mother Church, though it seems you're not too concerned with what your Mother thinks. I know there's 'Catholics for Dignity,' but Big Daddy Pope and his old boys haven't changed their tune on gays. There's the brow again; is that intentional or instinctive? It's no skin off my nose, personally or professionally. My denomination tries to ignore the whole thing in terms of policy. My last community assignment was in Spokane's version of Castro Street. Don't tell me you've never heard of 'gay-dar'— it's the gays who taught it to me. The nose ring is clue one; the double Venus tattoo on your neck is the clincher. Here now, crook your arms up and I can lay the medium-sized ones on top."

Anna staggered under the weight of the banners piled atop her outstretched arms. She steadied herself, silently savoring the snappy retort she'd never say aloud. *You forgot the buzz cut. But since your best friends are homos and you single-handedly ministered to the entire gay community of Eastern Washington, there's no problem, right?*

"About CDM." The woman slammed shut the van's door. "I cannot fathom the change in situation. It seemed to work well: residents had their own private rooms; there's a separate floor for more extensive services, but no round-the-clock care.

Those who began to need more than a daily laxative or Vitamin E had their leases bought out by the HMO and transferred to a facility in Sandpoint. This way, please."

Anna followed the woman, who carried two banners to Anna's twelve, and wondered what would give first, her engorged bladder or her urge to shriek SOMEONE PLEASE SHUT HER UP. A paperback fell out of the front pocket of Anna's oversized khaki cargo pants. The woman turned around, picked up the book, "Hmm-ed" at the cover, and stuck it back into Anna's pocket.

"Lucetta Vandehey's giving them the runaround—hasn't found another placement and won't sign transfer papers. Barring a miracle from Our Lady of Hip Replacement, Lucetta is not going to get out of that chair. 'I need it occasionally, to rest my feet,' she says. It started with Jared giving her a ride to the cafeteria every other day; now she thinks he's her chauffer, which is against policy. No personal attendants at CDM. When he's not having new body parts pierced Jared works the cafeteria and such. Jobs with minimal skill and personality requirements suit him; I suspect he'll try to stay on. CDM-ALC will be bought out by a local resort consortium. I do enjoy the sound of that: 'resort consortium.'"

Anna rested her chin on the banners she held and squirm-walked behind the woman. "Is the restroom ..."

"You knew nothing of this, obviously. What did they tell you at St. Stephens? Anyway, you're here. Best you find out right away I don't mince words." The Rev. Evelyn Lee laid her two banners on the sidewalk and opened the door to CDM-ALC.

Anna sighed with relief. "Where do I put these?"

"I get to the point, whether it's sharply obvious or one you must choose and focus upon. Set those on the bench inside the door. As for your earlier question, the one you didn't quite get to? Indeed, what shall you call me? You might call me what my first church's Sunday School kids called me. 'The Rev Ev.'"

"Rev Ev." Anna feigned bemusement, looking desperately right and left for the facilities. "I like that."

"I never did. Frankly, it annoyed the bejesus out of me. Impertinent snots; full of me-me-me. Self-esteem oozed from their disrespectful little pores, but how they're deified in church! 'Suffer the little children' and all. Call me Evelyn, for now. Bathroom's down the hall, on the left."

***

Evelyn Lee cherished the view from the Recreation Lounge of Coeur de Marie Assisted Living Center. The floor-to-ceiling glass panels that formed the lounge's south wall offered a spectacular vista of the northwest corner of Coeur d'Alene Lake. Although it had been several years since the last local lumber mill had closed, stray logs still found their way down the tributaries and into the northern Idaho lake. Shading her eyes against the harsh winter sunlight, Evelyn could make out strips of bark—sodden, red-brown, detritus that resembled shaggy ribbons of seaweed—strewn about the lake's gray, pebble-sand shore. She'd yet to spot one of the lake's celebrated osprey, but during a morning walk along the shore she'd seen a bald eagle emerge from the top of the pines rimming the lake. The eagle idly circled a cluster of trees before soaring north; it kept close to the tree line for twenty yards, ascended to a spot fifty yards off shore then made a sudden dive, skimming the lake's surface and making off with a thrashing salmon clutched in its talons.

Evelyn turned toward the sound of footsteps echoing down CDM's brown and white, speckled tile hallway. She pinched her fingers together and gestured to the lanky young woman who shuffled toward her.

"Yes, yes." Evelyn shushed Anna D'Onofrio's attempted greeting. She grabbed Anna's elbow, gently but insistently steering her to the window-wall.

"Amazing," Anna murmured. The women stood side by side in short-lived silence, gazing at the sunlight reflecting off the still lake waters.

"During the summer you can charter a sunset cruise at the pier," Evelyn said. "Coeur d'Alene was a gold rush town, did you know? Logging has all but bowed out; can't compete with overseas mills. There's the growing resort business, and still a bit of mining. Amateur rock hounds find the occasional gem. My Aunt Lily summered here for years, in a cabin north of the pier, where the condos are now. One year she found a star garnet by one of the streams at the southeast end of the lake.

"So! We can get a lot done before lunch." Evelyn turned her back to the lake and brushed her hands together. "CDM has its own chapel; small, but well-iconed. I'm not sure all of the residents know, or care for that matter, that their home is run by a Catholic Charities association. Well, it might matter to the two cranky Baptists, pardon my redundancy."

"Mrs. Dawes said something about the name, Coeur de Marie. Heart of Marie?" Anna said. "It's related to the lake, or town?"

"Also my guess, but no, according to Jayson," Evelyn said. "Jayson might be a good connection for you—he and Jared, the two remaining part-timers. They're your age, townies, both allegedly attending Northern Idaho College part-time. The other staff are friendly, if beholden to routine. Mrs. Dawes approved my request to hold Holy Week services here instead of in the chapel when I reminded her of the view." Evelyn rested her knuckles on her hips. "We'll need rows of folding chairs, with space up front for the wheelchairs."

"Whoa!" Anna folded her hands across her chest and forced a laugh. "I need a clue about what's going on. Mrs.

Dawes told me to meet you here. I brought some materials my advisor gave me, for an Easter service, and the one on Maundy Thursday ..."

"Tenebrae."

"A Tenebrae service; that's it. But, what am I going to be doing here? Who's in charge of me?"

"Ah yes—no time for official intros yesterday before you scurried off to the Little Girls' room." Evelyn Lee looked carefully at the young woman she had acknowledged so transiently the previous afternoon. Tall and thin, pale skin, dykeishly cropped, salt and pepper hair—Anna D'Onofrio looked much older than her twenty-two years. "I'm Evelyn Lee, as you know by now. The Right Reverend and such, who is officially pleased to meet Anna D'Onofrio."

"I appreciate the pronunciation." Anna blushed. "I usually get 'don-free-oo,' or ..."

"Call me Rev. Lee in front of others. It's generational, a matter of respect. Always use the resident's surnames, unless they indicate otherwise. The staff call me Pastor Lee; when it's just us it'll be Evelyn and Anna. We'll set up for the Thursday service while you tell me about your trip from Boise."

Evelyn steeled herself for what she'd knowingly solicited: a recap of the trials of a college student who'd had to drive three hundred miles in a car with no CD player—forget the spectacular scenery afforded one who might actually look out the window.

She crossed the Snake and the Salmon Rivers, skirted Hells' Canyon, and all she mentions with regard to aesthetics is the welcome sight of a Burgerville at the gas stop in Lewiston?

The two women pushed sagging ottomans and redwood burl coffee tables to the sides of the room. Emboldened by the view and the Rev. Lee's crusty but evident (to Anna) interest in such matters, Anna spoke of how she'd submitted the required internship proposals to her Social Services major advisor ...

Why do people assume a minister will listen to any story?

... who informed Anna that she had to have at least one choice that was out of the county. Her advisor was also her "Issues in Contemporary Theology" professor, a class Anna only took to fulfill the religious studies requirement ...

I can see where this is leading.

... and when in his class Anna had questioned for the fifth time the Cardinal's stand against pursuing full communion with the Lutherans ... you don't think that had anything to do with it, do you? Anna wanted to focus on family issues, which encompassed prison reform, education, just about anything, so why did it have to include geriatrics?

"Not that I'm opposed to the elderly. It's a simple matter of matching interests and skills."

A simple matter. For you, of course it is.

"So, about what I'm doing here. I thought I was supposed to work with them, the ones who are left." Anna grunted and pushed the last of four garishly striped ottomans against a wall. She wiped her damp brow on the sleeve of her shirt. "I don't care if CDM closes, as long as I get this requirement over with. Mrs. Dawes said she'd write my review ..."

Great god Ganesha, will it never end! Yesterday she wouldn't say piss if she had a mouthful. And she did. Perhaps Catholicism nurtures the confessional mode, Evelyn silently speculated. She looked about, realized they'd set up more chairs than would be needed, and let her ears go numb.

How can one with so little life experience blather on? The details she provides are mundane, ignoring the potentially interesting point – whatever she's being punished for.

"I was sent here as punishment? Did the others say that?"

"What others?" Evelyn grimaced, realizing she may have inadvertently mumbled her last thought aloud. "FYI, I don't know who'll write your review. I do know that what Claire Dawes says seldom jibes with what she does, but until she figures out what to do with you, you're mine. Just in time for Holy Week, which is quite the show for my Catholic brethren and sistren.

"'Nothing happens to which the Lord does not consent.' Sister Angela, CDM's visitation nun, told me that when I arrived here. This is noteworthy, considering her reaction when her Lord consented to her becoming a resident here. Keeping that in mind might be of comfort, the next time you find yourself arguing against the party line. What, exactly, did you do to antagonize your professor-advisor?"

Rev. Lee did not wait for Anna's answer, but looked around the Recreation Lounge and let out a low whistle. "Never mind. That's neither there nor here, but we are. Help me move the piano. It's heavy; three of its rollers are missing."

Evelyn and Anna pushed the nicked, faded brown upright to the back of the room. Evelyn ignored Anna's mumbled aside about how the Right Reverend was surprisingly strong for her size.

"I try to be ecumenical but it's difficult to keep track—I forget the hierarchy of R.C. transgressions. Disagreeing with church policy, might that be blasphemy? Heresy? Hirsutism?" Rev. Lee ran her fingers over the piano's dusty, once-white keys. "I assume the latter would be a venial sin?"

Anna wiped the sweat from her brow through her spiky hair. "I'm not sure there's that distinction anymore."

"Pity; such an amusing little doctrine. We need an altar. Ah, one of the card tables." Evelyn pointed to the front of the lounge. "Move those chairs to the side; leave space up front. Most of them use wheelchairs or walkers. We'll prepare the façade of optimism regarding possible attendance. Jared owes me; he'll get a few here. We'll have them in body if not spirit."

"Do you think that's wise?" Anna clasped her hands behind her back. "If they don't want to ..."

"Very few have come to my services. I'm lucky to get one or two." Evelyn grinned. "The oriental lady preacher, you see. Even the non-Catholic shy away."

"That's awful," Anna said. "I know they're older, but that's no excuse. It's prejudice, pure and simple."

"My dear, nothing in this world is pure and even less is simple." Evelyn leaned against a folding chair, her hands grasping the backrest. "Their hostility isn't overt." She spoke as if realizing for the first time what she was saying. "It's mostly postural; more attitude than oral, for those who even bother to speak to me. Though I have heard the proverbial, 'Go back to where you came from.' My first day here; I forgot his name. The old gent stroked out a week later."

Anna clucked her tongue. "He actually said, 'Go back where you came from?'"

Evelyn nodded. "I exhumed my serene, Person of The Cloth voice for my reply: 'Poor dear, you don't get out much, do you? I'd love to return from whence I came, but according to the census, Montana is full. They closed the borders last week.'"

Anna caught herself and morphed her laugh into a cough. "Still, it doesn't bother you?"

"This is a duck's back. This is water." Evelyn feigned pouring liquid down her back. "It is what it is. Lack of attendance at services is an annoyance, as that is what I'm supposedly here for. The cheap thrill of having Jayson or Jared wheel a squirming Sister to the services wore off a month ago."

Rev. Lee wiped her dusty hands against the seat of her pants. "This is it for now. I'm usually at CDM three days a week, but this week I'll be in every day. Be at the lake, tomorrow morning at eight. We'll discuss the service."

***

"You're on time, so I'll assume you slept well." Evelyn waved at Anna, who was picking her way down the path to the lake shore. "There's room."

Evelyn scooted to the side and patted the spot on the boulder where she'd been sitting. "It's even warm; I've been here for almost an hour. It's a nice drive from Spokane; I like to get an early start. The only thing that tops a lakeside sunset is a lakeside sunrise."

Anna yawned and rubbed her eyes. She wavered between blaming sleep deprivation or a lake reflection's optical illusion for what she saw when she beheld Evelyn Lee's face. "I think I need to remain standing," she said.

"I looked over the notebook you lent me." Evelyn hugged her arms against her chest. "I appreciate you bringing materials. More foresight than I'd expect from an undergrad ... but it was your advisor's idea, that's right.

"About tonight. The old guys' and gals' religions are written on the information forms in the office, on the line under 'allergic reactions.' I keep services as general as possible, with nothing to provoke offense over any perceived denominational preference."

Anna rubbed her eyes again and silently vowed to start drinking a better class of coffee. She took another look; it was no hallucination. The Rev. Ev, sitting on a boulder, holding a hymnal and the notebook Anna had lent her the previous evening, had a red dot in the center of her forehead.

"I must have left my 'bindi' on," Evelyn said, in response to Anna's bewildered stare. She licked her finger and rubbed the cherry blotch above the bridge of her nose. "Got a Kleenex?"

Anna removed a book, a pocketknife, coins, pens, tubes of Chapstick and her car keys from her pants and parka pockets.

She laid each item on the boulder before finally producing a linty, wadded piece of tissue. "It's unused," Anna said.

"Thank you. I use watercolor. It's easy to remove, when I have a mirror and can see what I'm doing." Evelyn pointed at her forehead. "This is to honor Mr. Singh. Ravi Singh, second floor. The non-Indian Indian, Jayson calls him. I visit Ravi first thing in the morning, to help him light his incense. He lived most of his life as Gerald Larsson, converted to Hinduism at age seventy-one and took a new name. Drove the Social Security and Medicare people nuts, according to Claire Dawes."

Evelyn rapped the hymnal against her knee. "What a life! He starts out Lutheran, then becomes a Mormon 'elder' at age nineteen when his entire family converts. Now he lights incense for Brahma, Vishnu and Shiva, and yesterday says he's thinking of converting to agnosticism.' You'll meet Ravi tonight; he's one of the few who attends my services." Evelyn tapped her finger against her temple. "Something's missing, but he's a sweet soul. I play the dot-head for him and we light the incense and flaunt the fire regulations—no flame of any kind in the rooms."

Anna scratched her nose. "Isn't that sort of patronizing?"

"Ask Ravi." Evelyn sighed. "Really, he's no more Hindu that you or I, although I do think he enjoys the accoutrements. A grownup plays dress-up; or, perhaps he's repudiating his clan and their conversion. They were un-churched Lutherans, now they're Latter Day Saints who dumped their present-day apostate. He has no visitors, other than me."

"That's unusual, isn't it?" Anna began refilling her pockets. "I thought Mormons took care of their own."

"LDS are almost unknown for charity to non-Mormons— they call us 'gentiles,' did you know that?—but, as you said, they do take care of their own. Still, his family never comes." A wistful veil descended in Evelyn's eyes. "A friend gave me some interesting advice during my second year at seminary.

She'd returned to finish her senior thesis after taking two years to do a one-year practicum at a Presbyterian church in Salt Lake City. She didn't talk much about the Utah years, except to say that if I ever had to be in that state for longer than a weekend I should remember to bring my own spices, tampons, and beer."

The dreaminess faded from Evelyn's voice. "They're closer than you might think, Mormons and Hindus. Here's something to bedevil your professor: 'twas only when I studied Hinduism that I began to understand Catholicism; specifically, the passion for saints and icons." Evelyn slowly slid down from the boulder. "Now, what is this sacred text you carry?" She tapped the book Anna was attempting to jam back into her pants' pocket.

"'A Bridge to Camelot.'" Anna grinned sheepishly. "My friend calls it 'Camelot for Dummies.' It's on the reading list for a class I need to take." Anna tugged at her eyebrow ring. "I'm almost embarrassed to admit I like it. A lot."

"I've just the thing for you." Evelyn jerked her chin in the direction of Couer de Marie. "If you like the Camelot tales, you'll enjoy 'Drapudi's Dance.' It's from The Mahabharata, one of the Hindu classics. I've been reading it to Mr. Singh.

"Drapudi was a princess who lived thousands of years ago." Evelyn ascended the path back to CDM, Anna by her side. "She had five husbands who were brothers, members of a powerful clan. One day in the royal court her eldest husband played a dice game with a hated enemy. His luck was terrible, but he played on, wagering possession after possession. He lost everything, but was too proud to quit. He even bet his own brothers! Finally, desperate to regain everything, he wagered Drapudi, and lost.

"Drapudi was in the women's quarters of the court while this was going on. The man who'd won her sent his emissary to claim her. When she refused his summons, the emissary dragged her out of her quarters and began to tear at her clothes."

Evelyn stopped at the knoll and turned to look back at the lake. "Drapudi was very beautiful. No great surprise; does any culture celebrate the adventures of the wall-eyed princess? But Drapudi was also renowned for her wisdom, and piety. She tried to defend herself; she held on to her sari and called out to Lord Krishna, but the goon was too strong. It seemed she would be humiliated in front of everyone. Drapudi stopped fighting. She closed her eyes and raised her hands. Her attacker thought he was home free; he pulled at her sari ... and pulled and pulled. The sari unfurled with no end. Drapudi spun as the goon pulled at her sari; she danced, her hands raised in supplication and rapture, until the man had pulled himself into exhaustion and collapsed upon the pile of her clothing."

Evelyn took a deep breath, looking, Anna thought, as if she herself wished to tumble onto a pile of silks. "Wow," was all Anna could bring herself to say.

"Yes." Evelyn looked down at the lake. "Wow." She spoke so softly Anna wondered if she might be speaking to herself. "The bird that just swooped down and skimmed the surface, like a cross between a duck and a raptor? I must get a field guide." Evelyn rubbed the back of her neck, her voice resuming its normal tone and volume. "You go on. I'm not ready to return yet. The book I mentioned is in the Rec Lounge, on top of the piano."

Evelyn opened the hymnal. "Lucetta Vandehey will be at the service. I want to find a song she'll like."

"What do you and Mrs. Vandehey talk about when you're by the lake?" Anna asked.

"Nothing. She won't attend my services but lets me take her to the lake. Come with us this afternoon, at three-thirty. It's a pain to get her there by myself; her wheels get stuck."

Evelyn crouched on her heels and picked up a handful of tiny pebbles. "From the windows of the Rec Lounge, it looks finer, doesn't it? Like sand on an ocean beach. Lucetta and I go to the end of the path, then another ten feet or so. I get tired of playing tow truck but she wants to get close to the lake. For weeks I've been telling her that if I take her down to the lake she must come to at least one of my services. I've made arrangements for Jared to ... escort her, shall we say, tonight."

"She doesn't want to be there, right?" Anna kicked at a pebble. "I met Jared; I bet he'd jump at the chance to literally push her around. It's like she's being punished."

"Petty and spiteful, isn't it?" Evelyn dropped the pebbles and stood up. "If you think ill of Jared, now's the time to apply the Christ-like compassion Mother Church loves to talk about, and to apply it both ways. Lucetta Vandehey has been nothing but disdainful of and rude to Jared. Naturally, there is a bit of payback involved."

Evelyn flipped through the hymnal, humming a tune that was vaguely familiar to Anna. "'Bring forth the royal diadem and crown Him Lord of all ...'

"Old guys and gals want old songs. I have to look up them up. Odd, though, that this particular request came from Ravi. He must be having a Lutheran flashback."

Anna jammed her hands into her pants pockets. "I might as well tell you this now," she said.

Evelyn closed the hymnal. Looking deep and hard into Anna's eyes, she detected the jumbled spark of tension and relief.

Of course you're not staying. What was I thinking?

"I can help with ... we haven't worked out the details of tonight's service, and I'll gladly help with that. But for your planning, I thought it only fair ..." Anna swallowed hard. "I've already told Mrs. Dawes. I'll be here tomorrow, to help clean up after the service, but I'm leaving on Saturday."

Evelyn appraised the vitals of the young thing before her: the natural givens of height and coloring; the modifications of hair, clothing and bodily decorations—attempts at distinction, or compensation for unformed intellect and unexceptional persona. In two days she'd given a short life's worth of consideration and conversation to Anna D'Onofrio, and for what?

"What were you expecting?" Evelyn asked.

"Nothing." Anna jingled coins in her pocket. "I mean, not this. It's been two days and I've barely met the residents."

"They're being transferred."

"They live here!" Anna sputtered.

"Not for long."

Anna caught the 'pay attention' tone in Evelyn's voice. She'd have made a great professor, Anna sneered to herself. She tried to counter Evelyn's impenetrable gaze. At least I'm taller than she is, Anna reassured herself.

"'A Contemporary Tenebrae.'" Evelyn cleared her throat and tapped her finger against the notebook Anna had given her. "Hardly practical, given our facilities and what passes for a congregation. Which is exactly why we're going to do it."

***

Rev. Evelyn Lee surveyed her flock—all five of them, not counting Jayson, Jared and Anna D'Onofrio. She looked at her congregation and thought of shoes. Their faces reminded her of boot soles, scuffed and weathered; of leather uppers from a once grand pair of wingtips that now sported fraying laces and rebuilt heels. Her Aunt Lily said, "As you age you get the face you deserve." Evelyn considered that aphorism as unfair as it was inaccurate. Was Karl Landry's face indicative of dourness? Were the ruts in his cheeks the result of a lifetime of tramping over those closest to him, or were they the genetic evocation of his Swedish parents and the fifty years he'd spent outdoors, farming Montana red wheat? Could Lucetta Vandehey somehow have earned such an extraordinary countenance, at once so stern and silken?

Fire regulations ruled out doing the part with the candles, Evelyn had informed Anna, but other than that, they would follow the suggestions in Anna's notebook for a Contemporary Tenebrae Mass. The austerity and brevity of the Thursday evening ceremony was to be in contrast with Sunday's joyful Resurrection service. Anna and Evelyn covered the windows in the Rec Lounge with black cloths and draped a mud brown tablecloth over a wobbly, folding card table, which would serve as the altar. Evelyn made copies of the appropriate scripture readings and placed them inside the biggest, heaviest book she could find—an over-sized Physician's Desk Reference from Mrs. Dawes' office. Evelyn wrapped the book in black cloth and placed it atop the altar.

Sister Angela and another female resident of CDM—both of whom, Evelyn triumphantly noted, had come of their own accord—were the sole ambulatory residents at the service. The two women eschewed their walkers for the evening; arm in arm, they ambled into the lounge and took seats in the back row of the folding chairs. Anna sat alone, on the right side of the first row, behind the space cleared for the wheelchairs. Ravi Singh deftly wheeled himself into the lounge, waving off Jayson's offer of assistance, and parked his chair in front of Anna. Jayson stood to the left of Mr. Singh, between the wheelchairs of Mrs. Vandehey and the heavy-eyed Mr. Landry, while Jared slouched in one of the chairs in the first row.

"I'm a devout atheist," Karl Landry mumbled to Jayson, "and a tired one to boot." He fumbled with the joystick on his wheelchair's armrest. "I'll take myself back to my room, seeing as how Bingo has been cancelled. We can play Yahtzee."

"Sorry." Jayson smirked. "It's this or nothing tonight."

A hymn was sung a cappella, and then another. Mr. Landry promptly and loudly fell asleep, his snores punctuating Rev. Lee's readings of the accounts of the Last Supper. The Messiah was betrayed and crucified.

Reverend Lee closed the *Physician's Desk Reference*. She slowly lifted the heavy tome above her head, then released it. The book plummeted onto the makeshift altar as she uttered the solemn words:

"It is finished!"

The book hit the table with a massive thud. The table's front legs buckled, and the book tumbled onto the floor.

"Jesus Christ!" Mr. Landry jolted into wakefulness.

Lucetta Vandehey gasped and reached out with her shaky but determined arm. She tried to slap Karl Landry's hand but instead hit the control panel and the joystick on his wheelchair's armrest, and his chair began to spin in a tight circle.

"What the f..." Jared jumped to his feet, knocking his chair over. The two women in the back row whimpered in unison.

"Hey now!" Jayson stepped aside, dodging the whirling wheelchair. He grabbed the chair on its fifth loop, deftly pulled a cable from the battery below the seat, and whistled appreciatively. "Dig it, Jared. Dude's a pagan and his chair speaks in tongues."

Mrs. Vandehey clutched at her bosom. She removed a vial from her sweater pocket and shook pills into her quavering palm.

"No, don't—that's not the nitro," Jared yelled. Lucetta Vandehey glared at him and tossed the pills into her mouth.

"Shit! Oh, man, that was her laxative." Jared jabbed his thick fingers at the non-plussed Rev. Lee, who was attempting to right the card table, and the drop-jawed Anna, who remained rooted to her chair. "There's going to be an industrial strength accident later, and you two are helpin' clean up. Hey, no more!" He snatched the vial from Mrs. Vandehey.

"Damn it, she has rights," Mr. Landry roared. He punched his fist toward Mrs. Vandehey. "She can take 'em; we all can. You plug that thing back in." He punched the buttons on his armrest and then flailed his arms to the side, reaching for the back of his chair. "She can take as many pills as she chooses, and she can put a bag over her head, goddamn! We voted it in!"

"That's right," Mr. Singh piped up.

"You oughta start the chair up again," Jared snickered to Jayson. "Spin some sense into his old wheezer head." Jared grabbed both armrests of Mr. Landry's wheelchair and leaned close to the old man's face. "We didn't vote nothing in; that was Oregon. Don't you know Oregon from Idaho?"

"Fine!" Landry's roar wilted into a defiant snivel. "Alright, then. Damnation; take me home!"

"Excuse me, Rev. Lee?" Anna approached the disheveled altar.

"Yes, my child?" The Reverend Lee bowed her head, her voice dripping with solicitude.

"Should I leave a note for Mrs. Dawes? If she hears about..."

"Yes yes." Evelyn dismissed Anna, haphazardly waving her hand in the form of a cross. "Vaya con Dios."

"Bless me." Mr. Singh leaned forward in his wheelchair and grabbed Anna's hand. "You could bless me, and I'd feel better."

"Oh, no," Anna stammered, "it's Rev. Lee, she's the priest—the pastor here, I mean. I'm just ..."

"Go, then," Mr. Singh snorted. "Like you say: go in peace, serve the Lord. But don't come back. Get your own folks to abandon. But you can't do that, can you? Papist pederasts tell us how to live, but can't have your own life, can you?"

***

Working side by side in silence, Evelyn and Anna straightened up the Recreation Lounge. "Ravi thinks you're a priest," Evelyn finally said, as she pushed an armchair from the back wall to the center of the room. "Or one in training."

"Yeah, right. I'd be kicked out of anyone's seminary after something like this. Or maybe just lose my internship, ha ha." Anna flopped down on one of the couches.

"One can always hope." Evelyn smacked the couch's cushions, raising a small cloud of dust. She motioned for Anna to get up and push the couch to the center of the room.

"I helped Jayson walk the two ladies back to their rooms, the Sister and the other one with the sore-looking nose," Anna said. "They wanted to go to the office and file a complaint. Can they do that? Your denomination may not believe in the same particulars as mine, but if we're not going to hell for this we deserve at least an hour in purgatory."

"I don't believe in anyone's particulars, nor in purgatory. I have, however, peeked at hell." Evelyn's smile was abrupt and thin. "Ms. D, this isn't even close. Help me fold these sheets."

***

Evelyn tucked her hands under her armpits and walked up the path to the knoll. She lifted her chin and exhaled in short puffs, her breath rising like smoke rings in the morning air.

"You left out so much."

Evelyn turned around. Anna was ascending the path to the knoll. "You're up early," Evelyn said. "Especially for someone who's leaving the next day. Not much packing to do, I suppose."

Anna reached the knoll. "I said, you left out so much."

"It made no sense to do the entire service, considering the interest level of the attendees."

"I meant about Drapudi. I read it last night. I almost did-n't; I thought you'd already told me the story, so why bother."

But you did.

"Her family, the relationships, the politics ... you left out so much, and the important parts, like how the respected princess was ultimately treated.

"She was traded, like a possession. The sari that was pulled by her attacker—her would-be rapist, by the way. He wasn't just going to strip her. The sari is ... it's not a story; not just a story. It's so obviously an allegory."

"Obviously?" Evelyn thrust her hands into her parka's pockets and regretted leaving her mittens in her car.

"About the situation of women in India. Women every-where. The way you told it, Drapudi's reaction was appropri-ate, even admirable. Like it was an effective response to re-pression, to being assaulted just because of what she was."

Evelyn's eyes narrowed; Anna stomped her feet to warm them and wondered what it would be like to really cross the Rev. Lee.

"Drapudi's story is five thousand years old." Evelyn's voice was as glassy as the surface of Couer d'Alene Lake. "No one was repressed, then. They did not think in such terms."

"So, when a woman is being attacked, no matter what cen-tury, she should just go limp and pray?"

"She did not go limp. She let go."

"You think I'm missing the point, but I ..."

"I never said there was a point; I said there was a story." Evelyn patted Anna's jacket pocket. "May I have it back?"

Anna clutched her hands over her pocket. "I put your book back on the piano. This one's mine."

"Of course it is." Evelyn turned her back to Anna and looked down at the lake.

Evelyn's head was backlit by the delicate dawn light, and Anna noticed for the first time a faint, patchy, white line, zigzagging from temple to chin on the left side of Evelyn's hair. It was as though someone had tried to finger-paint a lightning bolt on the Right Reverend's head. Anna was flustered by her sudden desire to reach out and stroke the white strands, to see if they were any softer than rest of Evelyn's coarse black mane. Anna willed her hands to stay in her pockets and warm themselves.

The Rev. Evelyn Lee cupped her hands over her eyes and peered through her circled fingers, as if looking through a pair of binoculars. "I've a lake to appease, and an Easter service to plan," she murmured. "Enjoy your journey back to Camelot."

❄

David Flood

LADYBUG

A four-year-old prodigy once said that reality is the ultimate fantasy. Maybe that's true. Some of the best things in life seem impossible—too hokey for good fiction. This is one of them. Every word is true, at least to the best of my recollection (except for changing the names and some of the dialogue about a billboard). So bear with me, I want to get this so you believe it as fully as I do.

Let's call him Gordon. He was a friend of mine, a fellow English tutor at the local community college. (If you must know, Seattle Central Community College). He died from AIDS on December 15. Yes, another one, but this one I cannot ignore.

He was not pure by any means. He had a good wit, he seemed to be comfortable with who he was, and toward the end, he spoke his mind freely. When we were tutoring, for example, he'd read a student's composition and say to her quickly, "Oh good Lord this is awful." Somehow, coming from Gordon, the student wouldn't be hurt. He could say what he felt without offending them; the honesty was refreshing.

Gordon had some uncanny experiences before he died. One I cannot dismiss, one involving, of all things, a ladybug.

I really would rather not risk my credence as a writer, an ex-advertising copywriter for science textbooks for that matter, by revealing that there are certain things that cannot be explained without making one sound, well, nuts. The best I can do is tell you the events and let you decide for yourself. Example. Just now, as I write this story to you, a ladybug appears on this coffee shop marble tabletop again. This is still winter for crying out loud. I'm preparing a story based on a ladybug. A coincidence?

The last time it occurred was after drafting a letter to a pastor about Gordon's death. The insect came out of nowhere and crawled across my typewriter. And the time before that, a few months before Gordon's death, it happened again. It occurred after Gordon posed the question: Is there a God? We were having lunch at a restaurant on Broadway in Capitol Hill. He exclaimed, "I want three-dimensional proof that God exists!"

To show his conviction, he started to pound the back of his hand with his fork. "This is my pain—I am tired of feeling this pain!"

The next day he left a message on my answering machine: "Thadeus, you won't believe what just happened. I had just gotten a cup of coffee as I usually do before class, and I'm walking up the stairs leading to Red Square and I hear this

411

voice. It says, 'Here's your 3-dimensional proof ...' and my fingers closed upon something. I looked between my thumb and forefinger and there was a ladybug ..."

The voice on the tape was shrill, excited, like a little kid stumbling across an unbelievable discovery. I replayed the tape. He didn't sound like he was making this up.

Gordon was a realist. With a finance degree, he traveled to Japan to teach classes in business and English. He was not exactly a religious person and had a pretty hard-core view of the world. He tolerated prejudice both here and in Japan. Once while we were walking down Pine Street toward Capital Hill some people in a passing car spat on him and yelled, "Fucking Faggot." He wiped the saliva off his shoulder and continued the conversation without missing a beat.

I was in shock. I said, "I've never seen anything like that. Has that ever happened to you before?"

"Oh, yes," he said, "It happens a lot."

I wondered how they picked him out of the crowd—the guy doesn't look gay—how do you look gay? He wasn't a jock by any means. He was scrawny, probably more from being HIV positive for eight years than anything else. He played violin as a child, Suzuki trained, he wrote Elizabethan poetry, did abstract wall sculptures. OKAY, so what if he doesn't meet your image of a stereotypical heterosexual. Neither do I for that matter. His real name was Adam Bartholomew Rochester III. He changed the name after his parents kicked him out of the house when they discovered he was gay. I would change my name too if my parents cut me off. He talked of the whole affair matter-of-factly.

"Don't you ever call your mom?" I said.

"I don't know where she lives."

"And where's your dad? Doesn't he care about you? Does he know you tested HIV positive?"

"No, he wouldn't care."

"But maybe he's changed. Does he live near here?"

He lives in New York.

"What does he do?"

"He's a surgeon."

We kept walking. I thought about his dad's occupation. Now here's a parent, obviously educated, unable to accept his own son's lifestyle. Now he may be soon dying of a disease and there's no attempt to communicate. I had read somewhere that thirty percent of diseases occur because of abandonment of loved ones.

After his ladybug experience left on my answering machine, I called him right back. "Gordon, what happened!"

"You won't believe it. I was on my way to class—I was walking up the steps to Red Square, and I'm scraping my finger between the rows of bricks along the wall beside the stairs. I heard a voice. It whispered, 'Here's your three-dimensional proof,' and my fingers were closed around a ladybug."

"What does that mean?"

"I don't know, but what a beautiful gesture, wouldn't you say?"

"I can't believe that ... did you ask who the voice was?"

He paused and said, "I think it said it was the wind."

After that, every day between tutoring students at the local community college I was playing twenty questions with the voice. I am a terribly curious person, and if God had manifested in Gordon, I was going to be sure.

"Is the voice still with you?"

"I think so."

"Can I ask it a question?"

"Go ahead."

"Is there life after death?"

"It said, 'yes.'"

"Why is there so much evil in the world."

"It says, 'He was evil, but he has learned.'"

"Does he think I'm a good person?"

"He paused and said it knew I was kind to animals."

"Would it be okay if I wrote about nature?"

He paused, leaned his head back as if listening to something I could not hear, and said, "You want to write about nature?"

And on I went, treating poor Gordon like some sort of Ouija board. I wondered what it looked like, and he told me that it seemed bigger than the universe—the personality was often sprite, excited in the morning. He said it would get him up early. It said, "The sun is up, let's play!" He also said it responded to music. It loved dance. Yet, on other days, he described it as something like the hash-smoking caterpillar from Baum's *Alice in Wonderland*. A slow thing, infinitely knowledgeable, but detached from the world.

I asked how something like the Holocaust could happen in a world with a God. He said it didn't give an answer. He could see in his mind a picture of something, telepictures, as he called them, and said "it" just shrugged. I got freaked out after that. I didn't want to know any more. I wasn't even sure if he was possessed by a deity or a demon. How could "it" be indifferent to such violence. I remembered a Buddhist Koan: if you see a Buddha in the road, kill him. In other words, don't be easily fooled by authority.

Gordon, too, got freaked. One day he announced that it wanted him to build up his body with good nutrition and weight lifting, then to go into nature and fast. He was afraid that it was calling him to be some kind of oracle. He had shifted his reading at that time, I noticed, from literature to spiritual texts ... the Bible, writings on Moses, and books on Indian shamans. He was also seeing a therapist and going to support groups for people with HIV. He told them about the voice, but they didn't believe him. One therapist was supportive, however, and recommended he read more texts on Indian spirituality.

Shortly thereafter he said the voice told him a name. He said it was Cloud Reflected on River; he thought it was an Indian shaman. I grew more skeptical. I felt he was being influenced by the literature. I also tried to trap him by asking it questions to see if it could read my mind.

"Am I thinking of a square or a circle?"

"A circle."

"No, it's a square."

Gordon frowned and didn't want to play anymore.

He grew weaker in the ensuing months, but he still kept up work as a tutor. He dropped all his classes except for a course in Italian, and shortly before his death, we had one of the most regrettable conversations of my life. I challenged him that if the voice was directing him back to health, he should get off financial aid and work full time.

"But I have a disease," he said emphatically, confessing the seriousness of his illness to me for the first time.

"I know, but you're getting dependent on the money. If you are getting better, you should start increasing your workload."

At the time he was maybe working ten hours a week. He was still proofreading once a week at SGN (Seattle Gay News). I was too, we both traded off at times.

Ultimately, I had no business prying into his financial life, but still I pushed it: "And you borrow money from your sister..."

"So what? She can spare it, she doesn't mind."

"But you said you're getting better."

I was stupidly trying to cover up my growing disillusionment with the voice, yes, but I was also afraid he would become dependent on others—such as me.

"Listen," I said, "Naoko is going to be coming back from Japan soon ... I won't be able to spend as much time together. It's been a whole summer since I've seen her, and, you know, we have a lot of catching up to do."

It was a very hurtful thing to say, but I wanted to prepare him for what probably would happen. I smiled, but Gordon didn't. He had said once that he loved me, but I'd interpreted it only in a friendly way.

I was wrong.

Gordon loved me. He wrote me a sonnet. Though time had passed, the sonnet was based on a conversation on metaphysics we'd had several years ago in a coffee shop on Broadway. We were both exploring the idea of becoming teachers, and I said the most important aspect of a teacher in assisting student growth is to admit how much is not known: the intellect becomes stunted with the fallacy that the great philosophers and the world's religions have already cornered the market on the truth, and a licensed teacher tends to dole out the truth in confident tones, as if the real inquiry into the basics of life, such as "Why are we here?" had been resolved some time ago. Gordon thought about this and wrote this poem:

> For Thadeus,
> How deep into unknowing can we go,
> As divers deep descend into the sea?
> While they have lamps to chart the ocean's flow,
> For us enigma it will always be.
> For sunken galleon's treasure we both search.
> We have no spears; we have no rubber skin,
> To help us in the realm of ocean's church,

Ladybug

To know unknowing if it is within
  Yes, some of us, sometimes, the ocean drowns.
The fragile souls who cannot hold their breath:
Unknowing panic, then Sargasso bound,
Exhale their lives and flounder into death.
  And if sea air is unconditioned love,
Let's both hold hands and make it back above.

The poem was written in iambic pentameter. Gordon said that since he had a feeling he was "punctured" by that spirit, the sonnets would come out of him with hardly any revision, one after the other. He ended up writing a total of twenty-three.

Shortly after that, we attended the first Baptist church for a time. The pastor was an English teacher, a good model for English tutors. Gordon appeared to be lifted by the sermons. At first he resisted the whole idea, but I convinced him there was something healing about being in this place—you can feel the collective love of these people. The pastor spoke strongly against discrimination, including homosexuality. While in the church, Gordon commented how the presence of that spirit within him seemed brightened in this place, a light turned up a few notches.

So for most of the Sundays during that summer, we'd sit up on the left balcony of this church, Gordon always punctual, me rolling in a few minutes late. Gordon would be really tuned in to the minister. He would be able to read between the lines. "He's angry about something today."

As the Sundays wore on, I noticed him beginning to cheer up, laugh. Once, he felt relaxed enough to wear a black tee-shirt, revealing his arms to the church. His left wrist had three distinct scars across the veins. He tried to take his life earlier that year.

417

After one service, without fear, Gordon charged down the aisle and asked the pastor that if the "voice" beckons you to do something—can you say no? The pastor was kind and tried to convey some of his own experiences with a "voice," but the congregation was pushing their way through and we had to leave.

Gordon seemed dissatisfied.

The next week I announced that my mother was coming to town and probably would attend church. Gordon didn't show up for church that Sunday. I thought that since his own mother had disowned him, the presence of mine must be painful. We never spoke of this.

Soon after, he told me he had fainted in a pharmacy. He did a Hollywood fall, grabbing at hundreds of bottles of drugs as he fell backwards. They called an ambulance and he was hospitalized for a day.

"Why didn't you tell me this?" I said.

He shrugged indifferently. All during this period his mood tended to shift; he had good days, he had bad days.

On a good day, we bought Dick's burgers and watched the sun set at an obscure Capitol Hill park. Fireflies were everywhere. We said anything and everything that swept through our minds. The porch lights began to brighten.

"Tell me," I said, "How did you find out that you were gay? Did you always know?"

"I had a defining moment. I was twenty-two; I met a biker. He wore leather, chains, the whole bit. Late that evening I remember lying on top of him after the most fantastic orgasm of my life. I said to myself that there's no doubt about who I am."

I contemplated this. His discovery seemed later than many. Some gays I knew were aware of their "difference" as early as age ten. We walked from the park under a canopy of stars and smoked clove cigarettes. We stopped on the I-5 overpass.

"It's poetry," he said.

"Poetry?"

"The night traffic. Squint at the red and white streams. Can you see it?"

I never considered I-5 traffic poetry. I squinted, but felt bothered by a Gilbey's Gin billboard looming above us. A brunette in a low-cut black velvet dress playfully eyed a man in a black tuxedo.

"But look, Gordon, doesn't it bug you how the media is so blatantly heterosexual?"

Gordon continued squinting.

"It's a heterosexual world."

"But what an intrusion it all is. TV, magazines, billboards, you can't get away. How do you stand it?"

"I fantasize."

"Fantasize?"

"I 'queer' the images." He looked up at the billboard. "To me, right now, that woman is a man, a sultry, long-haired male with flowing locks looking seductively into the eyes of another man."

Gordon looked back into the traffic, his eyes were red from the reflection. I pulled on a clove introspectively.

The two-story high billboard bathed us in a harsh white light, but we continued to lean against the cement protectors of the overpass and looked out at the traffic. I took another drag off the cigarette and tried to squint to see the red and white streams, but the light from the billboard made it difficult to see.

On a bad day, Gordon was terribly frightened. He was bothered by the tenacity of this same spirit that had entered him. We had just finished tutoring and while we were passing each other in the hall he said with trepidation in his eyes, "I'm going up into it. When I die, I go up into it."

The next day we saw the movie, "Sister Act." Gordon had seen it before, but wanted to see it again with me. Gordon began to enjoy uplifting movies. We walked toward his apartment after the movie. He looked up at the sky.

"Do you believe in reincarnation?"

I thought a moment and said, "I think we are born daily, and we die daily."

I talked some more, but Gordon stayed quiet. Finally he said, "You know, it's so refreshing being around someone who thinks so differently than other people."

I didn't know what to say. We got to his apartment and he gave me a sudden hug.

"You know I love you, Thadeus," he said painfully.

I hugged him back and said stiffly, "I love you, too." I really did—I loved him as a friend. He disappeared into the apartment.

When Naoko returned from Japan I still invited him to church, but he never showed up. I enrolled in the evening school and got involved with courses. At the tutoring center, he started to avoid me. I remember him distinctly walking toward me, then mechanically turning away as if I didn't exist. I felt like I was yet another in a long line of people who had abandoned him. I went over to his tutoring table and said, "Naoko and I are having some people over for Thanksgiving turkey. Would you like to come over?"

He pulled out a Kleenex, blew his nose carefully and quickly, and told me he would if he felt strong enough.

He never showed up.

Later, he changed his telephone number. I lost track of him. I saw him one more time. I was coming out of Japanese class in Savory hall, and he was heading into it.

"Hey how are you." He looked dazed.

"Hey," he mirrored my smile. "I passed out again."

"Oh no."

"No it's okay."

I don't remember what all we said after that, but I can still see him, standing where the crosswalk converged as if he was not sure where he was headed.

For the ensuing weeks our schedules at the tutoring center no longer overlapped. Oh yes, I remember him coming once to kindly deliver a paycheck from Seattle Gay News. But beyond that, I didn't see him again. Later, just as I got into finals week, I saw a sign up at the tutoring center. Written in computer type, it said, "In Memory of Gordon Adler, loving tutor and friend." Below the message, a plastic rose was stapled to the sign.

I couldn't believe it. Gordon never told me he was even hospitalized. And the tutorial coordinator, knowing full well we were friends, never even bothered to mention to me about a previous memorial service. One of the other tutors said that many of his Elizabethan sonnets were read, including the one he had written "for Thadeus."

Several months ago I got a call from the university. They said Gordon listed me as one of his financial references. They wanted to know if he was around in order to pay his bills.

"He died," I said.

She paused, "Oh ... I'm sorry."

"His real name was Adam Bartholomew Rochester III. I'm not sure where his parents are. I'm sorry."

I hung up the phone.

I wrote about Gordon's story to the minister at the First Baptist Church. There was no response for weeks. Then one morning over coffee, Naoko and I heard the tail end of the following sermon broadcast over the radio:

"... A young man began attending this church a year or so ago. Gordon was severely depressed and questioning whether there was a God, and if so, not at all sure of being loved by that God. He had been disowned by his family when he told them he was gay. For several months, he sat quietly in the balcony, keeping to himself but listening carefully and absorbing as much of the worship as he could. One day when his despair was almost overwhelming, he asked for a gift, some visible sign that would be an assurance of God's caring. At that very moment, a ladybug flew onto his hand. For some reason, not known to us, Gordon chose to accept that as the sign he needed, and life began to brighten for him.

"He began to write exquisite poetry.

"Gordon died recently of AIDS. A friend sat down to write to me about his death and how this church had been a strong and redeeming force in bringing Gordon out of darkness and depression to a place of faith and trust. As his friend finished his letter to me, which included that transforming moment when the lady bug came and sat on Gordon's hand, another ladybug walked across the page of his letter. And the friend in writing about it, said simply, 'Coincidence?' I do not think so. I think a tender God sent a sign to let us know that Gordon was now home and that all was well."

Naoko and I could hardly believe our ears. The sermon was called, "A Tender God Reveals a Tender Self." Later we went to the church office to get some printed copies of the sermon. I wanted to send them to Gordon's family, but could only find the address of his sister in Capitol Hill. The letter came back, "Return to sender." Apparently she had moved.

Ladybug

When I walk the city streets, I find myself unconsciously looking for Gordon. One time I saw a guy that looked just like him: scrawny, plastic-framed glasses, short hair-cut, earring. I did a double-take.

Now, as I pen my recollections of Gordon, a ladybug appears. This is the third appearance of a ladybug. The thing is still resting on my English 425 folder. I carefully tilt the folder and let the insect slide onto my upturned hand. Two dots dapple the back. The guy at the espresso machine watches me as I stare into my palm; I must appear insane. I carefully walk out of the coffee shop and into the fresh air. The bug tenderly lights, splits open the reddish shell, and tests the wings. A few moments later my palm is empty. The bug just vanishes, taken by the wind.

❄

J. Jumbelic
Three Rivers Review

FALLING INTO WATER

I whisper, "Take off your shoes."

I whisper, "Dig your toes into loamy soil."

I whisper, "Quiet, you'll scare him."

I whisper, "He's close enough to touch."

I whisper, "It's just a fawn." You stare into black eyes. You hold your breath.

I whisper, "You're looking into god's eyes."

Everything glows green. It's late July.

"His white spots are starting to fade," I whisper.

I whisper, "He can smell you. Don't move."

The fawn blinks once …twice … his ears twitch right, left. He blinks again and takes a few steps away. Stops. Nibbles grass; moves on.

I whisper, "The world still spins."

You shoulder your backpack: the rustle of shoes in a plastic bag; the gentle clink of glass on metal. You uncap your Nalgene bottle and sip. Under trees, the earth is cold on your calloused soles. Sweat drips down your back.

I whisper, "Unclench your teeth."

The narrow path is a mosaic of rock and dirt, light and shadow; clouds glide across dark blue. An airplane slices through silence, streaming parallel lines.

I whisper, "Nearly there."

You round the bend and hear the creek an instant before your eye catches a flicker-flash of noon sun.

I whisper, "Listen."

Leaves touch lovers; the creek gurgles; small stones rub together under your feet; the creek gushes; something crashes in the underbrush; the creek stalls in soft eddies. Always the creek under and over and through everything.

I whisper, "Get closer. Down the path between the ferns."

I whisper, "Run your toes over slick roots."

I whisper, "Veins." I whisper, "Clutch them with your toes."

I whisper, "Anchor," and "Hold fast."

I whisper, "Climb down to water."

There is the creek and the cairns on the other side; smooth limestone rocks stacked like fine china one on top of the other. I whisper, "I built one once. We built one—we touched the curve of the sky."

You step onto a slick shelf of stone. You feel out each step. You mumble, *ass-over-teakettle…*

I whisper, "We laughed so hard we cracked sky."

…sore for a week.

You follow the narrow path down stream. Ferns brush bare legs. Toes on roots anchor each step. You grab at roots and limbs and stone; dig your toes into downy dirt. Water sparkles. The creek roars. Falls. Grinds down chutes too narrow.

I whisper, "We camped up here. We left our bikes chained to trees and carried tents and sandwiches, cans of soda and beer."

You poke a fallen branch into a coal black fire ring. You mumble, *Carry in – Carry out.* You prod a scorched beer can; tap a ball of foil that disintegrates like an old puffball.

I whisper, "It's a long way back."

You kick stones into a pile; you bury the beer can. The creek sucks at you. Drags you to the edge. Water falls. Haystacks of stone. Chutes too narrow. Eddies of light. Worn basins and slabs of cracked stone.

You look at water falling. The sun is warm. You plant your foot firmly between two mossy roots, step. You plant your foot between two mossy roots, step. And again. And again down ancient stairs. You clutch a tree; reach for purchase in a spiderweb of soft roots. You plant your foot on stone.

There's dirt under your nails, wedged in the creases of your palm; it smells dark and raw, alive with decay and sun.

I whisper, "This creek is the maker of music; the dreamer of dreams."

You walk into the mountain's water. You break out in goose bumps in sun and in water. Your feet are paler now. Smaller. A minnow darts over your hairy big toe. Tadpoles swim about, protozoic, in an algae-green basin. You stick your hand in it: it's warm, living.

I whisper, "I collected rocks from every stream or ocean I ever put my feet in. They glowed so brilliantly under water."

You dunk your other hand into the creek, fingers and toes tingling. You adjust. You pull a smooth red stone into air. The brilliant red color fades to dull rust as it dries in your palm.

I whisper, "The brilliance fades so fast."

You skip the stone across the pool of water into the churning mass of a thousand snowfalls. The trees whisper to each other around you. *Done bun can't be undone.* You strip off your shirt and tuck it in your back pocket.

I whisper, "It was so hot that night. We drank bottled water by the gallon. You glistened. We danced until the sun rose over water. We watched it from the beach."

You cross the shallow end, toes testing each slick step. You cut **v**'s in the rippled surface as the water flows over and around your ankles. You stop and stare off at the Cyclopean boulders, at the haystacks of stone, at the flood of water rushing between them.

I whisper, "You remember sliding down the rocks and into the water. The rush of water and adrenaline that threatened to split our skulls open."

I whisper, "I remember shoving you so you'd go. You screamed. But when you popped up like a cork at the bottom, you flashed that fourteen-karat smile. I remember. I remember the sunrise. I remember it now."

Your knees pop as you fill your water bottle.

You hoist the straps of your backpack – the muffled rustle of the bag, the clink of metal on glass. Pull. Swallow. Take another careful step, then glance upstream again for snakes sunning themselves.

I whisper, "We threw rocks till it slithered into a crack. You wouldn't go near the water. So we built towers of stone to touch the curve of sky."

The mottled shade of leaves welcomes you to the other side. The cool of another worn path. Startled, you jump and spin around. Damn squirrels!

The trees laugh at you. A dog in the shape of a cloud crosses the sun as you wrap your toes around another root now. It's cold and stiff and rough. A jagged stone pokes the arch of your foot. A plane glides around the sky's curve. You swear.

I whisper, "Please."

I whisper, "Nearly there."

I whisper, "Our soles are worn clean from walking in rain."

You tighten the straps of your backpack and put one sore foot in front of the other up another fern-lined path, collecting dew on your leg hairs.

I whisper, "You're shining."

You wipe it all away with your age-speckled hand. You round the curve of the creek and our private swimming hole spreads out like quick silver. It never used to take this long.

I whisper, "You're nearly there."

The trees on the cliff still over hang the calm water. A decrepit stone wall, faceless, with only the stubble of dirt for hair. Dead leaves molder on craggy shelves. Twenty feet we climbed. Twenty feet we fell. The cold water knocks the air from our lungs. We struggled for air. We scissor-kicked. We clawed. We doggy-paddled. We laughed so hard we cracked sky.

I whisper, "The sky is blue. The sun is burning and right there, and…"

You climb the sloped path up the backside of the cliff. The leaves still. The smell of sweat and dirt. You stop and put your backpack down and lean against oak. You pull the white cotton shirt from your pocket and wipe the sweat from your forehead and sallow chest.

It never used to take this long.

I whisper, "Just a little further."

One bare foot in front of the other. And you're looking down into the dark blue water, colder in shade.

I whisper, "Remember sitting over there, where we'd leave our clothes, and swimming across the slow current and climbing up the cliff?"

I whisper, "I remember everything now."

Like that sunrise on the beach, I whisper, "Unarm, Eros; the long day's task is done, and we must sleep." I can feel everything now: the padding of the backpack; the smooth surface of the urn; your hands; the grains of dirt and bark and silica. I can smell everything: the sweat on your body; the salt breeze; the ground between your toes; the water … the cold water, the mountain water, and I'm falling.

I'm falling into water.

I'm touching the sky's curve.

You whisper, "The bright day is done, and we are for the dark."

❈

Janice Levy

SIDESHOW

"THE tomah-toes are fab," my mother mimics. "The ginger's lovely. Are you a fan of hhh-erbs?"

My mother prances like a circus poodle, then flops on the hotel bed. On BBC 2's *Saturday Kitchen*, the *Two Fat Ladies* cook dinner for a Welsh choir.

"Crack on." She wiggles her pinky, sipping imaginary tea. "This spoon looks a bit fiddly but it works quick."

We have come to Wales to bring home my brother. My mother says she will stuff him into a suitcase, perhaps punch holes in the top so he can breathe, perhaps not. In his latest photo, Matt looks pale and bony; a red and green dragon tattooed on his chest spits out the words *cymru byth*; she thinks a carry-on bag will be good enough.

"Hug," she pouts.

I am the "good child," she reminds me again-again-again; without me she would die. "My sugar-pie-honey-bun," she coos. "My cookie-pookie, my—"

"Eye of the tiger," I suggest, slipping free. "The lion's roar." I pound my chest, suck in my breath. I lift my shirt and move my stomach like a snake. I have been doing sit-ups and using Matt's ankle weights. I'll show him the cleat marks on the back of my thigh, I think, the karate scar shaped like Tennessee under my chin.

"Squid, duuuuude," Matt will say, when he's back in New Jersey. "Kick ass." Then he'll swing me by the ankles if he's feeling good, maybe dig his knuckles into my neck if he's not. I'll ask him a million questions and he'll answer each one, while I strike matches off the sole of his boot and inhale the smokey balloons he blows from his lips.

I'll have to be careful, though, show Matt I remember the rules; like never to interrupt, even when his eyes close, his head goes back and he sounds like he's snoring; he's not, it's his brain grinding, shifting gears like a bicycle. I'm not to brush the ashes from his shirt or take off his shoes and swing his legs together so he doesn't fall off the couch when he's had too much to drink. Matt doesn't like to be touched. Around him, even Mom's supposed to be quiet.

"Not keen on whip cream?" My mother strikes a pose, flutters her eyelashes. "Life's too short to dance with an ugly man." She laughs too loudly, reaches for me and misses.

I take a step back. If we don't find Matt soon, my mother will soak up all the air, fill the room like a black cloud, burst and drown us both. *The Two Fat Ladies* grab helmets and rev the engine of their bucking motorbike.

"Remember the story about the rodeo?" she asks.

I almost nod but don't. My mother's stories are the good-bad kind, like a sugar rush that turns to puke.

"Listen," she says, squeezing my chin. Her voice goes back, back to when Matt was 10 and I was a baby, and Friday nights meant *challah* bread so fresh you could paste it on your nose and my dad banged the table, pushing the *Siddur* aside, saying, "The Jewish people were surrounded. They fought the war. They won. Let's eat."

My mom was so skinny my father wrapped his arms around her like a necklace; her face framed under the fancy *Shabbat* wig that made her scalp itch. Her real hair was the color of a starless night, thick as lentil soup; hair that waited for my father, hair that waited for later.

"Your father liked to hold the bobby pins," she says. "He looked like a pin cushion." She rubs her jaw, as if waiting for novocaine to kick in.

"Suddenly there's a scream like the sky's falling," she says. "Your whole life you never heard such a noise; you're on the floor with your head half off, like a regular Tower of Pisa. Your father says don't make such a *tzimmis*, the soup is like ice and the brisket, by now it's dry. He tries to straighten you up, but you collapse like a sack of potatoes. Your brother, like a *meshuggeneh* he's laughing; a real lunatic, holding his stomach like he's gonna *plats.*"

"'We were playing rodeo,' Matt says. 'I was the bull.'"

"Your father takes off his belt, I'm afraid right away he's gonna have a stroke."

"'Blame her,' Matt says. 'She didn't hold on.'"

"Then he swings a rubber sword over his head. *'En garde,'* he yells. 'Die.' Tells your father to die. Matt leaps off the furniture, slides down the bannister, he's a regular Captain Hoodnick."

"'Collarbone, schmollarbone,' your father tells the ambulance driver who straps you up. 'Me, I'm having a heart attack.'" My mother pauses, her eyes searching the room as if playing to a crowd. "Which he did. Two weeks later he was dead. End of story."

"Tell the rest," I say.

"Your brother, that little *mamzer*, good-for-nothing, slept under your crib until your sling came off. I'd see him in the morning, cracking pistachio nuts with his teeth, slipping food through the bars like you were in the zoo."

My mother laughs without moving her lips. "I always said Matt had a heart, but not the regular kind, more like something floating in formaldehyde you'd keep on your desk."

"We'll find him," I say.

"Good child," she says.

I think of when Matt threatened to sprinkle gunpowder on his cereal and wash it down with warm blood.

"We'll bring him home," I say out loud, but shut my lips for the rest.

"There's this seaweed," I read from the guidebook. "It's called *laverbread* and you spread it on fried cockles and crisps. They recommend the faggots and peas."

"What are they talking, faggots. *Fagelehs?*" My mother flings a towel. She can't figure out how the shower works. "Promise me I die here you'll keep away the sheep. All night long with the baa-ing, a person can go deaf."

We have eaten too many Welsh cakes and Anglesey cakes. Our fingers are sticky from *Bara Brith* crumbs; our tongues burned from pots of tea. We have gotten lost going "up the road and turn for left," waited too long for "toilets not engaged." A man without teeth called my mother a "fucking tart."

We've tilted the Big Cheese Slot Machine with ten pence and bought a broomstick witch too long for our suitcase.

We've ordered a wooden love spoon with three carved hearts under a bird that looks like it's taking a piss.

My mother jabs the air with her new walking stick, then throws it across the hotel room like a javelin, cracking its silvery King Arthur's head.

"*Croeso i Gymru,*" she says, welcoming me to Wales. "*Ddyd da.* And a fucking good day to you, too."

People ask where we're from. Their eyebrows move in sympathy.

"He's a handsome boy, until he let himself go." My mother shows Matt's photo. "Look at the bone structure." Outside the Church of St. Collen, she searches the missing person posters.

"Matt isn't missing," I say. "He just doesn't want to be found."

My mother narrows her eyes, pushes the visor off her forehead. "*Shemen zich in dein veiten haldz,*" she scolds. I should be ashamed down to the bottom of my throat.

In his last letter, Matt mentioned the *Llangollen Fringe Festival* and checked off concerts in a brochure, so my mother and I have listened to an Afghan band, a *fado* singer from Portugal, a Dai Davies' talk on Welsh cuisine, while scanning the crowd at the Fringe Shed. We've pushed our way down Parade Street, holding vanilla with pod ice cream cones over our heads, our eyes squinting, staring, straining.

"Matt didn't call," I say. "He didn't tell us to come."

"He sent me a recipe," she says. "For stuffed leeks with cheese and mustard sauce."

My mother thinks it's a sign; a sign Matt's slipping, a sign the black sheep is ready to be shorn.

We walk alongside the River Dee, listening to the clip-clop of the horses that pull the canal boats full of tourists. My mother's feet hurt, mine hurt more.

I concentrate on the night Matt left, when he'd given me a hunting whistle and said it didn't matter where he was; he could be farting in the next room or a thousand miles away. Blowing the whistle would make him feel better, he said. Big deal, I said, big fucking deal, and he told me to stop being a cry-baby *putz* or he'd beat the shit out of me, and then he was gone.

The next morning my mother asked why I wasn't crying, too, and I told her I was too old, but that made her cry more, so I closed my eyes and thought of my legs being chopped off and squeezed out a few tears. I searched Matt's room, but he had taken all the good stuff, like the nails and pieces of glass, bloody band-aids, the *Listerine* and cooking oil, stuff only I knew he hid under his bed.

"Side-show," he whispered one day, scrolling the Internet, whipping past a boy with his legs tied around his head, a girl with web feet like flippers swimming in a tank. Then he hooted like a pirate, turned his eye inside out and stuck a flashlight in his mouth.

When Matt left, my mother threw herself around; her body wrinkly and soggy, her eyes disappearing into her face. I waited for the dried-up huh-huh-huh sounds, then the a-whole-day-you-can't-go-without-eating-you'll-first-make-yourself-sick sounds, as she clanged and banged, mixed and fixed, glopping food onto my plate, more and more, forcing me, forcing me; she a sweaty, smelly mess, snorting in satisfaction, blowing her nose on her sleeve.

Afterwards, she took my temperature, held the thermometer out of reach. I had a 104 fever, she said, you could fry an egg on my forehead and didn't I see the rash on my arms and legs and back. She said it was malaria and made me scratch and scratch and not stop scratching until we got to the emergency room. She drove very fast and parked in a handicapped spot.

A canal horse whinnies. My mother neighs back.

"May the road rise to meet you." She chants the Celtic blessing, spinning around, her arms sweeping the air. "May the wind be always at your back."

"The rain fall soft upon your face," I continue. "And until we meet again—"

"The good child," she says and almost smiles, but then the tears come and my kisses are too late, my arms too weak, and I shoot curses at the sky for the stars to fall down and crush my brother, for the gray metal moon to slice through his chest.

Neither of us finishes the line about the holding us in His Hand stuff.

"En garde," I mouth the words. "En garde."

His mail came in spurts: scenes of Seattle, Toronto, London, web sites of snake charmers and fakirs, ticket stubs and pub menus, breezy jokes typed in Gothic fonts; never with a return address. Our dining room table became Matt's place. My mother called it the "Placematt." At night I'd find her there, bent over and fussing, as if planting a garden.

My brother sent a poster of George the Giant swallowing a 33-inch sword and a "congenital division of the stomach" x-ray of the Space Cowboy. On tape Matt hawked the act of a man sleeping on a bed of nails with 120 pints of beer on his belly.

He scribbled quotes in red ink: "I'll make thee eat iron like an ostrich and swallow my sword like a great pin. King Henry VI," said one. *"Ars longa, vita bre-vis.* Art is long, life is short," said another.

"Twenty pounds they pay him, what's that in dollars, *ver vaist*, who knows, he calls himself an artist," my mother said one night, shaking her head. "Artist, shmartist, I'll give him an artist, all these years he couldn't color in the lines; everything he drew it looked like a fish."

I played a game flipping his postcards. "He who lives by the sword dies by the sword," I read. "Who is Matthew 26:52?"

"Nobody from our neighborhood, trust me."

My mother stood tall, her voice puffy. "He laughs at fear, afraid of nothing; He does not shy away from the sword," she boomed.

"Your brother was little he wrote backwards like Leonardo da Vinci; he ran out of fingers, he stopped counting. All of a sudden he's a scholar, a regular *rebbe* yet, quoting Job."

My mother slumped as if her bones snapped. Then she'd hugged me, always too tightly, but I never moved. I was afraid if she let go we would fall through the floor, pass through the center of the earth and be buried alive.

"If anyone asks," she reminded me. "Your brother's in international finance." She stroked my face as if rearranging my features.

"This one's son is a doctor, that one's a lawyer. Hammering a nail into your nose, from this you can earn a living? I'm glad he's watching his weight, all these light bulbs he's eating. I can't tell you the embarrassment; if your father was alive he'd wish he was dead."

We eavesdrop on a tour group. The guide talks about a giantess who killed men trying to cross Horseshoe Pass. When the warrior, Cullen, used his mighty sword to cut off her arm, she picked it up and hit him with it.

"The picture of the girl with the ax," I ask. "Do you think she's Matt's girlfriend?"

"With that sheet over her head I don't know where she's going so *farputst,* all dressed up, she looks like a ghost. Must be those holes in her face, drains out the blood. I'm sure her parents are also thrilled. They say the wrong thing, she saws them in half."

My mother sighs. "I love your brother so much," she says. "If we can't find him, I'll die."

I suddenly feel very tired, tired of *Delia's How to Cook No Lump Flour* and stiff hotel beds, tired of *Brodyr's* electronic music, tired of everything dragons and daffodils and red and green.

"Let's go home," I say and before I can take it back she grabs my face, says the whites of my eyes are yellow, my lids too droopy, my fingernails not pink enough but if she can find a place for a blood test; jaundice perhaps, a problem with my liver, blood in my stool. She chews her lip, getting worked up.

I do a deep knee bend, a jumping jack, run in place to show her I am not anemic, that all my vitamins are in place. "Look," I say, opening a bag of pretzels I've kept from the plane trip. "Salt for dehydration." I shove a fistful into my mouth, but she doesn't look convinced.

"Matt was a baby he was always putting things in his mouth. One time he swallowed a roll of quarters, the doctor lifted him with a magnet."

"True story," we say at the same time.

"All real, all steel!" I open my mouth and throw my head back.

"Down the hatch without a scratch," she shouts back. Then we laugh until there's nothing left.

If Matt won't come home, I'll stay here with him, I think. He'll see that I've grown three inches this year and cut my bangs to look older.

"Whassup, Squid," he'll say and he'll mean it and I'll take him aside and tell him things; about police escorts and hospital beds, shots and made-up names, the pills I hide in my cheek. I'll show him I can throw up on command, twitch my limbs, nearly swallow my tongue. I can moan like a dying cat until even in Wales all the nurses bring my mother tea, tuck a blanket around her shoulders and pat her hand.

Matt meets us in the lobby of the Chainbridge Hotel. He sits closest to the door. He doesn't mention my bangs. The girl with the ax doesn't speak.

He says it was easy to find us and I ask him so what took him so long and he fixes me a look and asks if I've just dropped out of an airplane and landed in Oz, which I remind him is really Australia doesn't he know anything and he says shit, Squid, oh yeah, what have you been doing all these months, you sure are one smart fish.

I wait for my mother to put Matt in a chokehold, to squeeze him until his eyes pop out, to shoot them like dice across the wooden floor. "Craps," she'll yell, and then I'll roll a pair of sevens because I am the lucky child, the good child, the one she can't live without. My mother will pounce on his bones, how could you, why did you, how dare you, crraaaaack, wrong answer. Then she'll flame the ax-girl, whip her dragon's tail around her neck.

My mother fiddles with her hair, smooths the creases of her jeans. Her voice is gentle, half pleasing, half-teasing, a voice she doesn't use with me; a voice that reminds me of Sabbath and bobby pins. When Matt goes to the bathroom, she reapplies lipstick, freshens her eyes with mascara, smiling at the ax-girl, who doesn't smile back.

My mother rambles on about Mrs. Cohen, the next door neighbor, how she's suing for malpractice because the doctor left a sponge in her spleen and how much the house across the street is going for he wouldn't believe it even with the original kitchen and *feh*, that ugly orange wallpaper and re-member, she says, the Kosher butcher you liked the lamb chops—it closed, the Rabbi wouldn't bless the meat.

"What are you doing here," he asks me.

"I'm on holiday," I say. "Cheers."

Matt laughs and pokes me in the shoulder and for a mo-ment it's like nothing's changed; like I'm riding on his han-dlebars, bouncing on potholes, jumping curbs, and I'm not afraid, can't be afraid because those are the rules. Then we're stopping for burgers and he's smashing mine down and mix-ing all the sodas together from the pump and daring me to drink, and then I'm crying about Lee Weiss calling me "fish hook" because of my cleft and Matt's walking me to the bus stop, his hand shoved forward in his football jacket as if hold-ing a gun and in a low, slow voice threatening to set the girl's house on fire.

My mother is still talking about the price of chicken breasts.

"What's your stage name," I ask.

"I'm just an apprentice."

"The Sorcerer's Apprentice," I say and Matt throws his arms out and I lean into him and Wales turns into New Jersey and we're watching *Fantasia* for the hundredth time, filling buckets of water, jabbing each other with brooms, until our mother slips on the floor and curses that *no goodnick* mouse, that Mickey, but then helloooo, my mother interrupts; her voice whiny, "what am I, chopped liver?" and the cord is pulled, the power out.

The ax-girl moves her lips at me in what might be a smile.

Matt talks of esophageal sphincter, the gag reflex, stomach acids, as if reporting for the *BBC News*. The watering of his eyes, the taste of metal in his mouth.

My mother omigods, shrinks to half her size.

"Once I couldn't swallow solid foods for three days," he says. "The germs, bacteria—"

"Shmuts."

"Talk English."

My mother sits back as if slapped.

"She took care of me," Matt says.

The ax-girl closes her eyes, begins to snore.

I tug my earlobe. "Fifteen," I whisper loudly. "Each ear."

My mother fans herself as if she will faint.

"You'll come home," she says. "For a few days, a visit. I know a specialist."

"I have one." Matt kisses the ax-girl on the lips until I have to turn away.

While my mother settles our hotel bill, Matt tells me life is a double-edged sword; you stick with it, suck it up and swallow what you can. "The swords are real," he says, "it's the throats that are fake."

"I cut my bangs."

"You look older," he says and I wait for more but it doesn't come.

"Mom is just—" He shrugs and blows air out of his mouth.

"She's a lousy cook." We both laugh.

"I've still got your hunting whistle," I say.

Matt pauses. "Sure, Squid. Kick ass." Then he turns and walks away, the ax-girl trotting to keep up.

I blow my whistle. Matt squeezes her ass.

The flight attendant doesn't know if the cookies contain animal lard. There is nothing he can do about the smell of his aftershave. He won't give my mother a third pillow.

She is not allowed to see the pilot who sounds like her old hairdresser; such soft hands, like butter, but that new girl, you shouldn't know from the bruises like she's cutting sugar cane so just a little visit he'll be glad to see an old friend she always tipped him double and what are you talking shouting, who's shouting, she'll first give you shouting you'll wish you were deaf such shouting, maybe then you'll open a window?

I take off my sneakers and slip down the aisle. I do laps around the cabin, sucking my hunting whistle, matching my breathing to my steps so there's no room to think. But somebody calls out the time and I remember the night Matt left, when he promised to be rich and famous and buy me a pair of watchdogs.

"Rolex and Timex," I said and he answered "en garde!" and we barked at the moon.

My mother is still being shushed; there's no toilet paper left, the lettuce is wilted, if she's blocking the movie screen it should be bigger. The flight attendant asks her to spell the word *shmock.*

The lights flutter, the plane dips. I hurry back towards my seat.

And then it happens. A leg, a sharp-heeled foot juts out, rising like a limbo stick and I trip. My head hits the serving cart, my chin smacks into metal, the whistle cuts my gum. My mother leans down, whispering, her face full of teeth. "Concussion, blurry vision, ringing in the ear," she instructs. "Like the Liberty Bell."

A doctor on board comes running; he's a gynecologist but my mother says that's ok, *abi gezunt,* as long as he's healthy, everyone's a specialist these days. She smiles too much, shakes his hand too long and *danken Got!* he also knows from teeth because my tooth is loose, my best tooth, the one I use for chewing, blood's sprouting, *oy vey*! everyone move back, especially the flight attendant who smells like cabbage and yes, she'll take those extra pillows now, a drink on the house, of course, whatever the pilot's having ha-ha and if the roast beef in First Class is fresh, they should cut her a piece. Finally it is quiet.

"Good child," she says, kissing my forehead.

I shift in my seat. The pieces of the hunting whistle look like a jagged sword in my palm.

"I wonder where your brother got his intelligence," she says. "Must be from your father because I still have mine." She smiles and taps the side of her head.

"I think I have a sword throat," I say.

My mother stiffens.

"On April 28, 1999, Amy Saunders swallowed five swords. It's in the *Guinness Book Of Records.*"

"Enough."

"Edna Price was the first to swallow a neon sword."

"Stop it."

"Natasha Veruschka belly dances and her stomach glows."

"Shut up."

"They say it's the fastest way to get iron into your system."

My mother wipes the sweat above her lip. "Only mourners walk in their stocking feet," she growls. "I'm not dead yet. You're lucky you didn't break your leg." She opens a magazine. "Next time—"

"No," I say and then she shoots me a look but I shoot it right back.

Everything in her face moves, then stops.

"Toad-In-The-Hole," she reads from a recipe, gathering her voice, as if flipping up the collar of a coat. "With a roasted onion gravy. Pop the sausages in, piggedly piggedly in the pan."

She turns the page. Her hand shakes.

❄

Laura Resau
Pilgrimage Magazine

BEES BORN OF TEARS

CRISTINA shifts her baby to the other hip and tosses me a stick. "Here, Sarita," she says, breathless. "For the dogs."

The main street of Huajolotitlan—"Turkeyland" in the language of the Aztecs—is a forty-five degree angle, so steep you want to use your hands to crawl up. Brutal mid-afternoon sunlight glares off the pavement. Low buildings line the street, cement and adobe shops painted pastels and stained with urine. I catch a whiff of fresh blood from a pink *pollería* with its plastic bowls of goopy, featherless, dead chickens. Other shops sell only a handful of bare necessities—tiny packets of chili peanuts, toilet paper, cooking oil, Coke, warm beer, all neatly lined up on shelves behind the counter. Shop owners peer out of the cool interiors; a man in the shadows hisses at me, *güera, güera*—white girl, white girl. Cristina and I walk in silence, keeping our mouths closed to seal in the moisture.

We are on our way to see Lupita Chiquita—Lupita the Very Little One. All I know about her is this: She is tiny. She is nearly a century old. She is a *curandera*—a traditional healer.

I've been staying in a nearby Mixtec town in Oaxaca, Mexico; it is nearly home. It is the same place where I lived and taught English two years earlier. This summer I'm visiting villages, talking to women and healers for my Master's fieldwork. Cristina, a former student with family in Huajolotitlan, has offered to take me to Lupita Chiquita.

Two years ago I would have been bursting with the anticipation of meeting this *curandera*, but now my forehead is furrowed and my eyes stinging from the dry heat. Despite the constant presence of people, I feel alone, an observer of life more than a participant. I have just turned twenty-seven and nearly every woman my age here has several kids already. During my interviews, women shake their heads and cluck sympathetically when they discover I have no children. Around me, despite poverty, people are having families, living their lives.

On this trip, my former students, who haven't seen me for two years, seem worried about me. *You look different*, they say, *pale, thin, sickly*. Just before today's journey, a poet friend said with deep concern, "Sarita, you seem *demacrada*." I'd never heard that word before—it is a poet's word, not something I could pick up on the street. "Something is missing," he explained. "Your *chispa*." Your spark.

I tried to joke about it. "Oh, it's the bad food up North. No fresh mangoes and chilies and tortillas."

He didn't laugh.

I finally said, in a naked, shaky voice, that the two years with my ex-boyfriend, Miguel, were hard, very hard. The half year since the break-up has been just as hard, in a different way. Miguel's words come back like a curse, each syllable punctuated in precise Spanish-accented consonants: "You will never be in love again."

***

Cristina and I veer onto a dirt path, where turkeys peck at old plastic bottles and silver potato chip packages.

"We're here," she says, motioning to a small reed hut with a woven palm roof. It is a quaint, lopsided structure, suggesting the home of a witch, a fairy, an elf, some other-worldly creature. A horde of dogs guard the dwelling, their skin stretched taut over the ribs, sparse fur standing up angrily. They begin a cacophony of barks and growls, which makes the baby wail.

Cristina quickly pulls the blanket over her daughter's head and whispers, "*Chchch, m'hija,* don't cry." There is urgency in her voice. I wonder if she worries that her daughter could get sick from *espanto*—fright—from the dogs. This belief is so pervasive that even mini-skirt-wearing, web-surfing, 21-year-old Cristina probably feels it in her bones. When a person is frightened, her spirit separates from her body; at that moment, the spirit-owner of the land captures her spirit and holds it prisoner. The person grows ill and could even die unless a healer performs a ritual to retrieve the spirit. Most people I know here say they have been afflicted with *espanto* at one time or another, often from encounters with the ubiquitous, vicious dogs in Mixtec communities.

I wave the stick in the air like a sword, and the dogs keep their distance. Cristina and I huddle in a sparse bit of shade under a mesquite tree, waiting for someone to call off the dogs. She murmurs under the blanket all the while, into that intimate space between baby and mother.

After the conversation with my poet friend, I looked up *demacrada* in my dictionary. Emaciated. What he meant was spiritually emaciated. I tell myself that life is a series of little deaths and re-births—part of yourself dies; a new part is born. But what if some essential part of yourself disappears, and there's nothing to replace it?

***

Maybe the heat is making me delirious, launching me into the dreamy beginnings of heat exhaustion. . . but something odd is seeping into this scene in Lupita Chiquita's yard . . . the ancient, musty odor of a folk tale. A wanderer approaches a hut, thirsty and exhausted, having climbed a nearly endless hill and confronted savage beasts, hoping to see the mysterious wise woman who will bestow upon her. . . ? For a moment, life takes on the crystalline structure of a myth, the pattern of a snowflake, the spiral of a shell. Everything is part of the movement drawing me closer to the center, closer to some truth.

Two girls appear at the door of the hut—about three and eight years old—and walk toward us. They're wearing jelly shoes and well-worn dresses a few sizes too big. Their brown twig legs are scaly with dust.

Cristina shifts her baby to the other hip. "*Buenas tardes, niñas.* We're looking for Doña Lupita Chiquita."

Whispering together excitedly about *la gringuita*, the girls lead us to the door of the hut, protecting us from the dogs with well-aimed stones, and call out *"Tía!"*

A tiny woman appears at the door. She barely reaches my shoulder, which would put her at about 4'4". She wears a pink polyester dress, a blue checked cotton apron, a red cable knit cardigan, and a heap of tangled necklaces—plastic pearls and gold chains and leather strings, each holding its medley of saints and crucifixes. A round pair of glasses with thick lenses, eighties-style, covers much of her face. Intricate networks of wrinkles spread out from her mouth and eyes, like the dried-up, folded skirts of mountains. Age spots a shade darker than her brown skin speckle her face. Her thick, muscular hands seem out of proportion to her bird-like body.

"*María Purísima Santísima!*" She smiles a toothless smile and gives me a tight hug saturated with wood smoke and copal incense.

Cristina glances at me with raised eyebrows and a shrug that says she has no idea what's going on.

It *is* strange. Lupita Chiquita had no way of knowing we were coming, yet she acts as though she's known us all our lives, as though she's been expecting us. She is overflowing with something, exploding with it, even. No doubt about it, this woman has *chispa*.

"*Ay, muchachita!*" she says to me. "Come in, come in! Sit down, *m'hija*, my daughter!" Her voice is nasal and urgent.

I duck through the doorway and follow her into a dark, windowless room with parallel slivers of sunlight spilling through the walls onto the dirt floor. There's an altar to the right, a wooden table crowded with candles flickering in small glasses, and a multitude of framed saints and Virgins amidst vases of carnations and daisies. A clay incense pot with charred remains of pine and copal holds a lingering smell of smoky resin. A few *petates*—woven palm mats—are rolled up in the corner. Clay pots with their bottoms burnt black hang from the wall. The only furniture is a small stool and two wooden chairs. The air smells cool and earthy like a cave.

Lupita Chiquita gestures to the chairs. "Sit down, sit down, *muchachita!*" She is barefoot, her century-old feet caked with dust and dry as leather, rough as paws or hooves.

Here in the Mixteca, people tell a story of a spirit woman called the *bandolera*, a beautiful woman with the feet of an animal—in some versions, turkey claws, in others, *burro* or horse hooves. She lives in a cave full of candles, each representing a life. The short candles are lives about to end, the long ones, newborn babies. In my favorite version, she brings certain people to her cave to teach them the secrets of life and death.

A woman appears at another door that leads to a dirt courtyard where people are milling around, engaged in various tasks. The woman is middle-aged, a bit taller than Lupita Chiquita and much wider. She introduces herself as Lupita Chiquita's daughter, visiting from Mexico City. "Remedios Gomez Rodriguez. *Para servirle*." Light from the doorway illuminates her face, round and damp with sweat from some exertion in the courtyard.

The girls carry in an extra chair—a plastic one with a Sol beer logo—and a bottle of Coke. The older girl pours me a glass and the little one offers it to me with both hands. "Here you are, *gringuita*." The warm syrup feels sweet on my tongue, the bubbles sharp.

Now Remedios and Lupita Chiquita let the questions fly. *Where are you from!? What are you doing all the way out here? Do you like our food? Do you like our village? Where is your mother? Are you married? Do you have children?* Wave after wave of sheer, giddy exhilaration. The air is electric.

Remedios tells us that her mother doesn't hear well, so I talk loudly, imitating Remedios's loud, slow voice. "I'm from the United States," I say. "Maryland." I translate the state's name as "*Tierra de María*."

"*María Santísima Purísima*!" Lupita Chiquita shrieks. "You traveled far!"

I answer the rest of the questions, explaining that I have not lived with my mother for nearly ten years, that I like spicy food, I like Turkeyland, and that I'm an old maid, childless and husbandless.

As we talk, bees spiral and dip around our heads, attracted, I guess, to the Coke. Cristina shoos them away from her baby, who has fallen asleep. I move my head around in a dance to get out of the bees' paths. The last time I was stung, years ago, on my finger, my entire hand ballooned up. Lupita Chiquita and her daughter let the bees land on their shoulders, rest in their hair.

"And what are you doing all the way out here, *m'hija*?" Lupita Chiquita asks.

"Cristina tells me you're a *curandera*. I wanted to meet you."

"Ah! So that's why!" Remedios shouts. "My *mamacita* is ninety-six years old! Can you believe it? Ninety-six! And look! Still strong, isn't she?!"

Lupita Chiquita nods vigorously.

She does look strong. More than strong. The whirlwind inside her nearly lifts her small body off the floor. There is something I can learn from this woman, with her candles, with her secrets of life and death.

***

Remedios turns to Cristina. "Who is your mother?" she asks, trying to place her in the web of families of Huajolotitlan.

Cristina tells them and adds, "My mother brought me and my sister here when we had *espanto*.

"Ah, yes, *muchacha*!" Lupita Chiquita says. "I remember you."

"What gave you *espanto*?" I ask Cristina.

"Some dogs." She kisses her baby, who is asleep now. "They scared me, and after that I couldn't sleep. I cried a lot. I didn't feel like eating."

People say that unless a child with *espanto* is cured she might die, or continue to live in a weakened state, missing the essential part of herself. I wonder if you can get used to living without parts of your spirit, like someone who's missing a finger and compensates with others. How many bits of my spirit have I lost over the years? Is my spirit scarred and mutilated, with chunks missing here and there? Or have they grown back, like the arms of a starfish, the tails of lizards?

When I was nine, one day I was rollerskating in the alley near my house, when two Dobermans—trained attack dogs—were let out of a parked car to enter their cage. The dogs bolted toward me and pounced. I clung to a splintery telephone pole as the dogs tore into my upper arm and thigh. The owner retrieved them, and, ignoring the blood and tears, told me to go home. "You're okay," he insisted, probably afraid of being sued. I skated home in shock.

That's when I started acting weird. I was terrified of any door clicking shut, convinced I would get locked in. I refused to be left without an adult for even a minute. I tolerated no dark corners, and frantically turned on all the lights in the house. My weirdness tapered off after a year, replaced by occasional dreams of wandering lost in a labyrinth of alleys. They were eerie dreams, very real, as though some part of myself was stuck amidst the trash cans and wire fences and weeds poking through cracked concrete.

I wonder now if I needed someone to retrieve my spirit and return it to my body. Literally or symbolically, it didn't matter. And now, after this relationship with Miguel has left me *demacrada*, I need a ritual, too. A part of myself got lost, and I need to find it.

***

452

Lupita Chiquita must notice that part of my spirit is missing, because she announces, "I'm going to give you a *limpia, m'hija.*"

"Good," I say. "I need one."

Cristina stares at me. "Are you sure?" She lowers her voice. "You know what she's going to do to you?"

"Más o menos." More or less.

"But Sarita, your clothes will get soaked. You don't have to do it."

"I want to. Really." Anyway, Remedios and the girls are already spreading out the *petate.*

"Take off your clothes, *muchachita,*" Lupita Chiquita orders.

This is an unexpected twist. I hesitate, trying to remember which underwear I have on.

"Down to your underwear!"

I take off my sandals. At least my clothes won't get wet this way.

Cristina bites her lip and watches, amused.

Voices float in from outside, where men and women are doing chores in the dirt courtyard. Hopefully, they can't see me undressing.

I strip. My underwear turns out to be an ancient pair, once white, now grayish, mis-matched with a grubby, frayed bra. I sit like a skinny plucked chicken on the *petate,* goose-bumped and shivering. The dried palm itches my thighs. I wonder if tiny bugs live between the fibers.

Lupita Chiquita pulls a bottle of neon green liquid from a crate in the corner. I've seen *limpias* done with clear mezcal— fermented agave nectar—but I don't recognize this stuff. *"Agua de Siete Machos,"* she calls it. Water of the Seven Macho Males? She holds it under my nose. It smells like cheap cologne. I sneeze.

Remedios hurries out the door and returns moments later with a handful of fresh *sauco* leaves and hands it to her mother.

Lupita Chiquita prays at her altar, then rubs the herbs over me, in my hair, my shoulder, arms, back, legs, the soles of my feet. The *sauco* smells fragrant, potent. She prays to God, the Virgins, the saints, punctuating her chanting with "Sara." My self-consciousness fades, and I focus on her voice, on the leaves' friction over my skin.

Then she murmurs, like a stage direction between prayers, "Take off your glasses, *muchachita.*"

The older girl carefully takes them for safe-keeping.

"Close your eyes!" Lupita Chiquita whispers.

I obey. I feel the shock of cool alcohol spit onto my skin. It is a jarring sensation, pulling me out of a certain dullness. I imagine all the *mal aire*—bad air—blown away with these great bursts. I imagine my spirit, something iridescent and alive, something like a blue butterfly, flying through the door and into my open chest, nestling where it belongs.

When the spitting ends, I open my eyes. The girl hands me my glasses. I look down at my ratty underwear, now spotted with lime green. I shiver and smile at Lupita Chiquita, her eyes huge and wild behind her thick lenses.

***

The bees seem even more attracted to me now that I'm covered in neon green stuff. I'm fully clothed again. I'd like to stand up to have more space to dodge the bees, but in a gesture of politeness typical in Mixtec villages, Remedios insists I stay glued to the chair. The bees zoom around my head. I pray they don't sting. Who knows if the local hospital is stocked with epinephrine.

"Don't mind the bees," Lupita Chiquita says. "They are good, these bees!"

The bees are buzzing around our heads like crazy now, two bees in particular, circling each other, spiraling around each other as if dancing. I duck out of their way.

"Don't worry," Remedios says. "They won't sting you."

"But I'm allergic."

"Look! Look how those two bees are staying near you and my *mamacita*."

Sure enough, the two bees seem to be doing figure eights around Lupita Chiquita's and my heads. Urgent, frenetic spirals.

"The bees are your spirits. See, they have met before, your spirits. They met each other first and they led your bodies together."

Lupita Chiquita nods.

The wings inside my chest move, I can feel them. They move with a thrill, a sense of discovering layers of meaning like ribbons intermingling in the wind. They move with the sudden knowledge that the world is a strange, deep, rich place.

***

Cristina's baby starts to fuss, and I realize it's nearly dark. "We should go, Sarita," Cristina says.

I hand Lupita Chiquita thirty pesos—about three dollars—her charge for a *limpia.* She hugs me hard and grasps my hand, unwilling to let me go.

"You'll come back tomorrow, right?" Her eyes are full of tears. Her grip is as powerful and genuine as a three-month-old baby's.

"In a few days," I promise.

"Last night," she says, "I was kneeling in front of my altar, crying because of how we suffer. Because we are poor, my family. I asked *Nuestro Señor* to look after us. *Señor Jesús, ayúdame!*, I prayed. *Help me!* And in my sleep, a baby came to me. A fat white baby in green clothes. Really fat, and really white, like your skin!"

There is a framed picture of a fat white baby in green on the altar, I notice. *El Santo Niño*, the holy baby Jesus.

"And he told me, Lupita, *m'hija*, have faith. Just wait until tomorrow."

She looks at me dramatically. "And today, you come to my door, *muchacha*! He was right, *El Niño Jesús!*"

I think about the three dollars I gave her—possibly enough for a small sack of beans, some eggs, dried corn—enough food for a few days if they really stretched it. Is that what she means? Or is she referring to our new friendship involving bees and spirits, a friendship with its own momentum that won't let a seventy-year age difference and thousands of miles stop it?

***

A few days later I'm back in the hut, on the plastic Sol chair, with bees once again circling my head, although I don't mind them as much now. Since the *limpia*, I've felt elated. I don't care exactly how the *limpia* worked. I simply enjoy the feeling that my *chispa*—my spark—is returning.

"You remind me of the gypsies!" Lupita Chiquita announces. "They traveled from far away, too." She turns to her daughter for confirmation.

Remedios nods. "*Muy buena gente*, the gypsies, really good people."

"They don't come anymore!" Lupita Chiquita's eyes fill with tears. "*Ay*, how I miss them!"

"Your skin is white like theirs," Remedios says.

"And you speak our language in a strange manner, too!" Lupita Chiquita adds, laughing. Her fluidity of emotion amazes me, how she cries at any hint of sadness and laughs heartily at the smallest joke.

"And you're so tall!"

Reminiscing about the gypsies inspires Lupita Chiquita to tell us her story. When she was about six years old, a gypsy woman read her palm and predicted she would live to be a very, very old lady. Soon afterward, Lupita Chiquita came down with a severe and sudden sickness.

Remedios jumps in. "She died, the poor thing."

"What?" I thought I'd mastered my verb conjugations. "Who died?"

"My poor *mamacita, pobrecita.*"

I turn to Lupita Chiquita. "You died?"

Lupita Chiquita nods solemnly. "I died."

The family mourned her and put white candles all over the room as villagers came to pray and cry over her. In the midst of the darkness and smoke and tears, a drop of candle wax fell onto Lupita Chiquita's arm. She flinched. She woke up. People say that her experience with death gave her the power to heal.

She doesn't remember what happened to her while she was dead, but I wonder if she met the spirit woman of death and life inside her cave of candles. Maybe she taught her how to heal. I imagine each of us with our own cave of candles, parts of ourselves burning down to wax pools, dying, other parts of us just beginning, the candles freshly lit.

***

It is nearly dark, time for me to leave. I tell Lupita Chiquita and her daughter that I won't see them again for a while. In a few days I'll be heading back to Arizona to finish grad school.

From her altar, Lupita Chiquita takes a photo of a statue of San Sebastián and puts it in my hands. He is dressed royally in a sequined, flowered outfit of turquoise, red, and gold, draped with gold chains and bracelets, flowers and ribbons. His arms are tied to a lopsided cross flanked by two small dark-skinned Jesus crucifixes. Small daggers pierce the man's throat and limbs and his wounds drip blood. Remedios's reverent look makes me realize this is a very special thing her mother is giving me.

Suffering saints usually frighten me a little, but this one doesn't look in pain so much as wistful. No, this tortured saint is not creepy. It is oddly comforting, actually, to see how he endures his suffering, trusting that his pain will be a flash in eternity, knowing that his wounds will heal, only flowers and sparkles and ribbons remaining.

I think about all the prayers focused on this photo, all the energy directed to it. It is a sacred thing, a thing of power for Lupita Chiquita, and she has given it to me.

We hug. She cries and moans and sobs and chants and prays, making small crosses over me with her hands. *Que Dios te bendiga, muchacha,* God bless you, girl. Over and over and over again, for a long time.

I'm embarrassed by the attention, unsure how to respond. Not even my own mother has ever given me such a farewell. Then I realize that neither Lupita Chiquita nor her daughter can read or write, so letters won't be possible. She has no phone. She has no money to visit me, no visa. And she is ninety-six years old. Of course she's worried this is the last time we'll see each other.

I am used to traveling, meeting people, saying goodbye. I naively believe that we will see each other in a year or two.

Bees Born of Tears

***

Within days, I get an email from Owen, the man I've known for years and will eventually marry. Our relationship is a stream that surfaces, goes underground a bit, and resurfaces. His email now comes after years of little or no communication, since Miguel discouraged our friendship.

Owen's email is three lines. It says he has been remembering the way sunshine smells on my skin. I imagine my spirit, a velvety bee, flying up to Colorado to confer with his spirit. I write back to Owen, and we arrange for him to visit me in Tucson. The following year, we are living together, engaged, in Colorado.

Bees, I discover, are associated with gods of love—Cupid among the Greeks and Kama among Indians. The Welsh believe that bees came from paradise down to earth to give humans gifts of wax and honey—honey to nourish them, and wax to make candles for altars. A bee entering the house is lucky, and one flying around a sleeping child is a sign of a happy life to come. And in Egypt, bees were born of the tears of the Sun-God, Ra, and symbolize the afterlife and rebirth.

***

A year and a half later, Owen and I walk up the hill in Huajolotitlan, just at dusk, when the air is blue and magical and tinged with sadness. We have heard from Cristina that Lupita Chiquita passed away last year, although Cristina is not completely sure; it could be a rumor. I remember how Lupita Chiquita defied death as a six year old. I hope it's another mistake.

I pick up a stick to fend off the barking dogs. Someone is walking toward us, a stout woman. Remedios.

"*Jesús María José!*" She hugs us, moaning and crying, and then leads us to her siblings, who have come from other villages. They know my name although we've never met, and hug us with the same force that Remedios does.

"How we prayed you'd come!" she says. "My poor *mamacita* always remembered you!"

It turns out we have arrived precisely on the night of Lupita Chiquita's *cabo de año*—the one-year anniversary of her death, where family members and friends spend a week mourning her. I can guess Remedios's explanation—that the spirit of her *mamacita* buzzed up to the U.S. to invite my spirit to the *cabo de año*.

Remedios ushers us into the hut and gives us sweet cinnamon coffee and sugary pastries.

The altar is overflowing with carnations and roses. The light from the candles is stronger than that of the bare bulb dangling overhead. In back of the hut are shadows of people milling around, talking quietly. Other relatives wander into the room and greet us. They have heard of me, Lupita Chiquita's dear friend from the United States. They have heard how our spirits flew together as bees.

The sugar, the caffeine, the shadows, the candlelight—they lend a surreal quality to the night, and I can almost see, in the midst of so many flames, a tiny body laid out. I tip over a candle, let a drop of beeswax fall, and wake her up, knowing that resurrections happen all the time.

❄

Silas Zobal

AND WE SAW LIGHT

Divinity is behind our failures and follies also.

–Ralph Waldo Emerson

WE feel the tremor of approach. On the paved road lined by wheat, the boy and dog come. Chained men collect trash among the roadside poppies. The scent of fire. The sky races with clouds. The foretaste of blood hangs in the air. The dog whines and rakes her nails on cement. Against the skyline, a tree burns.

The boy calls himself Gil. He breathes hard. He smells the phantom of his mother's sweat, of boxelder, of anise and cinnamon, of the smoke of green wood. Gil's thoughts out pace him. Gil sweats. The bloodscent raises images—the stillborn he'd found in the compost, the rotting meat, the decaying child, the spindle arms exposing bone, the maggots, the mulch and feces. The soil of this valley. Gil's stomach reminds him he hasn't had supper. Ham hock and mustard greens. Home lies behind him. The chained men sing in low and graveled voices. The dog jerks on her rope. Wine-red drops thicken on the cement. Blood. Bloodtrail leading toward the fire in the tree.

Gil, kneeling on the sidewalk, dips his index finger. Sniffs. Recoils.

—*What's it, girl?*

Dog doesn't know. She lowers her nose, widens her nostrils, breathes. She's a greyhound; she's a gazehound. She knows she's bigger than the boy. She eats ground. Pulls on her leash.

—*C'mon, girl, let's go.*

The gazehound drags Gil across the cement. She stops. She licks.

—*No, girl, no.*

Dog doesn't listen. Dog pants. Points her nose forward. Cocks one front paw. Leans her whole frame. Stiffens.

Boy doesn't listen. He squares his shoulders. Braces his feet. Takes the rope two-handed. Pulls. Pulls her toward.

—*Home, girl. Home.*

***

—*Think she dead, High?*
—*Don't much care.*
—*Yeah. Yeah, fuck 'er.*
—*We done that already.*

***

We hear her voice as she's walking. He. She. Journey-woman. She. Journeywoman singing the dirge, the hymn, the plainsong. A heartbeat and echo along the roadside, a worn-skinned mirage in a blue, lily-printed dress—*yes*, this far-traveled figure whose hand strangles the gunnysack by her side. We hear the sound of bared feet against road. We see the moon rising above fields of wheatgrass. We watch. How long must she walk? Large-bellied and singing. The road rolls with foothills. The winds quarrel with one another. The willows flail and lash. Night bleeds across the sky like ink.

We. We are unbeguiled by time; we are that which casts no shadow; we are without want. We are the dust and stones, and we are the street. We are.

The gunnysack. Coarse-fibered. Wet. The bottom that leaks. The dark ovals that trail in the dirt of the road. We, we who shall know neither the day nor the hour, we watch. To the left, a cemetery; to the right, a river. The sweep of the wind; the tangle of leaves; the hush of moving water. The cemetery gives off visions of the grave. Jaundiced children with distended bellies; skeletal old women; drowned and bloated men; blood. Shredded throats, carved breasts. The milk swollen. The promise choked. The scent of remorse.

And she walks past. Past strains of faraway drinking songs echoing between hills. Past the smell of burnt corn, of lamb on the spit, of woodfire. She walks past white-gowned choirboys trickling towards homes; past the ailanthus tree where a girl, hair in cornrows, lies beneath an umbrella; past the noise of someone loving someone else among the azal-eas. Past the strained and plaintive cries for more and more—she walks, beneath a thunderhead. Past the light rain come for the peonies once planted by lovers or fathers at the bases of graves. She walks by. Past wind-bent trees, a barn and silo, small clothes pinned to a line. Past men with love-bemisted minds, past a grandfather perched on an undersized rocker, humming off-key and knitting stockings for the smallest granddaughter.

We watch the journeywoman walk by, head low, eyes narrow. Listen to the patter of that which drips from the gunnysack. Twilight swarms behind the drum of barefeet. The sun's light fails to blind us to the stars. We watch the walk into darkness. Swollen woman. Womb's contents feel a part. And apart. Twinned heartbeats. Wind in gales—she walks. Trembling aspen leaves; watchfires dotting hills behind the cemetery; gravestones looming in shallow light. Walking past a pit dug for the wicked. The downcast eye. Walk past—*yes*, walk past. Arms cup her belly. Her. She. Journeywoman. Mother. Sundress colored by blue potatoes, knees bruised by falls, feet cut by stones. Legs as long-standing as religion. We, we who know nothing but the watch of the mother, see the shadows converge behind her. See the haze of clouds against the horizon as she walks. As she walks on the dirt road. Walks against the flow of the river. Face lifted. Footsteps. We. We who walk through the valley. Mottled light against leaves under wind. Nightbirds. Her voice may sound like grace. Singing. Come, now. We follow.

***

Two men find the countryroad woman. Two men. High and Ollie. High and Ollie dirtroading, shooting at crows through truck windows, sharing a half-empty thermos of homebrew.

—*Hey, High, we pass a sweet bitch picking berries?*
—*Pull on over.*

So it happens. Narrow evergreens border the road. Town lights blink distantly. Countryroad woman reaches tall for blackberries, lily blue dress slips up on thighs, body tenses and curves as she leans to the brambles. Pickup bounces by, trailing dust, men at the windows. Bored and waiting men. Men who wait for all the things they're sure they should have got but didn't.

Here she is. Shoulder-tossed. Bitch-whipped. Limbs pressed against the flatbed. Handsewn dress a yellow rag.

—*What's yer name?*

Countryroad woman mumbles. Crosses bare legs. Closes eyes. Trembles.

—*What it say, Ollie?*

—*Think it say Elly.*

—*Elly ain't yer name no more.*

***

Cecilia and Grandmother Furne walk toward town. They walk through forest. The path is worn, leaf laden, heavy with light. The sound of footfall resounds between hills. Grandmother Furne wears black woolens. She walks with an oak cane and breathes heavily. With one hand, Cecilia clutches a bead purse. With the other, she holds her Grandmother's dress.

—*Gammy Furne, where mama been?*

—*Well. What age you at?*

—*Nine, Gammy.*

—*You're gettin' on then.*

—*My mama. Where she go?*

—*Ain't for us to know, child.*

They stop beneath the shade of a hornbeam tree. The sun casts long shadows. The air's flavored of strawberries. Shrub fires dot the hills. Cecilia points to the hornbeam.

—*Gammy, that tree's losing its skin.*

—*Seems to be.*

Spreading her skirt neatly beneath her, Grandmother Furne sits beneath the tree. She takes two red pears from her jacket pocket, rubs them against her thigh, passes one to Cecilia. Cecilia pulls her own skirt above one knee to fuss with a scab.

—*Your pear, child. Eat.*

—*Mama dead. Isn't she, Gammy Furne?*

—*Don't speak such things.*

—*I knowed it, she gone.*

—*No telling, child. We wait and see.*

***

Countryroad woman. Elly. Nylons in ribbons.

Mouth stretching into the shape of the sound in whore or howl. Hands reach toward townlight. Across the ground flies the shadow of outstretched wings. What vista is this? Who brings these visions? What else may come?

—*Show 'er yer shit, Ollie.*

—*Hold 'er good.*

—*Make the bitch holler.*

Faint shrill cries. Hurt. Shuddering hips. They take turns lying on top of her.

—*Get off, mutherfucker. Fair's fair.*

—*Hold 'er legs open.*

Two men. High and Ollie. Kick her out of the flatbed. Have at her in the mud. They're out to bury themselves in this woman. To answer all questions of capacity. How much can be borne? The void belongs to whom? Who among us wears the face of the deep?

Faraway bells toll. Bootheels dig against kidneys. Hands are wet by mouth.

—*Flip 'er over, Ollie. Grease 'er with yer finger.*

Countryroad woman. Elly. White skin naked against mud. Low screams. Fainting. Intestinal shuffle and shudder. Hands rake mud; nails break against stone. Mosquitoes circle. Owl calls penetrate the twilight.

***

She still walks. She. Her. Mother. Journeywoman singing to the unborn, limping yet lightfoot, stride as remorseless as the seasons. The cold twilight air smells of rain. She walks by us. The sack leaks. Two loaves of bread, the space it takes— the gunnysack. Brown near her hand; black near the curved bottom. Air thickens. The strain of the sack's weight gathers, stretches, releases another drop for the trail that follows. Bare feet treat the earth like a drumhead. Must she walk until the singing fails to cease? We listen. Listen to the haunt of the wind; the birthcry of nightbirds; the swell of the river. Moonlight. Listen as she walks past a chorus of women singing songs to relieve grief. Past the gentle glow of kerosene lamps. Past a shirtless boy, hands full of river agates, wading the edgewater. Past the open-doored chapel, the men in dark coattails, the women in veils. Past the rose wreath, the eulogy, the mourning song.

She walks past the well-lit kitchen. Past the kitchen turned birthing room where the midwife sweats to the muscle heave and uterine clench, to the ghostwalk of communal heartbreak, until, so sudden, the highabove screaming of a voice where once there was none. She walks past the hollow, overwhelming emptiness of division, of one becoming two. Past two held together by the string of the umbilical connection; past the highgloss of steel and loss; and then, in the bittersweet moment of panting and cleaning and whisking away in porcelains of tissue and blood, *sweet Jesus*, the shudderache of separation. The journeywoman walks past. The girlchild. Who does she belong to now? What waters shall bear her? What toward? What ghosts will watch her walk? Can our footsteps lead anywhere but home?

***

Fingers tear at folds of skin. Sweatslick bodies fumble. The longitude of belief stretches; mouths cut breasts; knuckles loosen teeth. Blood vapor. The forgotten business of sacks and organs. The piss and shit vales.

—*Bitch ain't pretty no more.*
—*Listen to 'er grunt.*
—*What a tongue on 'er.*

Countryroad woman. Elly. Knee-jerked, bedraggled. Wet-thighed. Time drains away and returns twisted. Colors reduce to mutter, the glide of pain's measure, introduction and reintroduction, space reduced to the ring of emptiness, the sound of a belt unbuckling again. Open-mouthed. Saliva.

What will be left behind? Whimpers cease. Tears recede. Legs stiffen. Encroaching visions of the church steeple and stained glass; the lime and granite rectory; translucent women—ageless, long-haired figures of habits and crosses—with light angling through them. The blood rises. Days pass away like smoke. Bones burn like a furnace. The spit and slap of love overridden by choral singing. Hands clamp over bloodied mouth. By the distant townlights, above lime and granite, bells toll. What songs might she sing would her mouth open?

—*Why's she gone quiet, High?*
—*Don't know.*
—*Ain't so good no more.*
—*Let's string 'er up.*
—*String 'er?*

String her by jumper cables and joined wrists from a pine tree. Open her stomach with a hunting knife.

—*Cut the slut's feets.*

Terrorscreams. Highpitched. Endtrailing.

—*Not 'er toes, shitass.*

—*Didn't say that, High.*

—*Go at it again.*

Two men. High and Ollie. Pickup kicking dust behind spinning wheels. Leaving to the song of gunfire. Who will stay behind to mourn?

Here she is. Elly. Countryroad woman left to dangle until bad knots and bloodslick set her loose. Holding her stomach. Drunk on hurt. Spilling organs. Limping toward the river where, around her feet, angelfish will swim.

***

The boy. The dog. The blood. Darkness has come upon him like a stranger. The moon blanches fields of wheat. Indigo sky shows through cloudbreaks. Nightfires. The boy, this Gil, smells the bloodwinds. He cries. He thinks that the fire behind him at home's hearth might warm him; that the stillborn in the compost came in foretelling; that he's been dog-dragged to the valley where the dead belong; that spirits rather than winds cause the wheat to bend and wave. The gazehound drags him forward. The dog eats ground. The boy yaws through the night past the chained men among the poppies singing of the weary years coming to end like a sigh. Past opossums and nightbirds. Past the rounded hill that blocks the view of the horizon and the tree that still burns. Gill sees the wheat sway and fall before spectral feet. He sees the shades among the fields, but he closes his eyes. He doesn't want to see us. What are we but visions come in blessing?

***

Grandmother Furne and Cecilia come near town. The forest gives way to crops. Alfalfa fields lie cut. Grandmother Furne stops to rest often. She sweats.
—*Cecilia, what songs you know?*
—*Just church ones.*
—*Them'll do. Go on now.*
—*You too, Gammy?*
—*My voice ain't here. You're solo.*
The alfalfa flats lie cut. The heavy late-day light casts the fields in orange. Grandmother Furne gasps, shudders, sits in the aftergrass, asks Cecilia if grace might be found in the singing or in the song.
—*Gammy? Gammy, you okay?*
—*Could be I'll sleep a minute. Get on, Cecilia. Sing.*

***

We. We are the air in the fields of wheat. We are. We are following the journeywoman past a whirlwind of dirt and leaves. Past a tree stump where a knotted seamstress, head handkerchiefed and body aproned, sits with three children on her knees. Past the barrelfire where grangers gather to croon; past the mouthharp, the mandolin, the fiddle; past the middle-C chorus that begins, *She bled and died for me.* Past the unharnessing of oxen; past the mountebank selling glitz and miracle; past families whose more gentle members call out in question—call in voices that are ours: What might be carried in a gunnysack? Why does she clutch at her throat, gag, spit in the road? What words does she sing? A dog howls. She stops, rubs her hands low against her back, gazes on distant systems of light. The low-lying fringe of the blue dress is wet. Did she wade the river? Does she have shoes? Did she cut her feet on sharp riverstones? Has she been crying? Has she been loved? Has she a name?

***

Here she is. Countryroad woman. Elly.

Naked as the new born.

She is standing by the river.

Gutted. Quiet. Trembling. Skin streaked by blood and spit and semen. Whitewater. Angelfish swim the shallows; willows line the riverbank; windswept leaves rasp across ground. High above, in an ailanthus tree, a snow owl spreads its wings.

What might be left behind? The puddles of fluids; the furrows left by fingernails; the imprint of a face in the mud.

Whose eyes will spill the summary of a life's grief?

She is standing in the river. Angelfish. Bluegill. Ankles touched by shallows. Bloodclouds mask her feet; the snow owl glides upriver; the angelfish swim. We. We are the dust and stones, and we are the street. We are the roots and reeds, and when angels leap high. Over lilies. We. We see. Watergleam. Translucence. Light behind snow-white wings.

❄

Christopher Kritwise Doyle
Margins

THE MISSING SCROLL

IN Harper's Ferry, West Virginia, during the night of the 16th of October 1859, John Brown, a free man and abolitionist, descended with eighteen armed conspirators on the national armory housed there, in a bid to ignite a widespread slave revolt. During the ensuing day, a local army of townspeople forced these desperate guerillas into a small fire engine building off the armory. Either by the ferocity of this resistance or by the absence of a mounting insurgency, Brown was confused. With his options dwindling, and a family history of insanity, he proceeded to trade gunfire for the next thirty-two hours. This delay allowed federal authorities in nearby Washington to deploy a unit of Marines led by Colonel Robert E. Lee.

In the early chill of the second day of the revolt, the Marines rushed the engine house. Ten of the conspirators were killed; two of which were Brown's sons. Brown himself was cut by a saber and beat unconscious with the hilt. Amidst the destruction of cobblestone that morning, many historians claim the Civil War was ignited. What these same historians overlook is a small apothecary jar unearthed during the siege, a jar now on display at the Harper's Ferry Visitors Museum. Inside this clay jar, a jar known for storing crushed ox bone and lineament oil—a 17th century scroll, that until then hadn't seen the light of sun since it crossed the Atlantic Ocean with a certain Spanish druggist, one Escarcega Nogales—was discovered. The significance of this scroll cannot be overstated for our purposes of literary reclamation.

Not much is known about Escarcega Romante Nogales. We do know he immigrated to America from Tujillo, Spain, a region in Extramadura, toward the end of his life. He was 78 years old when he died of malaria in the Castillo de San Marcos in St. Augustine, Florida, in 1713. Escarcega's son, Leon Hernandez Nogales, intent on establishing his father's apothecary business in the more prosperous northern territories, found himself in Harper's Ferry by either 1745 or 1747, depending on varying accounts. Collaborating with Robert Harper, a Philadelphia builder, Nogales quickly became the main purveyor of pharmaceuticals in the region, and prospered as the town grew in stature after Harper built his ferry across the Potomac River in 1761. That Nogales carried with him a particular clay jar housing this 17th century scroll is beyond suspicion. Why he carried it and how his grandfather Dante Almos Nogales first came into its possession might only be understood after investigating the following commentary found in the same jar with the scroll. The original is written in Spanish and replete with romantic flourishes. This translation, we feel, is literal.

I

The guards are at it again, beating the *desconocidos*. Along with the rise and fall of the sun and the rise and fall of the moon, I have become dependent on the beatings of the *desconocidos*. There is an enthusiasm in the guards during these moments, an enthusiasm frightening to behold. That they could find such pleasure in beating those beneath them, chained to stakes in the yard, is a sickening indictment of this ritual—yet it is a ritual I find myself unable to look away from. Others, prisoners on the higher levels (1), those from Andalusia, Sevilla and La Mancha, often cheer in these moments. That it is not their flesh being lashed surely must add a contagious joy to their admonishments. Though once it is over, I have observed a melancholy accompany their echoing voices, once the other enticements of prison life have recaptured our attentions, and we wander back to our cells.

There is one though, "a man of letters" he is called, a man who does not shout with the rest of them: *Miguel de Cervantes y Saavedra*. I have ascertained his name after accosting him directly, when I thought he had stared long enough at the monthly scroll I purchased from the Santa Hermandad (2), with the profit my wife Alamadeira delivered from my apothecary stall, profits alleviating my boredom during my year's internment. That I refused to pay tribute to the Vicar on the occasion of his daughter's fifth birthday is an oversight I shall only briefly discuss. The customs of my region seem to change as dramatically as the leadership in the house of the honorable Josue Garcia Calabra—the Duke of these lands—and others failing to adhere to these ridiculous tributes have met the same fate. Though with the many scrolls I have accumulated, I feel I have insulated myself in a way from the dismal surroundings of this place, and I think Señor Cervantes envied the stunning scrolls at my disposal.

"Sir, I wonder if I could be afforded the distinct pleasure of touching the fine parchment you hold between your fingers. I have not seen its like since I was shown to my cell several months ago, and since the wall in my cell is almost completely covered with my meandering prose, I would hope to purchase some of your fine parchment for a fair price."

The nerve of him, I thought, this arrogant dandy approaching me across ranks, without an introduction or express word of intent (3). "No you cannot sir," I spat back at him, tightening my hold on the aforementioned scroll.

He slumped back against the common bench we stood beside, his gnarled left hand raised to his creased vest. His internment thus far had not the same soiled effect as the clothes on those surrounding us; he looked as clean and prim as a carnation and I laughed to see him so wounded at my dismissal of his offer.

"How much could you offer anyway?" I continued. "My only pleasure here is the scroll you see beneath my arm, and the dozen more like them in my bunk. Words are the only payment I could consider, and as you say so yourself, your cell wall is covered with prose. Well, I do not want your cell wall or any crumbling portion of it. I have my own cell to consider, now don't I?"

"But I could show you what I've written and in that manner make partial payment for the few blank spaces you may not happen to use." And he bowed to me, during which I watched Rudimeo Machado circle behind him and pluck the fine silk handkerchief from Señor Cervantes' velvet trousers.

"Ha! You bow so low as to show your colors!" I laughed as he righted himself and felt for his missing silk. "The comic figure you pose may be payment enough. One so seldom laughs inside Argamasilla, even in these relatively light rooms (4). At the very least, I should now entertain the meandering prose of this wall you keep."

II

Returning to my cell before I followed Cervantes to his, I hid my new scroll with the dozen others I kept for the letters I wrote to my wife, for my journals, for the ideas I might develop for my apothecary business. I kept my financial accounts ordered on a particular scroll, updating the figures regularly to give to my wife when she visited on the first and third Thursday of each month. By being able to correspond with a majority of my suppliers, I was kept abreast of my financial concerns, and with the neighbor boy Dante Nogales still working with Alamadeira, I did not fear for the continuity of services, but rather, for the quality of product. It was true Dante was almost a man in his own right, and that Alamadeira was a quick-witted woman, but they both lacked to me the long-range vision one must have in managing a business as temperamental as mine. So each night I prayed with my rosaries that my year's absence might not burden my business in some undefined way. But as of yet, the rosaries had remained quiet about any unforeseen complication.

"Lord," I would plead in those sacred moments. "Lord, it is I, Merced Cesares Jimenez Alfonseca, and I am in need of your munificent guidance." And here I recited a dozen *Ave Marias* before continuing. "Lord, I am once again interred not for any sin against Your Kingdom, but due to the greed of Man, and You will excuse me if this circumstance prompts in my demeanor an inclination toward the severe, the vulgar, the cruel. It is also this place Lord, this Argamasilla, with its savage beatings and the crude levels of treatment. So Lord, let me see this Cervantes' wall, let me not pass judgment too swiftly on this man, for perhaps his words are the words You have always wanted me to see."

III

With his crippled left hand he pointed to the first words on his stonewall. It was a small cell, no bigger than my own nine-by-six space, but with an altogether different atmosphere. An unending inscription of words decorated the walls, to the extent that even the narrow slit letting in a sparse breeze and described by Cervantes as his "open horizon" was outlined in the most delicate sentences.

"You see my open horizon looks upon the wooden acreage surrounding Argamasilla to the east. This is important because of one essential factor supporting my sanity: color."

"*Color?*" I replied, dumbfounded by the riddles the man spoke with. His crippled left hand was waving as he spoke and it took all my reserve to not ask of its ruined cause, until perhaps, when he finished his discourse on the depth of his "open horizon."

"*Color?*" I repeated.

"Why yes...the sunlight, man—what other color could I mean?"

"Señor Cervantes, listen, I have come here out of courtesy to your request regarding my scrolls. It does you no service to speak to me in this way. *By the Lord Almighty I pray for the patience of Your indomitable will.*" This whispered prayer helped steady my hand from lashing back at this incredulous dandy. "So continue please with your comments on the magnificent colors of the sunrise, which must surely give you hope and inspiration in your efforts, but please do not talk down to me in this way again. Or the charity of the scrolls I might find in my favor to grant you will surely distill."

"Ha! But you must have meant *dissolve* just now," he offered, a ridiculous smile on his face. " '*Of the scrolls I might find in my favor to grant you will surely dissolve,*' not *distill.* I think it's just a matter of finding the appropriate word in that instance, in expressing your intentions."

"Señor Cervantes, still you persist in mocking me after I have just told you the risk you run in proceeding with this line of discourse."

"Oh no, no, no Señor Alfonseca," and he crouched on one knee in front of his neatly attended bunk. "Señor Alfonseca, please, hear me out when I say I mean no disrespect to you. It is only my mania I suppose, that makes me correct the misuse of words. Words to me like words to you may be the only soulful payment to which I might ever respond. So you must understand the correct usage of words I find of utmost importance in aspiring to my chosen craft."

"What craft?"

"Of poetics, of pastoral books, of theater, plays, and on the larger project which you see behind me on this Spanish stone." Still crouched on one knee—his arms stretched across the expanse of the most intricate handwriting I had ever seen. "This is my obsession Señor Alfonseca; this is *Don Quixote*, a book unlike any before. These are the words I wish to transcribe on the back of your pristine scrolls. And if you permit me the gift of your fine parchment, I am sure some particular payment could be made instead of the monetary abundance I lack, a payment benefiting us both."

" '*A book unlike any before,*' you say." I was intrigued. To see the intricate design of that script, of his precise hand and how it scrawled across each available inch of the narrow cell, held me in wonderment. I couldn't breathe. Reaching out to the east wall, with its "open horizon," it was as if my body had entered a maze of brightened emotion. In the darker corners it was more difficult to see the passages, but when I inched closer it seemed as if in the shadows I read about violent beatings, confused battles, epic jealousies, while on the brighter sections, flourishing speeches of beauty, of love and humor spoke back to me. And I wanted to touch this world; I wanted to know it.

"I can see you are trying to discern the organizing principle of the piece. That my friend, and I may call you my friend can't I, now that we have crossed the boundary of a still undefined agreement, now that we may freely meditate on the importance of the word? That this organizing principle might still remain unknown to you resides in the description I started earlier, a description that has everything to do with this *open horizon* and the intensity of the sun's growing color as it happens to fall on the four corners of my cell."

It was many minutes later when Señor Cervantes continued with his description. In the interval, I had found myself at a passage detailing an encounter with this delusional Don Quixote, with this *Knight of the Sorrowful Face*, as he wanted himself to be called throughout the course of the text. He had come upon a gang of galley slaves, prisoners like us but with a much more severe punishment (5). And the freedom of speech Cervantes employed, the easy way he captured the everyday language of these prisoners, the same everyday words I heard in the levels and yard below me, was astounding, a triumph of replication, of art, and it took me another fifteen minutes to regain my composure.

"These voices, these prisoners," and I pointed to the dark passage I knelt before. "This is the language of Argamasilla; this is the language all around us, and that you mean to include these lowly speeches, this slang and profanity in this book will certainly constitute a design unlike any I have read before." And I reached out to touch his slender shoulder, to in some way display the empathy I felt for his artistic intentions, but he leaned back from me and turned away. So I continued anyway, in spite of his reluctance to my warmer enthusiasm.

"What do you do? Do you stand secretly at the railing when the beatings of the *desconocidos* begin and take notes? But you have no paper. Is it in your mind then, this vast capacity for mimicry, this vast recitation? Do you question the prisoners around you? Do others write what they say for you? Maybe you point to a spot on the wall and say, 'Okay, Rudimeo Machado, now I want you to write why you are here in Argamasilla, in your own words, in how you would speak to a friend.' But this cannot be either. Besides you, I might be the only other soul who could write in this place. This cannot be it at all. You have done all this yourself. You have conjured all these voices. It is you, isn't it, Señor Cervantes? It is you."

"Your intuition serves you well, Señor Alfonseca. Yes, I have written all these voices. I have conjured each word, each impression and dream. And I will tell you how I do it, sir, because it is no more a power of divination or augury than you might think. I simply listen to the sounds. I listen as some men must pray, as perhaps even you must pray. I listen to the sufferings and truths of my fellow man as if this whole vast prison were one large confessional. And yes, this *Don Quixote* is filled with violent beatings and battle scenes, with petty confrontations and vulgar indiscretions, but I have tried to balance the rudest portions of life, the lowest examples, with the highest and most noble pursuits: with love, beauty and honor. And I only wonder sir, if after you have read for a few days the extent of my musings, if you will think I have succeeded."

IV

The next three days passed around me in a haze. I remained in Señor Cervantes' cell, ate my bread, drank my water, while I read and never once broke the literary trance I established with his words. Even when the guards beat the *desconocidos* during their daily routine, I was steadfast in my undertaking. The world of this *Don Quixote* was like one I recognized but couldn't place. If it was Spain, it was a mythic Spain, a Spain populated by a world of imaginary beings that hovered on the cusp of the absurd. And yet, the words were true; the words were described with a new clarity, with a reality I could hear and feel in the voices all around me. So that this, *Don Quixote*—as imaginary and mythic as it seemed— was also familiar and recognizable and tumbled from my tongue with the same words I might have used, if I, too, were to describe such people and adventures.

Señor Cervantes, during these three fevered days of reading, lingered quietly in his bunk. He wandered out to the common room (6); he retrieved my food; he answered any questions I might ask. But largely, he watched as I moved from lighted patch to lighted patch of stone as I followed the path the sun made as it arched and refracted in strange configurations on the walls. During the course of those three days, each single section of the cell evolved through a different shade and gradation, an evolution that I would come to distinguish for its singular effect on me.

For instance, I remember in the early morning, a section of the stone above the narrow doorway, how it passed through a spectrum of orange and blue and how it warmed me reading it. Or the narrow stone ledge above his bunk, the morning light draped it in a warm golden hum, radiating with a luster I could scarcely imagine then, and which I find difficult to fathom now, in recalling its otherworldly radiance. In the afternoon though, at the height of the heat, the upper-corners of each wall were held beneath a hard white pulse. How this piercing whiteness reached across the wall with the "open horizon," the wall with the window permitting the motion of the sun, I do not know. There were several instances of an illusory nature that I thought impossible, even as I stood there witnessing the phantasmal play of light, my arms outstretched touching both sides of this mysteriously construed chamber. The moonlight was another instance of this shadowy enchantment.

A blue-white moonlight appeared as if spilled from a milky bowl. Its creamy rivulets clung in puddles to the blackened stone and I stood mesmerized beneath its ethereal glow. I cherished reading the almost dreamlike sections outlined by these milky currents, almost as much as I cherished the colors of the vastly swollen evening. And as much as I wanted to absorb each flowing drop of moonlight, to make each my own, to hold them inside me—these ivory rays, which I couldn't imagine equaled for the purity of their presence—frightened me a bit. Something of the ghost world lingered in their translucence, and I clung more heartily to the evolving twilight. A medley of greens, blues, violets and browns all converged beside Señor Cervantes' bed then, after dinner. Wisps of an indigo-blue pulsed to the left of a leather chair. A cloud of lavender hung above the gray paper shoes dangling from a nail in the ceiling. Chords of maroon and burgundy fell in diagonal bars across his bunk, and I felt more grounded because of it. I felt I inhabited the colors of a different world, that the cold, steely prison was far away, and the more welcoming sections of travel, of the open road and the mountains with their ardent meadows overwhelmed me. I felt the warmer colors of the earth rise from the evening and this earthly abundance helped fortify me for the ghost-hued night to come.

Señor Cervantes, for his part, couldn't help but pace in the hallway outside his cell in these moonlit hours. And I thought that perhaps something of the ghost world preyed on him, a demonic mania? He was scribbling on the outside hallway. A milky puddle illuminated the blackened stone where he stood on the third and final night of my reading, and I whispered to him when I was done that he didn't have to proceed with this futile stone-scribbling anymore:

"The guards will surely scratch your words away if you write outside your cell, so I do not think you should continue."

"I have bribed them with all the money I had left to let me write on the walls of my cell, and now that I have covered each moist inch with my ink I must continue elsewhere. The words will not wait for me to acquire the correct medium, Señor Alfonseca. The words will not wait!"

And he loomed above me in the milky light, his narrow shoulders tense marble columns. I had never seen him so large, so furiously imposing. His crippled left hand looked like a dagger in the sharp way he carved the air when he raved about the power of these infinite words that must have been pouring into his skull even then; words borne from moonlight and sunset; words moving on orange and blue waves through his mind and fingertips to the more solid catalogue of stone.

"The words will not wait for me to understand or order them in any way. The words come to me as miracles must come to the faithful—unknown of origin, unbound by law, incomprehensible in their form. It is only the hand that deciphers their shape for me. It is only the hand torn in the Battle of Lepanto, shot across the dark-spreading sea that translates this energy into a more knowable voice, into these scrawled symbols you see surrounding us," and he wiped his face clear of sweat, whispering now. *"The hand is the priest and the pen is the sacrament and the ink is the blood."*

"Lord," I whispered back, my teeth clenched at the heresy I heard from the pruned white lips in front of me, heresy I understood then as perhaps only another voice of Your greater design. "Lord, he does not know what he speaks, but may only speak with Your voice now, for the divination of Your design. Forgive him for this artistic sensibility, for this impulse to think he is truly the creator of Your words."

"But I don't think I'm the creator, Señor Alfonseca. Haven't you been listening to me?" And he moved closer to me now, the last moist drops wiped from his brow by the dagger of his left hand. "I am only a conduit for a more divine passage of night and day, a more divine annunciation of virtue and pain, of heat and cold, and that is all I could ever be, Señor Alfonseca—a conduit for the duality of life."

V

I stayed in my own cell after that night for the next week. Giving all my scrolls to Señor Cervantes, my only request was that he not write over the financial figures I had kept until then. With the other scrolls, I allowed him total freedom of transcription. He could write over my words, under my words, on the backs of the scrolls which I hadn't used; he could do anything to my scrolls because they were his scrolls now—his scrolls—that was of course, until we decided on a payment for my generosity, because as of yet, we had not come to any explicit agreement. You see; the events were so fevered in those days, that I feared obstructing his mania in any way. The last of the money I had I gave to the Santa Hermandad for half a dozen more scrolls. The scrolls I gave to Señor Cervantes without question.

My year's internment was almost up, and during the last three weeks I saw very little of Señor Cervantes, but the world he created, this *Don Quixote*, continued to rise before me like a shimmering spell, with wholly real shapes and fears. And I thought that maybe this *Don Quixote* was really a vast enchantment. Perhaps it was a dark magic Señor Cervantes was involved with, and I had only helped his enchantments by bringing a portable medium to their form, with the scrolls I gave him. Because I must admit, I began to experience a host of hallucinations in those last three weeks, hallucinations I could not ascribe to my continual state of dehydration and exhaustion. Instead, the words of Señor Cervantes seemed to build up a world of recurring illusions in my mind. At first it was only a minor distraction to me, and I thought that I had only caught one of the many sicknesses circulating a prison of less then adequate cleanliness. My bunk felt like the gentle grass of a green pasture, and upon rolling over one evening I thought I heard the sounds of an epic battle, with the *Knight of the Sorrowful Face* requesting my assistance in smiting a giant holding the kingdom of the Princess Micomicona for ransom. Each morning when I looked at my gray paper shoes, shoes that all of the prisoners in the higher levels had, I saw them instead as polished leather boots, with the gray paper dissolving into the chain mail of a Knights' gallant armor. I seemed singly infested with the ideals of chivalry, so that when I watched the guards beat the *desconocidos* during my last week, I saw instead a mythic clash of armies. I saw their arms full of scimitars and wands; I saw their tears like wells of souls. I saw the stakes they were chained to turn to snakes. I saw the sand and gravel melt with the sun, and found myself screaming for the lowly *desconocidos* to fight back, to fight back with all their strength, and in this way the guards turned their eyes on me, and I was brought before the warden. My last day of internment was less than a week away and he eyed me with an intoxicated humor. His breath smelled of onion and cognac, and as he leaned closer to me, I saw his face dissolve into the color of moist clay.

"Guards, leave us. Señor Alfonseca is no threat to me, and I must speak to him privately about the odd behavior he has adopted on the point of his release."

The warden was an obese man and rested his sausage-fingers on a swollen belly. A plate of *carnitas* was on his desk and with an indistinct gesture from him I was meant to devour the few scraps he was unable to finish.

"Wine?" he asked, his left eye drifting from where his right eye focused.

I nodded greedily and drained my glass before he could return his bottle to the table. He spun his mustache between his greasy fingertips. It was my first real taste of food and drink in a year; the bread and water until then had since dissolved from my conscious mind, their taste useless to me for comprising the whole of my diet. He laughed to see me drain my cup, and refilled it without a word.

"Senor Alfonseca, slower my friend, slower. Calm yourself, man; you are to be released in four days and once again the common taste of pork and wine will meet your lips. You cannot let them affect you this way. You must not be overwhelmed by my generosity either. I only wish to speak to you, nothing more, and then you can return to your cell. I only want to understand why it is you who shouted at the guards this morning. It was all I could do to keep them from lashing you for the *desconocidos* you wanted to support."

"Thank you sir, thank you," and I bowed to the floor before him, not knowing if I thanked him for keeping the guards from beating me or for the generous food and wine, but already I felt giddy with the rush of alcohol. My head was moist and I felt a sound welling up in my throat, one that I hadn't heard during this long year. I hadn't sung since I'd been here, but now with my release so close, and with the wine working through the loose layers of my soul, I felt a gaiety I had not experienced before lifting my voice in harmonious waves.

"It is only this other world I now see, sir," I practically sang out to him. "This other Spain occupying my senses with its dark enchantment." And I was up now, pacing around the room, with the warden urging me to drink more, so I drained my second glass of wine licking the last drops from my lips.

"This other Spain?" he asked, drumming his sausage fingers on his belly. "But my friend, a cigar." And he lit a cigar handing it to me. I breathed the sweet rich smoke and felt a countless parade of images twirling around me in the air. I saw the blue light in Cervantes' cell, the march of the guards, rain dripping from the cornice in the yard beyond my window like so many etched words. The room swarmed around me. My tongue knew no limits.

"This *other* Spain of Cervantes with his *Don Quixote*. This *other* Spain is a dream I keep seeing in the stone and in the yard when I thought the guards were an army with scimitars and snakes in the sand. And I shouted for the *desconocidos* because who else would shout for them now that they were lost to the war of the sun?"

"Cervantes, eh? He writes, no? He has the use of words, it is said. But one so seldom inspects the cells for all the responsibilities of my charge," and he motioned to his elevated post as if to excuse his removal from our more-immediate activities.

"He writes of dreams and adventures and of an enchanted knight, and I can only hope to see this other Spain cast its spell on those fortunate enough to read its pages. Because it is magic, sir, a deep vast magic spun with stone and silk, with pearl and gold."

"You say there are pages then, pages of gold?" And the warden edged closer to his desk, his round belly resting on a dusty ledger. The deception he had intended all along was now at hand, and had I been a stronger man, Lord, a man more in line with my pharmaceutical profession, I might have divined his darker purpose. But my weakness was made evident by the sweetened pork, by the red wine and easy manner we had established between ourselves, which of course mixed with the vanilla rich smoke of the cigar to craft a heady elixir. My senses were overwhelmed by then, and I reacted as if strings were controlling my tongue and hands, that the well-crafted strings the warden had attached to me were now working against what I should have never done.

"Yes, pages of gold, words of gold on the scrolls I gave him. He must be finished by now, transcribing it all from the walls he keeps. He must be finished with his *Don Quixote,* and he must be excited as well about the prospect of having it printed with maybe even King Phillip III reading in good favor its meandering tale."

"The favor of the King you say," the warden grinned, and poured another glassful. "And all because of your efforts ,Señor Alfonseca, all because of your efforts, my charity, and our new partnership."

"Partnership?"

"Yes, of course, for the benefit of Señor Cervantes, my man, and for the benefit of this *Don Quixote.*"

VI

Over the last four days of my sentence I ordered all of the scrolls as Señor Cervantes had numbered them. The deal, in principle, he agreed to almost before the offer was uttered from my trembling lips. Not mentioning the warden in all of this, for fear Señor Cervantes would feel less obliged to cooperate with the dismal authority of this place, I expressly stated I would take his manuscript to a printer friend of mine I knew through dealings at my apothecary stall.

"How do you know him again?" he asked. It seemed the only reservation he held was with my somewhat coincidental relationship to this printer.

"Because of the crushed ox bone I give him for his ulcers," I repeated. "This printer is well known in Extramadura and Madrid; I'm surprised you have not heard of him before."

"But how will we pay for the printing, and how will we distribute the book to the proper critics and libraries in Madrid?" We were in his cell; the blue light of evening revealed a passage by the doorway and in its dreamy light I read about Dulcinea, the idealized love of Don Quixote, a love who was really just another illusion in the vast simulacrum of his chivalric vision. And Lord, in that moment, had I known then the warden's true deception, I would have seen I was only crafting another illusory realm for Señor Cervantes, a realm of literary riches, of wealth and ease, a realm impossible to realize. But I proceeded anyway; so eager was I to invest the total value of my apothecary business into the printing costs of *Don Quixote*, so firmly did I believe in its success.

My wife Alamadeira met me when I was released and we stood for an hour in each other's arms outside the prison gates, tears diffusing the wan clouds of an overcast day. And for a moment I felt like I was still in Señor Cervantes' cell, that I stood in a dreamy blue patch of light moving across his meticulous wall. I felt the satchel slung across my shoulder, the satchel containing the two-dozen scrolls comprising *Don Quixote*, this monumental work, and I saw the next steps that I would have to take in getting it printed outlined in this same blue light.

At my apothecary stall the neighbor boy Dante Nogales stood distributing herbs to Señora Gaela Domingez Santaurus, and I greeted her as I had a year ago before entering Argamasilla. A pink hue saturated her skin and my hands when we touched, and it was as if the intervening months had fallen into a black nothingness. I only heard her kind words then, and how she smiled at my soiled clothes and the exhausted glow on my lined face, a smile which somehow helped align me in my present endeavor. I spread the scrolls on a table behind a curtain where we kept the clay jars of our supplies. Dried mimosa petals, sassafras root, oleander extract and tortoise shells hung in clusters above my head and I asked Dante to bring an empty jar and the heated wax and glue we kept by the glowing coals. I thought of Senor Cervantes' parting words, when he watched as I gathered the extent of his book in my arms. A certain energy had left him as he slumped in his cot. The white pulse of noon flashed in the corners of the walls and the strange configuration of his cell disoriented me momentarily, for I thought I heard him thank me for my efforts.

"You will hear from me shortly," I replied, not acknowledging his apparent gratitude. "But there is still the matter of payment, my friend. It is true I am investing the value of my livelihood into this publishing venture, but I wondered if I might take away something more substantial from the historical and artistic occurrence I feel this *Don Quixote* might someday represent."

"Ha!" he scoffed at me, this dandy who had once knelt before me. His warm graciousness from before had collapsed into a fleeting spark. "Señor Alfonseca, is it not enough that you are involved at all, that your scrolls now house the extent of my life, the intrigue of my soul? What you carry in your arms is really me from this place, and isn't it enough for you to free my soul, to bring me to a more unencumbered state?"

"I was just thinking of my…"

"You were just thinking of yourself," he spat at me. "Have you not listened to Don Quixote, to this Knight errant you say enchanted you with his humor and purpose? Have you not learned anything from this abandoned code of chivalry, of truth? Because I think the occasion of reading my words before any other is payment enough. And surely this venture, as you have told me, will be financially beneficial for you and for me, and I think only your greed now guides your decisions when before I thought it was your generosity," and he had turned from me with that, and I hoped this wouldn't be our last words, our final parting.

Back at my apothecary stall, behind the curtain, I found my favorite scroll, the one reminding me the most of the characters inhabiting Argamasilla for the last year, the one comprising the scene of the theft of Don Quixote's sword and his squire's mule. I wanted this scroll for myself and pulled it from its numbered order. The sword of Don Quixote seemed symbolic to me of Spain's larger power, of an older order lost or in decline. The words were spread out beneath my fingertips with an imaginative power I could touch, leaping from description to description with the swift wit of his piercing mind, and I held the scroll up beneath a burnt-orange sunset. This was the one, my true payment, and I looked into Dante's eyes as I placed it in the jar.

That this scroll happened to contain a description of the infamous desperado Ginesillio de Pasamonte did not pass my notice either. The descriptions of nefarious legends brought a hefty price on the collector's market, and in the event this venture and the unseemly partnership I had struck up with the warden proceeded in any way other than I expected, I felt I might need to be compensated. That I was interrupting the story of this *Don Quixote* by one whole chapter was of little concern to me. The breadth of the chapters before and after this omission, I thought, would surely compensate for the illogical gap this scroll might create. For you see, Lord, I was not thinking clearly, about the aim of art. Instead, I could still taste the warden's wine on my lips; I could still feel the tight strings he had attached to me. The more honorable decisions I might have been capable of making before my year in Argamasilla, before watching the beating of the *desconocidos* each day, had left me. A defeating wind accompanied these beatings I tell you, an echoed cruelty I might have internalized. To see that men could hold such power over other men, that their lives could be reduced to chains and stakes in the sand, made me wince when I remembered what a terrific hold it cast on me then, and I feared I might have fallen into that vicious cycle of behavior too. I might have even felt I held some sort of power over Señor Cervantes by taking this scroll, that I stood on some higher step.

For his *Don Quixote* had released me from my prison life, if only during the three days I was able to read it. I had fallen into that idealized realm so easily, in his brightly configured cell then, and maybe I thought if I had a scroll of my own to turn back to whenever I needed to, the beautiful enchantment of that realm might be mine to experience again and again, whenever the tedium of my daily life became too much, too repetitive to bear. Though now that I am writing this, I am not so sure. My own greedy mania might as well be to blame, and I can only ask now for forgiveness, Lord, with these words I hope You must surely hear, and of how I even enlisted my young apprentice into my dishonesty.

"This jar, Dante," and I pointed to the jar we both touched now on the table. "I want you to keep this jar for me in your house. Do not tell your parents what it is, only that it is yours to keep for me alone. I will send for it when the mood strikes me. Now go, Dante; take it at once and return tomorrow as usual. Tell no one of this scroll, Dante, no one."

VII

Of course the warden cheated us, took most of the profits. I barely made enough to keep my apothecary stall in opera-tion, and was only able to do that by allowing Dante Nogales, my apprentice, to buy into the business. I had no children with Alamadeira, so we both looked on Dante as our progeny. Over the next three years we had little difficulty in allowing the responsibilities of the shop to move increasingly under his careful eye. The boy had a head for numbers and was able to expand my services into villages and homes where before I had deemed it impossible.

Don Quixote became a national triumph. Everyone in the mountains and on the coasts seemed to have read or heard of this fanatical knight and the madness of his antics. Señor Cervantes, for his part, was much celebrated now in the Spanish countryside, and I only saw him once more after the book was first printed. It was in Madrid, three years after we last spoke.

After leaving the day-to-day operations of the business to Dante, I went to Madrid once a month to trade for some of the supplies more difficult to come by: bergamot, agate, hibiscus, sweet marjoram, mercury, elephant tusk. And once, after purchasing what I needed, I saw a notice describing the events of a curious incident. It seemed an esteemed nobleman, Gaspar de Ezpeleta, was mortally wounded on the street in front of Señor Cervantes' home. Gaspar had been transporting a chest full of taxed monies for King Phillip III, and Cervantes and the woman in his household were jailed on suspicion of having something to do with Gaspar's unfortunate end.

I went immediately to Argamasilla. He was in the same cell. The vile warden who had cheated me before had been killed in a prison riot the year before and it only took me a few cuartillos (7) to bribe my way in. It was early evening when I found him in his bunk. The same blue light I remembered from before was focused by the doorway on the same dreamy passage concerning Dulcinea—the idealized love. He recognized me immediately but did not stir. A white scroll was stretched before him and in his crippled left hand he held a bit of dark chocolate. He seemed heavier in the face, well fed and tan. His skin was a deep leathery-brown, but I didn't feel this weight agreed with the more manic man I remembered. If his fame had kept his stomach full it had also garnered him some preferential treatment from the new warden. A new quill, a fresh pail of water, half-a-dozen wine bottles, a wool blanket adorned his cell. Having a celebrated author to look after did wonders for the behavior of the guards as well, but I was shocked to see the same aimless group of *desconocidos* in the lower yard, their legs in chains.

"They do not beat them as often," he mumbled. He had watched me approach and placed my sympathies immediately. I had lingered at the railing for a few minutes, and was amazed to see, upon looking down on the same deplorable conditions, that the older mesmerizing power from those years before still captivated me.

"At least some things have improved," I whispered back to him, eyeing his wool blanket. And by standing in that blue light again I felt like I had entered some darker sanctuary. The world of the prison dissolved behind me. I felt a respectful silence crowd my tongue. I knew I had to speak to him like a man; he would not respect me otherwise. "You seem to have as many scrolls as you'd like," and he watched me for a moment. Our eyes searched the depths of the other, and by dipping his quill into his inkpot he broke the spell that had been cast between us.

"Señor Cervantes, I apologize for the check, for the royalty check and the abrupt nature of my correspondence before, in the weeks after your book was printed. I knew you wanted to hear more of my words, but I was afraid to write you—to you, who now write for everyone with such power…"

"I know all about the deal with the first warden," he replied, scribbling on his scroll without looking up. A dozen other scrolls were stacked in a wooden box beneath his bed, and I felt the same strange racing pulse in my heart when I looked at them. And it felt like before, when I had the scrolls of *Don Quixote* spread before me, and I almost expected him to hand these newer ones over to me, once our dialogue paused awkwardly.

"Not these, Señor Alfonseca, not these. I'm afraid experience has taught me how badly free men keep their promises made in captivity."

I wanted to protest, to tell him of the warden's duplicity, but the words would have been meaningless to him anyway. Money was meaningless to him; I saw that then. It wasn't the wealth that I had promised him that he regretted believing in, but the honesty he had accepted from me as a true sign of my friendship, of my honor. That bond I had broken. It could never be regained, no matter how much I wanted to grovel at his feet then and there, no matter how much I wanted to repent for my greed, but his cold scribbling silence kept me from saying anything more. What could I say that might have brought me back into the graces of this already mythic figure?

I edged towards the doorway and raised my hand for a moment. The evening light had shifted a degree and now a warm orange pulse radiated in the doorway. I touched the rosaries in my pocket out of habit. I wanted to whisper to Senor Cervantes about the inexplicable shading, about the rich color absorbing me, about each remembered voice, but he was already looking beyond me. I might have already been a ghost of memory, a fading wisp on the imperceptible edge of his vast repository of need, of use.

"Listen…listen," he whispered back, balancing on the rim of his bunk. I strained to hear what must have caught his attention, and it was only when his incessant scribbling stopped that I caught the faintest trace of what might have captivated his very being. A lone voice was crying in the darkness. The echo of a rusty chain rattled across a stone walkway. A door was opened and closed in rapid succession; and, in the pulse of an orange light, I thought I heard the chorus of some indecipherable song rise up to us before dying to a trembling silence.

"It's the *desconocidos*," he hesitated, as I strained to hear more. "Even the *desconocidos* have found it in their place to sing when the orange sunset reaches their depth. Yes, my dear Alfonseca, even the *desconocidos* can sing about the light of the world beyond these walls."

Editor's Note—

John Osawatowie Brown was arrested and charged with treason on October 18th, 1859. His family begged for his life, openly stating he was insane. To remove any doubt of this claim, they provided the following information on his ancestry and the people having reared him:

¤ Nine relatives on Brown's mother's side were insane.
¤ Six of Brown's cousins were insane.
¤ Two of his own children were insane.

By December 2nd, 1859, when John Brown was hanged for treason, no records remained of the Nogales pharmaceutical business, or of Leon Hernandez Nogales. We do know that Leon and Robert Harper had a falling out in 1780, two years before Harper died. It was rumored Nogales owed Harper a vast sum of money resulting from a failed investment in the now defunct Bolivar Mining Company.

In the intervening 82 years, from the last reasonable possession of Cervantes' missing scroll to its rediscovery after John Brown's capture and hanging was made, we can only surmise its history. It's quite conceivable Robert Harper hoped to conceal its value in the most auspicious structure he could find—in the cobblestone wall of the newly remodeled armory. How could he have known that in less than two centuries almost half a million tourists would visit it a year, touching the same walls he once envisioned as an anonymous vault? Because for all those 82 years, not a word was known of the contents hidden therein, where once ox bone and lineament oil cured the common maladies of the 17th century man. We can only guess the missing scroll was afforded the patience Cervantes himself seemed solely consumed with—the patience of waiting, of watching, and of listening between the walls to the sounds the world offered him.

❄

FOOTNOTES FOR "THE MISSING SCROLL"

1   Prisoners in Argamasilla were kept on different levels. The *desconocidos*, or unknown men, those without position or place, were kept on the ground floor and the most abused because of it.

2   Or Holy Brotherhood, an armed force that policed the countryside and prisons.

3   Another instance of prison etiquette, whereby inmates from different geographic regions rarely commingled.

4   Our narrator and Cervantes were both jailed for malfeasance and placed in minimally secure rooms.

5   Galley slaves had the often more brutal sentence of serving in the Spanish Armada.

6   In the upper levels of Argamasilla, the common room functioned as cafeteria, bathroom and laundry.

7   A *cuartillo* is one-fourth a *real*.

Notes on Contributors

OUR AUTHORS

Katherine Grace Bond ("Sailing to Babylon") has written or contributed to 17 books, including the bestselling *Legend of the Valentine* (Zonderkidz), and also *Sleepy-Time Dance,* and two collections of poetry, *Yielding to Calliope,* and *The Sudden Drown of Knowing* (Brass Weight Press). Katherine is a contributing editor for *Beyond* Magazine and has published extensively in children's and family magazines, and anthologies. Katherine is secretary to PEN Washington and mentor to The Inducers of Insanity Young Writers Cooperative. She is currently at work on a Young Adult novel.

Jaimee Wriston Colbert ("Waking in Sacred Places") is the author of *Dream Lives of Butterflies* and *Climbing The God Tree,* a novel which won Colbert the Willa Cather Prize. She has been nominated twice for both the Pushcart Prize and the Katherine Anne Porter Fiction Prize, and she is a winner of the Zephyr Prize and the Delogue Award for "Outstanding Woman Fiction Writer." Her stories have appeared in numerous journals, including *Louisiana Literature, Prairie Schooner, Natural Bridge, Connecticut Review,* and many others. She is an Assistant Professor at Binghamton University, where she teaches creative writing.

John Dalton is the author of the novel *Heaven Lake*, published by Scribner, and the winner of the Barnes and Noble 2004 Discover Award in fiction. *Heaven Lake* was also awarded the Sue Kaufman Prize for best first fiction of 2004 from the American Academy of Arts and Letters. John's short fiction has appeared in *Western Humanities Review, Story*, and *Alaska Quarterly Review*. He is an Assistant Professor in the MFA writing program at the University of Missouri - St. Louis.

Quinn Dalton ("Lennie Remembers The Angels") has published a novel, *High Strung*, and a collection of short stories, *Bulletproof Girl*. Her stories have appeared or are forthcoming in literary magazines such as *ACM (Another Chicago Magazine), The Baltimore Review, Cottonwood, Emrys Journal, Glimmer Train, Indiana Review, Ink, The Kenyon Review, Mangrove, One Story* and *StoryQuarterly*, and in anthologies such as *Sex And Sensibility* and *American Girls About Town*. She is the winner of the *Pearl* 2002 Fiction Prize and a North Carolina Arts Council fellowship. The story in this anthology, "Lennie Remembers The Angels" (*Kenyon Review*) also appears in her story collection, *Bulletproof Girl* (Washington Square Press, 2005).

Christopher Kritwise Doyle ("The Missing Scroll") is pursuing his Master of Fine Arts, specializing in creative writing at the University of Baltimore. His story, "The Missing Scroll," was chosen by *Margins* for his debut publication because of the unique way the story contemplates, through a blending of historical fact and invention, how Miguel de Cervantes y Saavedra might have written Don Quixote.

Anthony Farrington ("Bartleby") currently teaches creative writing at the Indiana University of Pennsylvania. He is a graduate of the Iowa Writers' Workshop. His most recent work has been nominated for several significant literary distinctions—most notably the Pushcart Prize and Best New American Voices. His work either already appears or is forthcoming in *The Cream City Review, Glimmer Train Stories, Gulf Coast, Hayden's Ferry Review, Salt Hill,* and others.

David Flood ("Ladybug") is a book reviewer for *The Seattle Times,* the author of a novella, *Unfolding Texas,* and *Two Doctors,* a novel in progress, and several short stories. He is currently at work putting together his first book of cartoons: *The Best Medicine.* His numerous feature stories and book reviews have been published in *The Seattle Times,* and a sampling of his cartoons, book reviews, articles, and fiction can be seen at his website, "The Flood Files", at www.davidflood.com, along with an inspiring, often funny, online journal, "Small Steps: Inspirations from a Cancer Survivor", which chronicles his spiritual sojourn as a cancer survivor battling multiple myeloma.

Alice Fulton ("Happy Dust" and "The Real Eleanor Rigby") is the recipient of numerous fellowships including the John D. and Catherine T. MacArthur and the National Endowment for the Arts. Her work has been included in six editions of the *Best American Poetry* series, the *Best American Short Stories* and *Cabbage and Bones: An Anthology of Irish-American Women's Fiction.* "Happy Dust" was first published in the *Missouri Review* as winner of the Editor's Prize in Fiction. "The Real Eleanor Rigby" was first published in the *Gettysburg Review* and was selected for *The Pushcart Prize XXIX: The Best of the Small Presses* (2005). Her collection of stories is forthcoming from W.W. Norton in 2007.

Angela Hamilton ("Rusted Nails") teaches creative writing for St. Louis Community College at Meramec. She received her MFA from the University of Missouri in St. Louis where she won the graduate prose award and was nominated for *Best New American Voices*. Her work has appeared in *Natural Bridge, Passionfruit* and *Opium Magazine*. She is currently working on a collection of personal essays.

J. Jumbelic ("Falling Into Water") has had fiction published in *Caketrain* and *Three Rivers Review*. At the time this story was selected, he was enrolled in the University of Pittsburgh's Master of Fine Arts program, where his focus is on Creative Writing. There he has come in contact with a multi-dimensional cast of wordslingers to whom he is deeply indebted.

Kathy J. Karlson ("Cleopatra and The Great Apes") has been the recipient of an NEA grant for fiction writing, and her stories have been published in *Chiron Review, Madison Review, Worldview, Calyx, SNReview,* and *Stories With Grace,* with ones forthcoming in *The McGuffin* and *13th Warrior*. "Cleopatra and The Great Apes" first appeared in *SNReview*. In addition, her paintings appear in more than thirty private collections.

David Evans Katz ("The Wandering Bard of Nether Sawrey") is the author of the novel, *Sin of Omission*, a literary mystery (Koenisha Publications), and many short stories, both literary and genre, that have appeared in such publications as *Skyline, Whistling Shade, Zahir, Peeks & Valleys, All Hallows* and *Hardboiled*. He was educated at Columbia University in New York and at Northeastern University in Boston.

Mary Kenagy ("Meeting The Family") graduated from Stanford University and holds an MFA in creative writing from Arizona State. She has published short stories in *The Georgia Review, Image,* and *Beloit Fiction Journal*. She is the recipient of an individual artist's grant in fiction from the Seattle Arts

Commission and had a special mention in the 2003 Pushcart Prize Anthology. She now serves as Managing Editor of the quarterly *Image: A Journal of the Arts and Religion* and teaches fiction writing at Seattle Pacific University. She is currently working on a novel.

Valerie Laken ("Covenant") received her MFA from the University of Michigan, where she teaches creative writing and composition. Her stories have appeared in *Ploughshares*, the *Antioch Review, Alaska Quarterly Review,* and *Meridian*, and have received a Pushcart Prize and the *Missouri Review* Editors' Prize. Her first novel, *Dream House*, is being published by William Morrow / Harper Collins, followed by a short story collection, *Separate Kingdoms*.

Janice Levy ("Sideshow") is the author of eight children's books: *Finding the Right Spot, Alley Oops, The Man Who Lived In A Hat, The Spirit of Tio Fernando, (accent on the i), Abuelito Eats With His Fingers, Abuelito Goes Home*, and *Totally Uncool*. Her adult fiction has won the Writer's Digest Competition for Best Literary Short Story three times. Her work has been published in numerous anthologies and magazines, such as *Glimmer Train, Alaska Quarterly, Iowa Review, StoryQuarterly, The Sun, Mid-American Review, Chattahoochee Review*, and *Green Mountains Review*.

Alice Mattison's "The Bad Jew" first appeared in *Glimmer Train* and can now be found in her new book of connected stories, *In Case We're Separated* (William Morrow, 2005), which was picked up as an Editor's Choice by the NYT Book Review at its debut. She is the author of four novels, including *Hilda and Pearl* and *The Wedding of The Two-Headed Woman*. She is also the author of three more short story collections, and a volume of poetry. Her work has appeared in *The New Yorker, Ms.*

magazine, *Glimmer Train, Ploughshares, Agni, The Threepenny Review, The Michigan Quarterly Review,* and *Shenandoah.*

Erin McGraw ("The History of the Miracle") is the author of three collections of short stories and a novel: *The Good Life, The Baby Tree, Lies of The Saints,* and *Bodies at Sea.* Her stories and essays have appeared in a number of journals such as *The Atlantic Monthly, Image, STORY, Good Housekeeping, Daedalus, The Kenyon Review, The Southern Review, The Georgia Review.* "The History of the Miracle," originally published in *Image*; appeared in *Lies of The Saints* as "A Suburban Story"; copyright © 1994 by Erin McGraw; reprinted by permission of Brandt & Hochman Literary Agents, Inc. A new novel called *Ain't We Got Fun* is slated for publication in 2007 from Houghton-Mifflin.

Rose Rappoport Moss ("The Path of Lightning") is slated to have a collection of stories, *IN COURT,* published by Penguin South Africa as a Modern Classic in 2007. She has published two novels, *The Family Reunion*, which was short-listed for a National Book Award, and *The Terrorist*, which was a featured selection by the New Fiction Society, and a non-fiction book, *Shouting at The Crocodile*. Among her more than forty short stories, one won a Quill Prize from the *Massachusetts Review* and another a PEN Syndicated Fiction Award. Several have been cited in *Best American Short Stories*, been nominated for Pushcart prizes, selected for anthologies in the United States and abroad and have been translated. "The Path of Lightning" first appeared in *ONE BLOOD*, an issue of the *Alaska Quarterly Review.*

Robyn Parnell ("Coeur d'Evelyn") is the author of two books, including *My Closet Threw a Party* (Sterling Publishers) and a short fiction collection entitled *This Here and Now* (Scrivenery

503

Press). An author of essay, poetry and drama, her primary focus is fiction. Her works have appeared in a variety of journals, books, magazines and anthologies, most recently including *The Seattle Review* and the British magazine *Mslexia.*

Laura Resau ("Bees Born of Tears") is a writer, anthropologist, and ESL teacher living in Fort Collins, Colorado. Her experiences with women healers in rural Oaxaca inspired her first novel, *What the Moon Saw* (Delacorte Press, 2006). Her travel essays and stories for youth and adults have appeared in a number of popular magazines and anthologies. "Bees Born of Tears" was first published in *Pilgrimage Magazine.* Visit her website at www.LauraResau.com.

Julie Rose ("Stunt for Two") received her MFA from the Iowa Writers' Workshop, where she was the recipient of a Teaching-Writing Fellowship, and a Ph.D. from NYU. She has published her fiction in *Antioch Review* and *Glimmer Train*, where she was the first prize winner of the New Writers' Short Story Award 2005. She teaches creative writing and American literature at Vassar College. She is currently at work on a novel.

Melanie Rae Thon ("Heavenly Creatures" and "Letters in the Snow") is the author of the novels *Sweet Hearts* (Houghton Mifflin); *Iona Moon* (Poseidon/Simon & Schuster/ Viking/Plume/Penguin); *Meteors in August* (Random House/Viking/Faber & Faber/ Penguin); as well as the following short story collections: *First, Body* (Houghton Mifflin/Henry Holt); *Girls in The Grass* (Random House/Faber & Faber/Penguin/Henry Holt). She has also had a number of stories published in a variety of literary journals including *Paris Review, One Story, Bomb, Ontario Review, Five Points, Story*, and others.

Lee Upton ("You Know You've Made It When They Hate You") has published stories in numerous literary journals, including the *Antioch Review,* the *Denver Quarterly, Glimmer Train, Del Sol Review, Shenandoah,* and others. Her poetry has appeared in the *American Poetry Review,* the *Atlantic Monthly,* and in the *New Republic.* She is the author of four books of poetry, most recently *Civilian Histories.* Her fourth book of literary criticism, *Defensive Measures,* is forthcoming this year. She is the recipient of a Pushcart Prize, a National Poetry Series Award, and was twice a winner of the Georgia Contemporary Poetry Series. She is a Professor of English and Writer-in-Residence at Lafayette College.

Silas Zobal ("And We Saw Light") has been the recipient of the Binghamton University Newhouse Award for best new fiction author and the Link Fellowship for creative writing. He has published stories in a number of literary journals including *New Orleans Review, Missouri Review, Wisconsin Review, and Shenandoah,* among others, and the journals *Glimmer Train* and *Iron Horse* have chosen his work for awards for new writers. He has also served as fiction editor and reader of the literary journal *Harper Palate.* Silas holds an MFA from the University of Washington and a PhD from Binghamton University.

Editorial Team

Debra Dean is author of *The Madonnas of Leningrad* (Wm. Morrow, 2006), which is a current nominee for the Quill Book Award. Isabel Allende (author of *The House of The Spirits*) says of Debra's novel that it is "...the rare kind of book that you want to keep but have to share." Chang-rae Lee (*A Gesture Life*) says "...Dean's exquisite prose shimmers with a haunting glow, illuminating us to the notion that art itself is perhaps our most necessary nourishment." Debra lives in Seattle with her husband, poet Clifford Paul Fetters, and has taught writing at colleges in the Northwest for fifteen years.

Ron Ebest is a former journalist and the author of *Private Histories: The Writing of Irish-Americans, 1900-1935*, published in 2005 by the University of Notre Dame Press. He is also the co-editor, with his wife, Sally Barr Ebest, of a collection of essays entitled *Reconciling Feminism and Catholicism? Personal Reflections on Tradition and Change.* He teaches English and journalism at St. Louis Community College at Florissant Valley.

Sally Barr Ebest is Associate Professor of English at the University of Missouri-St.Louis. Sally and her husband Ron are co-editors of *Reconciling Catholicism and Feminism?* (Notre Dame Press). Sally is also author of *Changing the Way We Teach: Writing and Resistance in the Training of TAs* (SIU Press), co-author of *Writing From A to Z* (McGraw Hill), co-editor of *Writing With: New Directions in Collaborative Teaching, Learning, and Research* (SUNY), and co-editor of *Too Smart to Be Sentimental: Irish-American Women Writers* (in progress).

Jenni Ferrari-Adler is the editor of *Alone in The Kitchen with An Eggplant*, an anthology of essays about cooking for one and dining alone, forthcoming from Riverhead/Penguin. Her stories have been published in *Glimmer Train, Hampton Shorts, Bellevue Literary Review, Literal Latte,* and *Happy.* She received a special mention in the 2002 Pushcart Prize and a nomination for the 2003 Pushcart Prize. She has an MFA in fiction from The University of Michigan where she received the Chamberlain Award for Creative Writing, a Zell MFA-Thesis Research Grant, and a Farrar Memorial Summer Playwriting Grant. She's at work on her first novel.

Jackie Gross is the founder of One-on-One Tutoring, is on faculty at John Burroughs School, and is a Writing Instructor off and on for Washington University and Webster University, where she also teaches seminars for teachers on how to teach children with specialized learning disabilities. She is the author of a novel-in-progress and author of two lovely boys, Max and Leo.

Cathy Lichti is a founding member of "The Three G's," one of the most long-running literary book clubs in the city of St. Louis and is the Most Voracious Reader that this book's editor has ever known. She is a manager of *Plowsharing Crafts,* a Fair Trade store, which sends her periodically to places like India, Bangladesh, Peru, Ecuador, Nicaragua & El Salvador with such organizations as Ten Thousand Villages, Project Salvador, and other Fair Trade vendors to meet with the artisans and artists whose works she sells. She has some post grad in Library Science under her belt—all this while being a mother of 7 children and grandmother of 15.

Marlene Muller has just finished up a joyful sojourn as Poetry Editor for *Mars Hill Review,* a journey for which she is grateful. Her poems have appeared in the *Cistercian Studies Quarterly, Crab Creek Review, Pontoon: An Anthology of Washington State Poets,* and in other journals, and she has recently completed her first chapbook. She is a retreat leader and spiritual director/companion in Seattle and at Holden Village in the North Cascades.

Sarah Steinke is Program Director Emerita for *Image: A Journal of Religion and The Arts* with the Milton Center at Seattle Pacific University. She has her MFA from the University of Washington, specializing in poetry, and this May, in the middle of reading mounds of excellent stories for the anthology, she gave birth to a baby boy, Rayne Pierce Barakh Steinke. Rayne has not yet commented on the quality of our stories, but he seems to be a very peaceful soul, which we take as a sign of tacit approval.

Lonnie Whitaker was 2004 Recipient of the Fred Starr Writer's Fellowship; 2004–2005 Writer-in-Residence for The Writers' Colony at Dairy Hollow; 2003 Winner of the Quincy Writers Guild Fiction Contest. Other publications: *Out of the Ozarks Writers Guild Journal*: 2000, 2001, 2005; *Missouri Life Magazine*: April/May 2001, August 2002; *The Ozark Mountaineer*: March, August & November 2005.

Linda Wendling has been a Starr Fellow, a Milton Fellow, and an H.E. Butt Foundation Writer-in-Residence. Wendling was awarded the Heartland Fiction Prize for The Short Story (*New Letters*), and Algonquin's *New Stories From The South—The Year's Best*. She has been a Ploughshares "Emerging Writers" nominee and an AWP Emerging Writers nominee. Her novel-in-progress has been a finalist in The William Faulkner Novel Competition (Pirate's Alley Faulkner Society and Barnes & Noble); The Bellwether Prize for Literature for Social Change (Barbara Kingsolver and Harper/Collins), and the James Jones First Novel Fellowship. Her stories have been published and anthologized in *The Norton Anthology of Microfiction* (W.W. Norton), *New Letters, River Styx, Sundog—The Southeast Review*, and *New Stories from The South* (Algonquin). Wendling is currently at work on a novel.

❋

Gregory Wolfe –SPECIAL THANKS! We are honored to have a Foreword from the publisher and editor of *Image* and the Director of the Center for Religious Humanism. He also serves as Writer in Residence and Director of the MFA in Creative

Writing program at Seattle Pacific University. Wolfe has been a judge in nonfiction for the National Book Awards. Among his books are *Malcolm Muggeridge: A Biography* (ISI Books); *Sacred Passion: The Art of William Schickel* (University of Notre Dame Press; *Intruding Upon the Timeless: Meditations on Art, Faith, and Mystery* (Square Halo Books); *Beauty Will Save the World: Art, Faith, and the Stewardship of Culture* (ISI Books). Wolfe is also the editor of *The New Religious Humanists: A Reader* (Free Press) and the co-author of *Bless This House: Prayers for Families and Children* (Jossey-Bass), *Circle of Grace: Praying with — and for — Your Children* (Ballantine Books), *Books That Build Character* (Touchstone), *Climb High, Climb Far* (Fireside), and *The Family New Media Guide* (Touchstone). He has published essays, reviews, and articles in numerous journals, including *Commonweal, First Things, National Review, Crisis, Modern Age,* and *New Oxford Review.* He received his B.A., summa cum laude, from Hillsdale College and his M.A. in English literature from Oxford University. Wolfe is currently writing a book tentatively titled *Christian Humanism: A Faith for All Seasons.*

❊

*SPECIAL THANKS to our Cover Artist, Randi Layne Scheu*rer. Randi's painting "Front Yard At Night" was specially requested by the editor because it perfectly reflects the mysterious nature held in common among all of our contributors' stories. While greatly diverse, these stories all hold in common a type of pilgrimage and a deep sense of mystery—best reflected in this beautiful work. Music and nature and night all play in concert in this painting—notice the tambourine circling the moon—conveying a playful, unpredictable, otherworldly Presence over, among, and within us. Thank you, Randi. You are amazing and generous.